the
kokopelli
theory
a novel

Kevin Correa

Lone Peak Press ▪ Boston, MA

Lone Peak Press, LLC
Boston, Massachusetts

Publisher's Cataloging-in-Publication
(*Provided by Quality Books, Inc.*)

Correa, Kevin.
The Kokopelli theory / Kevin Correa.
p. cm.
LCCN 2002112530
ISBN 0-9724814-7-8

1. Hepatitis C--Fiction. 2. Kokopelli (Pueblo deity)
--Fiction. 3. Conspiracies--Fiction. I. Title.

PS3603.O6846K65 2002 813'.6
QBI02-701993

for P

1

Los Angeles, California, February 1978

A solitary vehicle sat invisible in the shadowy recess of the empty parking lot. In it, Marcus Tran lit another cigarette, taking a long deep drag. He had waited patiently for forty minutes, watching countless raindrops bead on the windshield. A soggy mist blurred the overhead lamps, creating eerie fluorescent canopies of light in the otherwise pitch-black night sky.

Tran's eyes wandered around the parking lot before resting on the silver figure centered on the dashboard. He tapped it, causing it to wobble back and forth a few times. When driving, it amused Tran the way the tiny creature danced along with the slightest bump in the road. Now, motionless in the cool night, light flickered off the metallic figure as streaks of rain raced down the windshield.

From his car tucked in the far corner of the lot, Tran watched the front doors of the building. He checked his watch again—10:48 PM. Tran knew that shortly, the security guard would begin his exterior rounds of The Sierra Institute for Serological Studies.

Tran took a final drag from his cigarette, the burning tip reflecting bright orange on the windshield. Like clockwork, the guard exited the building and rounded the east corner of the lab. As he faded slowly into the darkness, Tran stepped quietly out of the sports car.

Just as he had on the previous two occasions, Tran walked toward the building in the protected darkness on the edge of the lot. No lights volunteered his location.

The SISS lab was housed in a single story building, designed with function in mind much more than aesthetics. The lack of windows exacerbated the drabness of the exterior. The only glimpse inside was through the glass doors at the front entrance.

The brown walls of the lab were foreboding to outsiders. The public had limited insight into what really occurred behind the windowless walls. Rumors abounded, but few knew the nature of the lab's true mission: creating vaccines and antitoxins from the captive animals.

Like the other employees, Tran ignored the rumors, instead concentrating on performing his duties. He received high praise for his work as a Live Animal Technician, and was recently promoted to his present status of Section Supervisor. In this capacity, he had sole responsibility for the care of the lab's adult chimpanzees, two vervet monkeys, a large male African lion, and one of only three captive Komodo dragons in the United States.

Tran made his way to the front of the building. As he fumbled nervously with the keys, his reflection stared back at him from the glass doors. He had a young, slender build, common to the Vietnamese men of his family; none of whom he had seen since 1970. In the fall of that year, American missionaries evacuated hundreds of orphans from Vietnam. Tran was among them. When he arrived on American soil, he was half the world away from any relatives that might still have been alive.

Stepping through the door, he felt more like a teenager sneaking back home after curfew than an intruder. Strong zoo-like odors welcomed him as he entered the lobby at the front of the lab.

Tran inhaled the warm aroma. Soon, he thought, he would owe much of everything he had to these animals.

He passed quickly through the carpeted lobby. In twelve minutes the guard would return to his cold coffee and an episode of *Sanford and Son* on the small black-and-white television. Once through another set of double doors, Tran walked swiftly down a dimly lit tiled corridor, lined with offices on both sides.

Hatari, the massive African lion, was the object of Tran's visit. Tran knew that many people would shell out plenty of cash for the powerful substance produced deep within Hatari's soul. With no education beyond a high school diploma, he had found an ideal way to make extra money. SISS paid him well, but his last two after-hours visits to the lab had each earned him two weeks' pay.

The squeaks from his wet shoes echoed off the sterile walls of the hallway. The red light of the holding area shined through the square window on the door at the end of the corridor.

Reaching the door, he slid through the heavy steel barrier and was engulfed in the sea of red light. He stood for a second in the doorway, imagining that hell was something like the sight before his eyes. Shrieks and cries reverberated off the high ceilings and red-lit walls of the warehouse-sized holding area. During the day, the holding area was a pristine white color, but at night, the red light allowed viewing of the animals without subjecting them to artificial daylight.

Tran walked directly to the tranquilizer cabinet. He had watched Dr. Cameron closely and knew he needed a combination of fifteen cc's of both xylazine and ketamine to put the lion down comfortably. He filled the large eighteen-gauge syringe and prepared to secure it to the spring-loaded prod. Similar to a baton, the prod had a handle on one end and a large coiled spring on the other. To the spring, Tran attached the syringe, which, upon forceful contact, would automatically inject the tranquilizer into the lion. Satisfied that the prod was ready, Tran slipped an empty syringe into his jacket pocket.

The sleeping lion looked demonic in the flat red lighting. His chest rose and fell rhythmically with every breath, a low grumble in his throat following the cadence.

"No roaring," Tran whispered, the words colored with the slightest hint of a Vietnamese accent. He maneuvered the steel prod through the bars toward the lion's thigh, clanking it against the metal cage. He stiffened, holding his breath. The lion didn't stir. He repositioned the prod.

Tran closed his eyes tight, braced for the roar and thrust the prod, hitting the lion square in the thigh ...

The shock of the roar knocked Tran to the floor, hands covering his ears. The smaller cages rattled with the shattering sound, and pandemonium broke loose among the other animals. All of the animals woke, joining the litany of screams filling the red air.

Tran propped himself onto his knees, inches from the lion's cage. Hatari faced him growling, lips curled back, bearing his hefty canine teeth. The lion's name, Tran knew, was Swahili for "danger", and now, as he stood face to face with the lion glowing red with anger, he understood why. Tran stared intensely into the lion's eyes as his growl grew deeper and more subdued.

The drug took effect. Slowly the lion lay back down, desperately attempting to focus on Tran. It was a losing battle and the lion soon surrendered. His eyes grew vacant, his breathing more relaxed.

Tran slipped the empty syringe from his jacket pocket, uncapped it and again pierced the lion's flesh, drawing a quarter pint of blood. As he pulled the plunger of the syringe, he felt the warmth of the lion's thick blood filling the glass vial.

He retreated quickly from the lion into an anteroom that housed a centrifuge and a large steel cooler. He placed the vial into the centrifuge and set it in motion.

Following the tiny second hand on his watch for an eternity, he waited. The machine separated the clear plasma serum from the platelets, red and white blood cells.

Tran felt the separation was necessary as a precaution—if caught, anyone would be suspicious of blood, but almost no one would recognize the plasma serum. And on the street, the plasma would bring in just as much money as the blood.

Tran removed the vial from the centrifuge, holding it up to the light to examine it. It had two distinct layers, one clear, the other red; he smiled and separated the two layers, pouring the clear plasma serum into another vial, and the remainder down the sink's drain. He then further divided the plasma serum into a half dozen smaller vials, which he capped and tucked into his jacket. He glanced at his watch—11:00 PM. Three minutes to get back to the car.

Calm to this point, his heart raced wildly, pounding in his chest and head. He shut the light and made for the door. A quick check of the red holding area confirmed that he left no signs of his visit. He flew down the corridor again, shoes squeaking loudly as he ran. In ten quick steps he was through the lobby and outside the door. Again he fumbled with the keys, trying to lock the door. The lock wouldn't catch. The guard would round the corner at any second. After several attempts, Tran finally gave up, running to the darkness in the bushes on the edge of the lot.

After reaching the safety of his car, he lit a cigarette for warmth, as the security guard, satisfied that the building had not been breached, returned to his cold coffee.

OVER the next six hours, Marcus Tran reverted to his life of risks and experimentation.

As on the past two occasions when he had "goods" from the lab to pawn, he ventured to the back-alley shops of Los Angeles's Chinatown. The streets teemed with activity late into the night. In the small Asian universe within the city, everything had a price. And when dealing in commodities associated with the flesh, that price could be extremely high.

Lions are legendary for their sexual virility. Tran knew that men from around the world sought to acquire that power. The secret may or may not have resided in the serum. Regardless, many men would pay top dollar to find out.

The shop merchants bartered with Tran, offering him heroin or cocaine for the serum, but he wasn't interested. He wanted cash.

An hour after entering Chinatown, Tran found a small vendor operating in a shop the size of a large closet. The storeowner was writing a sign advertising bowls of shark fin soup as Tran entered the shop. The elderly Chinese merchant looked suspiciously at Tran and the vials.

"What's that?" the merchant asked in a quick Chinese accent.

"Serum from a lion," Tran answered.

"Let me see," the merchant said, his hand outstretched.

Tran handed him the serum. "Two thousand, no less."

"I give you five hundred."

"We both know you can resell it for three times that," Tran replied.

"I give you one thousand now, and if it sells, two thousand next time. You come back. We see then."

Tran nodded and handed the old man five of the six vials. The merchant smiled. From under the counter he retrieved a small brown paper bag. He withdrew ten crisp one hundred dollar bills and handed them to Tran. Tran left without another word.

Five vials replete with the volatile spirit of Hatari, sold on the black market for the handsome sum of one thousand dollars.

Satisfied with his night's productivity, Tran turned his thoughts to the partying to be done. The cash and the remaining vial nestled safely in a pocket close to his chest, he hopped into his Datsun and scurried out of Chinatown, happy that the rains had stopped. As the late-night hassle of the dirty city faded into his rearview mirror, he smiled at the bouncing figure on his dashboard, dreaming of the bright future to come.

What Marcus Tran failed to see in that future, what he could not have seen, was the storm he had already unleashed.

2

Two Decades Later
Cambridge, Massachusetts, September 9

"WHAT can I get you, gentlemen?" the young waitress asked.

"Lemonade, please," Ian Nielson replied.

"And I'll have one of those margaritas everyone always raves about," Sean Graham added, trying to keep a straight face.

"Blended or on the rocks?"

"Blended, please."

"Salt?"

"Definitely. Thanks."

"Anything else? Nachos, maybe?"

"No thanks, we're in a hurry," answered Ian.

The waitress left the two men at their table on the sidewalk of one of Harvard Square's trendy cafes. The best friends graduated together from Georgetown two years earlier, but their paths had diverged greatly upon leaving the confines of the Washington, DC campus.

Sean had boyish good looks. He lounged comfortably in blue jeans and a baseball cap. His white polo shirt stood out against his deeply tanned arms and face. Ian, in contrast, wore his favorite charcoal gray Brooks Brothers suit. While sharply dressed, Ian was terribly pale. No doubt, Sean thought, a result of the long hours of study at Harvard Law School, coupled with the stress of working at one of Boston's most prestigious law firms. In spite of the law school's grueling second year curriculum, in his "free time", Ian managed to squeeze in two days, and sometimes nights, of work for the firm. One of the best researchers the partners at Donovan, Pratt & Kelly had seen in a number of years, a handsome salary awaited Ian upon graduation.

The friends sat juxtaposed in their chosen lifestyles. Just two short years had pushed their lives worlds apart.

Autumn was slowly taking the reins from summer for control over the Boston area. The heat of August still lingered in the air, but the cool winds of fall whistled through the treetops.

"Margarita, huh?" Ian said. "Don't you have a class this afternoon?"

"Yes, but I can't begin to tell you how long I've dreamt about a cold margarita. I'm telling you, sitting in the insanely hot and humid Serengeti, you become completely overrun by thoughts of anything cold; things from home that you can barely remember. Ice cream, a cold shower, margaritas. Especially margaritas. Anything that can give you a brain freeze."

Ian was right, Sean had both a class to attend and a class to teach, or at least assist in teaching. Back from Tanzania only two days, Sean began the process of proving himself to Professor Richard Fulsonmayer. Nine months earlier, Fulsonmayer gave Sean a much coveted spot on his Tanzania field research team. Now, Sean jumped at the opportunity to demonstrate to Fulsonmayer that the professor had made a sound decision. As is the protocol in most graduate programs, Sean earned his keep by assisting in the teaching of undergraduate courses. When Fulsonmayer offered the graduate assistant position for his freshman seminar in conservation ecology, Sean took the post without hesitation.

As a teaching fellow, Sean was given much of the responsibility for the administration of classes. He knew that the time commitment for TFs was hefty. The freshman class, in addition to his own course-load, would be taxing, but he couldn't summon a single complaint. All he could think about was the Serengeti and life on the East African plains. He couldn't suppress the smile.

"It's great to see you," Ian said. "You left in what, January?"

"December thirtieth, just a bit over eight months ago."

"That's right, you missed my New Year's party. That was a mess." Ian laughed, "Has Michelle forgiven you for that fiasco yet?"

"Hasn't brought it up since March, and I'd like to keep it that way."

"Man was she pissed. How's she doing now that you're back in the states?"

"I'm not sure," Sean said, pausing as a police car sped by, lights flashing. He followed it with his eyes. "I haven't seen her yet."

"You've been back from Africa for two days! That's simply outlandish."

Sean had hoped that the two-day lapse wouldn't be significant. Judging by Ian's reaction, it was.

"We're having dinner tonight. I'm not sure how it'll go."

The waitress returned with their drinks, her eyes locked on Ian.

"Let me know if I can get you anything else," she said.

"Thanks. We will," Sean replied. When she had left their table, he turned back to Ian. "She wants you."

Ian ignored the comment. "You'll have to tell me how dinner with Michelle goes."

Sean stared at the tall glass and its slushy yellow contents. He really had dreamt about the margarita. He felt sad now that it was finally in front of him. It was as if it represented the end of his time in Tanzania. Cold drops of condensation ran down the glass from just beneath the salted rim. The glass was cool to his touch. He felt guilty sitting in complete comfort at the small sidewalk cafe. Sam was probably sitting in the Land Rover at that very instant. That hot and dusty Land Rover. He wished he had taken Sam's advice and put off "the real world" for just a few more months. The real world would always be there.

"Not that I wasn't paying attention as you babbled on about it, but what were you doing over there again?" Ian asked.

"Professor Fulsonmayer is doing hepatitis research. He was the first to document a feline version of the disease in lions. I helped initiate a study to determine how lions' immune systems cope with it in an effort to understand how the human immune system can better cope with our various strains."

"You're telling me lions drink booze?"

"Really funny. No, they have a viral hepatitis similar to hepatitis C."

"Of course," Ian joked. "But why study a disease we already have a vaccine for?"

"There's no vaccine for the hep C virus. Hep A and B yes, but not C. We know very little about it. About ninety percent of the lions in the Serengeti have feline hepatitis. But it seems to have no detrimental impact on their lives. Lions with hepatitis live just as long as those without the virus. So we're hoping that maybe there are some hints in lions that can help us with humans."

"And how did you go about collecting information for this study?"

"We took blood and semen samples from the lions."

"You handled lion semen?" Ian asked, a disgusted look crossing his face.

"Yep. But mostly we studied blood."

"Fascinating," Ian said rolling his eyes. "And somehow, I suppose, this is related to your pursuit of a master's degree in anthropology and public health?"

"Absolutely," Sean answered.

"At some point I'll want you to explain how, but I'll pass for now," Ian said raising his lemonade. "Allow me to propose a toast. To my best friend, who has finally seen the other side of the world and some of its many cultures, possibly one that might even accept him as its own. It's good to have you back, even if you are a bit skinny."

"It's great to be back," Sean replied unconvincingly.

"Please tell me that I'm not the only person you've talked to since you got home. You've at least called your brother."

"Yeah, I spoke to Pete yesterday. He's off in Alaska climbing Denali of all things," Sean said. "He called me an idiot for coming back so soon. He knew how much I enjoyed it over there."

Ian shook his head slowly. "We both know exactly why you came back. Have you spoken to him?"

Sean sighed. "No, but I got a 'Memo From the Desk of Martin Graham' yesterday welcoming me home."

"Did he at least sign it this time?"

"No, it was one of his secretaries again. Let's trade parents. My father's been trying to get you into the family for years. And when you graduate, I'm sure that he'll scheme as much as he can to get you to work for him in Manhattan. 'Why work at one of those little outfits up in Boston when you can work for the real guns in the Big City?'" Sean said, imitating his father's voice. "He's so full of shit."

"Enough about the big man. How's Pete doing?" Ian asked, changing the subject.

"I think he's doing alright. He said that his treatments are moving along fine, and that he feels relatively healthy." Sean paused. "You know what I don't get? My father turns his back on Pete, and I'm the one who gets angry. I don't know how Pete handles it."

Ian finished his lemonade and spun the ice cubes around in his glass. He started to say something but cut himself off.

"What?" Sean asked.

"Nothing really. I just don't want to talk about your dad. But I think that you have to realize that even though Pete's only a few years older, after all he's had to deal with, he's got a hell of a lot more than a few years of maturity on us."

Sean slouched back into the chair and took in the hectic atmosphere of Harvard Square. Young and old people alike rushed across streets, into stores and banks. Everyone had some place to be and something to do. "This place is too crazy."

"Yep, and you chose to come back," Ian said smiling. "I have to run downtown to help Sarah finish a motion she's filing tomorrow at Middlesex. Seriously, let me know how dinner with Michelle goes." Ian stood up, dropping a ten dollar bill on the table. He headed for the cab stand. "That margarita is on me."

"Thanks. Catch you later."

AFTER dozing in and out of a long afternoon of classes, Sean sought refuge in the activity he loved most: running. Since arriving at Harvard a year earlier, Sean had found running along the Charles River relaxing, in spite of the heavy traffic that buffeted both of its banks.

The early autumn grass crackled lightly under his feet, and with every footfall, Sean drifted further away from the ivory towers of Cambridge and back into the panoramic world of the East African savanna. As he ran, the sounds of the rush hour traffic faded into winds rustling through knee-high golden grasses ...

JUST over two hours late, Egypt Air flight 273 arrived from New York City after a twelve-hour layover in Cairo. Two hundred eighteen weary travelers of numerous ethnic backgrounds and in various states of jet lag emerged from the jumbo jet.

Situated on the outskirts of Nairobi, Kenya, Jomo Kenyatta Airport is fairly typical of ports of entry into Third World countries. A cacophonous mixture of languages rises from people from every imaginable walk of life. Street vendors peddle their goods on unsuspecting tourists fresh from the West. Chickens desperately try to free themselves from tiny crates. Cabbies use their best English to lure fares into their rickety vehicles. And ever-present thieves scan the terminals for those tourists most nonchalant with their belongings.

In the sea of skin darkened by millennia of sun, the pale Western tourists stand out like tapioca against chocolate. Even in a world blind to skin color, their dress would give them away. For most Westerners, a trip to East Africa is made with the intent of capturing images of the virgin wildlife, free from the man-made confines of urban zoos. And for these people on safari, the dress code is derived from Hemingway novels and old films documenting the exploits of the Great White Hunter. They come decked out in khaki from head to toe, with a jacket or vest fully equipped with more pockets than one could ever find use for. As for headgear, Panama hats generally suffice.

Within the chaotic dance played out daily at Kenyatta Airport, it is always an easy task to separate the newcomer from the seasoned traveler. For this precise reason, Sam Ferson was immediately able to pick Sean out from the crowd.

Treading slowly from the baggage claim into the open greeting room, the stale humid air hit Sean full force. He almost passed out. It was just after noon and the temperature outside the terminal flirted with the ninety-degree mark. Inside the poorly ventilated terminal it was ten degrees hotter. Taxi drivers left their cabs idling for fear that, if stopped, the dilapidated cars would never see life again. Their exhaust fumes poured steadily through the terminal doors and mixed with the raw smell of life void of deodorants and perfumes.

Sleep had eluded Sean both on the plane and during his Cairo layover. He scanned the terminal in a deliberate and jet lagged daze, not sure whom exactly he was looking for.

Sam smiled and walked directly to him.

"Sean Graham?"

"Yes?" he replied.

"Have you collected all of your belongings?"

"Yes, I have."

"Then let's get you some fresh air, you look like you could use it."

"Right," Sean said, pleasantly surprised, "except that I'm supposed to meet a Dr. Sam Ferson here at the airport."

Sam smiled, extended a hand, "Of course, I'm sorry, I'm terrible with introductions. I'm Sam, Samantha, Ferson. I just get a bit nervous in airports. Too many strange run-ins, you know."

The two quickly made their way out of the bustling terminal and into the parking lot. It took Sean's sleep deprived brain a few seconds to fully comprehend that the person before him was Dr. Sam Ferson, this tall woman with her pony tail pulled through the back of her Detroit Tigers cap. Not what he was expecting.

Weaving between small cars in various stages of decay, Sam led Sean to an off-white colored 4x4. She tapped the hood. "This is our trusty Land Rover Defender. It's old and takes a bit of coaxing to get started, but it runs fine."

Standing on the running board of the truck, Sam deftly secured Sean's gear among the bags of equipment and supplies she had purchased at the markets in Nairobi. As she stood on her tiptoes, reaching into the middle of the rack, Sean couldn't help but admire the strong tanned calves that tensed and relaxed with Sam's slightest movement. Succumbing to the effects of jet lag, he failed to avert his stare from her legs when she turned to ask him a question; blood flowed quickly to his cheeks and ears.

"You're definitely feeling the time change aren't you?" Sam asked.

"It's that obvious?"

"Jump in, we've got a long day of driving ahead of us. You have all of your visas right?"

"Barely. One mishap after another, but I finally got everything in order."

"I only ask because sometimes crossing into Tanzania can be a hassle. If the customs officer you're dealt has a particularly large chip on his shoulder, you might get strip searched. Not fun."

"That's ... great."

"That's Africa."

Before Sam could start the engine, a police officer approached the vehicle. He tapped at Sam's window with his nightstick. As soon as she had rolled it down, he began yelling at her in Swahili, gesturing wildly toward the front of the truck. Sam waited patiently until he had finished. She replied to his tirade in a few calm Swahili words. Sean watched the exchange, having no idea what was being said. When Sam had finished, the officer peered past her, looking at Sean. Then without another word he walked away.

Sam turned the ignition and the Land Rover's engine coughed for a few seconds before roaring to life.

"What was that all about?" Sean asked.

"Nothing, really."

"How could all of that have been nothing?"

"It happens all the time. The police see some white people and think that we're all tourists. He said that my license plates had expired, and that he was going to impound the truck. Unless, of course, we paid him the appropriate fines."

Sean laughed. "A bribe?"

"Get used to it. Anyhow, I dropped the name of his boss on him, saying that if he didn't leave us alone, I'd be sure to talk to him today. I guess it worked."

Sean smiled at Sam's success. "That was great."

After letting the engine idle for a minute, Sam flicked on the radio and turned to Sean. "Before we get into the whole getting-to-know-you conversation, do you have any tapes? I'm sick of mine and this BBC guy can get to you pretty quickly."

"Yeah I brought a bunch, but I'm ashamed to admit that they're all cheesy mixes of eighties bands. A bunch of one-hit-wonders."

"Oh, the eighties. I was really hoping you might have some classical music, but eighties tunes are a close second to Mozart," Sam joked.

"Hey don't knock the eighties. I love these songs, even if they remind me of junior high—parachute pants, mesh jerseys, acid washed jeans and all."

"Well, there's our first difference, I hear the songs and think of college and med school, not junior high."

Sam caught Sean's surprised look.

"You don't have to ask, I know what you're thinking. I'm thirty-four."

No way, he thought. "I'm only surprised because I would

have guessed that you were, at most, thirty."

Sam laughed and steered the truck south toward Tanzania. Sean began to feel better as they pulled away from the airport and onto the freeway. The wind rushing through the windows brought relief from the hot afternoon sun. "I would never have imagined that they had major freeways in Africa," he said. "I've always pictured dirt roads crossing endless miles of open plains."

"Enjoy the pavement while it lasts. Plenty of dirt roads ahead."

Even the outskirts of Nairobi teemed with energy. Sean scanned the scene. Compact cars and overcrowded buses spewed dark clouds of exhaust into the air as they darted here and there.

For the next several hours Sam maneuvered the rotting Land Rover south, around innumerable potholes, toward the border Kenya shares with Tanzania. Nairobi's urban environs quickly melted away, yielding to the vast expanses of the Great Rift Valley. Large mud huts with grass roofs dotted the landscape. Sean could see men dressed in brilliant red clothing, carrying long spears while they tended their cattle.

"Those are the Masai," Sam said. "They believe that god entrusted them with the care of all of the cattle in the world."

"That's quite the responsibility. Why the spears?" Sean asked.

"The spears are carried by the great Masai Warriors. For the most part, the spears are used to protect the cattle from predators. They also act as a symbol that a Masai boy has completed his rite of passage into adulthood and become a warrior."

"And how does he do that?" Sean asked.

"He has to participate in the killing of a lion, with only his spear for protection."

"Does that still go on today?"

"Not to the extent that it used to, but it's still an essential part of Masai life."

Africa's highest mountain, Kilimanjaro, engulfed the entire southern horizon. The majestic volcano with its signature snowcapped dome stood out in stark contrast to the miles of gently rolling hills that surrounded it. Sean couldn't contain his excitement. Finally, this was Africa. "Kilimanjaro," he said, recognizing the mountain from photographs.

"Yep."

"It's beautiful."

"Isn't it?" Sam replied. "So why East Africa, Sean Graham?"

"I've answered that question so many times you'd think that I'd have an answer down pat by now. I don't. But I can tell you the standard answer I've given everyone else."

"Why don't you start with the standard, then get to the real reason. Everyone has a reason for coming here, and more often than not, people are running from something. Or someone."

Sean marveled at the landscape just outside of his window. "Where to start. Well first, I'm twenty-four years old. I graduated a year and a half ago from Georgetown with pretty good grades. I took a job as an analyst at a big name Wall Street firm."

"Ugh, how was that?"

"Well one morning, about a year after I took the job, I realized over my Corn Flakes that staring at a computer screen for seventeen hours a day wasn't the way one should live life. Or at least not the way that I should live mine."

"Good decision."

"Thanks. Anyhow, after a thorough berating from my uber-attorney father, I decided that I'd better get on track with something else. Now I had the question of 'What the hell am I going to do with my life?' staring me in the face for seventeen hours a day. Only slightly less unpleasant than stock quotes."

Sam laughed, "So young yet such angst."

"Right about the time I quit my job, my brother told me that he had HIV." Sean paused, and the squeaking of the truck's shock absorbers filled the air. "Pete, my brother, is two years older than me. Growing up he showed me everything. The two of us were inseparable. By all standards he was my hero; he is my hero. In high school and college he was always the superstar. But by the way he acted, you would never have known it. He always down-played his achievements."

"Mind my asking how he contracted the virus?"

"For a brief period in high school, Pete experimented with drugs. He assumes that's where he got it. You might think 'nice role model', but he got out of that scene quickly and made sure that I never did."

"How did the family take the news?" Sam asked. "I know it can be pretty tough."

"My family's held together by little more than Scotch tape. Pete's HIV really tested us. My father's a bit of a relic who longs for the puritanical days of the Reagan administration. He's convinced that my brother is gay, or a drug dealer, or both."

"So how does your—"

"My mother play into this?" Sean interrupted, finishing the thought. "Good question. When I was in fourth grade my mother, an aspiring travel writer, went to cover a story in Chamonix, France. After three months, we got a post card telling us that she wasn't coming home. My father never saw it coming. Apparently he spent more time building his legal empire than he did creating a stable household."

"Sean I'm sorry, this seems like it may be more than you want to tell me."

"Not at all. Back in high school, I used to be embarrassed by my mother's leaving, but not anymore. It's just one of the many things that've made me who I am today. Besides, it all plays into how I ended up here in this truck, on this deserted road. See, after my mom left, I was deprived of that person who would hang school projects on the refrigerator or listen all about my junior high crushes. She was supposed to do that. God knows that my father never had the time, so it all fell on Pete. He took me to little league and prepared me for my senior prom. He's only two years older, but he'd always been the stability in my life."

Sam looked at Sean and smiled. He calmly gazed out the window. "I think you chose a marvelous hero."

"Thanks. When Pete told me he had HIV, it made me realize how precious life was, and how little I knew about protecting it. His sickness gave me direction and drive. Though my grades at Georgetown might have been good enough, I never considered med school. I'm the type that faints at the sight of blood. So I began looking into public health programs. The most interesting one I found was at Harvard, combining public health and anthropology. So I'm working on a master's, with the option to continue on for my PhD. And as part of the program, I sit next to you today. My father's not the happiest with my decision. He thinks I'm wasting my time."

"Imagine what my parents think. They put me through medical school, and now I'm in Africa. They refuse to see how my work out here can possibly have an effect on medical science back home. Hopefully that'll change with this hepatitis project we'll be working on."

"I can't begin to tell you how excited I am to be here," Sean said.

Sam smiled. "So maybe I wasn't right about you. When I spotted you in that terminal, I was positive that you were one of the people that comes to Africa as an escape. You actually do have a reason to be here."

Sean nodded. "Ultimately I have a reason to be here, but I'm not so sure that I'm not running away as well."

"I'm continually running back here. I return year after year not because I'm afraid of anything back in the states, but because I never know what to expect when I'm out in the bush doing research. Every day brings new surprises. Being out here studying lions or baboons or whatever, the days all blend into one, but it never grows mundane. Life out here doesn't change much day to day. It hasn't changed much in the past million years. But nonetheless, I live for every sunrise, for every thunderstorm. Everything that happens out here seems to be on a grander scale. When its hot, its really hot, when it rains, you expect to see Noah and his boat float by.

"In the bush you feel so alive. More alive than I could ever feel in an office. Some people think that sitting in a hot car all day studying animals is a waste of time. In the end, maybe it is. But I don't think that anyone who says that really understands what happens out here." Sam paused, scanning the landscape ahead. "See that animal over there?" Sam asked, pointing to a small Thompson's Gazelle off the side of the road.

Sean nodded.

"That gazelle is more in tune with its life than any person I've ever met. His instincts tell him that every moment counts. The vast majority of his day he eats and avoids predators, and somewhere in the mix he has to find time to sleep. He's fully aware that should he drop his guard, it very well could be the last mistake he makes. Every moment counts," Sam repeated. "How many people that you know have come to that realization?" She stopped talking and stared out to the horizon. She removed the baseball cap and let her hair out of the pony tail.

Sean looked at her, waiting to see if she would continue the thought. Again, he noticed how attractive she was. Deep blue eyes accenting a beautiful face tucked under long straight brown hair. Her tanned skin gave away a small scar on her chin.

"How'd you get the scar?" Sean asked, surprising himself.

Sam smiled. "Aren't you supposed to phrase that in a positive way?"

"Such as?"

"Such as 'that little scar on your chin is really cute, how'd you get it?'" she said.

"Okay, that little scar on your chin is really cute, how'd you get it?"

Sam laughed. "Much better. It's nothing really. Back, maybe ten years ago, I was drawing blood on a lioness, and she woke up a bit too soon. She swatted me with her claw before staggering to her feet and running off."

"She woke up and didn't just eat you?"

"Lions aren't like that. They know how dangerous people are, so generally, when they see us, they'll walk away. The only time you can guarantee getting attacked is if you come between a mother and her cubs. And at night, well, all bets are off. It's hard to tell how a lion will react to you. As for this," Sam said touching the scar, "like I said, she took off as soon as she got to her feet."

"Did it hurt?"

"Only a little, but it was pretty scary. She knocked me six feet away while she was half asleep. Bruised my ego more than anything."

"Well it's left an endearing mark."

"So nice of you to say so," Sam laughed.

"Have you always worked with lions?"

"No. When I first started working over here, it was mostly with people, doing public health type work. The work mostly entailed bringing medical supplies to remote villages, and performing simple health exams on the people. But at the time that I got the scar, I had been working with lions and chimps for about a year. I've worked with them ever since. Most of the projects have dealt with different types of immunities that the animals possess. And as with this hepatitis project, we're always trying to figure out how animals' immune systems combat invaders."

Sean stared out the window. Beautiful acacia trees with their umbrella-like canopies dominated the landscape. Off the side of the road a faint sign indicated that the border town of Namanga was a kilometer away. This was their point of entry into Tanzania.

Namanga is a tourist trap. Nestled on the only major tourist travel route to the Serengeti, it is a haven for locals with trinkets to peddle. Everything from authentic Masai spears to faux ivory carvings are sold at the tiny African version of the Midwestern flea market.

Just as Sam had singled him out at the airport, the peddlers all made their way to Sean, recognizing in his expression that he was new to the game. At an even six feet tall, he towered over the tiny merchants tugging at his sleeves. With the deftness of a stateswoman, Sam politely escorted Sean to the customs office, leading him firmly away by the elbow. He had to keep himself from smiling.

After a painless forty-five minute wait, the two were back in the shuddering Land Rover, delighted to have been offered entry into Tanzania without having to disrobe.

Ten kilometers outside of Namanga, Sam and Sean jumped back into their conversation. "Sam," Sean began, "when I first saw you at the airport, I could have sworn that I'd seen you before. Specifically, I think it was the Tigers cap and the pony tail. But the more that I thought about it, the more I realized that it was impossible that we'd ever met before."

"I'm pretty sure we hadn't met before Nairobi."

"I agree. But seeing you surrounded by all of the merchants in Namanga, I realized where I'd seen you."

"Oh no," Sam moaned, shaking her head. "You didn't see it, did you?"

"So you *were* in the documentary I'm thinking about. What was it called? *Whispering Quietly*? *Walking Softly*?"

"*Treading Lightly: The Impacts of Tourism on Africa.* You recognized me from a cameo in a five year old documentary?"

"Like I said, it was the combination of the cap, the pony tail, and surroundings. The only thing that threw me was ... and I hope I'm not being too forward ... that at the time of the documentary you were engaged weren't you? At least I remember the narrator making a big deal out of the soon to be husband and wife team in the bush. And back at the airport I noticed you weren't wearing a ring."

"You looked to see if I was wearing a ring?" Sam laughed.

"Force of habit, sorry."

"Don't be sorry, I just thought that only women did that. Things have changed since that documentary. His name was Charlie. We worked closely together in Tanzania for about two years when he asked me to marry him. He was sweet and caring, intelligent and handsome—what more could I want?

"So I said 'yes'. Some time soon after a ring decorated my finger, he was offered a tenured position at a small liberal arts college in Oregon. Without even consulting me, he took the position, assuming that I would come along. From there, it didn't take too long for the situation to reach meltdown. I have my own ambitions and paths to follow, and unfortunately, none led me to Oregon."

"You don't seem bitter at all," Sean said.

"At first I was, and I thought long and hard about my priorities. Was I being too selfish? How often does love come knocking on your door? But the more I thought about it, the more I realized it was just loneliness making me question my decision. Although I love every night in the bush, it does get lonely when you think about the relationships you're missing out on."

For the first time in hours, an awkward silence filled the air. Sean thought about Michelle. They had been dating for three months before he told her about Pete's sickness.

"Maybe it's because I'm so tired from traveling," Sean said, "but I'm unusually comfortable talking to you about things that don't often come out in conversations on the first day people meet. I don't really discuss my brother's HIV with relative strangers, and I can imagine that you don't usually relate the details of your engagement with just anyone off the street."

Sam smiled. "We'll be in extremely close quarters with almost no one else to talk to for the better part of the next eight months. The lions we'll study are magnificent to watch, but they have difficulty keeping up with their end of a conversation. Our interaction so far is a good omen of things to come. I can't begin to tell you how many times I've made this trip with grad students fresh from the states, and the whole trip to the field was one long boring silence. So I'm happy to go on about my past if you're willing to listen."

After a quick stop for gas, Sam handed the Land Rover to Sean. After he adjusted to the steering wheel's location on the right side of the truck, the two headed west toward the Serengeti. The paved highway soon gave way to a wide dirt road. The dusty road wound its way through the Great Rift Valley and eventually led them to the eastern entrance of the Serengeti National Park.

The hassle of Nairobi seemed light years away as the Land Rover raced into the African dusk. The fleeting rays of the fading sun slowly danced across the wide horizon, leaving faint hints of the passing day on the wispy clouds to the west.

"I've been driving this road for what seems like a lifetime, and I'll never get over these sunsets," Sam said.

"How long has it been?"

Sean glanced at Sam as she calculated the time in her head. "Well, since my freshman year in college, which was, let's see, sixteen years ago."

"That's a good amount of time."

"A while back you asked if I was bitter about the breakup with Charlie. I think that by the time that we split, I'd already grown pretty accustomed to the fact that one way or another, my continually returning to Africa had the tendency of preventing me from having a stable relationship. Every serious boyfriend that I had, either in college or med school, found it too difficult to carry on a relationship with someone who was always gone for months on end. I can't say that I blame them. Long distance relationships can probably work between cities or even states, but between continents seems unlikely.

"Of all of my relationships, Charlie was the first guy I thought I might have had a future with, because he already knew about the hardships of being away from the states for extended periods of time. I thought things might be different. But eventually, well, we already covered this," Sam cut herself off, shrugging her shoulders.

"I know what you mean about the distance. My girlfriend and I decided to stay together while I was over here only because eight months didn't really seem like too long of a time. If it were longer, I'm not sure what we would've done. Asking someone to wait for a long period of time is pretty unfair. And bottom line, if she wanted to see other people while I'm here, I don't think that I could have asked her not to."

"Ah-ha. We've known each other an entire, what, ten hours, and this is the first time that you've mentioned a girlfriend. I figured she was out there, but I was waiting for you to tell me."

Sean chuckled, "You may find this hard to believe, but this is the first time that I've thought about her since I arrived."

"Trouble in paradise?"

"I don't know. Africa may prove to be our unraveling, too. She's of the impression that I wasn't the most qualified person for this research position. Long story."

"We've got nothing but time."

"Well Michelle doesn't understand that my father has always tried to make up for his parental shortcomings with his money and connections. In his own way, he feels guilty about my mother's leaving. But instead of changing his workaholic ways, he tries to appease Pete and me with money. Michelle thinks that my father bought my way onto this field expedition. I worked for this opportunity more than I've worked for anything in my entire life, and it wasn't always fun. I can tell you the sounds you hear in the library at four in the morning, or what kind of people actually go to twenty-four hour convenience stores during the middle of the night. It's a scary crowd. And I was right there with them, drinking coffee by the gallon, writing grant proposals for twenty hours of the day. But it was all worth it. I met my deadlines and got the funding I needed. And now I'm here, and well, she's not. That's the issue," Sean said, slowing the truck as they rounded a sharp turn in the road.

"At some point I want to hear the end of that story, but you're in luck, because that shack up there on the left is the gate to the park. You'll have to sign in and show your research visa. Don't worry, no strip search."

Nearing the top of a short hill, the small wooden outpost began to take on shape as the Land Rover's head lights fell on it. The dark silhouette of a man was visible through a window on the side of the structure. He made his way outside.

"Samantha, you are back so soon!" the guard said in a heavy East African accent.

"A short trip to Nairobi to pick up supplies and a new researcher," she replied. "Thomas Kifaru, this is Sean Graham."

Kifaru extended his hand, "It is a pleasure to meet you Sean Graham. Welcome to Tanzania's jewel, the Serengeti."

"Thank you very much, I'm excited to be here."

"Just wait until tomorrow when the sun rises and you can truly see all of the Serengeti's beauty. You have brought your research visas with you?" Thomas asked.

"Yes, I have them right here," Sean said, handing over his passport.

"Excellent. Please come in and share a cup of tea with me, I have just now boiled the milk. While I prepare the tea you can fill out the research log," said Thomas, leading the two into the dimly lit patrol shack. "Please forgive me the mess, it is not too often that I receive company after sunset. Mr. Graham, the log is on that small table in the corner. Simply follow the years of examples in filling out your information."

Sean crossed the small room in four steps and found the log. The size of an enormous coffee table book, it was bound in leather, worn by years of relentless heat and humidity. The leather had faded into shades of brown and black. On the front, Sean could make out a faint inscription: *To The Serengeti National Park, Tanzania. A Donation Of The London Zoological Society. 1972.* He carefully turned back the cover revealing hundreds of pages of delicate ledgers containing the names of researchers and their project goals, dating back two and a half decades.

He could barely contain his excitement as he skimmed the pages for names he recognized. He had heard of many of the people contained on the book's pages, but none really caught his attention until he came to the year 1977. In March of that year, a rising star in the field of public health signed into the Serengeti with a small team of assistants. His name was Lawrence Needham. In 1977, not too many people knew of the driven young man, but his name would become known across the globe in 1988 when he was appointed Director-General of the World Health Organization. Needham took the helm of the organization just one year after launching the WHO's Global Program on AIDS.

Sean's smile spread from ear to ear. "Lawrence Needham," he said aloud.

Both Sam and Thomas looked up from their conversation and warm tea. "What about Lawrence Needham?" Sam asked.

"He stood here in this very room and signed into this log book twenty years ago. That's pretty cool."

"I didn't know that you were a fan of Dr. Needham. We've worked closely in the past, mostly on communicable disease projects. But, as you might know, he's primarily concerned with AIDS these days, and I've moved off to chase less glamorous diseases. If you stick with it, you'll see that this research community is fairly small and close-knit. I'm sure that you'd eventually be able to work with him."

Sean pondered the possibility for a moment. "His writings on AIDS are really incredible."

"I know what you mean, he's a great communicator. How's your entry coming?" Sam asked.

"Just finishing up." He looked at his entry. "A two sentence research goal that I'm sure I could build a career from."

"The first step of that career is getting a good night's sleep. Tomorrow you meet some lions, and to identify them, you'll need to be on your toes," Sam said.

Sean gently closed the book, running his fingers over the inscription. Sam thanked Thomas for the refreshments, and headed with Sean out the door.

They drove forty more miles of dirt roads to get to the lion research house—home for the next eight months. Built in the early 1970's by Texas A&M University, the three bedroom house had long since passed its prime. In its early years, all of the amenities of home had graced the simple single story building; but repeated thefts led to the replacement of only the bare essentials. Even the solar panels that provided electricity had been stolen. As a result, the noisy diesel generator was called back into action.

His first night in the bush, after the generator fell silent and the lights faded into darkness, Sean had a fitful sleep. He tossed at the rustling in the bushes outside and the strange cries in the night. Sam woke him early the next morning, eager to educate him in the ways of the Serengeti.

They devoted their first week together solely to teaching Sean how to identify the lions by both whisker patterns and distinctive scarring. During that week their relationship evolved from one of teacher and pupil into one of friendship. In the past, Sam often felt burdened by the inconvenience of showing students how to track and identify lions. This wasn't true of her experience with Sean. She felt more like she was showing an old friend around her office: sharing, rather than teaching.

Within two weeks, Sean could track, identify, tranquilize and draw blood from the lions. What had once been a mechanized routine for Sam was revitalized by Sean's presence. His wide-eyed enthusiasm for the research was refreshing for her. She had lacked a close friend in the bush for years.

Sam was excited to show Sean everything, and he was eager to see. The Serengeti is the size of the state of Connecticut, and Sam wanted to show every last inch of it to Sean. Early in the mornings, she would wake him and drive to one of the rolling hilltops. There they sat on a blanket atop the hood of the Land Rover, sipping tea from a thermos. In the valley below, the lingering morning fog drifted lazily among the sparse trees. Herds of elephants, led by their majestic matriarch, tread solemnly to the water holes. Giraffes grazed silently from the tree tops. In the distance, the lions roared in unison before falling asleep; another night of hunting behind them.

Late in the evenings, they lay atop the truck, gazing at the labyrinth of stars punctuating the black sky of the Southern Hemisphere. Sam had Sean close his eyes and listen to the sounds of the African night. They repeated the exercise every evening until he could identify all of the cries and howls in the darkness. For the eight months that he lived in the Serengeti, the two spent eighteen hours a day together, never growing tired of the other's company.

Those eight months proved to be the beginning of an obsession for Sean. Like Sam, he too fell in love with the sweet slow melodies of life on the African savanna. The magnificent wildlife, the generous people, and the limitless land all found a home in his soul. And as the expiration date of his visa grew near, he felt a strong conviction that he would return.

His last night in the Serengeti, after sharing a bottle of wine and a traditional East African meal with Sam, Sean fell into a deep and peaceful sleep. He dreamt happily through the night, safe from harm in the research dorm. He slept unaware that three decades earlier, less than one hundred miles from where he rested his head, the rhythmic sounds of the African night were shattered by a terrifying cry in the forest.

Not even Sam was aware of that long since forgotten night ...

DEEP in the overgrown forest, miles from anywhere, a drab green jeep, a remnant from the Second World War, sped noisily down a winding dirt road. Large crater-like puddles developed after a recent rain. Every jerk of the steering wheel jostled the American husband and wife researchers inside of the jeep.

"Darling, you're driving a bit fast for the conditions," the woman said.

"What's that?" the husband yelled, his voice barely audible over the roar of the engine.

"I said, 'you're driving a bit fast for the conditions,'" she shouted back.

He took his eyes off the road to shoot her a contemptuous glance. As he did, they smashed through a large pot hole, sending the jeep fishtailing toward the edge of the road. He recovered his steering and laughed at the terrified look on his wife's face.

As he stepped on the gas again, a loud bang rang out and the jeep swerved toward the edge of the road. Knowing that he'd blown a tire, the man quickly brought the jeep to a stop on the side of the road. He killed the engine, allowing silence to fill the night.

"What I was saying, was that perhaps you were driving too fast for the road conditions. And now, I believe you will have to agree with me," the woman said.

"Not another word."

The man looked around the back of the jeep until he found the tools he needed to change the flat tire. He knelt in the moist dirt waiting for his eyes to adjust to the dark night. His wife hummed a song from a musical they had seen on Broadway just before they left the states for Africa.

He began to hum along.

His heart jumped and the hair on his neck shot up when he saw the nails protruding from the tire. “Get the gun,” he said to his wife, trying to stand but finding no strength in his legs.

“What did you say, darling?”

Before he could answer, the machete crashed through his collar bone and three ribs. He blocked the second strike with his forearm as he fell, leaving his arm severed below the elbow. The third blow glanced the left side of his head removing the tanned skin of his cheek and his entire ear. The final swing brought the swift relief of the guillotine, his head separated from the shoulders.

From the darkness of the forest, six African assailants emerged to complete their ambush. The husband was lucky to have died first. The wife’s screams filled the forest for twenty minutes as the men raped her. When they had finished, they silenced her with a slit of the throat.

The attackers worked methodically removing their victims’ clothes. The blood stains would be cleaned, and the tears sewn. The men’s laughter echoed off the trees deep in the forest. They took inventory of the jeep, installed the spare tire, and drove off into the night. Their attacks were a very profitable enterprise, and would continue indefinitely. They were never caught.

Two days later, a farmer found the grisly naked remains. The tropical heat had accelerated the decay. Afraid to approach the bodies, the man returned to his remote village, and word was sent to the proper authorities. It would be a full twenty-eight days before the victims’ only child, at the request of the US consulate, arrived from college in the states to make positive identification.

Though Sean slept oblivious to this event, in the months to come, the fate of the couple would become entwined with his own.

AFTER eight months in the bush, Nairobi’s Jomo Kenyatta Airport wasn’t a welcome sight. Sean fiddled anxiously with his luggage as he prepared to clear customs for the last time until he reached America. “Why are you acting so funny?” Sam asked. “All this fidgeting, you’d think you were smuggling ivory out of the country.”

"I just realized that I'm not quite ready to go home yet."

"Then stay. We can go right now to get an extension of your visa. God knows there's plenty of work to do on the project. Stay until you're ready. You don't want to have any regrets." Sam looked steadily into Sean's eyes. He turned away.

"Why can't you look me in the eye?" she asked.

He looked up at her with her Tigers cap and pony tail. "Back home, I've always felt like I've had to prove myself. That wasn't the case out here with you in the bush. Just you, me and the research. Nobody staring over my shoulder. I'll miss it. The eight months flew by too fast."

"Sean, I have to admit that my wanting you to stay is for personal reasons. Do you remember that first morning I took you for a drive in the Serengeti? When we saw those lion cubs and you immediately fell in love with them, do you remember what I told you?"

"Not to get attached, because they may not be around forever."

"I broke that rule with you. I forgot that you weren't going to be around forever, and I grew too accustomed to having you here. I'll really miss you." Sam reached for Sean and they embraced. She wiped a tear from her eye while resting her head on his shoulder.

"I'll miss you too," Sean replied, realizing just how true his statement was.

"Alright kiddo," she said, slowly pulling away, "I don't want you to miss your plane. But I do want you to have this," she said, handing him her Tigers cap. "It'll keep the sun out of your eyes on those jogs along the Charles back in Cambridge."

"Thanks Sam, I'll take good care of it."

"Well, I'm not good at saying 'good-bye', so I guess I'll just see you around," Sam said, not taking her stare from Sean's eyes.

"Yeah. See you around," he replied, pulling her into a hug again. As he released her, she gently pulled him back, kissing him softly on the lips.

"I'll miss you," she said, before turning and walking away.

3

HAVING lost the time during his run, Sean was late for dinner. He got off Boston's subway, the "T", and ascended the stairs into Government Center. Though the late nights of summer had grown cooler, many post-Labor Day tourists still lingered about the city, taking in all of its historic sites. Street performers sang folk tunes with amplified acoustic guitars, while jugglers awed gaping crowds with fiery stunts.

Just as Sean had hoped, the flower vendors still manned the T stations, ready with bouquets for husbands to bring home after another late day at the office, or for the fledgling lover excited to make that first impression.

Sean found the perfect red rose for the evening and walked with an anxious gait toward the North End of Boston. Known for its narrow streets and apartments lined shoulder to shoulder, the North End houses some of the best Italian restaurants in New England. More important to Sean, it was the home of his girlfriend's favorite eatery—Fiamma's.

Just off Hanover Street, the North End's busiest thoroughfare, Fiamma's is a cozy restaurant nestled in the shadows cast by the Old North Church of Paul Revere fame. Through the restaurant window, Sean spotted Michelle. She wore blue jeans and a yellow V-neck sweater. She had a petite figure, standing just two inches over five feet. Her shiny black hair was shorter than Sean remembered, leaving nothing to obstruct her cool green eyes. Butterflies took flight in Sean's stomach. Hiding the rose behind his back, he made his way inside to her table.

"Hey stranger," he said from behind her.

"Hello to you too," she replied standing to hug him.

"Before it gets crushed, this is for you. I missed you," he said, revealing the rose, and handing it to her with a kiss.

"It's beautiful. Thank you. You said that you might be late, so I ordered you the Chicken Marsala."

"Sounds great."

"Aren't you the tanned one. When you told me you lost a little weight, you weren't kidding. How does it feel to be back?"

"It's been tough getting used to a strict hourly schedule again, you know with classes and everything, but it's also nice to be able to go to the refrigerator whenever I'm hungry, and to shower more than once a week."

"So, how was it?" Michelle asked apprehensively. "Monthly letters really didn't relate the experience too well."

Sean had hoped that somehow the subject of Africa wouldn't creep up until somewhere around dessert, giving them at least enough time to enjoy the entrees.

"Incredible. The land, the people, and the animals all surpassed my wildest imaginations."

"I really don't want to bring you down because I know you had an incredible experience, but it's hard being happy for you knowing that I could have been there instead."

The waiter brought their meals as Sean was about to reply. When he did, he had difficulty finding the right words. "I'm really at a loss here, knowing that an apology can't change the last eight months. But I also know that it's been bothering you, and that we should probably talk about it."

Michelle tore a piece of bread off a roll she had been picking at, and she changed the subject. "So what results did you get?"

Sean was somewhat relieved that the issue of his merits had, for the time, past. "We drew blood from about one hundred fifty adult lions and cubs. We sent the samples off for analysis to the Infectious Disease Division at the National Cancer Institute. We should hear back from them in the next week or so. Sam's confident that the samples will yield some interesting information."

"I'm not really concerned about what Sam thinks. I want to know what Professor Fulsonmayer has to say," Michelle said.

"You know the man. He's pretty tough to read. He'll be fairly tight-lipped until we get the results back, but he has me moving ahead with the project. He's given me a month to have the final report on the field research ready for him to submit for publication. To be better prepared to write the report, he's got me doing archival research on the hepatitis C virus."

"Research HCV? What for?"

"From what I gather, of the strains of hepatitis, HCV has the closest relationship to feline hepatitis. And I guess he just wants me to have a firm grasp of the vectors HCV uses to move from one host to another, and how the research and medical communities learn to combat them. I've been given the glorious task of studying the virus, from what we know about its origins to current treatments and research. I know the basics, but additional background material should help."

"Something specific that Fulsonmayer wants you to look into?"

"Yeah, it's actually pretty interesting. I guess he has some friends down in Atlanta at the Centers for Disease Control. I'm headed there tomorrow to get copies of the original case studies from what's commonly believed to be the primary outbreak in southern California back in 1981. I didn't know that anyone could get copies of that stuff."

Michelle laughed at him. "Not just anyone can get that type of material, but if you're doing legitimate research and have an insider at the CDC, it's not too difficult."

It was awkward being together again after eight months. The conversation jumped erratically from one topic to the next, each time grinding to a painful silence.

Sean struggled for an upbeat topic. "Did I tell you that I got season's tickets to the Celtics? Big hoops fan that you are, I figured it would be nice to know that we can go any time we want."

"Dad's money again?" Michelle said shaking her head.

"Not exactly. His firm helped close the deal on the Fleet Center. They gave him tickets."

"Same thing."

"Forget I mentioned it. Ian will be glad to know."

The two ate in silence until Michelle spoke up, the hostility gone from her voice. "So how's your class so far?"

"Which one?" Sean asked.

"The one you're teaching."

"We met for the first time outside of lecture today, and it didn't go well."

"How's that?"

"The students were supposed to hand in a paper Fulsonmayer assigned at the first lecture, and this goon on the hockey team didn't turn it in. He asked for an extension and I said 'no'. He absolutely flipped out," Sean said, still in disbelief.

"What's the big deal? It's one grade for the semester."

"I don't know, something about being on academic probation because he failed a course last spring. Oh, did I mention that this guy is a junior in a freshman class? Sharp as a marble, alright."

"Say anything to Fulsonmayer?"

"Not yet. I hope it's just an isolated incident." Sean laughed, "I survive all the perils of Africa, only to face death in the form of a kid the size of a tractor."

"I'd really rather not talk about Africa."

"Sorry."

"You know that I don't like feeling this way, but I can't help it. I'm just being honest. It eats me up inside knowing that your father's money was probably the reason that you were sent to Tanzania instead of me. I'm happy that you had the experience, but this was something that I've dreamed about my entire life, and you lived my dream."

Sean couldn't look her in the eyes. "Can we get something straight? Yes, my father is a wealthy man, and yes he has a number of connections. But that doesn't mean that I didn't deserve the trip. Michelle, I've busted my ass from day one. You know that. I'm sorry that only one of us had the chance to go to Tanzania, but I deserved it as much as you. We were both there when Fulsonmayer said that the deciding factor was that your research proposal failed to secure any federal grants. Mine did. I'm here, and I'm doing the best that I can. Don't you think that I know that Africa has been a dream of yours forever? I'm sorry that only one of us could go." He paused. "There's nothing I can say that will change the fact that I went instead of you. But we both know that my father had nothing to do with it."

Michelle took a deep breath, "I know that you're sorry, and it's not really you that I'm mad at. I'm frustrated with the school. I thought that by the time I got to grad school, getting ahead would be based entirely on merit. But over the last eight months I've had plenty of time to realize that's not necessarily the case—that's why I'm looking into a few other programs."

"Other programs?"

"You know how I've been working with Michael Sullivan

from the University of Michigan? Well I've spoken to him about transferring programs, and he said that they'd probably give me a full scholarship if I were to go to Ann Arbor."

"So what do you think? I mean that's great, scholarship and all ... but how do you feel about moving?" Sean asked.

"I'm not sure. All I know is that I'm really unhappy with the school's politics right now. Sullivan wants to know by the end of the month so that he can have the papers ready for next semester if I transfer. I just don't know."

The possibility of transferring to Michigan was a bomb that Michelle didn't know how to sugar coat, so she didn't try. The two sat uncomfortably, not knowing what to say. The remainder of the dinner was marked with small talk, skirting the bigger issues the two would eventually have to face. The check's arrival was a welcome sign that the evening was near an end.

"Sorry dinner didn't go as well as I'd hoped," Sean said. "The Michigan thing was a total surprise."

"I'm sorry too. There really wasn't a good way to bring it up."

"Listen, I'll be back from Atlanta in a couple of days, and I'd like to try this again, when we've both had a few days to think."

"That's a good idea," she replied with a small smile.

"Are you headed back to campus?"

"Yeah, do you need a ride?"

"No, thanks. I need to pick up a few things for this trip. I'll just take the T."

"Give me a call when you get back," she said, kissing him on the cheek.

"Sure thing."

Sean walked slowly out of the North End and through Government Center, oblivious to the tourists and street performers. He passed a couple walking as one, the woman snugly tucked under the man's arm. For no particular reason he walked into Boston Common. It offered a welcome reprieve from the busy streets of the North End. At the entrance to the Common, Sean passed a homeless man sleeping under a wool blanket. Sean slipped a couple dollars into the tin cup that sat by the man's head.

The pavement in the park was wet from a brief shower that passed through during dinner. The air was cool and the smell of autumn floated in the air. Sean's footsteps resounded over the fading sound of the downtown traffic. Far from the reaches of the overhead lamps, Sean found a bench near the center of the park. For the next hour he sat there to collect his thoughts.

IN June of the summer of 1981, five men from a single county in southern California came down with a previously unknown liver disease. One month later, another ten men in California, as well as four men in New York City, were diagnosed with the same disease. All would soon die, throwing the medical community into a frenzy. Red flags went up at the Centers for Disease Control, and small investigative teams were sent to Los Angeles and New York to search for answers. They were successful in their mission to discover why the disease spread, but ultimately they failed in finding its origin.

Sean thought about these puzzling deaths on his flight to Atlanta.

Arriving at the Centers for Disease Control, Sean grew nervous. He represented both Fulsonmayer and Harvard, and notwithstanding the research he performed in Tanzania, by all standards, he remained a rookie at the game.

A division of the US Department of Health and Human Services, the Centers for Disease Control and Prevention officially opened its doors in 1946. At the time, its primary mission was to combat diseases like malaria and typhus that were prevalent in the southern United States.

In the half-century since its inception, the CDC's areas of expertise broadened, leading to its involvement in public health battles across the globe. Over the years, the CDC continued to play an instrumental role in the fight against emerging diseases, both in the US and worldwide.

Sean entered the CDC's highly secure building at 1600 Clifton Road. He presented identification to the uniformed guards who issued him a visitor's identification badge. With no pockets on his shirt, Sean clipped the plastic badge to his belt. The security guard then ushered him to a check post, similar to that at an airport, where Sean's bag was scanned by x-ray. A tall square-jawed guard resembling a body builder ran a hand-held metal detector up and down Sean's body. Sean tried to make small talk, but the guard ignored him. After both Sean and his bag cleared security, the officer passed Sean on to a CDC intern.

Sean's contact at the CDC was a middle-aged doctor named Hector Mendoza. The intern escorted Sean to Mendoza's office. Sean notified the doctor's secretary of his appointment. He paced slowly around the anteroom, gazing at the poster-sized photos decorating the walls. From a short distance, he couldn't easily discern what the photos were. Each depicted crystalline images of various vibrant colors. He stepped closer to the wall, examining one photo in particular that resembled a fluorescent earthworm slightly tangled at one end. The caption under the photo: EBOLA RESTON VIRUS.

"Ebola. A beautiful, efficient and deadly virus," said a man with a Hispanic accent from behind Sean. Sean turned to face the man.

"I'm Hector Mendoza, you must be Mr. Graham from Professor Fulsonmayer's team."

"Yes, Sean Graham. It's a pleasure to meet you doctor," Sean said shaking Mendoza's hand.

"Ebola is deadly alright, but it's nothing compared to hepatitis C. Since the first documented case of Ebola, only a couple hundred people worldwide have died. There are a hundred seventy million people with hep C. That's three times more people than have AIDS." Mendoza let the numbers sink in. "Professor Fulsonmayer has asked me to grant you access to all of the early HCV files that we have," Mendoza said, speaking as much with words as with his great bushy eyebrows.

"Yes sir, he's sent me to learn everything about the virus's history, from the first case in the US, to what we know now."

"Excellent. Every couple of years Fulsonmayer has a grad student do exactly that. He sees the infectious disease case studies as solid teaching tools in both public health and anthropological respects. I agree, because to truly understand a disease, you must understand the cultures surrounding it. Now Mr. Graham—"

"Please, call me Sean."

"Right, Sean. Exactly how much knowledge of hep C do you have?"

"Just what I've learned from my grant research."

"Okay. I've prepared copies of the original five case files from Los Angeles County back in June of 1981, complete with color copies of any file photos that we have. You'll have to excuse my rush, but I have to run to a meeting that will unfortunately detain me for the rest of the day, but I've set aside some time tomorrow morning to meet with you. So if you review these files and come back tomorrow we can go into specifics about the virus and discuss any questions that you might have."

Sean took the box of files. "Thank you very much Dr. Mendoza, I appreciate your time and I'll be back tomorrow morning."

"You're very welcome. See you tomorrow," said a smiling Mendoza, before he raced out the door and down the hall.

IT was mid afternoon when Sean returned to his small hotel room on the sleepy outskirts of Atlanta. The room was poorly lit even with all five of its lights on, so he pulled back the shade. The bright southern sun illuminated the room. He stood at the window for a minute taking in the Atlanta skyline.

Sean took a deep breath, exhaling slowly, "Time to work."

Aware that the small hotel room would double as an office of sorts for the next day or two, Sean carefully arranged the work space. He spread the case files across one of the two double beds in the room.

Once he had arranged the room to his satisfaction, he jumped into a paper that Mendoza had included with the case files. It was from the CDC journal titled *Morbidity and Mortality Weekly Report*. According to the report, the five case files in front of Sean were of men from Los Angeles County, each of whom was diagnosed with liver disease caused by a previously unidentified agent. None of the men had any prior history of disease.

As Sean read, he couldn't help thinking of his brother. Pete told Sean about his disease on a week long trip to the mountains ...

IT was late spring. Pete bought Sean a ticket to Montana to go fly-fishing with him. Due some vacation time, Sean jumped at the opportunity. The rivers and creeks were high, the run-off from a long winter filling the waterways.

The brothers set up camp right at the Galatin River's edge, about seventy miles southeast of Bozeman. For seven days they did little more than fish, cook and talk. They slept under the stars outside the tent, by the small crackling fire. Conversation was easy and flowed on through the night.The impossibly fresh, cold mountain air bit at their lungs. It wasn't until the last day of fishing that Pete broke the news.

Sean had just caught a large trout when Pete called to him from down stream. "What is it?" Sean asked.

"We need to talk. Come on down," Pete yelled above the rolling water.

"You come up here, you've got to see this trout I landed. She's a beauty."

Pete walked slowly up to Sean, leaning slightly forward in his waders to fight the current. As he neared, Sean sensed that something was wrong. The smile slowly faded from his face.

"So let's see this trout," Pete said grinning.

Sean lifted it without saying a word, trying to read his brother's face.

"That's not so big. The one we ate last night was a good two pounds bigger," Pete said laughing. Sean stared blankly at him.

"What's wrong?" Sean asked.

Pete's grin disappeared. "What makes you think something's wrong?"

"Because you're wearing the same face you bluff with in poker. And we both know you've never won a hand."

Sean was devastated by the news. Pete comforted him, answering all of his younger brother's questions: When? How? How long do you have? As his brother spoke, Sean tried to pretend he understood the news, nodding his head at everything Pete said, though he heard almost nothing after "I have HIV".

"There've been a lot of advances Sean. I'm not going anywhere any time soon," Pete had promised.

Sean found strength in his brother's courage. Always close, the bond between the two grew stronger as they made their way back to the East Coast. Sean never forgot the image of Pete in his waders, struggling upstream to break the news. Sean gave his two week notice immediately upon returning to his tedious Wall Street job.

BACK in the Atlanta hotel room, Sean found himself frustrated at the dry clinical nature of the *MMWR* journal report. He wanted to know the human side of the men. They were all dead, but they too were somebody's brother, son or friend. They had stories to tell.

Sean decided to head into the case files. Each file was about an inch and a half thick, full of medical charts, patient histories, autopsy reports, and CDC analyses, among other things. Large manila folders held the files together, the inside cover of which listed all pertinent case information, including a photo or two of the individual.

Sean stared at the photos one by one. In each one, the men wore smiles. They were pictured with friends, families, dogs or even just leaning against a car. The men appeared full of life. Sean felt strange, like he was invading their lives and their privacy. Facing each picture was the file that told the story of each of the men, documenting even the most trivial of facts. How did these men come into contact with a disease that would eventually infect three percent of the world's population?

The detail of the reports was astounding. The CDC had investigated every detail of the men's lives: frequently visited restaurants, criminal records, types of pets, overseas travel, everything.

At first the language of the reports was tough to get through, but Sean deciphered what most of it meant. He tore through the reports, searching for similarities between the men. Before he knew it, his carefully organized room and meticulous study plan were both lost. He jumped from file to file, cross-referencing information.

The men in the pictures began to take on lives. The first to die of the five men was Jerry Famone. He was a struggling writer who longed to travel the world. His lack of success, however, kept him firmly anchored in Los Angeles. Close on his heels was Enrico Martinez. Martinez moved from Miami to LA where he became a successful dancer. According to the file, his encounters at the post production parties had probably led to his demise.

The third man to die was Syd "Trophy" Hollman. A playboy whose nickname stemmed from the fact that he always had a trophy on his arm—man or woman. He confessed that he couldn't turn anyone away from his bed. The youngest of the five men to die was Calvin Heindrich. Heindrich was the son of a brilliant German physicist immigrant who had fled to the United States in an effort to help stop Hitler. The son too was on his way to greatness, standing at the top of his UCLA class before the disease struck him down. Finally, the last of the files was that of a Vietnamese immigrant. He led a modest lifestyle working as a technician at a lab on the outskirts of Los Angeles. Marcus Tran had been fired for breaking and entering the facility only three weeks before his admittance to the hospital.

Their stories began in divergent ways, but through one common link they each met with the same fate, a death brought on by hepatitis C. Again, the thoroughness of the reports astounded Sean. For each man, every sexual contact was listed, every drug buddy recounted. Apparently there were no crossed paths between the men.

Sean poured over the reports, focusing on the interesting details. The information fascinated him. Looking up from the files, he noticed that the sun had set, and the lights of downtown Atlanta stood out against the black night sky. After having read for several hours, his eyes needed rest, and his stomach craved food.

Sean pulled the local phone directory from under the bible in the desk drawer, found a number and, as promised, had in his possession a pepperoni pizza half an hour later. Having skimmed all five of the files, he lounged on the previously untouched bed eating pizza and wondering how best to proceed.

He picked up the lab technician's file and began to browse through it again. The photo inside showed a man posing in front of a gray sports car. His name was Marcus Tran: born 3/15/57 in Buon Me Thuot, Vietnam; died 7/08/81 in Los Angeles, California. No known relatives. Cause of death: hepatocellular carcinoma, a form of cancer resulting from chronic infection of a "Non-A, Non-B virus".

Sean had never heard of the Non-A, Non-B virus, but

reading further he learned that it was the identification originally given to what years later became hepatitis C.

In 1989, after intensive international search, hepatitis C was identified and the name "Non-A, Non-B" was replaced. Hoping to curb the disease, the medical community listed high risk groups including: transfusion and transplant recipients, health care workers, intravenous drug users, and those with unsafe sexual contact with multiple partners.

Given the risk groups, Sean wondered where Tran had contracted the disease. The report suggested that he was promiscuous, but Tran repeatedly denied it, stating that he wasn't even sexually active. If he wasn't sleeping around, Sean reasoned, he was most likely an IV drug user. Sean flipped to the medical and autopsy reports. Tran's blood screens all turned up negative for use of narcotics like heroin. Yet both his physical exam, taken upon admission to the hospital, and his autopsy report noted that he had numerous pronounced needle tracks on and around his testicles, suggesting recent injection of some form of drug into the genitals.

"What were you thinking?" Sean said aloud, disturbed by the image. He looked back at the photo of Tran and his car. "Why would you do that?" he said to Tran, who's smile betrayed no confidences. Sean couldn't get the image of Tran sitting naked, with legs spread and syringe in hand, out of his head. He felt sick to his stomach.

But what was he injecting into his groin? Sean scoured the case file; nothing in any of the medical reports noted any unusual substances in his blood. He kept searching for answers for another hour, but it was an hour fraught with frustration. One dead end after another. Sean studied a police report from Tran's arrest. It said that he had stolen 'pharmaceutical paraphernalia', leading to his discharge from his job. Maybe this would lead somewhere, but at almost two in the morning, and with no second wind in sight, Sean reluctantly gave in to the urge to close his eyes.

THE morning sun poured heat and light into the room, waking Sean just after seven. He felt hung over. The room was a disaster with files and paper strewn everywhere. In two hours he would have to meet with Mendoza. He had plenty of time to clear his head with a run.

From his hotel, Sean sought out quiet side streets for his jog. The Atlanta morning had a nice summer warmth to it, not yet having grown into an oppressive afternoon heat. He ran slowly around the suburban area, watching the sleepy community rise with the sun. From his front porch, an old robed man crouched to pick up the morning paper. He waved to Sean. A group of small children rubbed their tired eyes while waiting on the corner for the arrival of their morning school bus. Sean smiled as he recalled the carefree days of his childhood.

He began mentally preparing for his meeting, carefully choosing the questions and topics he would address. Every question he thought of related directly to Tran's file. Sean considered focusing on the file, but then thought better of the idea. Perhaps the only things worth questioning were the origin of the genital track marks, and the nature of the pharmaceutical paraphernalia that Tran had stolen. The file seemed to lack significant insight into these two subjects. Otherwise, it was air tight.

JUST past nine o'clock, Mendoza called Sean into his office. "How did the reading go last night?" the doctor asked.

"It went well. I lost total track of time. I was really impressed by the amount of background research the CDC did on each of the files."

"That's what our epidemiologists do for a living, and they're the best in the business. So do you have any questions or anything you'd like to discuss?"

Sean wanted to say, "Yeah, what was this Tran guy injecting into his nuts?" but instead began with a more sedate topic. "If you don't mind, I think that a quick review of the virus's progression into disease would really help."

"Not a problem," Mendoza said. "Let's start from the beginning. You know the risk groups: transplants, transfusions, IV drugs, and risky sex, among others."

"Right," Sean nodded.

"Through some means the virus enters the body and attacks the liver. Bad news. This leaves the victim susceptible to diseases like cirrhosis and even worse, hepatocellular carcinoma."

"Cancer."

"That's right. Without treatment, most die within six months. Ninety-nine percent of people with the disease don't have access to treatment because they live in Third World poverty. And of the small percentage of people who can get treatment, it's only affective in about twenty percent."

"Pretty staggering figures," Sean said.

"It's a relatively unknown disease. I'm telling you, this will be a hell of a lot bigger problem than AIDS. Well more than half of the people with the virus are asymptomatic for up to thirty years. They pass it on for decades without knowing. Then it suddenly hits them. In the US, we're starting to see all of these middle-aged people who had a little youthful indiscretion two decades ago coming in and dying of some form of liver disease. They may have dodged the AIDS bullet, but hep C found its target."

"And there's no vaccine or cure?"

Mendoza shook his head, "There are some drugs in clinical trials, but nothing you'd call totally reliable." His expression grew distant as he pondered the scope of the problem.

"Dr. Mendoza," Sean said, "I have another question, but this one's about a specific file. Marcus Tran's." Stop while you're ahead, he thought.

"He was the lab technician, if I'm not mistaken."

"That's right. None of the medical or autopsy reports indicated that he had any narcotics in his system, yet they found track marks on his genitals from hypodermic needles. Have those ever been accounted for?"

"I'd have to look at the files again to refresh my memory, but I'm sure they have been. It's a very common practice for IV drug users to attempt to hide their track marks, most often between their toes, but maybe this Tran guy got a little more creative. I don't know, but, like I said, if I reread the file, I'm sure I could give you a sound answer. Why, what's your question?" said Mendoza, interested.

"Well in the file, it only *suggests* that Tran was promiscuous. When asked, he denied having sex at all. That denial, in conjunction with the fact that he had no narcotics in his system, is kind of strange, isn't it? These five cases were all chalked up to high risk sex and IV drug use, right?"

"That's right, it wasn't until later that transplants, transfusions and the others were seen as risk groups. What are you getting at?" Mendoza asked, looking at his watch.

"Well, you know, I probably just missed it in the report, but Tran said he wasn't sexually active, and no drugs were found in his system. However, his physical exam stated that the pronounced nature of the track marks on the genitals indicated that they were relatively recent. So what was he injecting into his groin?" Sean stopped, hoping for an answer.

"Sean, like I said, if I had another look at—"

"Dr. Mendoza, is there any way that something was missed in this file? Or that maybe I didn't get all of the pages? The track marks aren't accounted for, and neither is the nature of the material he stole from the lab."

Mendoza's eyes stared at Sean from under a stern brow, "As I was saying, Mr. Graham, if I were to read the file again, I'm certain that I could find you more satisfactory answers. What are you suggesting? That none of the thousands of professionals who read this file over the past two decades saw a mistake that you just happened to find after one night of review? Let's not be foolish." He paused letting the weight of his comments take the air from the room. Then, with a smile he continued, "Yes, Sean, I guess you've uncovered the great hepatitis conspiracy. CDC actually stands for Centers for Disease Cover-ups. We knew that one day you would come along and find us out. And now that I've let you in on the secret, I must ask you to swallow this cyanide pill. I assure you, your death will be instantaneous and painless."

Sean sank into the very depths of the plush leather chair in front of Mendoza's desk. He was speechless.

"I'm just yanking your chain Sean. I really haven't reviewed the file closely for quite a while now. If I had, I'm sure I could give you better answers." He patted Sean on the shoulder, "By the way, did you happen to notice who the primary CDC researcher was for this investigation?"

"No, I hadn't," Sean responded.

"It's at the bottom of the inside cover there."

Sean looked. Had he seen it before, the discussion would have been moot. "Lawrence Needham, M.D."

"By your expression, you know who he is then?"

"Yes I do, and I'm really sorry to have wasted your time with the lesson on being thorough in your investigations."

"Not at all, it was an honest mistake."

Sensing Sean's embarrassment, Mendoza changed the subject to the next set of case files he had prepared for Sean's review. Ten more files in the same arrangement. Sean took the files, thanking Mendoza for his time.

"Don't mention it. Send my greetings to Professor Fulsonmayer," Mendoza said.

"I will."

Mendoza walked Sean to the door of his office. After seeing him off, he closed the door and walked slowly toward his desk. Disturbed, he replayed the conversation over in his head. With a few minutes to spare before his weekly staff meeting, he picked up the phone and placed a call to an old friend with whom he hadn't spoken in years.

4

SEAN'S return flight to Boston was delayed two hours. When he finally made it home he was ready to collapse. His apartment was a welcome sight after his morning at the CDC. Several framed photographs decorated the walls of the bright apartment. Most were pictures of Sean and Pete together at various times while growing up. Sean walked to his couch and dropped the box of material Mendoza had prepared, vowing not to touch it until the next day.

Below the National Geographic map of the world, the light on his answering machine blinked twice. He played the messages while watering his plants. The first was Ian letting Sean know that he would stop by later that night; the second was Michelle, saying she had gone to Ann Arbor for informal interviews with the anthropology department.

Sean rubbed his temples as if to deter the onset of a migraine. Opening the refrigerator revealed that he desperately needed groceries. There were, however, a few bottles of beer calling to him. He opened a bottle and reclined on the couch. He found himself running through the conversation with Mendoza again.

Sean was convinced that he hadn't missed anything in the file. He looked at the CDC box sitting next to the couch. Giving in to the temptation, he reached for Tran's file. For the next two hours he read it in its entirety.

Just after seven o'clock, Ian knocked on the door, waking Sean from the couch. Sean staggered to the door in a post-nap daze.

"Hey, come on in."

"Brought something for you," Ian said, handing Sean a six pack. "Imported fresh from Wisconsin."

"Great," Sean said rolling his eyes. "You're not hiding any Chinese take-out, are you?"

"Sorry. So how was Atlanta—no, first, how was dinner with Michelle?"

Sean explained how dinner had turned into a disaster, and that Michelle was in Michigan interviewing with faculty. Then he proceeded to relate the details of his meeting with Mendoza.

"He really laughed at you?" Ian said.

Sean nodded.

"What did you say?"

"I just sat there. What could I say?"

"What do you think they missed?"

Sean shrugged. "I'm not sure, but this guy Tran said that he wasn't sleeping with anyone. Next, he'd been injecting something into his groin, yet his blood screens all tested negative for narcotics. So how did he get HCV? I mean, sure, there are innumerable ways, but the ones suggested by the CDC just don't seem to work."

"And?"

"Maybe nothing. That's just it, I'm not sure. I could be miles out in left field on this. Tran's file doesn't make its way to a tidy resolution like the others, and because it doesn't, it sticks out like a sore thumb."

"I'm not sure what to tell you. My guess is, and don't take this the wrong way, that you probably just missed something," Ian said.

"Normally I'd agree with you, but I've read this file several times now, and everything, everything, is in it. That is, except for an explanation of the track marks on his balls, and the nature of the material he stole from the lab. Each may be insignificant, but all of the other insignificant leads were tracked down. I mean they even knew the guy wore Fruit of the Loom tighty-whities. How is that significant?"

"I think it affects your sperm count," Ian laughed. "Mendoza's right Sean. Not to say that you're not a smart guy, but literally thousands of academics have read that file, and none that we know of has questioned its accuracy."

"I know."

"But," Ian continued, "we both know that you won't let it rest until you have your answers. And you won't get answers unless you pursue it."

"So you think I should?"

"I didn't say that. Do what you have to do, and then move on."

"Have you ever questioned a professor's judgment?" Sean asked. "I mean to his face."

Ian thought for a moment and laughed. "Yeah, back in my first semester of law school, I was sitting in a lecture and the professor made what I thought to be an outrageous observation, about ... what was it, maybe maritime law ... it's not important. Anyhow, it was so outlandish that I commented to the girl next to me, and the professor saw. Well, you know what happened next, he proceeded to make me stand and repeat my comment, which I did. He then tore me and my astute observation to shreds in front of the class."

"What did you get for a grade?"

"Let's just say it almost cost me law review."

The two sat silent for a few seconds, pensively drinking their beer.

Ian broke the silence, "These are very intelligent people you're dealing with. When people on the other side of the world start dying of some unknown disease, the CDC is the first team sent in. They're the best."

"I know. It's just that I've read this guy's file a few times now, and it doesn't add up. Every possible avenue was investigated for all of the other files—dotted I's and crossed T's. They all reach a logical conclusion. This one doesn't."

"I don't know what to tell you," Ian said.

"Do me a favor."

"Oh no, what is it?"

"Would you take a look at the file for me? It's probably right there in front of my eyes, and I'm just missing it."

"You've piqued my interest, so I'll look at it, but not tonight."

"No problem," Sean said. "Do you think that this guy's employer would remember him seventeen years after he died? I'm just thinking that maybe they'd have some insight into who this guy was."

"Well how often did this place get broken into? Couldn't have been too common, especially by an employee. I'm pretty sure they'd remember him. But before you go calling anyone, why don't you let me read this file," Ian said, waving Tran's file at Sean. "Don't go embarrassing yourself."

"You mean more than I already have," Sean said shaking his head. "Since you're such an ace at research, you think you could do me another favor?"

"Flattery's the way to my heart. What do you need?" Ian asked.

"There's a lab in that file called SISS. Think you could track down the phone number for me?"

"Sure but it'll cost you," Ian replied. "Listen, I have to run. Up for a game of hoops tomorrow afternoon?" he asked, heading for the door.

"I don't think so. I have to prepare a quiz for Fulsonmayer's undergrads to take, and I really should read all of these other files that Mendoza made for me. But give me a call, I'm sure I could be persuaded."

IAN hopped into a cab and went home to his apartment on Boston's Beacon Hill. Known for its notoriously high rents and dearth of parking spaces, it is a haven for young urban professionals. Most of the property in the area is well out of the price range for most students. Realizing his earnings potential after graduating, however, Ian took out a loan to pay for his fourth floor, one bedroom palace. He sat down at his desk, tucked into a large bay window overlooking Boston Common.

In college as well as law school, Ian stood out among his peers as a student with a genuine thirst for knowledge. His studies often took him beyond the assigned readings, which never failed to impress teachers. Sean's hepatitis research fascinated Ian. Had Sean really stumbled onto something significant? Odds were against the possibility, but Ian couldn't resist the opportunity to find out.

He cracked open Tran's file and studied the photos on the inside cover. Tran was taller and thinner than Ian had imagined. He studied Tran's face. Something about the smile wasn't right. It looked like it was manufactured just for the photograph. Was he a happy guy? Ian doubted it. Ian recognized the car in the photo as a Datsun 240Z. Great car, he thought. Tran leaned against the hood of the car. Over his right shoulder, Ian saw a silver figure mounted on the dashboard. He recalled it from a cross country trip he and Sean had taken the summer before their senior year in college. "Kokopelli," he said aloud. He stared at the photo for another minute, then made his way into the file.

At midnight, he finished the file. Like Sean said, Ian couldn't find answers about the track marks or the stolen goods from the SISS labs. Ian, however, doubted their significance. Jotting down a few notes, he closed the file. He was heading to bed when he remembered Sean's second request.

Sitting back at his computer, he planned his search. Ian felt that Sean was probably correct, that Sierra Institute for Serological Studies could shed some light on Marcus Tran. Odds were strong that someone at the lab would remember Tran as the technician fired for breaking and entering.

Searching the Internet, Ian found no current listing for SISS. It took him another hour to locate a database called Baker International which catalogued all scientific research firms in the United States from 1965 to the present. The database listed SISS as a pharmaceutical firm that folded in 1982 due to a lack of government funding.

Ian became pessimistic that SISS could lead him to any answers until he ran a search under the name of the lab's director—Dr. Valerie Chapeau. After SISS closed in '82, Chapeau had taken a position as chief researcher at a major pharmaceutical firm in Stamford, Connecticut. The lab was called New England Integration Laboratories. Unlike SISS, NEIL was still in business, and doing well, having posted the sixth highest revenues in the industry for the previous fiscal year.

It may not answer any questions, but it was a start, Ian thought. First thing in the morning he would call Sean with the news.

THE right knee of Trevor Matthews' pants grew damp as he knelt on the moist, sponge-like floor of the rain forest. His latest research project led him one hundred seventy miles to the east of the city of Kinshasa, the capital of the Democratic Republic of the Congo. A sturdy forty-three years old, Matthews was in great shape. An MD specializing in communicable diseases, Matthews hadn't worked in the comfort of a lab in almost a decade. Instead, he'd grown accustomed to the heat and humidity of the rain forest. His students, on the other hand, had not. As Matthews negotiated a map of the area, he could hear two of his students fumbling through the thick foliage somewhere just out of sight.

Matthews was an independent researcher. He went about

his investigations without any tangible affiliation or loyalty to any university. Though an American, Matthews sought research funding primarily from South African sources. In a unique arrangement with The Crown University of Johannesburg, Matthews secured grants in exchange for providing the school's graduate students the opportunity to perform field research.

CUJ was one of the oldest universities in South Africa, established early in the country's Dutch colonial days. In the late 1980s, the university fell on hard times. Several outspoken pro-apartheid faculty members stood their ground as the world watched Nelson Mandela fight for black rights in South Africa. The small faculty at the school was torn in two when the institution was labeled racist by the world press. The school closed its doors for two years. When it reopened in 1991, its faculty was completely new. The fresh start was applauded by civil rights activists from around the world. On the downside, the caliber of the school's faculty was widely questioned. Most of the professors had never taught a college class in their lives. The need for experienced mentors was highly publicized. Matthews jumped at the opportunity, seeing that he could get funding without taking time out for campus lectures. On his current trip, Matthews had three students along from CUJ. They were busy studying chimpanzees.

Matthews uncapped his water bottle and took a sip. The water was warm and had the strong taste of the iodine tablets added to kill any infectious invaders in the water.

Kenneth Fields, one of Matthews' assistants, emerged from the bushes off the side of the trail. He was a very lean young black man. He wore a blue bandanna around his forehead. Matthews offered him his water bottle.

"Thanks," Fields said, before taking a sip. He had a South African accent. "Kim found an adult female with an infant."

"Where?" Matthews asked.

Fields pointed. "About three-quarters of a kilometer out that way."

"Are they alone?"

"She couldn't see. She didn't want to get too close before she told you."

"That's good work," Matthews said. "Do me a favor, Ken. Go back to camp and help Mark set up the tents. It's going to get dark soon, and we want to have it all done before sunset."

Fields nodded. "Can you answer a question for me?"

"Sure," Matthews said.

"When I applied to be on your field team, the university said that I'd be working with a Dr. Wilmott. Who's Dr. Wilmott?"

An awkward half-smile crossed Matthews' face. "That's me. I don't use my real name because I don't want any real ties to the university."

"Because of its apartheid history," Fields said.

Matthews nodded, though the school's history wasn't the real reason. "The people at the school that need to know are aware that Wilmott is a pseudonym. It was part of our agreement. As far as the school's concerned, Dr. Matthews doesn't exist."

"I'm glad you worked out an agreement with the school. You're a good teacher," Fields said before he turned and disappeared back into the jungle.

Matthews returned his attention to the map. Nothing about performing research in the rain forest was easy. All supplies were carried into camp on the researchers' backs. Base camp for the current project was about fifteen kilometers from the nearest road. And calling the muddy, overgrown path a road was being generous. It was another eighty kilometers along the path before it intersected with a paved highway.

For Matthews, there had been many years of research without a significant reward. Exacerbating the dry spell was the fact that there was no real reward in sight.

He walked in the direction that Fields had pointed. A mosquito landed on his forearm. He quickly smashed it. Malaria was prevalent in the area. The only way to prevent exposure was to avoid getting bitten in the first place; a task easier said than done in the rain forest.

He walked blindly through the wet vegetation, his shoes and socks water-logged. In the past few years he'd convinced himself that he was happy with the way things turned out. Now, with the most recent news, he wasn't so sure anymore.

A single phone call had torn open old wounds.

ON the fifth floor of Harvard's Peabody Museum, Richard Fulsonmayer sat comfortably in the oversized, faded leather chair in his office. The warm, early morning sun peeked through his office window. The fifty-two year old professor reviewed his lecture notes under the watchful eyes of artifacts collected from his travels across the world. Ritual masks, totems and tapestries gave the office the feel of an overseas travel bureau.

While working in his office, his wire-rimmed glasses and tweed blazer grounded him firmly in academia. Yet his students were more familiar with the rugged unkempt look depicted in the lecture slides he used displaying his work in the field. It was widely known across campus that his office hours were more often spent recounting his global adventures than answering questions about his most recent lectures. Richard Fulsonmayer had groupies.

Despite his widespread popularity among the student body, a tenured position in the anthropology department had eluded him for years. A respected mind among his associates, he felt that his quest for the grail of tenure was nearing fruition. It was imperative that upon publication, his latest research project meet widespread enthusiasm. Fulsonmayer felt he had the deck stacked in his favor. His latest Serengeti research project was original in both its design and application. Sean Graham had done an excellent job in the field collecting data. All that was left undone, prior to publication, was the data analysis and the final report. Fulsonmayer was making great progress on the data analysis, and Sean was to be working diligently on a draft of the report. Finally the stability of tenure was tangible.

He edited his notes over his morning coffee when Sean appeared in his doorway. "Good morning professor."

"Good morning, Sean. Come in. Take a seat."

"Thank you," Sean said sitting across from Fulsonmayer.

"How was your class this morning?"

"Actually, I've rescheduled it for this evening at my apartment. That is, if that's alright with you."

"Your apartment? Strange setting for a class, isn't it?" Fulsonmayer said, removing his glasses and placing them on his desk.

"I wanted a more informal environment. Last meeting

we had the class was pretty reserved, and I had to force the dialogue along."

"Let me know how it goes." Fulsonmayer's face revealed that he was skeptical about the idea. "How's your research progressing?"

"I've been busy reviewing Dr. Mendoza's files. The information is fascinating."

"Having any problems making your way through the medical jargon?"

"Not in general."

"But?"

"But there are some things that aren't accounted for in one of the reports."

"And your question is?"

"Well, I want to know if I'm way off base to think that I might have found an oversight in the CDC's investigation."

"I suppose that you know what I'm going to tell you. Of course you realize that these are professionals standing at the top of the game that you're suggesting may have overlooked a thing or two. I don't want to know what you think they overlooked because I haven't read the files in years and wouldn't be of any assistance to you. However, part of the value of having you perform this research exercise is that you will learn, as a researcher, that it doesn't matter how many people are satisfied with a given project if you aren't. Until you are satisfied, everyone else's opinions aren't worth a dime. So my advice to you is that you seek explanations for your questions from sources that can provide them. I only caution you during this exercise not to lose sight of the bigger picture here which is ..." he stopped, waiting for Sean to finish the sentence.

"Which is to prepare the draft report for your Serengeti lion research project."

"Correct. So do what you must to satisfy yourself with the HCV background material, but do it quickly and don't lose focus of the task at hand. Ideally I would like at least a rough draft of the Serengeti report on my desk a week from today. We're on a tight schedule here in terms of getting this thing published in time for the winter lecture circuit. Let's not stray too far."

Sean knew that the tight schedule was for the tenure

committee, not the lecture circuit, but he just nodded his head. Fulsonmayer reached for his glasses, Sean's cue that the meeting was over. "Give me a call tomorrow and tell me how this class in your apartment goes."

"Yes sir."

IMMEDIATELY after leaving Fulsonmayer's office, Sean jumped into his car and headed west on the Massachusetts Turnpike. The rolling hills on the sides of the highway were already showing abnormally early signs of change. Every few hundred yards, large patches of orange trees stood out from the sea of green. Mesmerized by the New England hills, Sean sped west past Framingham and Worcester, happy to get away from campus again.

Just before turning south off the Pike, traffic ground to a halt as motorists picked their way through a massive ten car accident. A driver trying to cross four lanes of traffic to make his exit, clipped a minivan, sending it careening into two other cars.

It was five minutes before Sean made his way to the accident scene. Eight of the cars were on the shoulder and the slow lane when Sean got there. The remaining two vehicles sat in the middle of the highway, shattered beyond recognition. A small crowd gathered around each of the wrecked cars. A number of people ran about doing what they could until the authorities arrived. Like most drivers, Sean just slowly made his way around the crushed cars and broken glass. Once the highway opened up again, he stepped on the gas, the accident already a distant memory.

An hour later, Sean's cellphone rang as he drove south, about ten minutes outside of Stamford, Connecticut.

"What's up with your cellphone?" Ian asked.

"I don't know. What's wrong with it?"

"This is the fourth time I've tried to get through."

"It never rang," Sean said.

"Well get it checked out."

"Yes sir."

"Did you get my message this morning?" Ian asked.

"Yeah, I did. Thanks for getting that phone number for me."

"No problem."

"So what did you think about the file?" Sean asked.

"I don't know. Like you said, I couldn't find any answers referring to the track marks or the stolen pharmaceuticals. But then I also don't really see the significance."

"But the missing information stuck out, right?"

"Only because you'd told me about it. Had I read the file without your bias, I doubt that I would've questioned it," Ian said.

"Maybe I'm crazy."

"You are, but I know you'll never be happy unless you hear it from someone in authority."

"That's what I'm about to do."

"What?" Ian asked.

"I'm in Stamford, pulling into the lot of New England Integration Laboratories," Sean said. "This morning I spoke to that doctor that used to work for SISS out in LA. She remembers Tran."

"I figured she would, with the break in and all. Just don't say anything stupid while you're down there."

"I'll try not to. Listen, I'll call you later. Thanks again."

Overstepping his bounds, Sean had arranged his meeting with Dr. Chapeau under the pretense of performing further research for Fulsonmayer.

Sean turned into the parking lot. New England Integration Laboratories was housed in an inconspicuous two floor building in the heart of Stamford. Sean parked his car and headed for the doors. Security cameras followed his approach to the building. Once inside, an armed guard buzzed him through a second set of thick glass doors.

"Can I help you?" the large guard asked from behind an array of security monitors.

"I'm here to see Dr. Chapeau. She's expecting me," Sean replied.

"One moment. Please wait over there," the guard said, motioning to a black leather couch sitting in the shade of a large artificial fern.

A few moments later, the guard called Sean to his desk. "This is your visitor's pass. Wear it at all times inside the building. Proceed through the door on my left to the third office on the right. She'll meet you there." The guard pressed a button and a door behind him opened.

"Left door, then third on right. Thanks," Sean said.

Walking through the door, he entered an extremely bright and immaculate hallway. Valerie Chapeau met him outside her office, her voice echoing down the long corridor. After exchanging polite greetings, Chapeau showed Sean into her office. "Quite a bit of security you have here," Sean said.

"Indeed. Industry standard. A pain, but it's necessary. The pharmaceutical industry is becoming so competitive today that you can't take any chances. There're billions of dollars to be won in medical patents, you know. Please, have a seat."

The small room was cluttered with books and scientific journals. Sean removed a stack of papers from a chair in order to sit.

"Just toss those on the floor," Chapeau said to Sean. "My colleagues say that I'm disheveled. I prefer to think of this as creative organization."

Sean smiled, looking at the mess. "I'm not the neatest person either."

"Tell me, how is Richard Fulsonmayer these days? I'm afraid we've fallen out of touch as of late."

"He's feeling some pressure to publish his latest study, but otherwise I think he's fine."

"Poor Richard. We worked together on malaria projects back in ninety-two and then in ninety-four. Afraid neither met the greatest success. He was quite distraught. It's no wonder he's concerned about getting something successfully published. He's in the wrong business. More money and far less stress here."

"I think this latest project is heading in the right direction, but he'll be relieved when he sees it in a journal," Sean said smiling.

"So how is it that I can help you Mr. Graham?"

"I have some questions regarding some background research I'm working on."

"When you mentioned Marcus Tran on the phone, I have to admit I was extremely intrigued. He certainly raised some hell back when he worked for us at SISS."

"That's what I'm here to learn about. What both SISS and Tran did."

"SISS was primarily concerned with the creating pharmaceutical products from wildlife. Today, most pharmaceutical firms utilize plants and synthetics rather than wildlife. SISS was one of the last government funded research institutes to successfully patent pharmaceuticals derived from animals," Chapeau explained.

She went on to describe Tran's duties at the lab, which consisted almost exclusively of caring for the live animals. "He was a good employee, and, if I'm not mistaken, he was a supervisor at the time of his termination. If our security guard hadn't caught him sneaking in one night, who knows how long he would have stolen from us. As it is, we think that he'd been stealing from us for a few years."

"In the police report from his arrest, it stated only that 'pharmaceutical paraphernalia' was recovered from his residence. What exactly had he stolen?" Sean asked.

"Hard to say, because we didn't know how long Tran had been stealing from the lab. But after he was arrested, the police recovered a number of vials of some test serum and a few hypodermic needles from his apartment."

"What was the serum?"

"It was from a lion imported from Africa that we routinely ran through a battery of tests," Chapeau responded. "When I look back at it now, I'm glad that I'm not working with live animals anymore. That poor lion eventually died from all of the radiation we exposed it to." She sat silent, staring out the window and into the past. "I'm much happier now. And the money. The money from SISS isn't even in the same ballpark as the money one can make here."

Sean was taken aback by the comment, but went on. "How well did you know Tran?"

"Not very well, I knew who he was, but that was about the extent of our relationship," she paused. "Why are you so interested in Tran?"

"As I told you on the phone this morning, I'm reviewing the early case studies of hepatitis C, and Tran's doesn't fit into the same molds as the others," Sean said.

"And what is it that you're hoping to find out from me?"

He explained how he felt that the reports failed to sufficiently investigate the track marks on Tran's groin and the stolen goods from her lab.

Chapeau sat thinking about Sean's questions. "That's the first I ever heard about Tran having hep C or injecting something into his groin. As for the stolen material, well at least you know what that was."

"Is there any way that the serum from Tran's apartment was contaminated with HCV?" Sean asked.

Chapeau laughed. "Heavens no. Larry Needham—do you know who he is?" she asked. Sean nodded. "Well he was in charge of the investigation into Tran's death, and he had the serum sent to the CDC for analysis. If there was anything suspicious, he would have told me."

"You know Dr. Needham personally?"

"Yes, we went to medical school together. But we had a falling out in the early eighties. SISS was up for review for its federal grants, and knowing that Needham was a rising star in public health, I turned to my old friend, hoping to have a good word strategically placed in Washington, but he turned his back on me. The lab closed less than a year later."

"I'm sorry to hear that," Sean said.

"Don't be. I'm much happier with my job now, and it got me away from Los Angeles and the land of fruits and nuts. And like I said, much more money here than there ever was in LA. I just bought a brand new car. Couldn't do that on the beans SISS paid me. And I even have a parking space with my name posted in front of it," Chapeau said smiling.

"I guess that's all I came to ask," Sean said.

"Tell you what. Put all of your concerns to rest by calling your friend at the CDC and asking for the file on the lion serum that Needham sent down there to be analyzed. All potentially biohazardous material sent to the CDC is catalogued under a strict protocol. That file will put your inquiry to rest."

"Thanks for the advice," Sean said, standing to leave.

"Hope I've been of some assistance."

"You have. That's a big fish," Sean said, pointing to a photo on the wall of Chapeau with three men and a large fish. "Swordfish?"

"It's a marlin. Biggest fish I've ever hauled in."

"Should think so. Thanks again for seeing me Dr. Chapeau."

"Don't mention it," she said opening her office door. "You've really piqued my interest with this Tran thing. Keep me updated if you find any answers, or call if you have any more questions."

"I will. Thanks."

Having gained all of the insight into Tran and SISS that Chapeau had to offer, Sean headed back north to Boston.

SEAN'S phone call caught the CDC intake clerk half an hour before the business day ended. After an extremely slow day, Stan was reluctant to put his book of *New York Times* crossword puzzles down. The last thing he wanted to do was to begin the arduous task of a catalog search. He attempted to persuade Sean to call back the following morning, but Sean politely dropped Mendoza's name, and Stan complied with his request.

Though still a painstaking ordeal, locating the file for an incoming shipment of biohazardous material was easier after the implementation of the CDC's computer networking system. In the past, Stan thumbed through a card catalog system to locate a file. Now it was just a matter of filling in fields on a computer screen, and narrowing down the files to examine.

Sean gave Stan all of the information that he could think of to help the clerk complete the computer's query: the name of the lab, a date range for the shipment, and Needham as the CDC investigator in charge.

"Sure those are the dates?" Stan asked, entering the data into the computer.

"Yes, it's accurate. I'm positive."

"Because it's not finding any profiles that match your query."

"Can you increase the date range a few months, just in case I'm mistaken?" Sean asked.

"Already done it. Nothing matches. You sure about the name of the lab and the investigator in charge?"

"Yeah, I'm positive about those too," Sean said, stumped. "Is there any possibility that this shipment didn't make it onto your database?"

"Absolutely not. Whenever we've had a discrepancy, it has always been on the part of the person making the query, not the computer. Sir, this thing is always right. Never once had a mistake. You know, they sent us a bunch of computer people from Seattle to implement this system. They said it was one hundred percent accurate. And they certainly know computers."

Sean thanked Stan for his time and retired to his couch to think. Where had that serum gone? It could have been misplaced, it could have been misfiled. The possibilities were endless. But this was the CDC, and somewhere, its loss should have been noted. Sean worked his brain in a circular frenzy, not knowing what to do next.

Having run up against a brick wall with respect to Tran, he decided to prepare his apartment for his evening meeting with his class. He put out some chips and a few two liter bottles of soda.

The phone rang as he placed napkins on the coffee table. Picking it up, the poor reception made it obvious that the call was from a cellphone. "Sean?" the voice on the other end asked.

"Yes?"

"It's your father. I'm on Storrow Drive about two minutes away. I'd like to have a talk with you."

Sean shook his head. It was very common of his father to drop in unexpectedly. "I'm really busy. I don't think I have the time. What are you doing in town?"

"Last minute meeting with a client. Just got out of there. Listen, I'll meet you at that nice restaurant by the Charles Hotel."

"I really don't have time for dinner," Sean protested.

"Then we'll just have drinks. See you there in five minutes," his father said hanging up.

Sean stood with the phone in his hand. He wanted to throw it against the wall. His father had always run the family in the same dictatorial fashion that he ran his law firm. It worked in Manhattan but failed miserably on the home front. Sean checked his watch and left his apartment.

Entering the restaurant, Sean found the bar. Three well dressed couples sat in an improvised circle of bar stools as they waited for their table. Sean's father sat at a table off to the side. Sean made his way over to him and took a seat.

"How slow do you walk? You live two blocks from here," Martin Graham said.

"I really don't have time for this."

Sean's father had an empty glass in front of him. The waitress stopped at the table and gave him another Scotch. "Bring him one too, honey," his father said.

Sean rolled his eyes. "So what is it that you want to talk about?"

His father took a sip from his drink. "This program you're in here."

"What about it?"

"I've spoken to a guy down at Hopkins. When you're done with your master's here, he said that he thought you would be a strong candidate for their PhD program in public health. All we have to do is say the word. So bust your ass and finish your work up here. If this public health business is what you want to do, the opportunity is there."

The waitress brought Sean the glass of Scotch. She placed it on the table. He pushed it away. "Are you kidding me? I'm doing great here. I appreciate the effort, but I really don't need your help. Don't you get it? I'm an adult, and I can take care of myself."

His father chuckled. "Right."

"What's that supposed to mean?"

"You and your brother are adults, taking care of yourselves. That's a load. You stumble your way through Georgetown and your brother manages to catch a disease reserved for degenerates. Without my direction, you two would probably be living in a gutter somewhere."

Sean shook his head. In the past, he always found himself arguing with his father. But in the last few years, he had learned to temper his father's delusions. "Both Pete and I have had our problems along the way, but we've gotten by just fine."

"Having HIV is hardly 'just fine'. You and your brother seem to have forgotten that I've gotten you to where you find yourselves today. Well, not including your brother's disease. And neither of you is grateful. It's mind-boggling. Kids today don't know how to express gratitude. You all expect to have everything handed to you. And when it is, you walk away without a single word of thanks. I came here with good news. I got you into Hopkins for a PhD. God knows you never could have done that on your own. Without me you'd be twiddling your thumbs out in the Square, asking people for spare change. I still can't believe that you quit the job with the brokerage firm. What were you thinking? That was a good job. In ten years you would've been making millions. But no, you'd rather be out playing with the natives in Africa. My lord, where did I go wrong?"

Sean stood from the table, not wanting to be too disrespectful. "I'm out of here. Thanks for stopping by." He walked out of the restaurant without saying another word.

Martin Graham remained at the table. He shook his head. Then, spotting the extra Scotch, he tossed it down his throat.

SEAN sat in his apartment, trying to calm himself. Only on the rarest of occasions did a meeting with his father end in a different way. He lay back on the couch and closed his eyes. When the phone rang, he considered letting the answering machine take the call. But then he thought it might be Michelle. He picked up the receiver on the fourth ring.

A warm voice greeted him from the Serengeti. "Hey kiddo!"

"Sam! How are things in the bush?" Sean asked excitedly.

"Life's moving along more slowly now that I'm out here alone again. Have I caught you at a bad time?"

"No, not at all, I was just preparing for a class, but it can wait. God it's great to hear your voice. What time is it there? It's almost five here, so it's almost what, midnight there?" he said.

"I'm not exactly sure, but it's pretty late. I'm at one of the safari lodges, and I figured I'd make a quick call while I had a chance. I won't be near a phone again for at least a couple weeks. I just wanted to see how you were adapting to life again in the states. So how are things going?" she asked.

"The comforts of home are still nice, of course, but I'm incredibly busy, with research and classes and deadlines. The worst part of it is that I've spent the majority of my time chasing a ghost." Sean proceeded to tell Sam all that he had done in relation to the Marcus Tran file, including the most recent dead end with the lost serum.

"So is that the end of the road then?" Sam asked.

"I'm not sure yet. I know that I should let it all drop, and get on with my classes and with the draft report Fulsonmayer wants, but every time I try to do something else, I find myself working my way through this Tran puzzle. It's all engrossing. I'm beginning to feel a bit obsessed."

"Obsessions aren't necessarily bad things. You need to learn to trust your instincts. If you don't think that the CDC and Needham were thorough, pursue it. If you look hard enough, you'll find an answer. It might not be the one you're looking for, but it's out there. Open all closed doors until there aren't any more to open. It won't go away until you have. Trust me."

Sean set out napkins next to the soda and chips. "You said that you'd worked with Needham in the past. What kind of guy is he? Is he a crazy perfectionist, meticulous about everything? Or does he barrel ahead full throttle at everything, bowling over everyone in his path? I just want to know if I'm barking up the wrong tree here."

"Needham is definitely the meticulous type. He's very deliberate, not one to rush any decision. And he's one of the most brilliant men I know. He's not one of those people who simply stumbles upon success. He's the type of person who would have risen to the top of any field he pursued, he just happened to choose public health."

"How long ago was it that you worked with him?" Sean asked.

"Quite a while back. Early eighties mostly. I really haven't worked with him in a number of years."

"Did you do hepatitis research with him?"

"No, not at all. Almost all of his hepatitis work was in the US. When we worked together, it was almost exclusively in Africa, on women's health initiatives. At the time, AIDS was gaining public health attention and he was doing sporadic work on it, so he left much of the work in the women's health projects up to me. It was during those early years that the hepatitis cases you're studying sprang up. Eventually, AIDS was all he did. Who knows what would have happened had he stayed with the hepatitis field? Anyhow, AIDS is how he got to where he is today. An obsession, you might say."

Sean slouched more comfortably into his sofa. "So what project had the two of you been working on?"

"We initiated grass roots programs all over sub-Saharan Africa attempting to curb the spread of syphilis by prostitutes. It wasn't the most glorious program, but it was worthwhile, and I was able to see the world, or more correctly, a large amount of Africa. We went from Zaire in the west to Tanzania in the east, making a short side trip to Egypt as well. We hit every town on the way. I get excited thinking about it. That project was the first time I was published in a scientific journal, even if only as a footnote. *Syphilis Directive in Sub-Saharan Africa 1981-1984.* My name's on the fourth page. You should check it out."

Sean could see her smile from the other side of the world as he jotted the title down. "It's really nice to hear your voice again," he said. "Planning any guest lectures on this side of the globe any time soon?"

"Unfortunately I'm not. I'm out here with the lions for at least another three months, no breaks. Impending deadlines to meet before the grant money disappears. Hopefully I'll make it back to the states some time before the New Year. Not much hope for a white Christmas here. But enough about life out here. How are things with Michelle?"

"Not the best. She's thinking about transferring to Michigan in January."

"Good program. What are your thoughts on the transfer?"

"It's probably best that she go. She's not happy here anymore."

"Is she happy with you?"

"I don't think so. I think I'm just part of a larger problem." Sean glanced at his watch. "Listen, I'd better let you go. The charge for this call could fund another month out in the bush."

"You're right, I should get going. It was great talking with you, and like I said, trust your instincts. I'll give you a call next time I make it to civilization to see how things are going. Take care of yourself."

"I will."

"Miss you."

"Me too, take care," Sean said hanging up the phone.

SEAN found that having twelve people in his apartment at one time may not have been the best idea, if only due to a lack of adequate seating. The oversight left a few of his students shifting uncomfortably on the hardwood floor for an hour. One of them was Michael Rubicon. He was an extremely shy but friendly student who never failed to wave or say hello to Sean when passing on campus. As he sat on the floor behind the coffee table, Sean caught his eye.

Rubicon smiled to conceal his discomfort.

Aside from the seating, the class was much more successful than their first meeting. Everyone seemed to find the atmosphere more relaxing. The group discussion flowed over music from the stereo. The environment lent itself to a more conversational tone, not simply students answering Sean's questions about assigned readings. Everyone appeared to be more relaxed, except for Ankur Gustav.

After Sean announced the next week's readings, the class began to depart. Michael Rubicon stopped to talk to Sean. "*Asante sana*," he said, shaking Sean's hand.

"You're welcome," Sean replied, a bit surprised. "You know Swahili?"

"Just a bit. I know that you just got back from East Africa so I thought I'd try some on you."

"Why do you know Swahili?"

"I don't really. But my concentration is linguistics, so I've already had a smattering of foreign languages."

"Keep up the good work," Sean said as Rubicon left his apartment.

As the student departed, one of the young women in the class stopped to ask Sean a question. The way she looked at Sean made him suspect that she had a crush on him. She asked him something about one of the readings, but Sean wasn't really listening. He was too busy watching Gustav milling about his kitchen. "That's a good question Courtney. I'll talk to Professor Fulsonmayer and get back to you tomorrow."

"Oh, okay. Would you like me to stop by in the afternoon?" she said with the helpless look of a lost puppy.

"Uh, sure. Where would you like to meet?"

"It's up to you."

"How about down at Peabody Museum? Around two PM," he said, still watching Gustav.

"Great. I'll see you then," she replied, flipping her long blonde hair as she turned through the door.

Sean approached Gustav in the kitchen. "Can I help you Ankur?"

"I'm sure you can," the ox-like student said peering down at Sean. His voice was deep and forceful with an eastern European accent.

"Listen, I think we got off on the wrong foot the other

day, but I had to give you the 'F' on the paper because you didn't hand it in."

"I'm on academic probation this semester, and that 'F' isn't helping my cause. If I don't get a 'C' in this course I won't be able to play hockey this winter." He paused looking Sean directly in the eye. "I will play hockey this winter."

"I hope you can, but you're not exactly making the greatest effort so far. Class participation is part of your grade, and you haven't said a word in the two classes we've had. You don't even pay attention during lecture."

"You're the one who needs to pay attention. No more bad grades. You hear me? I know your daily routine and now I know where you live. I'll be watching." Gustav stepped forward until their faces were inches apart. Sean could feel the giant's breath on his forehead.

"Are you threatening me?"

Gustav only stared.

"Get the hell out of here," Sean said, not backing down. Gustav didn't move. "Did you hear me? Get the hell out of here."

"Oh I heard you. And I hope you heard me," Gustav said walking slowly out the door. Sean locked it behind him, his heart pounding wildly. A poor end to a good class.

TWO hours later, Gustav sat with an acquaintance at a table in the back of one of Harvard Square's sports bars. He poured himself a beer from a large pitcher. He downed it and poured another. "I think I just made a big mistake," he said.

"Did you really threaten him?"

"More or less. When I thought about the possibility of missing the hockey season, I just lost it."

"Maybe you should apologize."

"I don't know. I just wanted him to know that no matter what, I will play this season."

"Well, I wouldn't do anything foolish."

Gustav shook his head. "We'll see."

SEAN woke early the next morning, eager to work on anything other than the frustrating Tran file. After grabbing a coffee and a scone in Harvard Square, he made his way to Tozzer, the anthropology library on the north end of campus.

He enjoyed working at his carrel in the basement of the

discreet library because there were rarely any disturbances. A disorganized student during college, he learned in graduate school that it paid to be neat. His desk in the library was well organized. Tidy stacks of papers and books sat just as he had left them. Upon returning from Tanzania, he had decorated the enclosed workspace with colorful photographs of the research lions. His favorite photo was of himself and Sam sitting on the hood of the Land Rover. To be out in the middle of nowhere, he thought.

Stuck to the shelf of the desk, Sean found a Post-It Note. Unfolding the small yellow note, he recognized the writing as Fulsonmayer's. In a three inch by three inch space, the professor had managed to squeeze a detailed outline of tasks he expected Sean to accomplish "in the near future". As a post script, the words "Let's Discuss, Tomorrow, Noon."

Sean sighed. Plenty of work to do before that meeting with Fulsonmayer. He had yet to begin the draft report. His procrastination could be overlooked if he could at least give the professor a strong summary of his research. But this too was doubtful.

Having read all of the case files Mendoza had prepared, Sean followed the doctor's advice and began reading up on the CDC's locational timeline for the spread of known HCV cases. Once the CDC zeroed in on the causative factors involved in the transmission of the hepatitis C virus, they initiated an exhaustive global search for the disease. The locational timeline gave a detailed account of the first known occurrence of HCV for a given geographical location, be it a large city or small town.

Sean scanned the chart which spanned numerous pages in the book. A few of the town names stuck out for Sean, but still sleepy from a late night of reading, he couldn't figure out why. He brainstormed for a while, but then gave up. He made a photocopy of the chart and highlighted the names that stuck out in the event that he might remember them in the future.

Deep in thought, he didn't hear the footsteps approaching from behind. The tap on the shoulder startled him. He turned to see the aging and wilted figure of Chester Hamilton smiling from ear to ear.

"Mr. Graham, what on earth are you doing here so early in the morning?"

"Good morning Professor Hamilton. I'm just doing some research for Professor Fulsonmayer."

"Come join me at the cafe across the way for my morning tea."

"I would love to except—"

"Nonsense. Lad, you'll come to understand one day that you learn much more from talking with people than you ever could from books. Now ship out," Hamilton said, whacking Sean in the leg with his cane.

The two slowly crossed the street to the cafe. Hamilton took tiny steps as he leaned over his wooden cane, gripping Sean's elbow for added support. Sean was very fond of the aged professor. Tenured since the sixties, he still taught one seminar a year and had been Sean's first graduate school professor. Though he had fascinating tales to tell of his adventures living with tribes from across the globe, Sean had difficulty grasping exactly what insight students were supposed to gain from the class. Nonetheless, the old man was charming.

"If Richard Fulsonmayer gives you trouble for not finishing whatever you were doing, blame me. He thinks I'm crazy, you know," Hamilton said when they found seats at a table. He carefully poured three packets of sugar into his tea, brushing his wild bushy white hair back from his face.

"He doesn't think you're crazy," Sean reassured him.

"Bahh. Everyone does. I see them turn and run when they catch sight of me. Even my close friends. Maybe it's time to cut this mop. I'm beginning to look like one of your rock-and-roll stars."

Sean laughed. "Not quite."

"So what is it you're working on these days?"

Sean explained Fulsonmayer's project with the lions, and the background research on hepatitis C.

"Hep C," Hamilton said stirring his tea slowly. "Such a strange disease. They know how it spreads, yet they can't stop it. Kind of like AIDS that way; except from what I understand the fallout will be much, much worse."

Sean nodded in agreement. "Professor Hamilton, have you ever said or done something professionally, only to find out later that you were wrong?"

The professor laughed, "I can't count how many times I've been wrong. I've been teaching since the forties. So many times I've been wrong."

"And did you realize yourself that you were wrong, or did someone tell you?"

"Sometimes I found my mistakes myself, but most often others have to tell you."

"Did any of your students ever find mistakes you made?"

"Certainly."

"How did it make you feel?"

"Embarrassed. I was the teacher. I'm not supposed to be wrong. But when I look back at it now, I realize that both student and teacher seek the same thing—the truth. And if the student can help the teacher find the truth, then both are better off. Today, I'm not sure that the teachers have the same relationship with the students. Teachers are preoccupied. There's too much outside influence—books to write, interviews to give, and of course competition for tenure. It was much simpler back then."

"Did you feel threatened by the students?"

"Of course not. Knowledge is like any other commodity out there. If something I say to a class doesn't make sense, if nobody asks me to clarify, it's assumed that they understand. I don't think that students today were taught that it's their responsibility to make their teachers justify what they say. The act of learning isn't simply about going home and memorizing notes from lectures. That's not learning. To learn you have to create a dialogue of questions. Each question brings about an answer, which in turn begets another question. This is the road toward fully understanding. Not simply repeating things over and over until you can recite them in your sleep." He stopped and Sean waited quietly for him to continue.

"Let me give you an example. A few years ago I went to the hospital because I had a lump in my neck. After hours of tests, this young lady doctor says that I have an angiolypoma, and then uses a bunch of other medical jargon to describe my condition. I'm an educated man, but I had no idea what she was talking about. I thought I was dying, and this young woman let me go on thinking this for a half hour before she told me I was fine. I didn't believe her because I had this giant lump on my neck. So I pushed her and pushed her until she explained, in English, just exactly what was going on in this old body of mine. That's what a student is supposed to do. Push and push until you get satisfactory answers. Your job is to ask questions, their job is to give you the answers.

"It's like going to get your car fixed. Some fella named Mel tells you that your car needs a catalytic converter which costs many thousands of dollars. How the hell do I know what a catalytic converter is? I haven't looked under the hood of my car since the sixties. Had a mustang, you know. Now it's all computer chips and global positioning something-or-others. Anyhow, make him tell you exactly why you need one and what it does. Odds are he'll say that your car really only needs a new spark plug."

Sean laughed as Hamilton ranted about car parts.

"So why this question about me ever being wrong? Is the dean talking about me again?" Hamilton asked, blowing on his tea before taking a sip.

Sean explained how he felt that Needham and the CDC were insufficient in their investigation of the genital track marks and the stolen serum. "I found some answers regarding the serum, but the track marks remain a total mystery. It was suggested to me that the track marks were on the genitals to conceal drug use, but there were no drugs in the guy."

"What did you say the nature of the serum was?"

"Extract from lion's blood."

Hamilton leaned back in his chair, rubbing the handle of his cane. The cane was made of a polished wood with intricate animal carvings on it from the ground to the elephant-head handle. The handle had worn a different color from the many years the old man rubbed it while deep in thought.

"For three years back in the forties I lived with the warmest people I have ever encountered. It was in a little village in the rain forests of western Brazil. No roads in. Just a one hundred mile hike. It's no longer there, I think because of logging. A shame. As I said, these were the most beautiful people in the world, the *Moh-hoa*, which roughly translated means 'Man of the Trees'. I showed you some slides last year in class."

"I remember," Sean said.

"At first they saw me as just this crazy white outsider. I had to watch everything from the edge of the village. My hair wasn't white then. It was brown, and let me tell you, it got long. Looked like a hippie. Not like you. Your hair is just right for a young man," Hamilton said reaching across the table and tapping Sean's head.

"Thank you," Sean said with a chuckle.

"So where was I?"

"Living on the edge of the village."

"Right, thank you. So I was living on the edge of the village for quite some time. But then one day, I remember it was after two weeks of nonstop rain, I came down with a terrible fever, chills and all. They took me in. They knew I was sick, and come to think of it, maybe even a bit delirious. Some might say I'm still delirious, but you know that I'm not."

Sean smiled.

"I was in a bad way for quite a while, and they nursed me back to health. They watched me for about a week, until I finally was able to get about on my own. Point of my rambling is that they cured me you see. With their own medicine."

"That's wonderful," Sean said, humoring the old professor.

"You don't see what I'm getting at, lad. They didn't give me our traditional medicines from the states. There was no corner pharmacy. And even if there was, this was the forties. Antibiotics weren't easy to come by. No sir. They fed me cassava laced with boar's blood." He stopped to let the image sink in. "You see Sean, these people are in touch with nature. They believe in the power that rests within every animal, and they're not alone. Many cultures from across the world look to nature when the human body goes awry. This tribe had uses for parts of every animal. They used diluted snake venom as a pain killer. And it worked."

"I'm not exactly sure what you're getting at," Sean said.

"It's obvious. This fellow of yours was trying to tap the powerful rhythms that occur in nature."

Sean sighed, "You're suggesting that this guy was participating in some kind of ritual?"

"Not just any ritual, perhaps the most powerful—a fertility ritual."

"I'm not so sure."

"I think it's obvious," Hamilton said.

"I think most people would call it a coincidence."

"Calling it a coincidence would be naive. Don't be afraid to see life through the eyes of another culture. That's what anthropology is about; shedding the barriers of your culture in order to better understand another."

"I don't know," Sean said, shaking his head.

"As Westerners, we have difficulty imagining life in a way that is not our own. Take cats and dogs. In Western culture, we keep these animals as pets, spending hundreds of dollars every year on food and vets and whatever else the critters might need. This is an absurd notion to many other cultures. The only time any of these animals would even be let in the house would be on a dinner plate. It's all in the cultural perspective.

"Why do you think that tigers are nearing extinction?" Hamilton continued, "The market for tiger skins is no longer booming. Much more money can be derived from what's under that skin. Bring that tiger to Bangkok and you could sell its organs for over fifty thousand dollars. Why? Because there's a market in Far East countries that seeks to capture the raw essence of nature. Ground tiger eyes can be mixed into food to cure glaucoma. Tiger claw cures rheumatism. And tiger testicle soup cures impotence and acts as an aphrodisiac. Our culture doesn't celebrate the spiritual links between man and nature. Now we have little blue pills and Bobby Dole. We can't imagine curing impotence with testicle soup. But I bet this man of yours did, and he sought to embody the power within the king of beasts. My money says he was impotent or into strange sex."

"That's an interesting theory, I'm just not so sure I can swallow it."

"Ask Fulsonmayer what he thinks. You'll knock his socks off."

"That's what I'm afraid of."

STEPPING out of his palatial island homestead, Barnard Claris gingerly placed the wide-brimmed hat onto his head. The sun above the island of Tutuila in American Samoa was unforgiving. He grimaced as the straw scraped along the sunburn of his increasingly noticeable bald spot. Just the day before, he had forgotten to wear the hat. Now he paid the price. Hovering in the mid-eighties, the temperature was moderate, but the humidity was suffocating.

As usual, the sweat began before he made it to the towering palm tree where his bike rested. He undid another button on his linen shirt. Sweat dripped into his eyes. He removed his glasses, wiping the perspiration from his sun-aged face. He threw his leather pouch over his shoulder and began the short bicycle journey to town. The ride was always paradoxical. The faster he rode, the cooler the wind felt, but the more he sweat. By the time he reached the semi-paved road leading to the town of Pago Pago, the soaked linen shirt clung to his body.

His large estate sat dwarfed against the backdrop of the island's volcanic ridgeline. From his home, it was a twenty minute bike ride through a sparsely populated forest to the island's main road. Other than the capital city of Pago Pago, and a few satellite towns, the Polynesian island was, for the most part, only minimally developed—except for the tuna canning factories. When Star-Kist and Chicken of the Sea landed on the island, not a single person could escape their broad-reaching Western influence.

Claris passed a rusted sign indicating the side road leading to the Star-Kist plant. He looked down the road, but continued into town.

Riding down the middle of the street, local school boys chased the sweating Claris, calling him what they heard their parents call him, the "Dripping Expatriate".

He stopped in front of the small post office, leaning his bike against a street light. The boys caught up to him, sticking their hands out and laughing.

"Just a moment," Claris said, again removing his glasses and wiping the sweat from his eyes. He reached into the pocket of his tattered shorts. He handed each of the boys a quarter and sent them on their way.

When the last of the boys had left his side, he opened the door to the post office, expecting to be hit with the cold blast of air conditioning. But it was only hotter inside. He walked past the counter, avoiding eye contact with anyone. He inserted the key into his PO box and opened it. Bending over to peer inside, he was greeted by the ordinary emptiness of its stainless steel walls.

He closed the box and walked outside. He looked up at the cloudless sky, wiping the sweat from his brow.

"The rain will come late this year," a man said as he

passed Claris on the sidewalk. Claris watched the man walk away. The large dark skinned man was not sweating.

The open market was a block away. Locals brought in all of the produce from the hills daily. Claris walked the block, trying to stay in the shade of the buildings. Browsing among the fruit and vegetable stands, he made his decision. He bought a mango and retired to a park bench in the square opposite the government building.

He reached into his leather pouch and removed a pocket knife. He cut the mango and ate the pieces slowly. His linen shirt had dried in the heat. When he'd finished his mango, he wiped his hands in the grass at his feet, removing the sticky mango juice.

Satisfied that his hands were clean, he again reached into the weathered leather pouch, removing a cellphone and a laptop computer. He ran a cable between the two and turned on the computer. Its modem whirred to life and within seconds, Claris was back in touch with the western world.

He leaned back against the stiff park bench, ready to read *The New York Times*. An hour after he began, Claris read the international news briefs:

Lusaka, Zambia — Dr. Lawrence Needham, Director-General of the World Health Organization, did not attend yesterday's AIDS panel discussion at the Conference of African Public Health Workers. Needham was to lead the discussion, but was forced to return to the United States, citing medical reasons. Conference organizers voiced their disappointment in his absence, but called the meeting a success.

Claris reread the article. When he finished, he spoke softly to the computer screen, "My dear friend Lawrence, what seems to be ailing you? You too could be living in this god-forsaken tropical paradise. Oh, the decisions that we make in life; sometimes they come back to haunt us."

A bitter Claris sat alone on the bench for another hour, staring skyward. The typhoon season would start soon. The cool rains would once again bring relief from the tropical heat. But not today.

He looked around the square. Large men and women milled about, fulfilling their daily routines. Claris recognized most of them. But in spite of having lived on the island for fourteen years, he was still an outsider. In a white minority comprising less than three percent of the population, he would always be a sweaty sore thumb. And no matter how much effort he gave to becoming one of the islanders, the locals would always see him for what he was: an expatriate running from the American mainland.

An elderly tourist couple dressed in matching short-sleeved pastel shirts approached Claris as he packed.

"My wife and I are on holiday from London," the man said in a British accent. "Could we bother you to snap our photo?" he said, holding his camera out to a visibly annoyed Claris.

Beginning to drip again, Claris looked at the two blankly. He slowly wiped his brow. "Fuck off, old man. Shove off to your stuffy fucking London, you limy."

5

SEAN spent the rest of the morning in the library, mulling over Hamilton's observations. The facts from Tran's file were consistent with what the old professor had suggested. Track marks yet no drugs, no admission of sex of any type, and the lion serum. To top it off, he was of Far Eastern descent and maybe even impotent. But Hamilton was probably certifiably crazy. There was no way that Sean was going to Fulsonmayer with that hypothesis. He needed more concrete research. He spent three hours scouring the library's texts, searching for other accounts of fertility rituals involving animals. To his surprise, he found plenty of evidence on the dusty library shelves.

There were examples from cultures across the globe of men using animal blood and body parts in ritual contexts. Gorillas in Central Africa, jaguars in South America, polar bears in Alaska. Hamilton's theory began looking ever more enticing and credible. With renewed hope, Sean left the library and headed back to his apartment. He needed to speak with Chapeau. The missing serum had taken on greater importance.

Sean walked home absentmindedly, running through new Tran scenarios in his head. Two blocks from his apartment he was almost knocked over by a man walking in the opposite direction. Stunned, Sean turned to look at the man, just in time to see Gustav duck around the corner.

Once back in his apartment, Sean called Chapeau. Her secretary said she was out of the office for the day, and that she'd be back in the morning. Sean then called Ian at home, but got his answering machine. He hung up realizing that Ian was probably working at the firm. He gave the office a call.

"Hello, this is Ian Nielson."

"Ian, I've got some crazy news."

"What is it?"

"There's too much to explain it all on the phone."

"You want to grab some dinner?"

"Sure. Where?"

"Can you come into Boston?" Ian asked. "I'm working late, but I could use the break. How's seven at The Cellar?"

"Sounds great. See you there."

With nobody to share his news with, Sean decided to start the draft report for Fulsonmayer. He booted up his computer before going into his bedroom to change into sweatpants. Finding his favorite pair of Georgetown sweats, he put them on.

Turning from his bedroom, a sharp pain hit Sean in the back, knocking him to the floor. The sound of the shattering window began to register in his head as the shards of glass crashed all around him. Instinctively he covered his head, waiting for more projectiles. None came. From the street below he heard footsteps running away. He started to sit up, using his hand for balance, but fell back shrieking in pain. A piece of glass had lodged itself deep in his palm. Scanning the bedroom, he grabbed the bed and eased himself up onto it, a shooting pain running the length of his back. He looked out the window. No one below. Sitting on the bed again, he saw the large brick amongst the broken glass.

Bending to pick it up, the pain returned. The words "BACK OFF" were written in block letters on the brick. He placed it on the bed. The wound on his hand was bleeding heavily. He gripped the piece of glass in his palm and jerked it out, wincing in pain. His back was starting to throb, and for the first time he could feel the warmth of his blood flowing down his spine. Removing his shirt he walked to the bathroom and looked over his shoulder into the mirror. A small triangular flap of skin dangled in the center of his back. He put another shirt on and called the police. They arrived as a skinny male paramedic finished his examination.

"The bandage on your back will be fine until you get to the hospital, but you have to get that hand looked at ASAP. That's a deep puncture wound. We can take you to Mount Auburn Hospital, or the campus police can take you to the University Health Services. It's up to you."

"If it's all the same, I'd rather just stay on campus," Sean replied.

"That's fine, you just need to sign this release form," the paramedic said, handing Sean a clipboard.

Sergeant Lyndon of Harvard's campus police had been looking around the apartment while the paramedics worked on Sean. Lyndon was a massive black man with his head shaved to the scalp. His years in the Marines were apparent in everything from the neatness of his uniform to the stiffness of his gait. When the paramedics left, he sat on the couch next to Sean. He was all business. "Name's Lyndon.Your super filled us in on what happened. Just the brick through the window, right?"

"That's right."

"Happen to see anyone?"

"No. But I heard someone running away."

"Did it sound like the person wore soft or hard soles?"

"Soft, I suppose."

"Do you have any idea who might have done this? Enemies, old girlfriends, or boyfriends?"

Sean shot Lyndon a look.

"You have to ask these days," Lyndon said, shrugging his shoulders.

"There's a student of mine who kind of threatened me last night. And I literally bumped into him a couple of blocks from here about five minutes before this happened."

"What's his name?" Lyndon asked, furiously scribbling notes.

"Ankur Gustav."

"Gustav, the defenseman on the hockey team?"

"One and the same."

"He's a very big boy. What's his beef with you?"

"I failed him on an assignment. He said that I'd better watch out."

"Anyone else?"

"Not that I can think of."

"Well, we'll take the brick and go have a talk with Mr. Gustav. We'll be in touch," Lyndon said. "Oh, I almost forgot. We'll give you a ride to health services."

"Appreciate it," Sean said.

IAN arrived at Sean's apartment as the building superintendent was leaving. "I'll have the window replaced by dinner tomorrow," he said to Sean, passing Ian in the doorway.

Ian's face was full of concern. "Are you alright?"

"Yeah, I'm fine. Just a bit scary getting hit with a brick in your own apartment. Worst of all, the brick smashed my stereo."

"How do you feel?"

Sean held up his palm. "They gave me six stitches in the hand and eight in the back. Both are throbbing, but they gave me some Tylenol with codeine and I'm feeling fine."

"Does Michelle know?"

"She's in Michigan for the weekend. I left a message with her roommate."

"Do you have any idea who did it?"

"It might've been that student I told you about. Cops are looking into it. I thought you had to work late."

Ian laughed, "Right. You call me frantically babbling about being attacked by brick-wielding assailants, and I'm going to stay at work all night. Have you eaten?"

"Not yet."

"Good, I brought over some burgers," Ian said tossing a paper sack on the coffee table.

"Thanks."

"Don't mention it. So what's the news that was so important that we just had to have dinner?"

"I made a possible break-through on the Tran puzzle."

"So you haven't dropped it yet."

"Not when it's heating up."

"Don't want to burst your bubble, but the guy's been dead for twenty years and they know how he died. There's nothing to heat up."

"Correction—they know what he died of, they're wrong about how he caught it."

"Let's hear the latest theory."

"First, we start with the facts. He's not promiscuous, possibly not even sexually active."

"Possibly."

"Possibly, that's what I said."

"Fine," Ian said.

"He had no drugs in his system, yet he had track marks."

"Right."

"He had strangely placed track marks."

"Admittedly strange."

"And then there's the matter of the lion serum," Sean

said, taking a cheeseburger from the paper bag.

"What?"

"That's what he stole from the lab. Serum derived from lion's blood."

"Really. So what's—"

"I'm getting to it. Hold onto your hat," Sean said, pausing for dramatic effect.

"Yes?"

"He was participating in a fertility ritual."

"What? That's simply outlandish. Who came up with that?"

"Professor Hamilton and I had a long talk this morning."

"Why is that name familiar?"

"He's the old man with the cane who's always feeding the squirrels in Harvard Yard."

Ian burst into laughter. "That guy's a professor? I always thought he was a homeless guy. I gave him a dollar once. He smiled and thanked me."

"You idiot," Sean laughed. "He happens to be an extremely intelligent man—with periodic lapses into insanity."

"I don't know."

"Don't worry, he was just the sounding board. I spent the morning doing research, and found several documented cases of this type of thing from across the world. People do it. For whatever reason, people do it."

"I guess it makes sense," Ian said.

"You're an easy sell. Shouldn't you be playing devil's advocate?"

"I think I might have seen this coming before you did."

"How so?"

"Remember the picture of Tran from the front of the file?"

"Sure, it's right here," Sean said, opening the file and removing the color copy of the photo. "What about it?"

"Tell me what you see."

"Tran in front of a sports car."

"Look closer."

"Uh, I don't know, some bushes in the background. What am I supposed to see?"

"Look closely at the car; the dashboard. What do you see?"

"A silver something-or-other. That little hunchbacked guy

who runs around the desert playing the flute. Oh, I know what it's called. No, don't tell me. It's a ... okay, tell me. I forgot."

"It's a kokopelli."

"Right, kokopelli. We saw plenty of those driving across the Southwest. So it's a kokopelli, what does that mean?" Sean asked.

"He's a prominent character in Native American mythology."

"And?"

"He's most widely known as a mischief-maker, but he's also a god of fertility."

"So why didn't you say something earlier?"

"Yeah right. The guy has a kokopelli on his dashboard, so it logically follows that the track marks on his balls are from a fertility ritual? Come on. I was supposed to make that leap? I don't think so."

"Wow. Good eye. I never would've seen that."

"It's all still pretty circumstantial."

"I would've said that before, but now with the kokopelli it's too much of a coincidence."

"So now what? Will you finally let it rest?" Ian asked.

"No way. Now, the missing serum is even more important. I think this guy gave himself HCV by injecting that serum into his nuts."

"Whoa. Hold on a second. You're saying that he caught HCV from a lion? You said lions have feline hepatitis, not hepatitis C."

"Right. What I don't know is whether its a close enough relative to HCV that it could actually mutate and infect humans. That's why I need to speak with Chapeau again."

"Fine, but, no offense, why does it even matter?" Ian asked.

Sean thought for a moment. "It matters because Tran was one of the first five people in the US, if not the world, to contract the virus. And I, we, seem to be on track to find out how he actually got it. If that missing serum turns out to contain HCV, then we might have found the precise moment when this little known plague jumped species into humans. That's huge."

"It's a long shot, is what it is."

"Maybe, but it's worth pursuing. God only knows what

good could come from knowing exactly where HCV came from. New treatments, a vaccine, maybe a cure."

"If hepatitis C is such a big deal, why isn't it all over the news?"

"Because it's not flashy like Ebola—it doesn't kill you in six days. But it's following the same media pattern that AIDS did. It'll start making big news when someone like Rock Hudson dies. By all accounts this is a horrific global problem."

"Take a step back. You, a graduate student in anthropology and public health, with the assistance of your strikingly handsome law student friend, have brilliantly stumbled upon the human origin of HCV; something that this guy Needham, who, might I add, is the Director-General of the World Health Organization, missed. Is that what you're proposing?"

"In a nut shell."

"Are you sure they gave you pain killers and not hallucinogens?"

"Pretty sure."

"Well, let's for the moment assume you've got Tran dead to rights. What next? You told me that the CDC said the serum was a no-show at their labs. How do you find out where the serum went?"

"That's where the next stumbling block is," Sean said. "I don't know where to look."

"What about Chapeau?"

"She said the last she heard of it was when she gave it to Needham."

"Did she personally give it to him, or was it couriered, or what?"

"I didn't think to ask."

"Ask her."

"I will," Sean said. "You know, Needham was the one who officially signed off on all of the reports, but a few other names turn up here and there as people collaborating on the files. If we could find these people now, I'd like to call them."

"What you meant to say was if I can find them, you'd like me to call them."

"Pretty much."

"If you give me names, I'll give them to the computer, and hopefully I can get you some numbers. I'll do it right now on your laptop."

Sean yawned as he wrote a list of six names from the file.

"Why don't you get some rest while I deal with this," Ian said.

"I'm just going to put my head down for a few minutes."

Sean was finishing propping pillows on the couch when the phone rang. It was Sergeant Lyndon. "How are you feeling Mr. Graham?"

"I'm fine. Any news?"

"We talked to Gustav. He denied seeing you today and has a few friends who vouch for him, saying he was playing basketball with them at the time of the incident. He really doesn't like you, and my money would say that he did it, but there's really no way to prove it."

"Great. So now what?"

"Without any other leads, it'll have to go in the books as vandalism, not assault."

"So that's that?"

"Like I said, unless something else turns up, that's all we can do. Just keep us informed if anything else should happen. I wouldn't worry though, it was probably just some school kid making good on a bet."

"Very reassuring."

"Sorry. Have a good evening."

Sean replaced the receiver and sighed.

"The police?" Ian said.

"Yeah. They have nothing on Gustav. Guess bricks aren't traceable."

"Not when all of the sidewalks around here are made of them."

"Good point. I'm beat," Sean said lying on the couch. "Let me know if you find anything."

A few hours later, Sean awoke to the buzz of his computer's printer. "You're still here? What time is it?"

Ian looked at his watch. "Quarter after two. I couldn't stop, I was on a roll."

"Find anything?"

"Yes. Of the names you gave me, I've got phone numbers for two. Of the others, one's dead, two are overseas, and I found nothing on the last. Take a look," Ian said, handing Sean the printout.

"Chicago and San Francisco. I guess those are the best bets, I'll call them tomorrow. Thanks Ian."

"No problem. I think I can find one of the guys overseas, but I'm not promising anything," Ian said rubbing his eyes. "Do you mind if I crash here? I don't want to deal with catching a cab right now."

"Sure, I'll stay out here on the couch, take my bed."

"You sure?"

"Positive."

WHEN Sean woke up a few minutes past eleven in the morning, Ian had already left. Sean went through the previous day's events again, until they all fell into place. Pouring himself a cup of coffee, he remembered his meeting with Fulsonmayer. He pondered over telling the professor about Gustav.

In half an hour he had showered and left his apartment for his meeting. The late morning air was cool in spite of the sun's presence high above a few scattered clouds. Sean walked slowly through Harvard Yard on his way to Fulsonmayer's office. Freshmen sat reading under trees in front of their dorms, taking advantage of the lingering late summer weather. A Frisbee floated silently over Sean's head. Twenty Japanese tourists each awaited their turn for a photo with the giant bronze statue of the college's namesake, John Harvard. From its towering white steeple, the ancient bell of Memorial Church rang out loudly, reverberating off the red brick buildings of the Yard. It was noon, and Sean was late.

The door to Fulsonmayer's office was open, and his secretary instructed Sean to go in. He knocked as he peered around the door frame. "Come in Sean," Fulsonmayer said looking at his watch.

"Sorry I'm late."

"Let's not make a habit of it. How's my draft coming along?"

"I don't have anything written other than a rough outline. But, I think I'll be able to write the draft quickly, as soon as the outline is solid."

"I can't emphasize enough how important it is that we get this paper ready for publication."

"I'm aware of it's importance, Professor Fulsonmayer."

"Then that's all we need say on the issue," the professor

said, turning his attention back to his paperwork.

"There's something I think I need to tell you," Sean began.

"Which is?"

"Ankur Gustav, from your ecology class, has become somewhat of a problem."

"How so?"

"Well, I failed him on the first paper because he didn't turn it in, and he sort of threatened me."

"He threatened you?" Fulsonmayer said removing his glasses.

"Yes. And yesterday I think he might have thrown a brick through my apartment window," Sean said revealing the stitches on his palm.

"Good lord, are you alright?"

"I'm fine. Campus police said he has an alibi. It's nothing really. I just thought you should know in the event that he should do anything in the future."

"I appreciate your telling me. If he even hints to you that he threw the brick, I'll be sure that he's expelled. Don't you worry," Fulsonmayer said sternly. "Are you sure you're alright?"

"I'm fine, thanks. There's just one other thing. I know you said to keep moving ahead on the draft report, and I have been. But I've also been looking deeper into that hep C file I'd spoken with you about."

Fulsonmayer smiled, "And what did you find?"

Sean related his latest theory in great detail, including everything down to the kokopelli. "The missing serum is now of some importance. Dr. Chapeau said that Needham was the last person to have it. He was supposed to send it to the CDC, but they never got it."

Fulsonmayer reclined in his large leather chair. "Allow me to preface the following by stating that I'm not particularly enthralled with your preoccupation with this file. However, it would seem that you're in luck. Although they're rarely there, the Needhams live right in Brookline, and Larry and his wife are in town getting the good doctor a medical exam. He thinks that he caught a bad spell of malaria over in Zambia. Anyhow, Mrs. Fulsonmayer and I are having the Needhams over for dinner. Why don't you join us? I'm sure that Larry would love to discuss this dilemma of yours. And it would help me to have you finally put this behind you so you could concentrate on more pressing matters. Tell you what, why don't you bring Michelle along with you?"

He obviously didn't know of her intentions of transferring, Sean thought. "That would be great."

"It's settled then. I'll give you a call with the specifics. Now be gone and get going on that draft."

"I will," Sean said leaving the office.

AFTER his meeting with Fulsonmayer, Sean stopped by the library, packed some of his notes in his bag and headed to his apartment. A message from Chapeau waited for him when he arrived. He called her.

"Dr. Chapeau, thanks for returning my call," Sean said.

"So what's new Mr. Graham?"

"I know this is out of the blue, but I think that there might be a connection between SISS and hepatitis C. I know that you dismissed the idea that anything in your lab was contaminated with HCV, but I think that you might have been mistaken."

"Is there any evidence that would support this theory of yours?" she asked.

"I'll admit, it's largely circumstantial, but I think it's becoming more possible the more that I learn about Tran. The evidence that I've found is supportive of the idea that Tran was engaging in some form of fertility ritual. But I need to be able to prove that something from your lab was contaminated with HCV."

"That's all but impossible to prove now, these many years after the lab closed. And as for circumstantial evidence, it doesn't really float in the world of science."

"I know." Sean thought for a minute. "You said that you had been irradiating the lion. Had you performed any blood work on it?"

"Of course."

"Any I could see?"

"The lab closed years ago. I have no idea where any of those files might be. Please tell me you're not suggesting that Tran caught a derivative of hepatitis C from the lion."

"Hear me out. From studying HCV, I know that a vaccine for the virus is difficult to find because of the fact that the virus is highly prone to mutations, making it difficult for a single vaccine to be effective. I also know that about ninety percent of African lions we studied are seropositive for feline hepatitis—"

"But I thought you said that the hepatitis isn't detrimental to a lion's health?" Chapeau interrupted.

"That's not what I was getting at. Given that the vast majority of lions have feline hepatitis, let's assume for a moment that your lion did. Is it then possible that subjecting the lion to radiation for your tests caused a mutation in the feline hepatitis, that could possibly have manifested itself as HCV?"

"Radiation does cause mutations in genetic material, and as you said, HCV does survive because of it's mutations, so theoretically, it's possible that feline hepatitis could have mutated into HCV. But it is highly, highly, unlikely."

"Unlikely, but possible," Sean reiterated.

"Look, viruses cross the species barrier all of the time. In 1993 hantavirus jumped from field mice to humans. A few years back in Hong Kong, avian flu jumped from chickens to humans. And of course we all know about mad cow disease over in Europe. But in almost all instances, the cross-species transfer of a disease follows relatively simple vectors—maybe it's something we breathe, maybe it's something we eat. What you're suggesting is intricate, and against the odds."

"I know," Sean admitted.

"Did you call the CDC to look into the serum?"

"I did, and that's why I called you again. The serum was a no-show. They have absolutely no record of its transfer."

"Really? Is there any way that there's some kind of mistake?"

"I asked the same thing, and I was assured that there was no mistake. They never received the serum. Which means that it was either lost, or it was never sent. If it was lost, I would think that there would have been some form of investigation into its disappearance."

"So you're suggesting that it was never sent. Is that what you're saying?" Chapeau asked.

"That's what it looks like."

"Yes, it does, doesn't it? You don't think that I didn't give it to Needham do you? Because I did, I can assure you. I specifically remember giving it to a young student he'd sent over. Needham was working in a lab over at UCLA. If this is really a concern of yours, I think you'll have to find a way to talk to Needham or one of his team members."

"That's the next step."

"I have to admit, when you first came looking for me, I never in a million years could have foreseen you coming up with this sequence of events. It's a somewhat logical series of events, yet unlikely. Hepatitis C from a lion. I hope you find that serum because, though finding HCV in it is unlikely, I want to know what you turn up. I guess Needham is the missing link between me and the CDC. He's a busy man and rarely in the country. Best of luck getting an audience with him."

"Thanks," Sean said, not revealing that he was soon to have dinner with the doctor.

"Let me know if you make any progress. Stranger things have happened. By the way, how is life as a teacher treating you?"

"Fine, except for this character named Gustav. He's just a punk who thinks he can intimidate me. What kind of student does that?"

Chapeau laughed. "Well I hope it all works out."

Sean thanked Chapeau for her time, and planned his next move. The deep orange light of late afternoon crept along the hardwood floor, casting long shadows across the apartment. He pulled the list of phone numbers Ian had found from a folder. James Mason and Carl Tessum were Needham's associates on the LA hepatitis cases that still lived in the US. Sean decided he would call Mason first in Chicago.

JAMES Mason lived in a small dingy apartment in the Rogers Park neighborhood on Chicago's north side. He lived alone except for the company of a cat that he hated. Empty beer bottles littered the floor of his apartment. The sink overflowed with dishes.

Mason despised keeping sober during the eight hours he taught high school biology for the Chicago Public Schools. The window shades in his apartment were drawn. He laid motionless on his couch before the muted television. The overweight gray cat nuzzled its way between Mason's legs, starved for attention. The phone's first two rings went unnoticed.

ON the East Coast, Sean sat patiently waiting for an answer.

A man retrieved the phone from what sounded like a deep sleep. Sean looked at his watch; it was too early to be asleep.

"Hello?" the man said with a gruff voice, still not quite awake.

"Hello, is James Mason there?" Sean asked.

"This is Mason. Who's this?"

"My name's Sean Graham, and I was hoping to ask you a few questions about some work you performed for the CDC back in the early eighties."

"What? Fuck the CDC. They're a bunch of high-brow assholes," Mason said, revealing his drunken state.

Sean was silent, not knowing how to proceed.

"You work for the CDC?" Mason asked.

"No I don't, I'm just a graduate student from Boston."

"What do you want to know?"

"Just a question about some work you did with Lawrence Needham."

"Fuck. I should've known this was about Needham. You work for that prick?"

"No, like I said, I'm just a student."

"So you want to know about those hepatitis cases back in LA, right?" Mason said.

"That's right, how did you know?"

"That's the only time I worked with Needham, and the last time I worked for the CDC. They fired me because of him."

"Sorry to hear that," Sean said.

"You're sorry? Try getting a good job after the CDC gives you the can. Assholes."

"Listen," Sean said, "I don't want to take up much of your time. Do you remember the Marcus Tran file?"

"Sure, Vietnamese lab rat."

"That's right, he worked at a lab outside of LA. Do you remember anything about that file?"

"Not really, other than he didn't fit into Needham's profile for the early cases."

"How so?"

"Originally Needham wanted everyone with this new disease to fall into the category of sex fiend or drug user. He said that all had disease consistent with a Non-A, Non-B viral infection. And whatever he said was gospel."

"Needham coined that phrase—Non-A, Non-B virus?"

"Sure as hell did. Got me fired over it, even though he ended up being wrong."

"What do you mean?"

"Maybe 'wrong' isn't the word I'm looking for. I think we knew right then that we could identify the new virus as type 'C', not some cryptic Non-A, Non-B bullshit that kept people guessing for years."

"So what happened?"

"He forced the closure of those five cases. The CDC was pressuring him to get answers. Four of them fit his profile: IV junkie, promiscuous sex, or both. But not that Tran guy. I made a stink when he closed the file. Got fired," Mason said. "Who the hell are you anyway? Calling me out of the blue and bringing up all this shit!" he barked into the phone.

"Mr. Mason, I told you I'm just a student looking for some answers."

"You don't work for Needham?"

"Absolutely not. Listen, just one more question."

"What now?"

"Regarding Tran. Do you remember if Needham, or anyone working with you, received lion serum from the lab that Tran worked at? Dr. Chapeau, from that lab, said she sent it to the CDC via Needham, yet the CDC's never heard of the serum."

Mason didn't answer immediately. All Sean could hear was the sound of Mason's labored breathing. "I couldn't tell you one way or the other. But I do remember that the serum was at issue for some reason. What the hell that reason was, I have no idea."

"You're sure you can't remember."

"I already lost one job because of Needham. I ain't fuckin' with his business again. This conversation is over," Mason said slamming down the receiver.

Though brief, Sean found the conversation mildly insightful. That was, only if Mason was of sound mind, which was far from clear. For what it was worth, Needham had apparently made some enemies for himself. And although Sean still didn't know if Needham had ever seen the serum, Sean now knew that the serum was the subject of some debate among the small team from the CDC. Sean hoped

Carl Tessum in San Francisco could shed some light on the nature of that debate.

Sean dialed the number from the printout.

A woman answered the phone.

"May I please speak with Carl Tessum?" Sean asked.

"One moment please," she said over the din of children playing loudly in the background.

"Hello," Tessum said picking up the phone.

"Dr. Tessum, my name is Sean Graham, and I have a few questions for you regarding work you did for the CDC several years back," Sean said.

"Oh, okay. Can you excuse me for just a second," Tessum said putting his hand over the receiver. Sean could hear him telling the kids to be quiet. "I'm sorry, the boys just got home from soccer practice and they're still a bit wound up."

"I remember those days."

"So what is it that I can help you with Mr. Graham?" Tessum asked.

"It's regarding the work you did with Lawrence Needham and the CDC out in LA," Sean said. He continued, explaining his desire to learn more about the missing serum.

"Wow, I haven't thought about that case in a long while. Marcus Tran," Tessum said, his voice growing distant. "Those were truly exhaustive weeks we spent down in LA. Needham worked us like dogs. Eighteen hour days."

"What was it like working with him?"

"He was a complete egomaniac, and he had some really extreme views."

"Such as?" Sean asked.

"Well, during our work down there I remember there being some violence in central Africa. The BBC was reporting that Americans were being targeted by guerrillas. Our State Department was urging the immediate evacuation of all Americans. I knew Needham had students over there so I relayed the news to him. All he could go on about was how barbaric Africans were. This really surprised me because I knew how much work he did over there. I was going to dismiss his comments as the utterances of a sleep deprived man, but he went on and on." Tessum paused for a second. "He really turned what should have been a friendly debate into much more."

"How's that?" Sean asked.

"Well I took the stance that it was Europe's fault that Africa is such a political and economic mess. Life had existed on the continent virtually untouched by outside sources until Westerners came along. For thousands of years, the people of Africa had recognized territorial boundaries passed down to them from their ancestors. Then came the Europeans, who arbitrarily divided the continent into countries, failing to recognize any of the traditional boundaries. Bitter enemies were suddenly expected to unite as a nation. It was doomed from the outset, and we continue to see its failings today: warring factions within the same country at civil war for the power of a Western-style government. It's only called a civil war because it occurs within the boundaries of a country. What people don't realize is that these different factions have been at war for centuries. Needham chose not to see this."

"So you were at odds."

"Hell yes, we were at odds. In his high and mighty way, he said, and I quote, 'The continent of Africa is in disarray, not because Western thinkers embarked on an ambitious mission of enlightenment, but rather because they abandoned that mission when faced with the slightest measure of adversity. It is the moral duty of educated men to provide the means of social enrichment for those less fortunate, lest disparity prevail.'"

"Wow," Sean muttered.

"Wow's right. This all came from an 'enlightened' man. I'm sure that in order to rise to where he is today, he didn't offer these social insights to many others. Pressure of the situation must have gotten to him."

"Not that that's not an interesting insight, but what do you know about Tran?" Sean asked.

"That was my file of ..." Tessum abruptly stopped. "Can I ask why you're so interested in this case?"

"I'm doing background research for a related project for one of my professors."

"And where is it that you study?"

"At Harvard."

"Oh, for whom?"

"This project is for Richard Fulsonmayer."

"Fulsonmayer, I met him at a seminar in Denver once. Interesting man. I'm sorry, I just wanted to know a little about you. What was I saying?"

"The Tran file."

"Oh yes, the Tran file. Of the five LA cases, Tran was my assignment. I conducted hundreds of hours of interviews with him. Knew almost everything there was to know about him."

"Almost everything?"

"Well, we were working with a certain profile that Needham had developed for the then unknown disease. What Needham labeled—"

"Non-A, Non-B," Sean interrupted.

"That's correct. Good to see you've done your homework. As you know from the case file, there was no recent drug use and no sex. Yet Tran had these unusual track marks on his groin. We never did resolve the nature of those marks."

"Why not?"

"The CDC was pressuring Needham for answers. They had a dozen new cases of the disease in New York, and the public health community needed answers. At Needham's demand, Tran went into the books as contracting the virus through promiscuous sex."

"Didn't you have any say in the matter?"

"Not really. Needham was top dog. We were all there as his lackeys. You don't understand, crossing Needham was career suicide."

"Like James Mason."

"Yes, like James Mason. I take it you've spoken to him?"

"This afternoon."

"I haven't heard from him in years. He really fell to pieces. I'm not sure he's playing with a full deck anymore. Getting fired from the CDC crushed him. Was he of any help to you?"

"Only marginally. You've answered one of my two questions, which the file didn't. I had gotten the impression from the file that the track marks were simply overlooked."

"No, I knew about them, and thought they were strange because there weren't any drugs, but like I said, Needham felt they weren't related to the hepatitis."

"My only other question is about the lion serum sent by Dr. Chapeau to the CDC via Needham, which the CDC claims never to have received. Mason said there was some controversy over the serum, but he couldn't remember why."

"The serum never made it to the CDC?" Tessum asked.

"No."

"Well I can tell you that Needham did have it at some point. I remember a student bringing it over to him where we were working at UCLA. Control freak that he was, he ran all of the CDC's standard screens on the serum right there in the university's lab."

"Really?"

"I asked if he found anything of value, and he said no. So that was the last I ever thought about the serum until now."

"So it wasn't HCV infected?"

"Hell no," Tessum laughed.

"Did you ever examine the serum?"

"No, but I know it wasn't HCV infected."

"How can you be sure?" Sean pushed.

"I can only assume that if it had been, Needham would've told someone."

"Would he?"

"Listen, Needham was an asshole, he wasn't crazy."

Sean thought for a moment, but couldn't think of any more questions for Tessum. The professor told Sean to call back if he could be of further assistance. Sean thanked him and hung up as the streetlights outside flickered to life.

TREVOR Matthews was exhausted. He stared out the window of the massive Boeing 747. The vast Atlantic Ocean swept from horizon to horizon thirty-seven thousand feet below the plane. It took the better part of a day to get from his research site in the rain forest to the airport in Kinshasa. His three novice research assistants were shocked when he said that he was leaving them for up to two weeks. He left them with explicit instructions for the time he would be away. They would either sink or swim, he told them. He hoped when he returned that they would at least be treading water.

The phone call had infested his thoughts. Matthews hadn't spoken with Hector Mendoza in almost ten years. Mendoza was fortunate. His name wasn't associated with the project. He had settled into an excellent job at the CDC. Matthews hadn't been so lucky. The opportunity to work with Needham in Los Angeles, at the time, seemed like a god-send. As it turned out, it was a curse. Matthews' name would forever be connected to the project.

A flight attendant walked down the aisle handing out blankets and pillows. Matthews took both, making himself comfortable in his seat.

A nauseating feeling came over him as he thought about the Los Angeles team. He wondered what had become of each of the men. Needham, of course had grown immensely successful. His Global Program on AIDS was one of the most successful international campaigns against any disease. And then there was his appointment to the post of Director-General of the World Health Organization. Success seemed to be a way of life for Needham.

What had become of the others? He knew of Claris only through their limited interaction in Los Angeles. He had also been present for a meeting between Claris and Needham. Threats, extortion, and bribery had all surfaced. In the end, Matthews figured that Claris was living comfortably in some secluded corner of the world, an anonymous person with an unknown past.

Unlike Claris, Matthews had simply disappeared. He packed all he could into two large travel bags and a foot-locker. Then he vanished. His only goal was to put as much distance as possible between himself and the US.

Matthews had been a promising young doctor. The CDC recognized his talent. The only drawback they could find in Matthews was his confidence. Would a recent graduate be able to hold his own in the company of Larry Needham? The CDC hoped he would, and made him the offer he couldn't refuse. He eagerly signed on to the LA research team, and in so doing, began what would become a slow journey that eventually led him to Africa. In those few months that he worked with the LA team from the CDC, he found his calling. He would search exhaustively until he found the vaccine and cure for HCV.

After fleeing the US in the 80's, Matthews began studying primates, looking for an HCV relative in the wild. Both Matthews and others found it. Chimpanzees harbor a relative of HCV. Matthews had studied the virus in chimps for several years. Although he made some advances in his research, the progress was painstakingly slow. Working without a large support staff made the process even slower. But in order to maintain relative anonymity, a large staff was something Matthews couldn't afford.

He closed his eyes, trying to catch some sleep on the long flight. He wasn't sure what he planned to do once he arrived in the US. He'd always avoided confrontations. Now he sat on a plane racing northwest, certain that he would find himself in the middle of a conflict. He didn't like the thought, but he knew that he had been silent for too long.

6

AFTER his conversation with Tessum, Sean began casting a suspicious eye toward Lawrence Needham. But he didn't want to jump the gun. Needham probably had a perfect explanation for the serum's apparent disappearance, and at dinner on Monday night, Sean would get to ask what that explanation was.

It began raining on Friday night, as Sean lay in bed trying to sleep. Rain drops pattered off the window throughout the night. The following morning, Sean woke to find that the showers continued, promising a dreary day. His back not too sore, he grabbed the Tiger's cap and went running down on the river. He ran for an hour on the soaked trail, returning to his apartment with mud caked up his legs and back. The deluge continued through Sunday night, providing Sean with no excuse for procrastination on the draft report. He forced Tran from his mind, concentrating on Fulsonmayer's beloved lion project instead.

Early Monday morning, the sun finally broke the rain spell. The wet trees glistened in the crisp dawn air. Michelle was due in at ten. Sean drove to the airport to meet her. He waited for an hour before deciding that she had probably taken a cab back to campus. He stopped by her apartment on his way home. She was not receptive, acting overly tired from the trip home from Michigan.

"So what did you think about the program?" Sean asked.

"It's great," Michelle replied, unpacking her bag.

"What about the faculty? What did they think of you?"

"I don't know."

Sean sat on the corner of her bed, not knowing what to say. He decided to tell her about the Tran file and all the sleuthing he'd done. Michelle walked to the bathroom disinterested, placing items in the medicine cabinet. She remained distant, not participating in the conversation. "So bottom line is," Sean said, "that at this juncture, all fingers point to Needham."

"I'm really tired, Sean, and I need a nap."

"There's one other thing," he said. "Needham's having dinner at Fulsonmayer's tonight and Fulsonmayer wants us to come."

"Us?"

"Yes."

"As in you and me?" Michelle asked for clarity.

"Yes."

"You told him I was out of town, right?"

"I told him you were getting back this morning. He insisted that you come along."

Michelle rolled her eyes, flopping into the chair beside the bed. "I have to go to this, don't I? What time?"

"Eight."

"I have several errands to run, so you'd better leave. I'll be ready at half past seven."

"Is everything alright?" Sean asked, knowing the answer.

Michelle simply looked at him. He left her apartment without another word.

SEAN spent the better part of the afternoon preparing notes for his next meeting with Fulsonmayer's class. It wouldn't be at his apartment. He was reviewing material on asexual reproduction when the phone rang. It was Chapeau.

"How's the research coming along?" she asked.

"The plot thickens. I spoke with two of the men who worked with Needham on the Tran file, and turns out, as you said, Needham did receive the serum from your lab."

"And you doubted me," Chapeau said laughing.

"No, I never doubted you. Maybe the courier got mugged. Anyhow, now Needham's my focus. I just can't imagine why he never turned the serum over to the CDC."

"Who were the men you spoke with?"

"Carl Tessum in San Francisco and James Mason in Chicago. Neither had the greatest things to say about Needham."

"He could certainly be difficult to get along with."

"Is there something else you thought of since we last spoke?" Sean asked.

"No not really. I was just sitting at home this weekend thinking about the things you'd said, and I was wondering if you made any progress."

"Nothing more than I just told you."

"Well keep me up to speed with what you find. Gives me something else to think about during the day."

"I will, thanks for calling," Sean said, hanging up the phone.

Chapeau's interest gave Sean faith that he was within the realm of possibility. Had his inquiry been completely baseless, Chapeau would have dismissed his calls. He needed that kind of encouragement if he was to ask Needham about the serum.

SHARPLY dressed, Sean stood before the mirror straightening his tie. The phone rang. It was Ian.

"What's up?" Sean asked.

"Who's the greatest?"

"The greatest what?"

"Just the greatest in general," Ian said.

"I don't know, but I suppose that Larry Bird has to be up there."

"No, idiot, it's me."

"Why are you the greatest?" Sean asked.

"Because I found Barnard Claris."

"Who?"

"Barnard Claris. Recognize the name?"

"Vaguely."

"He's one of the guys who worked with Needham in LA. It took me a while to find him because he's overseas."

"Where?" Sean asked.

"American Samoa."

"American Samoa," Sean repeated. "How'd you find him?"

"He may be on the other side of the world, but apparently he still likes to have a say in who runs the country. He's a registered voter."

"How do we get in contact with him?" Sean asked.

"All I found was a PO Box."

"No phone number?"

"Just the PO Box. If you give me whatever it is you want to send him, I'll overnight it from here at the firm."

"Alright, take this down," Sean said, giving Ian a five sentence note to write. "Do you think that covers everything?" Sean asked.

"Short and sweet."

"Like you said, you're the greatest," Sean said.

"Don't mention it," Ian laughed.

SEAN left his apartment at seven. He stopped at a liquor store in the Square to buy a bottle of wine. A late afternoon shower had passed through the area leaving puddles all along the red brick sidewalks. A man and his tiny son walked hand in hand on the other side of the street. The man swung the small child over each of the puddles. Sean smiled at the boy's contagious laughter.

The small white Ford Escort sat exhausted against the curb. While in college, Sean had purchased the car used for fifteen-hundred dollars. It was beaten up, had a hole in the floor, and the ceiling fabric drooped, but it moved—albeit slowly. Sean picked Michelle up at her apartment and they drove silently to Fulsonmayer's house.

Sean turned down Fulsonmayer's street. There were no street lights, leaving the road dark and silent except for the noise of the small white car. The professor's home was set well off the street, tucked deeply behind several large oak trees. Sean pulled into the long driveway, slowly driving up to the well-lit house.

"Are we ever going to talk tonight?" Sean asked as he killed the engine. "If not, this'll prove to be an awkward experience."

Michelle sat in silence. The cooling engine clicked under the hood. "I really don't want to be here," she said.

"I realize that, but we're here now, and I think we can make the best of it."

Michelle put her hand on Sean's. "I've decided to transfer to Michigan for the spring semester."

Sean didn't look at her; instead he fiddled with the car keys. "I figured as much."

"I decided that I'm not comfortable at a school that's so concerned with money and endowments and legacies. It's just not for me."

"I know."

"What do you know? You fit right in. Have you forgotten that your father endowed a department chair? This place loves people like you."

"That's not fair. That has nothing to do with me. My father can throw his money around any way he chooses. You can't hold it against me."

Michelle shook her head and took a deep breath. “Sean, I don’t think we should see each other after tonight.”

He was silent. He knew she was right, but the words, even when expected, weren’t pleasant. “Great timing.”

“There’s never a good time.”

The front door to the house opened and Fulsonmayer’s wife, Madeline, poked her head out. “Is that you Sean?”

“Let’s make the best of the evening,” Sean said to Michelle as they climbed from the car. He turned to the house, “Yes, it’s me and Michelle. How are you Mrs. Fulsonmayer?”

“I’m fine, please come in. You two look wonderful, let me take your coats,” she said.

The aromas of the kitchen had taken over the large foyer. Sean heard laughter from one of the nearby rooms. Fulsonmayer emerged with a glass of brandy in hand. “Welcome Sean and Michelle.” He looked much more vibrant away from his office. “Can I fix you something to drink? Or did you bring your own?” he asked pointing to the bottle in Sean’s hand.

“I forgot. Thank you for having us over tonight,” Sean said, handing Fulsonmayer the wine.

A tall handsome man with salt-and-peppered hair entered the foyer, followed closely by an equally attractive woman. “Michelle Connelly and Sean Graham this is Larry Needham, and his beautiful wife Gayle.” The four exchanged handshakes and polite greetings. Sean recognized immediately that Needham had a commanding presence. Not only was he handsome, but something drew all attention to his steel blue eyes. Michelle had shed her cocoon and was listening intently to Needham. Sean watched the exchange. She was totally absorbed by his words. He imagined that Needham exercised this charming power over many people.

“I almost forgot,” Fulsonmayer said, looking over Sean’s shoulder towards the kitchen. “You and Sean have already met, but Michelle Connelly this is—”

“Sam!” Sean blurted out, shocked.

He walked over to her and the two hugged, smiling ear to ear. “What are you doing here?” he asked.

“So you’re not happy to see me?”

“Of course I am,” Sean said, suddenly remembering the others in the room. “Samantha Ferson,” he took her by the hand and led her to the others, “this is Michelle Connelly.”

"Pleased to meet you Michelle, I've heard a lot about you," Sam said.

"Funny, I was under the impression that you were a man."

"What?" Sean said, causing the Fulsonmayers and Needhams to laugh.

Fulsonmayer saw the awkwardness of the situation and quickly diffused it, "Why don't we head into the living room where we can all sit comfortably in front of the fire." The group followed Fulsonmayer into a large room with soft lighting, decorated in a fashion similar to his office, with beautiful artifacts from around the world hanging from the walls.

Sam took the seat across from Sean. She wore a black skirt with a black sleeveless silk blouse cut low under her neck. Sean couldn't help staring at her as the conversation flowed around him. She was absolutely stunning. He followed the line from her smooth crossed legs up past the gentle contours of her skirt. In all the months together in the field, he had never seen her in anything other than dirty shorts and a T-shirt, her hair pulled into a pony tail. Now her hair fell softly off her shoulders. She wore a thin leather necklace, on the end of which hung a small jade stone. Sean traced the necklace down Sam's tanned neck to the tiny green stone, hanging just above her blouse.

Sam raised her glass of wine and caught Sean's eye as she sipped. She had sensed his gaze. She too had caught glimpses of him, though infinitely more discreetly.

Sean was surprised to hear Michelle deep in conversation with Fulsonmayer about Michigan. He would find out eventually, so why not get it out in the open. Good for her, he thought.

"You know, Sean, Sam was the best student I ever had. So you're really fortunate to have had her show you the ropes out in the field," Needham said, with a broad smile full of bright white teeth.

"I know that she had great patience with me. I can't tell you how many times I got lost in the Serengeti," Sean replied.

"It's a big place. It takes a while to get all of your bearings."

Mrs. Fulsonmayer appeared in the door to the living room. "Dinner's ready if you'd all like to have a seat at the dining room table; Richard and I will bring it out. Hope everyone likes fish, I've prepared grilled mahi-mahi. Richard, please lend a hand," she said. The two disappeared into the kitchen while their guests found places at the large dining room table.

Fulsonmayer arrived at the table with the fish steaming on a large plate. He served each of his guests and then took his place beside his wife at the head of the table.

"Before we dig in, allow me to make an announcement. Our friend Michelle has elected to transfer to the outstanding program at the University of Michigan. I'd like to congratulate you on the decision and wish you the best of luck, though we'll miss you dearly. Congratulations," he said raising his glass. The others followed suit. Everyone offered Michelle words of encouragement, raving about the school's programs. Nobody ventured to ask why she had chosen to transfer. Another awkward situation deftly side-stepped by Fulsonmayer.

Half an hour into dinner, the guests began showering their hosts with compliments on the meal. The conversation weaved its way from the origins of mahi-mahi to the historical background of the intricately designed dinner china. As talk around the table slowly ebbed, Needham took a sip of wine and looked down at Sean. "Richard tells me that you might have some questions for me about research I performed years ago."

Sean hoped the next words from his mouth would fall neatly into place. "Uh, yeah, I do have a few questions if you don't mind. But it can wait until after dinner."

"Nonsense. If our dear friends don't mind, go ahead," Needham said, looking around the table. Nobody objected.

"Well I'm sure you recall the initial five cases of hepatitis C out in Los Angeles," Sean said.

"Absolutely: Jerry Famone, Enrico Martinez, Trophy Hollman, Marcus Tran and Calvin Heindrich. I'll never forget them."

Sean was visibly impressed. "Regarding Marcus Tran. I had some questions that weren't addressed in the CDC case file. At least not in writing."

"Shoot."

"What was the nature of the track marks—" Sean stopped. "I'm not sure this is dinner conversation."

"Oh, please. This young fellow Tran had needle tracks on his scrotum," Needham said directly to Madeline Fulsonmayer. "There, I said it. We're all adults here."

It took a full five seconds for Fulsonmayer's wife to resume chewing. Sam smirked across from Sean.

"Right, he had these track marks. Yet, all of the blood screens returned negative for narcotics," Sean said.

"That's right. It was never determined what the nature of the track marks was."

"That's it? Nobody ever figured out what they were?" Sean had the sinking feeling that he would be revealing his kokopelli theory by the end of dinner.

"That's correct."

"Then, if you don't mind my asking, how did Tran fit into your profile?"

Needham answered without flinching. "With these initial cases, transfusions and transplants weren't an issue, so with regard to Tran, though he probably hadn't engaged in IV drug use, he was a rather sexually adventurous fellow."

"Not everyone shared that opinion."

"Who said otherwise?"

"Carl Tessum and James Mason."

Needham laughed. "They were both very green at the time. Tessum eventually came around; and as for Mason, well, he was a drunk. That's why the CDC let him go. You see, though Tran never admitted being sexually active, I'm certain that he was involved in gay sex. It's a common belief, and back me up on this Richard, that in many cultures, one is not gay and does not engage in gay sex if they participate as the penetrative partner rather than as the receiver. Tran was a penetrator. With that in mind, he didn't consider himself gay or even sexually active. And maybe struggling so hard to fit into American culture, he was afraid to admit it. Who knows?"

Sean didn't buy the story Needham was selling, but had nothing to refute it. He sat silent for a moment. "Mason also suggested that the label 'Non-A, Non-B virus' really hampered subsequent investigations."

"Non-A, Non-B virus—the single most embarrassing mistake of my career; thanks for reminding me. As we now know, that was a misnomer. What can I say? I missed identifying hepatitis C. But so did everyone else until 1989."

Again Sean didn't speak.

"You're having trouble with the gay sex issue, aren't you?" Needham said. "Well, if you have a theory about how he caught the disease, please entertain us."

Michelle shot a look at Sean—not the fertility ritual.

"I do, but I have another question first," Sean said, and for the moment Michelle relaxed.

"Then on to question number two," Needham smiled.

"The lion serum from Chapeau's lab. She said she'd sent it to you for examination, and that you were to forward it to the CDC. The CDC never got it. Where did it go?"

"Chapeau did send it, and I did examine it. There was absolutely nothing noteworthy about the serum, so I sent it back to her."

"Why didn't you send it to the CDC for further examination?"

"Why? It was my project and my call. I was the team leader and the CDC respected my authority. I felt there was no need to send it to Atlanta, and they trusted my decision."

"Chapeau didn't mention that you sent it back to SISS."

"She probably lost it. Valerie Chapeau and I went to medical school together. She was a strong student, but a poor doctor. Let's just say that organization was not her forte. Bottom line was that she was somewhat incompetent; that's why she went out of business. Saying that I lost it is just her way of painting me in a bad light. I didn't support her bid for government funding precisely because she didn't run a tight ship."

"She mentioned to me that you put her out of business."

"A bitter classmate. She wanted me to support her bid for the additional government grants. There was no way that I was going to support that lab. It was a mess. The closing of the lab had nothing to do with the serum. I sent it back to her, that's all I know. I mean, what would I possibly want with the serum?" Needham asked.

"I had asked myself that same question," Sean said, his theory falling apart at the seams.

"So let's hear your theory," Needham said, slowly raising his glass to his lips.

"It holds no water without the serum."

"Sean," Michelle said, hoping to save him from embarrassment.

"Don't worry, it's entertaining if nothing else," he assured her.

"You'll like this Larry," Fulsonmayer said.

Sean began. "From the facts presented in writing within the case file, there is no evidence that Tran was either a drug user or participant in homosexual or any other form of intercourse. The nature of the track marks on Tran's groin, in conjunction with the fact that he had stolen serum extracted from a lion, lead me to believe that he was involved in some form of fertility ritual, in which he injected the lion serum into his genitals. And I suspect that the serum was contaminated with hepatitis C."

"First of all, how is that a fertility ritual?" Needham asked.

"He hoped to embrace the virile sexual power of the great cat."

Needham laughed, "You thought this up on your own?"

"With a little supportive nudge from Chester Hamilton."

"Hamilton? Who's he?" Needham said.

"Chester Hamilton, old anthropologist. Best argument I've ever seen for forced retirement," Fulsonmayer said.

The table was silent, awaiting further response from Needham. He sat staring at his wine glass, swirling its contents. He took another sip. "Though patently absurd, your theory does fall within the realm of possibility, remote as it may be. Given the facts of the case, yours is a viable conclusion." He turned to Fulsonmayer, "Richard, you have a keeper in young Sean here. However, I assure you Sean, there was no HCV in that serum. I would love to prove it to you with serum in hand, but as the good Dr. Chapeau has apparently misplaced it, you'll simply have to trust me. Millions of people around the world do, I should hope you would too."

Sean nodded. And once again the table fell silent.

Content that everyone had finished their dinner, Madeline Fulsonmayer spoke up. "I hope each of you saved room for dessert. I made an apple pie."

"And I made sure to pick up some vanilla ice cream for those preferring their pie à la mode," Fulsonmayer added.

"Why doesn't everyone retire to the comfort of the living room? The fire should be perfect. Richard and I will bring in the dessert and coffee in a moment."

Sean grabbed his plate and silverware, helping clear the table.

"Sean, put those down. You're our guest," Mrs. Fulsonmayer said.

Sean complied, following the others into the living room.

Needham was standing with his palms extended to the fire, "I asked Richard to start up the fire. I've had quite a bad spell of the chills lately. I think that I caught a bad case of malaria overseas. My doctor drew some blood and I should get the results back soon. I told him I was positive it was malaria, but he insisted on doing the tests. Young guy, just being thorough."

"Malaria's no fun," Sam added.

"It certainly isn't. But considering some of the alternatives, I hope it's malaria," Needham said.

The two began comparing a long list of tropical diseases they had fallen victim to over the years. It stopped only when the hosts arrived with the desserts, which they placed on a coffee table. "Please help yourself," Fulsonmayer said, slicing the pie. He took a piece of apple pie and placed a giant pile of ice cream atop it, before sitting happily by the fire. The others followed his example. "Don't be shy with the ice cream. If you don't eat it, I'll have to. And Madeline has me on a diet," he said rubbing his stomach.

As before, the room slowly segregated into isolated conversations. Needham sat across the coffee table from Sean. "For some reason, you don't believe what I said at the dinner table. Why is that?" he asked.

Sean didn't know how to respond. "I believe you, Dr. Needham."

"I'm quite certain that you don't."

"Well, to tell you the truth, I'm in a bit of a pickle. Dr. Chapeau has been extremely forthcoming with any information she could find. I think she would've mentioned if you had sent the serum back to her. But it was a long time ago, and maybe she just forgot."

"I can't speak for Chapeau, but maybe it's as you say, that she simply forgot. Why is this case file of such interest to you?"

"Reading through the reports, I saw some things that I thought were glossed over. I just wanted answers—answers that I can live with."

"And you haven't found them yet," Needham said.

"No, I don't think I have."

"You're very thorough in your work. That's important. You're also the only person who's ever questioned me about that report. And in a sense, you were right to do so. The information you sought wasn't contained within its pages. But it's also irrelevant in light of the bigger picture. So to dwell on it any longer would be a waste of your time and considerable talent. You should let it drop and move on to more important things. Richard's getting very jumpy about getting his latest project published."

Sean nodded, and in doing so dropped a spoonful of ice cream onto his tie and down onto his lap. Needham laughed as Sean's face went crimson. "You can go clean yourself up before anyone notices," Needham said smiling. He then turned his attention to the others and effortlessly took command of the conversation.

Sean left the room, walking to the kitchen. The bathroom door opened as he passed. Sam and Sean came face to face. "Nice tie," she said.

"It's ice cream, I was just going to the kitchen to clean it up."

"I'll help."

Sam unbuttoned Sean's suit coat and dabbed at the spot of ice cream on his tie. He watched her closely. "You look beautiful tonight," he said.

"Thank you. You're rather handsome yourself, when you take the time," she replied without looking up from the tie. She saw the stitches in his hand for the first time. "How'd you get those?" she asked, running her fingers along the scar.

"It's a long story. I'll tell you later. So how did you arrange a stateside visit? You'd said you probably wouldn't be back for a few months."

"You could say it was complete luck. As you know, most of my research grants come from biotech and pharmaceutical firms from across the country. One of the major contributors is having their annual meeting, and my grant came up for review. They want me to present my findings and future goals. It's just a glorified setting for a grant review. And as for tonight, Richard invited me over to thank me for looking after you in the Serengeti."

"So where are you staying?"

"That's the downside. My sponsors paid for the flight

over here, but I have to pay my own room and board. The only place I could find on such short notice was a run-down hotel over in Brighton."

"Why don't you stay with me? My apartment's not the Parker House, but it's comfortable."

Sam finished with the tie and looked Sean in the eye. "Michelle wouldn't be concerned? Seems you forgot to mention that I was a woman. I wouldn't want to cause any more friction between you."

"You noticed?"

"How couldn't I? And those wandering eyes of yours," Sam said laughing.

"Give me a break. This is the first time I've seen you without an inch of dirt covering you. I mean in the bush, we were always filthy. As for Michelle, you needn't be concerned. She broke up with me before we came inside."

"I'm sorry."

Sean smiled. "I saw it coming a long time ago. It's for the best."

"I'll let you take care of the spot on the pants. If anyone walked in, they'd probably take it the wrong way." She straightened his tie before returning to the others.

After cleaning his pants, Sean reclaimed his seat across from Needham. "Much better," Needham said.

"Thanks."

Michelle walked over to Sean's side. "I'm a bit tired after the long day. Would you mind taking me home?" she asked.

"I'd hoped to speak with Sean about his plans after completion of his master's program. Another time, I guess," Needham said.

"You two talk. I'll drive Michelle home," Fulsonmayer said. "Would that be alright, Michelle?"

"That's fine, if it's no trouble."

"Not at all, let me get your coat."

"Sean, I'll speak with you later," she said.

Fulsonmayer returned with Michelle's coat. Michelle thanked Madeline Fulsonmayer for dinner and said goodnight to the guests.

For the remainder of the evening, Needham and Sean discussed Sean's background, motivations and long term goals. Needham shared stories from his early days in the field, captivating the small audience. As the grandfather clock worked its way toward midnight, the fire flickered, its supply of wood exhausted. Sean announced that he was going to leave.

"Sean, would you mind driving me to my hotel?" Sam asked.

"Of course not," he replied.

The two thanked the Fulsonmayers and excused themselves from the fading dinner party.

The night had grown considerably cooler. Sean turned on the heater in his car. The two didn't speak as they drove away from Fulsonmayer's house. Driving through Harvard Square, Sam finally spoke, "What's on your mind?"

"Sorry, I'm just a bit tired."

"No you're not. You're thinking about something."

"It's just strange having you next to me in my beaten down Ford. I mean, I'm so used to sitting in the Land Rover with you on a dirt road. Now we're in Cambridge. It's just strange." Sean parked in front of his apartment. "We're here."

Sam looked out the window. "This isn't my hotel."

"I'd really like you to stay with me."

"I'd like that, but all of my clothes are at the hotel."

"You can borrow mine until tomorrow."

"You're sure it's not an inconvenience?"

"Please. I missed you."

"Are you tired?" she asked.

"Not really."

"Let's go for a walk."

"I'd love to."

Sam looped her arm inside Sean's, and the two walked down Memorial Drive along the river. Sam shivered in the dark night air. She cozied up closer to Sean, resting her head against his shoulder.

"I thought you weren't tired," Sean said.

"I'm not, I'm just trying to stay warm."

Sean put his arm around her shoulders for added warmth. Her soft hair brushed gently against his cheek. Sam slid her arm around his waist; the two now walked slowly in a partial embrace. The air grew misty with the faintest trace of drizzle. Sean felt Sam squeeze him tightly. He pulled her closer to his side. He ran his fingers though her damp hair, pulling it away from her eyes. A pang of nervousness ran through his body in the anticipation of a kiss.

“What are you thinking about?” Sam whispered.

“Nothing really. Just how comfortable and happy I am right now.”

“Me too.”

Sam stopped and turned to face Sean, wrapping both arms around his waist. She stared up at him, a small smile crossing her face. She touched his cheek with an open palm. Her hand was cold, and Sean’s first instinct was to pull away. But within seconds the chill faded leaving the warmth of her soft caress.

Sam turned again, resuming her spot under Sean’s arm. They continued walking. “You don’t fully trust Needham, do you?” she said.

“My instincts tell me not to.”

“Even though I believe him, you have to go with your instincts.”

“I know, but it’s getting more difficult with Fulsonmayer breathing down my neck. I have very little leeway with the research I’m doing right now. Fulsonmayer’s not going to let me screw around with these LA cases anymore. He’s getting antsy for the draft lion report.”

“What would Needham’s motivation be for lying?” Sam asked.

“I have no idea. But Chapeau has no reason to lie either. At least not that I can think of. This thing won’t let me rest until I find out who’s lying, if anyone, and why.”

A strong wind blew off the river causing Sam to shiver again. Sean pulled her closer. “We should get you home. I don’t want you to get sick before your presentation,” Sean said.

Once back at his apartment, Sean gave Sam a T-shirt and a pair of sweatpants to wear for the night. The two sat talking on the bed until three in the morning. Sam yawned, struggling to stay awake.

“I’ll let you get some sleep. You stay here tonight. I’ll hit the couch,” Sean said.

Sam smiled at him from behind tired eyes. The two sat silently for a moment, before she took his hand and pulled him close, into a hug. “I’m so happy to see you,” she whispered in his ear.

He slowly pulled away from her, kissing her forehead as he stood. “I’ll wake you in the morning. Good night,” he said, turning out the light.

"Sweet dreams."

SEAN woke early the next morning, ready for a long day. After a quick run along the river, he returned to his apartment and showered. Attempting to be silent, he crept into his bedroom, towel around his waist. He gathered his clothes quietly.

"Do you always walk around in towels?" Sam asked, stretching in bed.

"I'm sorry I woke you."

"Don't be. Come here," she said, gesturing for him to sit next to her.

He saw the sweatpants he had given Sam the night before lying at the foot of the bed. Smiling, he picked them up and held them out to her. "Mrs. Robinson, you're trying to seduce me … aren't you?"

She laughed. "Who wears pants to bed?" Her smile suddenly faded. "What happened to your back?"

"I got hit with a brick," he said, sitting next to Sam on the bed.

"A brick?"

"Yep, right through that window."

"So that's why you let me sleep in here. Who threw it?"

"The police don't know. I think it was one of my students, but there's no proof."

"Does it hurt?" she asked, gently rubbing her hand over the stitches.

"Not anymore." Sean adjusted the towel around his waist. "Are you hungry? I'll make us some breakfast."

"Sounds great. I'd like to shower first."

"What would you like?"

"Surprise me."

After her shower, the two ate a breakfast of blueberry waffles together. Sam looked at her watch. "I should hit the road if I'm going to have time to change at my hotel before my first meeting."

"Are you planning to bring your luggage over here tonight?" Sean asked.

"Would you like me to?"

"Absolutely. We haven't done any catching up yet. And I want you to meet Ian."

"Then I will."

"Great. Why don't you grab my spare key from the hook

by the microwave? That way if I'm not here you can let yourself in."

Sam looked around the microwave. No keys. "I don't see them."

Sean looked, but he too failed to find the keys. "That's strange. Ian probably has them. No problem. Take mine and I'll pick one up from my landlord."

"Are you sure?"

"Positive."

She kissed Sean on the cheek. "Have I told you how happy I am to be here," she said walking to the door. "I'll see you tonight."

"See you tonight," Sean said closing the door behind her.

7

SEAN'S first order of business for the day was his meeting with Fulsonmayer's freshman class. It was a chilly day, thanks to a gusty northerly wind that made its way down the coast from Maine. An early autumn was on its way. Only a few tourists braved the cooling overcast weather to take a look around campus.

Sean found the class fairly uneventful. Not that he expected a festive atmosphere, but he was wary of Gustav. The mammoth hockey player sat next to Courtney Hillerman, the overly flirtatious blonde who always vied for Sean's attention. An attractive young woman, her wanton mannerisms made it difficult for Sean to avoid staring at her. He was concerned that Gustav would mistake his gazing at Courtney for stares at him. As he had before, Gustav sat silent as the class discussion proceeded around him. And as he had at Sean's apartment, Gustav milled about the room as the others departed.

Michael Rubicon passed Sean on his way out of the room. Sean barely noticed him. "Have a nice day, Sean," he said, smiling.

"You too Michael. I'll see you in lecture."

Sean continued to quietly pack his books when he felt a hand on his shoulder. He tensed and wheeled around quickly, ready for a confrontation.

"Oh, Courtney. What can I do for you?" Sean said, somewhat relieved.

"I have a bunch of questions about the Malinowski reading, and I was hoping that you could help me out," she said, holding her books against her chest while slowly swaying from side to side.

"I have a few minutes now if you'd like."

"Well I have a meeting I have to run to. I was hoping that we could meet over dinner or something. You know, to discuss Malinowski."

Sean found himself tempted. "I'm pretty busy right now, and dinner's just not the best time for me. Maybe coffee in the Science Center sometime?"

"I could always come by your apartment while you're studying and put together some dinner for the two of us. It's no problem, really," she said reaching out and opening his palm. She handed him a small piece of paper. "Call me if you want to get together."

Sean was speechless. "Courtney, I can't—"

"The offer's out there. You don't have to decide now," she said smiling before she turned and walked away.

Sean looked around the room to make sure that nobody else had heard the exchange. He opened the piece of paper in his hand. It was her phone number. He folded the paper, stuffing it into his pocket.

"Damn," he sighed. He finished packing his bag and stepped into the hallway. Again he felt a hand on his shoulder.

"Courtney," he said turning around. But instead he found himself staring at the chin of Ankur Gustav.

"No, not your little blonde freshman friend. But I'm sure you wish it was. You two have quite the secretive relationship going, don't you? Everyone can see the way that you look at each other. And how she always stays after class. I wonder what the administration would have to say about such a relationship," Gustav said.

"There's no relationship. She asks questions and I answer them. That's it."

"Then why so defensive? Am I getting to you? Who could blame you? She's quite attractive. And so young and innocent. I'm sure you could teach her things. But maybe seductive young women don't do it for you."

Sean struggled to keep his composure. "What is it that you want, Gustav?"

Gustav's eyes sharpened. "The police stopped by to talk the other day. Why would you send them? What could I possibly have to do with the brick? You're messing things up for me. My coach got on my case about the brick too. I'm telling you again, there's no way in hell that I'm missing the hockey season. Do you know how many pro scouts are watching me? Nobody's going to stand in my way. Not you, not anyone."

Sean stepped forward into Gustav's face. "You listen to

me, Gustav. You think you're pretty tough making threats. Well here's a news flash for you, tough guy. You won't be playing hockey anymore at Harvard, and that's a guarantee. I'm going to see to it that you're expelled. Don't think you scare me, punk," Sean turned and walked away, leaving Gustav to wonder if Sean was serious.

"This is far from over," Gustav yelled after Sean.

Sean didn't turn to reply. As he exited the building he took a deep breath. Gustav did scare him, but he wouldn't give the brute the satisfaction of knowing it. He walked directly to Fulsonmayer's office to relate Gustav's latest threats.

Fulsonmayer's secretary said that the professor was in a meeting with a student, and that he would be finished in a few minutes. Sean took the time to compose himself, still riled up from the exchange with Gustav. When Fulsonmayer's door opened, Sean stood and approached it, not wanting to waste time.

"Thanks for stopping by. Please don't hesitate to call me if I can help," Sean heard Fulsonmayer say.

"Oh, Sean," Fulsonmayer said surprised. "We were just talking about you." Sean looked through the door and saw Courtney putting on her jacket. His face flushed. "Miss Hillerman says that you're an extremely engaging teacher. It's good to hear. Now if we could only see some results with the lion report," Fulsonmayer laughed.

"Hi, Sean. I'd really appreciate if you could call me with a response to that question I asked you in class," Courtney said, her eyes fixed on Sean's.

"Uh, yeah. Sure, I'll call you later."

"Great. Thank you for your time Professor Fulsonmayer. And Sean, please give me a call," she said leaving the office.

Fulsonmayer looked at Sean, "I think she has a bit of a crush on you."

"I was under that impression too."

Fulsonmayer invited Sean into his office. "So what can I do for you?"

"It's Ankur Gustav again. He made another threat and I'd like to report it to the administration."

"What was it this time?"

"He threatened me because the police questioned him about the last incident. The thing with the brick."

"Okay, I'll initiate things from my end. You'll probably

have to answer a few questions for the Ad Board."

"Who?" Sean asked.

"The committee that deals with disciplinary proceedings."

"That's no problem."

"Anything else?"

"I was wondering if you could tell me how to get in touch with Dr. Needham. I wanted to thank him for humoring me last night."

"I'm afraid he's out of town for the day. I spoke to him this morning and he had some disquieting news."

"Really?"

"Well, it turns out that he doesn't have malaria. He caught what's called schistosomiasis. It's caused by a parasitic worm that lives in still water primarily in developing countries. Its symptoms can mimic those of malaria, and it can get pretty bad if it's not caught. There are all types of neurological problems if it goes unchecked."

"I hope he's okay."

"I'm sure he will be, but his doctor sent him to a specialist to have his liver checked out. So he's not around today, but I'm sure he'd appreciate the call tomorrow." Fulsonmayer found the number in his organizer and gave it to Sean. "I hope that draft is coming along as planned."

"It is," Sean lied.

"Then if you have no other questions, we both have work to do."

Sean left Fulsonmayer's office and walked slowly across campus back to his apartment, pondering what would come of Gustav. He wondered if Gustav would go down quietly. Unlikely, he thought.

On the way up to his apartment, Sean stopped by his building superintendent's to pick up a key. He struggled to get it onto his key chain as he neared his apartment door. Looking up at the lock, he realized that the door was open. Had he left it open? He'd never done that before. Was Sam back early? He checked his watch. She was scheduled to lecture for the entire afternoon. Sean exhausted the possibilities in his head.

He put his ear up to the door. He could hear rustling coming from what he thought to be the kitchen area. His heart started racing. He removed his jacket, quietly placing it down with his bag on the floor. Listening intently, he slowly opened the door. The intruder was rifling through drawers. Sean stopped, thinking he should leave and call the police. But then his emotions got the better of him. He looked around his doorway, spotting his baseball bat. Even the enormous Gustav wouldn't be foolish enough to go up against the polished wood of Sean's Louisville Slugger. He gripped the bat firmly in his hands, strangling it in his sweating palms. He crept slowly toward the kitchen; the intruder still moved from cabinet to cabinet. Taking a deep breath, he raised the bat above his head and jumped around the corner.

"Freeze!" Sean yelled, causing the intruder to drop a glass, which shattered across the floor, spraying both men's feet with small shards. "Pete? What the hell are you doing here?"

"Jesus Sean! Why did you sneak up on me like that? And what's with the bat?" Pete said, white as a ghost and holding his hand over his heart.

"I'm sorry, I just wasn't expecting anyone." Sean put the bat down and walked over to hug his brother.

"It's great to see you little brother. Still tan from Africa I see." Pete was two inches taller than Sean with the same strong facial features and a razor sharp crew cut.

"How do you feel? You look like you've lost some weight," Sean said, concerned by his brother's appearance.

"Relax Sean, I lost the weight climbing Denali, not because of the virus. Besides, you look a bit skinny yourself. Are you still running like a fiend?"

"Of course. So how was Denali?"

"Most incredible experience ever. Alaska was spectacular. After we finished our climb, we fished the creeks for a week. We would set up camp, find a nice spot to fish, and by nine in the morning we were sharing the area with half a dozen grizzlies not two hundred yards away. It was outrageous. But it's nice to be back in the Northeast."

"What are you talking about? It's freezing out."

"Stop your whining. Grab your jacket, we're going for a walk."

"A walk? I just got back from class," Sean said.

"Are you kidding me? I just climbed a mountain. Stop being a weasel."

"I'm not a weasel."

"Then shut your trap and put this on," Pete said seeing

Sean's jacket on the floor and tossing it to him.

Once on the street in front of his apartment, they headed down to the river.

"When did you get in?" Sean asked.

"I got to Manhattan last night, and I drove up here this morning. And you're welcome for the groceries."

"Was that what all the noise was about?"

"Well it certainly didn't merit being attacked with a baseball bat."

"Sorry about that. I've just been a bit jumpy."

"So I can see," Pete said. "What's got you on edge?"

"Just this problem I have with one of my students. He's been threatening me for failing him on an assignment. Then someone, I imagine it was him, threw a brick through my window and gave me these," Sean said, holding his hand out for Pete to see.

"Ouch," Pete said as the brothers walked out onto the footbridge that crossed the river.

"I've got a few stitches in my back as well. So you can see why I'm a bit edgy."

"Sure," Pete said propping himself up on the wall of the bridge. His feet dangled twenty feet above the water.

"Be careful Pete."

"What—are we changing roles now? You're going to start looking out for me?"

Sean hesitated before answering. He joined Pete on the wall. "If I have to."

Pete smiled at Sean and patted him on the leg. "I know you'll be there if and when I need you."

"So you're saying that right now you don't need me to look out for you?"

Pete frowned. "I had some blood work done before my trip, promising my doctor that I'd call as soon as we finished the climb. I had to cut my vacation short because he gave me some bad news. My CD4 count is way down. The virus has built up some resistance to the drugs I've been taking."

Sean sat silent, staring down to the waves on the river. "So what does that mean?"

"Maybe nothing. There are some other drugs they're going to try. But if they can't get this thing under control, I'll be sailing into some rough water."

The two sat without saying anything. Pete looked over

at Sean and saw his eyes beginning to fill with tears. "Don't worry Sean, I'm going to get through this. And when I do, we'll sit on this bridge again and laugh when we remember you sitting here crying and almost falling into the water." Pete put his arm around Sean's shoulder. Sean felt dizzy. His brother's grasp relieved him. "Enough about me. How are you and Michelle doing?"

Sean laughed. "That's a terrible way to change the subject. In the future, try to find something upbeat to talk about."

"What's the trouble?"

"She dumped me last night."

Pete chuckled. "Oh, sorry to hear that."

"Don't be. It just wasn't meant to be."

"When I last spoke with you, you said that you were doing some research for one of your professors. How's that coming along?"

"That's another great subject," Sean mumbled.

"Now what?"

"The research I'm doing is on hepatitis C. Not too dissimilar to HIV."

Pete chuckled again. "Is there anything that we're allowed to talk about?"

"The research is fine. In fact, I should be done with it soon."

"Why aren't you?"

"Well there are a few things that don't add up, and nobody seems to have the right answers. Not even the Director-General of the World Health Organization."

"You spoke with the Director-General?"

"I had dinner with him at my professor's house last night," Sean said. He went on to fill Pete in about all of the HCV research that he had done, and all of the questions the research left unanswered.

Pete took in all that Sean had to say. He paused before offering his input. "I agree that some things have been left unanswered, but what exactly are you looking for at this point? It seems like you're at a dead end."

"I need to find out what happened to that serum."

"Why?"

"Because if it contains some form of hep C, then it might shed some light on the virus. I mean, if that serum contains

HCV, then we know at least one place, if not the only one, where the virus jumped the species into humans."

Pete didn't want to dishearten his brother. "Sean, don't get me wrong, but don't you think that if Needham suspected even in the slightest way, that the serum had HCV in it, that he would have retested it. You said yourself that he told you that the serum definitely did not contain the virus. What more do you want?"

"I look at what Needham said in one of two ways: he's either wrong, or he's lying. I hope he's just wrong."

"Whoa. You're saying that the Director-General of the World Health Organization is lying?"

"Not necessarily, but he might be. I looked into his eyes last night, and he was hiding something. He just had this look in his eyes. You should see the command this guy has over people. I'm convinced he could cloak anything with his charm."

"Maybe he's a charming man, but this isn't an ordinary person we're talking about here. He's a doctor, and not just a guy out in the woods making house calls."

Sean began reciting from an argument he had been through in his head several times. "So what if he's a doctor? Do you think doctors have different morals and motivations? I'm not saying Needham's lying. I'm simply saying that you can't dismiss the possibility because of titles he holds and awards he's won."

Pete was at a loss for words. But as he always had in the past, he supported his younger brother. "All I can tell you is to follow your instincts. Growing up I recognized that while I may have been more adept when it came to studying books, you were always the one with the talent for reading people. Do whatever you feel you have to do. But don't let it get in the way of your responsibilities."

"Thanks Pete. I know I don't always make sense, but it's good to know that you're by my side."

Pete grabbed Sean's baseball cap from his head. "Since when are you a Detroit Tigers fan?"

"Sam gave it to me."

"Right, I remember you mentioning her. She was in Africa with you. So who is she?" Pete asked.

Sean smiled. "I'm not sure where to begin. First, well, she's older."

"How much older?"

"She's thirty-four."

"So?"

"So, nothing. She's intelligent, witty, and now that I've seen her without dirt all over, I think she's gorgeous."

"She's ten years older than you."

"I'm aware of that. We spent so much time together in Tanzania that I feel like she's one of my best friends, even though I've known her for less than a year. And now there's this attraction thing going on between us, or at least for me. But I'm sure that she's going to be off to Africa again in a few days, so who knows."

"Sounds like you've got yourself a little crush."

"I'm not sure what you'd call it, but something's going on. Why don't you stay for dinner and both you and Ian can meet her?"

"I'd really like to, but I have to get back to New York for some tests early in the morning. I just wanted to come by and let you know how everything's going with me."

"Keep me up to speed with your treatment. I want progress reports every time something changes," Sean said.

"You'll be the first one I call."

"Have you spoken to dad since you got back?"

"No, but I'll call him tonight."

"Why bother?" Sean asked.

"Because he's my father," Pete said, somewhat irritated. "Sean, I think you need to come to terms with the fact that the three of us are a family. We all have different priorities and ways of expressing ourselves. Dad's way is just a bit off."

"Way off."

"How's Ian doing?" Pete asked, again changing the subject.

"He's cruising right along. He'll graduate in the top ten of his class."

"That's great. Is he seeing anybody?"

"Of course not."

Pete shook his head, laughing. "I tell you, a guy with his looks, it's incredible that he's never dating anyone. What's the word he's always using?"

"Outlandish."

"That's it, 'simply outlandish'."

Sean looked at his watch. "If you're not sticking around

for dinner, you should probably hit the road. They're tearing up the highway down around Hartford and it can be a mess."

"Yeah, I should get going. Oh, I almost forgot," Pete said pulling from his pocket a smooth, jet black stone with a white band running around it. "This is for you."

Sean took the rock, looking quizzically at it. "Gee thanks, Pete. You brought me a rock all the way from Alaska."

"It's not just any rock, its a wishing stone."

"Oh, that's different, a wishing stone," Sean looked at Pete with his brow raised.

"It's part of a myth from a Native American tribe in the Northwest called the Kwakiutl. You see, there was this little boy who was orphaned at a very young age. Nobody looked after him, and nobody fed him. The great spirit of the sea took pity on the small child, and taught the boy to fish. From that point on, that's all he did, day in and day out. His only love was the sea.

"Now time passed and the little boy became a young man. The entire time that the boy was learning to fish, a beautiful young girl was blossoming into a woman."

"Blossoming?" Sean asked.

"Yes blossoming," Pete reiterated. "Now let me finish. Like the boy, she was orphaned at a young age. But instead of growing up on the sea, she was kidnapped by the spirit of the night, who, I should add, was not the friendliest of spirits. He let her wander the land, but only late at night, under a shroud of darkness. He dressed her in a beautiful white gown so that he could always find her, even when it was dark. The spirit of the night took care of the young girl, but she too was lonely. One day she asked the spirit if she could wander about the land during the day, for she couldn't remember what the land looked like under the warm rays of the sun. Thinking that no harm could come of it, he allowed her one day in the light, making her promise to return by sunset.

"That day, the young fisherman was weaving a new net when he saw the beautiful woman emerge from the forest. When their eyes met, they immediately fell in love, forgetting all of their years of loneliness. The fisherman made plans to run far away with the woman, but she told him she had to return to the forest by sunset. The young man said that after meeting the beautiful woman, he couldn't bear to be alone again, and he convinced her to run away with him. But the spirit of night knows every land, and only a few hours after sunset, he found the two on a boat, miles out to sea. He was very angry and he swept her from the boat, saying that if she wouldn't stay with him, then nobody could have her. And in an instant, he placed the woman, dressed in her glorious white gown, into a stone as black as the night.

"The spirit of the night then handed the stone to the fisherman to be a painful reminder of his actions. The man was distraught and cried for days, holding the stone to his heart. Finally, in despair, he threw the stone as far as he could, and it skipped on the waves past the horizon. The only thought on his mind was a wish that the beautiful woman would return to him. The great spirit of the sea saw the distress of his young fisherman and caught the rock when it sailed across the horizon. Hearing the man's desperate wish, the great spirit broke the woman from the stone, sending her back to the fisherman on a gently rolling wave. Once reunited, the two lived out their days without ever encountering the spirit of the night again." When Pete had finished his story he took the stone from Sean. "So what we take from this story is—"

"Don't steal women of the night or their pimps will turn you into stone," Sean interrupted.

"No, we take the wishing stone. For every white stripe on the stone, in this case only one, you get one wish. But the catch is that for the wish to come true, you have to make the stone skip on the water. You think you can handle that?"

"I'm fairly confident. Thanks for the stone. I'll save it for a rainy day."

"It's all about believing in the things that you do," Pete said, climbing down from the wall. "Walk me to my car and then I'm out of your hair."

"You're sure you can't stay for dinner?"

"I really need to get back to the city tonight. But thanks, I'll take a rain check."

The two walked back toward hectic Harvard Square and Sean's apartment. "I'll try to make my way back up here in a few weeks," Pete said, climbing into his black Jeep. "Or you could always come down to Manhattan. Bring Ian, we'll see if we can find him a woman." Pete started the Jeep.

"Sure thing," Sean replied. "By the way, how did you get into my apartment?"

"The door was open," Pete said, pulling away from the curb.

SEAN decided to spend the remainder of the afternoon working on the draft hepatitis report. He walked slowly to the library, running through every detail of the morning. Sam had left before he did, and he was certain that he closed and locked the door behind him. He ran his mind in circles and opted to forget about it until later.

He passed the circulation desk of the library on his way to his carrel. Ms. Pierce, the ancient librarian, addressed Sean without looking up from her newest periodical. "Mr. Graham? You're back again. How on earth do you ever see the sun?"

Sean stopped, confused by her remark. "Excuse me?"

"How can you enjoy fall if you're always here?"

"Ms. Pierce, I haven't been here in a few days."

"Nonsense. I saw you at your carrel this morning. Plugging away. So busy that you didn't even say 'hello'."

"Are you sure it was my carrel? There are quite a few down there."

"Mr. Graham, I've worked here for too many years not to know which carrel belongs to which student."

"I assure you, I was not here this morning."

"Well I only saw this person from behind, wearing a baseball cap like you always do."

"Thanks for letting me know, I'll go take a look," Sean said, making his way to his desk. He took inventory, and just as Ms. Pierce had said, Sean had the feeling that somebody had been there. Nothing seemed to be missing, but it was a bit too tidy. As if everything had been placed in a deliberately neat manner. Too neat. I'm going crazy, he thought. The desk is exactly how I left it. Then he began doubting the librarian's credibility. She probably didn't even know what year it was.

Sean opened one of his folders. In it, he found the photocopy of the CDC's locational timeline that he had highlighted. He looked at the city and town names silhouetted in fluorescent yellow. He still couldn't remember where he had seen the names before. He put the photocopied chart away and found the draft report that he had started.

Fulsonmayer wanted the completed draft soon, and Sean wasn't even a quarter of the way done. He pulled together all of the materials he needed and got to work again, writing vigorously. After two hours, his mind wandered. The highlighted names kept drifting into his thoughts. Another half-hour passed in which Sean failed to write a single word. Frustrated, he collected his belongings and stood to leave.

He stared at the desk with its tidy stacks of materials. His paranoia finally got the best of him. With his pen, he etched a tiny mark on the desk along the bottom edge of the book. It was barely visible, but if anyone moved the book, Sean would know. He left the library, convinced that he was going crazy.

YET again, the Chicago Public School system had to find a substitute teacher for James Mason. This time, Mason claimed to have caught a viral infection. And, as usual, the truth was that he had stayed out too late the previous night, partying with his friends José Cuervo and Jim Beam.

Mason lay on his couch still wearing the clothes from the day before. On the muted television, an episode of *CHiPs* neared its dramatic highway chase climax. The phone's ringing woke the cat sleeping on Mason's stomach. It dug its claws into the napping drunk as it ran away. "Damn it!" Mason shouted, throwing an empty beer can at the cat. He picked up the phone.

"Hello," he said in a gruff voice.

"Is this James Mason?"

"Yes. Who's this?"

"I'm calling from the Archival Research Division at the Centers for Disease Control down in Atlanta."

"Great. What the hell do you want?"

The caller proceeded to ask Mason questions regarding his recollection of the LA hepatitis cases.

"Listen," Mason said, "I'm not playing this game. I haven't heard from the CDC in fifteen years, and I have no intention of revamping that relationship now." He hung up the phone.

The cat sat in the corner, licking up beer that had spilled from the can Mason had thrown. Mason threw a magazine at the cat. "I'm gonna kill you, and then I'm gonna kill that motherfucker Needham."

WHEN Sean arrived back at his apartment building, he stopped by the building superintendent to ask if he'd been in Sean's apartment. The old Italian man said that he hadn't since fixing the broken window.

Sean proceeded to his apartment, where he unlocked the door and inspected it from top to bottom. There were no signs that it had been forced open; not that he knew what he was looking for, short of a gaping hole caused by a crow bar. Unsettled, he walked around his apartment peering into closets and under his bed. "I'm being ridiculous," he said aloud.

After watering his plants, he called Ian. "By any chance did you stop by my apartment this morning?" he asked.

"No, I was here at the firm. Sarah asked me to help her with an oral argument she's making tomorrow down at the federal court. Sean, I think she likes me."

"So what else is new?"

"No I mean it," Ian said.

"Of course she likes you. Have you ever met a woman that didn't? But enough about you. Do you think that maybe Michelle would have stopped by?"

"Not without leaving a note or calling first. Why don't you call and ask her?"

"I really don't feel like it."

"Trouble again?" Ian asked.

"You could say that. She dropped the ax last night."

"Sorry to hear that."

"We all know it was the best thing that could happen for us. We just weren't getting along."

"You didn't have to be Nostradamus to see it coming."

"So how about dinner tonight? Sam's in town and I'd like you to meet her."

"Sam's in town? I thought you said she was away at least until New Year's."

"That's what I thought, but her benefactors have her in town to speak at their annual meeting or something. Anyhow, she's here and I want you two to meet."

"Sounds great. Is she staying downtown, because I'll pick her up on my to Cambridge if you want."

"No, she's staying with me."

"It's a good thing that Michelle already dumped you. Any monkey business?"

"We're just friends, Ian."

"I forgot, she's almost forty."

"She's thirty-four," Sean corrected him. "And what does it matter?"

"I guess it doesn't. But back to your earlier question. Why do you think someone was in your apartment?"

"Because Pete stopped in, and when he got here, the door was open."

"Oh no, the evil hockey player is after you. Or maybe it's the CDC, or the CIA, or the Mafia," Ian laughed at Sean. "I think you're a bit too paranoid. You probably just left it open."

"Maybe," Sean admitted.

"Listen, I want to hear all about Pete, but I have to run. Sarah just peeked in and wants to talk. I'll see you tonight."

"See you later," Sean said, hanging up the phone.

JUST past seven in the evening, Ian arrived at Sean's apartment. "Come on in," Sean said.

"So where is she?" Ian asked.

"Calm down, she's not back from her meeting yet."

"Do you have anything to drink?" Ian asked.

"Check the refrigerator, Pete bought me some groceries."

Ian wandered off to the kitchen, returning with two beers. He handed one to Sean. "So how's Pete?"

"Not so great. His T-cell count is down. I guess that's an indicator that his drugs aren't working so well anymore." Sean saw that Ian didn't know what to say. "He's more concerned about you than he is with himself," Sean continued.

"Concerned about me?"

"Yeah. He wants to know why it is that you're never dating anyone."

"Well that could all change with Sarah."

"Do you know how often you've said that?"

"I know, but this time it's different."

"Right," Sean said rolling his eyes.

"So how was dinner last night?"

"Other than the Michelle thing, it was fine. Did I mention that she's transferring to Michigan for the spring semester?"

"That'll make the breakup easier, not being in each other's faces all day long," Ian observed.

"Always putting things in a positive light."

"That's me."

"So I asked Needham about the serum. He said that he examined it and that there was nothing noteworthy about it, so he sent it back to Chapeau."

"I thought that Chapeau said that Needham was the last one to have it."

"She did. Someone's lying, and for some reason I think it's Needham. Though Chapeau is a bit out there too."

"So now what?"

"Now I have to find the serum."

"Good luck."

The two sat silent, listening to a key entering the lock to Sean's apartment.

"Oh no, it's the k-k-killer h-h-hockey p-p-player," Ian said.

"Shut up already. I haven't even told you about the library yet."

Sam came through the door dressed in a dark navy business suit, with two pieces of luggage in her hands. Sean greeted her, taking her bags and placing them in his bedroom.

"Sam this is Ian," Sean said.

"Pleased to meet you Sam, I've heard all about your adventures in the Land Rover. How does it feel to be back in the US?" Ian asked.

"It's always nice to come home, but it takes a bit of getting used to."

"I thought we could all go out for dinner, if that's alright with you. There's this small bistro that I've been dying to try out on Commonwealth Ave. From what I've heard, they make incredible pizza and pasta," Sean said.

"That would be wonderful. Would you mind giving me a few minutes to shower?"

"Take your time, we'll be in the living room," Sean replied.

Sam disappeared into the bedroom while Ian and Sean returned to the couch down the hall.

"She's thirty-four?" Ian asked.

"That's what she told me."

"No way."

"Promise me that by the end of the night you'll have something intelligent to say."

A few minutes later, Sam emerged from the bathroom in

a towel before disappearing into Sean's bedroom.

"Wow," Ian said.

"Cut it out."

"Forget Sarah."

"You're not going near Sam," Sean said.

"What if she likes me?"

"It's not going to happen."

The door to the bedroom opened and Sam came out wearing khaki pants and a white blouse. Her damp hair left faint wet spots on her shoulders. Ian and Sean fell silent.

"Did I interrupt your conversation?" she asked.

"We were just arguing as usual," Sean said.

"Allow me to be the first to say that you look wonderful," Ian said.

"Oh man," Sean muttered.

"Thanks. The two of you look nice as well. Shall we?" Sam asked nodding to the door.

As Sean put on his jacket the phone rang. All three of them stood watching it. It rang again.

"Are you going to answer it?" Ian asked.

"Uh, no. I'll let the machine get it, but I want to see who it is."

After the fourth ring, the machine took the call. Sean's recorded voice filled the apartment.

On the other end of the line, background noise filled the air. The caller was either on a busy street corner or in front of a loud television. He spoke in an agitated and slurred voice, "This is a message for Sean Graham. This is Jim Mason. You called me the other day asking questions about Needham and some missing serum. Well somebody else called me today saying it was the CDC, asking what I had told you. Bunch of shit. They weren't from the CDC. Listen, I've got to keep moving, I think I'm being followed. I just sent you a note with some other information in it. It's too dangerous talking on the phone." There was a pause, the sound of machine gun fire erupting from the TV in the background. "I'm taking a big risk talking to you now. Be careful who you talk to, and watch your back. I have a feeling Needham is behind this. I'll be in touch." Mason hung up and the answering machine switched off again. On it, a single red light flashed intermittently.

"Who the hell was that?" Ian asked.

"That's James Mason, one of the guys I had you look up the other night," Sean answered.

"He's even more paranoid than you," Ian said.

"He's a drunk, but somebody's gotten to him." Sean stood staring at the machine for a moment. "Let's go eat."

MASON stood in his filthy apartment, running his hands through his greasy hair. He shut the television off and turned out the lights. He stepped to the window, pulling back the shade to look outside. A few teenagers loitered on the street corner below, harassing a young woman as she walked by. Mason scanned the other end of the street. I know you're out there, he thought. If he had any booze in the apartment he would never have considered leaving the building, but the tap had run dry and he was thirsty.

He walked to the door. He stuck his bloodshot eye to the peephole. The hall was empty. His enormous cat pawed at his pant leg. He kicked it away. Once into the hall he ran as quickly as his stout legs would take him. Sweating heavily in the Chicago night air, he climbed into his car and struggled with the ignition.

"Come on," he said, checking the mirrors. The car started and Mason screeched away from the curb. He let out a small nervous giggle. He passed all of the local bars he frequented. He figured that once they realized he wasn't at home, those would be the first places they would check. Fifteen minutes later, Mason was satisfied that he'd lost anyone that might have followed him. He parked in an alley and found a stool in a bar.

Except for the Michelob sign hanging above the stained green felt of the pool table, the bar was poorly lit. Mason sat as casually as possible, watching every patron who entered the bar. By his seventh shot, his vigilance had faded. With no one to look out for him, his paranoia grew.

THE bistro on Commonwealth Avenue was as advertised. Though comfortably small, the atmosphere inside the restaurant was very lively. Only a shoulder-high divider separated the kitchen from the dining area, giving the diners a bird's eye view of their meals' preparation.

The three enjoyed their dinners, sharing stories about random escapades. It was Ian who asked about Mason's bizarre phone call.

"I have no idea what to think about it," Sean answered.

"What are the chances that he's sincere?" Ian asked.

"I have no doubt that he's being sincere. My question is whether or not he's sane. I'll give him a call tomorrow and see what's got him so revved up."

"But it's not safe to use the phone," Ian said in a mocking tone.

"Yeah, I don't know what that was all about," Sean said. "But he did say that someone claiming to be from the CDC called him. Did he say if the caller was a man or a woman?"

"He didn't say," Sam replied.

"Well there are only a few people who knew I called him."

"Wasn't me," Ian said looking to Sam.

Sam shrugged. "Before you go accusing anyone of calling this man, I think you need to speak with him again. From the sound of that call, he seems like the type that believes in alien abductions."

"Sam's right," Ian said. "You need to talk to this guy again and see if the lights are on upstairs."

"Like I said, I'll call him first thing in the morning, assuming he can pull himself out of bed."

When they finished dinner, the waitress cleared the table and returned with coffee. Ian stirred a spoonful of sugar into his and looked at Sam. "Do you mind if I ask you a question?"

"Go ahead."

"It's a bit personal. Don't answer if you don't want to."

"Ian!" Sean said, shooting his friend a look.

"Don't worry, it's not that bad," he assured Sean.

"I hope not," Sam laughed.

"On the drive over here, you were talking about Needham," he said.

Sam nodded.

"You weren't ever involved with him, were you?"

Sean spoke before Sam could answer. "What the hell kind of question is that?"

"No, it's okay Sean. Ian's very observant. Yes, Dr. Needham and I were involved in the past."

Sean sat stirring his coffee, not looking at her.

"But that was a very long time ago." Sam looked at Sean. "Why so silent?"

"I, I don't know. I guess that I figured you might have said something about it before."

"You never asked. And that's not something that one simply volunteers to others."

"Oh I know, it's just ... surprising, that's all."

"It doesn't bother you, does it?" she asked, putting her hand on Sean's.

"No. But like I said, it was just surprising." Sean looked at Ian. "Any more questions, genius?"

Ian chuckled, "What are you complaining about? She's holding your hand, isn't she? Besides, you have a story of your own that falls along the same lines."

"Shut up, Ian," Sean said.

Ian ignored his friend. "Sam, when we were freshmen at Georgetown, Sean had this economics professor. A female professor. She was probably in her forties. Anyhow, being about as sharp as a spoon, Sean couldn't figure out the concept of present discounted value."

"I know what it is now," Sean interjected.

"That's great, Einstein. So he was always staying after class and asking the professor for help. Seeing that he was lost in the woods, they began having one-on-one sessions over coffee. Sean took this as an indication of the professor's suppressed obsession for his skinny teenage body."

"You guys all said that she wanted me," Sean said, blushing.

"So one day I told Sean to bring a bottle of wine and a dozen roses to their meeting, convincing him that it was what she wanted."

"Sean, please tell me you didn't do it," Sam said.

"Oh he did it all right," Ian said laughing.

"So what happened?" Sam asked.

Sean shook his head. "She yelled at me, saying that my behavior was totally inappropriate. She thought that I'd purposely done poorly in class just to seduce her. She stopped meeting me, and I almost failed the class."

Sam and Ian laughed as Sean buried his head in his hands. "I think that should about do it for dinner," Sam said. "That's probably all Sean can handle for the night."

SEAN and Sam dropped Ian off at his apartment. It was still fairly early, so the two rented a movie. Once back at his apartment, Sean attempted to discreetly check all of the usual hiding spaces for intruders.

"Why are you looking behind doors and under your bed?" Sam asked.

"To prove to myself that I'm just paranoid."

"And why, might I ask, do you want to do that?"

"I think in this case, it's better to be paranoid than to actually have someone hiding under my bed or in the closet."

Sam laughed, "An odd logic, but you have a point."

It wasn't until the first lines of the movie were spoken that Sean realized that it wasn't in English. "Sam, I thought you said this was a good movie?"

"It is."

"But they're speaking French. I don't speak French."

"That's why they put those little words at the bottom of the screen."

Sean sighed. "Must everyone mock me?"

Sam grabbed one of the throw pillows and put it on Sean's lap. "Mind if I lie down?" she asked.

"Not at all."

Just a few short minutes into the movie, Sean began gently running his hands through Sam's hair. "That feels nice," she said, without looking up at him. He slowly moved his hand onto the back of her bare neck, caressing her soft skin.

At midnight the movie was still trudging forward. Sam had fallen asleep long ago. Sean leaned down and whispered to her. "You should go to bed."

"Okay," she said, barely awake.

Sean walked her to his bedroom and sat her on the bed. "I'll let you change and come back to say 'goodnight.'"

Sam changed into her nightshirt and crawled under the covers. She called Sean back into the room. "Are you sure you don't want the bed?"

"I'll be fine on the couch."

Sam motioned for him to draw closer. She reached up and hugged him. "You're the sweetest guy around." He smiled as she kissed him on the cheek.

"Do you have anything planned for tomorrow?" he asked.

"No, what did you have in mind?"

"I thought we could picnic up at Cape Ann."

"Sounds like fun. It's a date."

"Sleep well," he said closing the door.

"I didn't get a quarter," the plump, dark-skinned boy said as he tugged at the back of Claris's shirt.

Claris turned around and reached into his pocket. "Here," he said, handing the boy the coin. "Now run along with your friends."

The American removed his hat as he entered the steamy tropical post office. He walked to his PO box. As usual, it was empty. He walked back past the other customers, heading for the door. Edmund, the head postman, called to him from behind the counter. "Mr. Claris, I have an urgent parcel for your attention."

Claris walked to the counter. He wiped the sweat from his brow.

Edmund disappeared into another room, returning with an envelope. He placed it on the counter, just out of Claris's reach. "I'll need to see some identification," the postman said.

"But you know who I am. I've been coming here for years."

"It's government policy. I need to see some identification."

"Government policy? Listen, you know I don't carry any ID. I ride my bicycle everywhere. Just give me the envelope," Claris protested, now drenched in sweat.

"No identification, no parcel," Edmund insisted.

Claris reached into his pocket, producing a twenty dollar bill. He slid it across the counter. Edmund pocketed the money, his hand remaining motionless on the envelope.

"For christ-sakes," Claris muttered. He slid another twenty across the counter. "That's all I've got."

The postman handed Claris the envelope, depositing the additional twenty into his pocket.

Claris placed the unopened envelope into his leather pouch and walked back outside. After a trip to the open market, he took a seat on his bench across from the government building. He leisurely ate a mango before returning to the envelope.

He looked at the return address: Boston, Massachusetts. Overnight delivery from the US. Must be important. With his pocketknife, he sliced open the top of the envelope. He removed the single sheet of stationary size paper and read the handwritten note. Once finished, he refolded the note, placing it back into the envelope. He leaned back on the bench, deep in thought.

Who are you, Sean Graham? And why are you asking questions about missing serums and hepatitis C? These issues haven't seen daylight in the many years I've lived on this island. Why now? I'm no longer in the disease business. Tuna is my life now, and it will be until I die. I've made a new life for myself, and I'll be damned if some student starts dredging up the past. Maybe Needham put you up to this. But why would he? Lawrence, my friend, would you do such a reckless thing?

Thinking quietly to himself, Claris found that he had dug a hole in the wood bench with his pocketknife. He placed the letter and the knife into his leather pouch. He sat silent for another few minutes, no longer interested in reading *The New York Times* over the Internet. His plan of action solidified in his head, he rode his bicycle through the oppressive heat back to his tropical estate.

8

WHERE the Chicago River snakes its way through the downtown section of the city, there is a fifty-foot drop from the roadway to the water below.

The divers pulled the body out of the river as Detective Ed Kwitkowski of the Chicago Police Department arrived on the scene. Kwitkowski was scheduled to end his shift at nine PM. He called his wife to let her know it would be a late night.

Exiting his car, Kwitkowski ducked the yellow police line tape and found the officer in charge.

"I'm Detective Kwitkowski.What do you have?"

The patrolman walked with Kwitkowski toward the gap in the barrier left by the car as it crashed through the guardrail before plunging into the water. A dozen high-powered floodlights lit the water below.

"As you can see," the patrolman said, "the divers just pulled the driver out of the water. He's DOA. They're looking for passengers, but the divers don't think there were any."

Kwitkowski watched as a fresh crew of divers plunged over the side of the police boat and entered the chilly water.

"Any idea what caused him to go into the drink?" Kwitkowski asked.

"No. We couldn't find any witnesses."

"No witnesses at this time of night?" Kwitkowski said.

"Sorry. We'll have a better idea what happened when they get the crane down here to haul the car out. Good money says that he was drunk. We ran a check on his ID. He has three DUIs in the last four years."

"Let's just wait and see what the medical examiner has to say before we go jumping to conclusions," Kwitkowski cautioned.

"If you're up to speed, I'm heading to home," the patrolman said. He walked with Kwitkowski to the gurney with the dead body on it. The body had a rubbery look to it. There was a deep laceration on the man's forehead. A small section of skull was clearly visible.

Kwitkowski nodded. "Yeah, I'll take it from here. Do me one favor. When you get back to the station have someone get the phone company to send us his phone log. If this turns out to be a homicide investigation, I want to get the ball rolling."

THE phone rang early the next morning, waking Sean from another fitful sleep. Standing to retrieve the phone, he felt a dull pain in his neck; the result of an uncomfortable night on the couch.

"Hello," Sean said picking up the phone. He looked at his watch: 7:06 AM.

"Mr. Graham, please," said the man on the other end.

"This is he."

"Mr. Graham, my name is Ed Kwitkowski. I'm a detective with the Chicago Police Department. Sorry to call so early, but I have a few questions I'd like to ask you."

Sean struggled to shake the sleep from his head. "Go ahead."

"Were you in Boston last night?" the detective asked.

"Not Boston proper. I was in the surrounding areas."

"Were you with anyone else?"

"Yes, I was with two friends."

"What are their names?"

"Ian Nielson and Samantha Ferson."

"Can you give me their phone numbers?"

Sean hesitated. "Can I ask what this is about?"

"I'll get to that in a minute. The numbers please."

Sean gave him Ian's number. "As for Samantha, she's staying with me right now. Could you please tell me what this is about?" Sean said, looking at the closed door of his bedroom.

"Mr. Graham, what was the nature of your relationship with James Mason?"

"I wouldn't really call it a relationship. I've only spoken with him once, and that was over the phone."

"Did he call you last night at about seven PM?"

"Yes he did."

"And what was the nature of your conversation?"

"It wasn't a conversation. He left a message on my answering machine."

"What did he say?"

"He was following up on some questions that I'd asked him about research he performed with the CDC back in the early eighties."

"Anything else?"

"He was acting all paranoid. He said that it wasn't safe for him to be talking to me."

"Why wasn't it safe?"

"I don't know. He never said," Sean lied. He wasn't going to bring Needham into the conversation based on Mason's crazed speculation. "I think he was a bit out of it. Did something happen to him?"

"Give me a second," Kwitkowski said. "Do you still have the message on tape?"

"No I don't. I erased it last night. Listen, detective, I would really like to know why you're asking me these questions."

"James Mason is dead."

"Dead?"

"That's right."

"How?"

"We're still trying to determine that. His car careened off of Wacker Drive, broke through a retaining wall, and plunged into the Chicago River late last night."

"Was it an accident?"

"Like I said, it's still under investigation. The medical examiner said that Mason had twice the legal limit of alcohol in him."

"So he was driving drunk."

"That's right. But we're still not sure that it was an accident."

"Why not?" Sean asked.

"Because he had no water in his lungs when the divers pulled him out of the river."

"What does that mean?"

"It means that he didn't drown. More often than not, when people drown, they essentially breath water into their lungs. No water in the lungs means that he was dead before he had a chance to drown."

"So how did he die?"

"The ME found a large gash on his head. Right now they're trying to determine whether or not the injury could have occurred when his car hit the guardrail or the water.

So far, the evidence is inconclusive either way."

"So this is a homicide investigation?"

"I'm a homicide detective, and I'm on the case, but it's not strictly a homicide investigation. I'm working it until we reach a conclusion."

"Why are you calling me?"

"Standard procedure. We got your name and number when we checked Mason's calls with the phone company. He died less than an hour after calling you."

Sean thought about the prior night. He was enjoying dinner with Ian and Sam when Mason died. It was an eerie thought. "Is there anything else I can help you with?" he asked.

"Not at the moment," Kwitkowski said. "We'll be in touch if we have any further questions. Thanks for your time."

"No problem," Sean said before hanging up the phone.

He lay back down on the couch, taking in all that Kwitkowski had said. The sun began to creep through the large bay window in his living room. He began to think that Mason might not have been paranoid. But Needham being responsible for Mason's death? Impossible, he thought. Sean wondered what he had gotten himself involved in, or even if he was truly involved. He sat silent on the couch.

The phone had awakened Sam as well. She approached from behind Sean, wearing her nightshirt and Sean's sweatpants.

"Good morning," she said.

He turned and looked at her over his shoulder. "Hi Sam."

"Who was that calling so early?"

"That was a detective from the Chicago Police Department. That guy who called last night, James Mason, he's dead."

"Oh my god. What happened?"

"Apparently he was driving drunk and crashed into the Chicago River."

"Why would the police call you?

"I guess he was dead before he hit the water, so they're not sure that it was an accident. They called me because Mason called me about an hour before the accident. The detective said it was standard procedure in a potential homicide."

"Homicide?"

"They don't know either way yet."

"I'm sure they'll find that it was just an accident," Sam said.

Sean shrugged. "It's probably all in my head, but what if this has something to do with me? A man I don't know dies less than an hour after leaving a crazed message on my answering machine. That's a little strange."

Sam rubbed Sean's shoulders. "They're going to find that it was just an accident."

He nodded.

"Go shower," Sam said, "I'll make some breakfast and pack lunches. The sun's out and we're going to have a great day up on Cape Ann. We'll put all of this in the past and enjoy a relaxing getaway."

"You're right, a change of scene will do wonders."

BARNARD Claris sat in the shade of a large palm tree, a tall glass of lemonade in his hand. An iguana slowly sauntered across the cream colored patio tile to his feet. Claris placed the lemonade on the table and picked up the large lizard. He rubbed the scales of the lizard's back. "How are you today?" Claris asked.

The lizard replied with a fluttering of his tongue. Claris kissed it on the head before replacing him on the floor.

From a pitcher on the table, he topped off his lemonade. He opened his electronic organizer and searched for a number. When he found it, he dialed it on his cellphone. Nobody knew why, but Claris was very particular about using his cellphone.

The phone on the other end had not finished ringing once when a man picked it up. "Santiago and Associates."

"Raoul, this is Salieri," Claris said.

"One moment. Let me change phones."

Raoul Santiago's title was Private Investigator. And for whatever reason, he claimed to have associates, though there were none. Santiago fancied himself a PI, but when the investigating business was slow, which was often the case for Santiago and Associates, he found work performing odd jobs. Frequently, Santiago played the role of bounty hunter, hauling in bail jumpers for a bondsman friend.

Santiago was Claris's only remaining contact in the continental United States. Whenever Claris needed anything done, he called Santiago. And whenever he called Santiago, he insisted on using the code name Salieri, after Wolfgang Amadeus Mozart's nemesis.

"Go ahead," Santiago said.

"I need you to look into a person for me."

"Where?"

"Boston."

"It'll cost you extra for the trip to the East Coast."

"You know that's not an issue."

"What's the name?" Santiago asked.

"Sean Graham. He's a student at Harvard."

"Do you want anything done, or just surveillance?"

"Just find out who he is and what he's up to. You'll be receiving a package in about an hour. It's a cellphone. That's the only phone I'll call you on. I'll check in later for an update. Mind you, this is time sensitive."

"It'll cost you."

"Just get it done."

"I'm already packing," Santiago said, placing his revolver into a duffel bag.

GETTING away from campus helped Sean's mood. As he drove north out of Boston, he found almost immediate relief. Every second put more distance between him and his worries. The sky was bright blue, not a single cloud as far as the eye could see. It was a bit brisk outside and promised to be even more so on the ocean.

As they drove, Sam and Sean passed north shore towns like Lynn and Peabody. Towns where the entire populations attend their local high school's homecoming football games.

Soon they found themselves on a curvy two-lane road hugging the coast. The waters were rough, rocking the fishing boats that sat idle in the harbor. They drove slowly through the small town of Gloucester with its weathered gray shingled shops and restaurants. Simple wooden signs hung off the buildings toward the street, advertising such things as their "World Famous Homemade Chowders".

"Do you have a place in mind for the picnic?" Sam asked.

"Ian said that there's a turnoff up here and then a small path to the beach."

"So he's taken many romantic interludes up here."

"No, there's a bike trail here that he likes to ride. I think this is it," Sean said turning onto a gravel road. Overhanging trees and shrubs quickly swallowed the road and brushed against the sides of the car. The gravel ended and opened into a small parking area. Sean and Sam got out of the car and walked to a thin dirt path. "I guess this is it," Sean said, leading Sam by the hand.

The path was heavily wooded and damp. Just before they gave up on the trail, the woods broke, revealing a small grassy outcropping bordering the water.

"Wow," Sam said. "This is beautiful."

A tiny peninsula, the grass stretched only twenty-five yards, sloping gently from the forest to the rock-lined ocean.

Sam set the large plaid blanket on the grass, weighting down the edges with small stones. Sean walked ahead to the wave-beaten rocks. As the waves rolled in and crashed on them, a salty mist sprayed Sean's face. A steady wind blew off the water. Sam came up to his side and handed him his sweater. "You should probably put this on." He pulled the sweater over his head and put his arm around her shoulder. They stood looking out onto the rolling swells of the Atlantic.

"I miss being able to find myself alone," Sean said. "It doesn't happen too much at school."

"So you drag me out here and then ask me to leave," Sam said joking.

"You know what I mean. It's good to get away."

Sean reached into his pocket and pulled out the stone Pete had given him.

"What's that," Sam asked.

"My brother brought it back from Alaska for me. It's a wishing stone. The white stripe is my wish waiting to come true. All I have to do is skip it into the water." He rubbed the smooth stone between his fingers.

"Do you have a wish?"

"Not yet."

"Are you thinking of using it today?"

Sean thought for a moment. "I just want to finish Fulsonmayer's paper and get on with my life."

"Then save your wish for another day. This will all pass. Trust me," she said, closing Sean's palm around the stone. Taking his hand, she led him back to the blanket.

"It's cooler than I thought it would be," he said.

Sean lay back on the blanket, staring up at the blue

sky. Sam sat cross-legged watching the waves march in. "This reminds me of growing up in Vancouver," she said. "There was this beautiful spot where my parents always used to take me for walks—Stanley Park. I loved walking down on the sea wall. The park was full of tall pines and bright flowers. It smelled wonderful. And every once in a while we would see a lazy sea lion sunning itself on the rocks of the harbor.

"And then there were the docks. I made my father sit with me for hours, just watching the fishermen unload their bounty. I loved it, the bearded men with their yellow slickers tossing fish through the air. They always looked so tired at the end of the day, but they never failed to smile and say hello."

While she reminisced, Sean opened the wicker basket and retrieved a bottle of wine and two glasses. He poured Sam a glass and handed it to her. "Thanks. Here's to getting away," she said, touching her glass to his. "Vancouver is one of the most beautiful places in the world. When my family moved when I was in junior high, I thought I would die. But it didn't take long to fall in love with San Francisco too. Mornings down on the bay can have a surreal quality to them. I loved walking down on the water just after dawn. Nobody's around. Just a few joggers starting their day. The fog blankets everything. It's like you're walking in a dense soundless cloud. And as the sun rises, the fog burns off, and the Golden Gate Bridge slowly emerges from the gray mist." Sam smiled, "You know, other than Vancouver, I had never left California before I went to Africa after my freshman year in college. I didn't think that there was any reason to leave California. We had everything right at our back door."

"You never wanted to see New York or DC or Chicago?" Sean asked.

"Why—so I could get mugged? No, San Francisco was just right."

"And let me guess, the logical choice of college for a San Francisco girl who was afraid to spread her wings, was Berkeley."

"The logical choice for anyone is Berkeley," she retorted.

"What's wrong with Georgetown?"

"Nothing, if you want a stuffy East Coast atmosphere."

"Ouch. I didn't want a stuffy East Coast atmosphere. I simply wanted all of the students to wear clothes to class."

"*Touché*," Sam laughed. "At times it could be a strange place, but we all had fun."

"And, of course, that's where you met Needham."

Sam looked down at Sean lying on his back. She sipped her wine and smiled. "Do you want to talk about this?"

"It's just one of those things that I think I should've known. Having lived together for eight months, I just thought that there really wasn't too much about you that I didn't know," Sean said.

"Surprises keep a relationship interesting."

"Yeah, but they're not supposed to make your stomach turn. So let's hear it all," he said, topping off her wine.

"During my freshman year, Needham gave a guest lecture for one of my classes at Berkeley. He talked about the rewards and challenges of field research. I was in awe and accosted him after class. I begged and begged for him to let me do research for him during the following summer. He said that it was highly unusual for him to take on a freshman, but that my enthusiasm won him over."

Sean rolled his eyes, "I can only imagine why he would want to work with an attractive young coed."

"It wasn't like that. At least not while I was an undergrad. I continued to work for him during the summers and sometimes over breaks, but nothing happened until later. I was in my third year of med school when a crush became a little something more. And after a very brief fling, and I emphasize brief, we both came to our senses and decided to call it off. No hard feelings."

Tired of sitting, Sam joined Sean, lying down on her back.

Sean rolled onto his side, propping himself up with an elbow. "So that was that," he said.

"That was that. I'm still fond of him. I have him to thank for giving me the opportunity to work on the other side of the world, in one of the most spectacular places around."

Sean looked at Sam. She had closed her eyes and continued to talk. She looked very peaceful.

"I love living in the Serengeti," she said. "I can't imagine life without it. That sweet smell that envelops you when you're walking in the open grasses. The brightest of blue skies, with soft fluffy clouds floating by. Listen to me, going on and on when you know precisely what I'm talking about." She stopped. A small smile grew across her face.

The wind blew a few strands of her long hair onto her cheek. Sean gently brushed them away. She reached for his hand, holding it against her cheek. It felt warm in the cool wind.

Sean sat perched on his elbow in indecision. She looked so beautiful lying by his side. He leaned toward her, her eyes still closed. She felt the warmth of his face nearing hers. She lifted her head slightly to meet him.

His heart raced. He pulled her closer and softly kissed her lips. Her hand found the back of his neck and pulled him closer. He was so warm. With both arms around him, she pulled him over her, squeezing and not wanting to let go. The wind blew gently around them, but they no longer felt the cold. Their kisses were long and slow, not rushed at all.

Sean began kissing her cheek until he was at her ear. She smiled. "I'm falling for you," he whispered, kissing her neck.

"Then we're in the same boat."

They lay on the blanket for the next two hours, kissing and holding each other, happy just being together. But inevitably, they had to return to Cambridge.

On the drive back to the city, Sam rubbed Sean's neck while he drove. He kept his hand on her knee. He wasn't excited to return to his problems at school, but having Sam by his side made it bearable. All of this craziness will pass, he kept reminding himself. Soon, it will all pass.

"GO ahead," Santiago said, standing on the corner opposite Sean's apartment.

"What do you have for me?"

"Sean Graham: turns twenty-five in a couple of days. Father's a big shot in Manhattan. Brother is no longer in the work force—health reasons. Mother is MIA somewhere over in Europe. Like you said, he's a grad student at Harvard studying under one Richard Fulsonmayer. He appears to be seriously involved with a young doctor named Samantha Ferson."

"Samantha Ferson, why is that name familiar?" Claris asked himself.

"Graham has a friend named Ian Nielson. I'm still getting the scoop on him. A guy over at the law school's getting back to me in an hour. Listen, Claris—"

"Salieri," Claris interrupted.

"Right, Salieri. Information out here isn't coming cheap."

"That's not an issue."

Santiago smiled. "How do you want me to proceed?" Santiago asked.

"As we discussed earlier."

"You're sure about that?" Santiago asked.

"I'm positive."

AS usual, the mid-afternoon sun found the Harvard campus in a flurry of activity. Sean parked about a block from his apartment. Walking along the brick sidewalk, he nervously took Sam's hand.

"Does this make you uncomfortable?" he asked.

"Of course not. It's a nice ending for our little trip. I had a great time," she said with a smile.

"Me too. So was that officially a date?"

"You could say that."

Sean smiled.

"What are you up to this afternoon?" Sam asked. The question had a subtle hint of tension behind it. The inevitable "now what" feeling after the first date.

Sean sensed it. "I have a few errands to run. How about you?"

"I have to pick up some research supplies while I'm in town. As you know, nothing's cheap in Africa. Other than that, I have no plans." She paused as Sean opened the door to his apartment. Sam's expression grew more serious. "I'd like to have dinner tonight so that we can talk."

"About Africa, right?"

"About Africa," she nodded, "and me and you and god knows whatever else."

"Dinner sounds great," he said, pulling Sam closer by the hand. He kissed her. "I can't begin to tell you how happy I am to have you around."

"You go run your errands, and I'll do my shopping. We'll meet back here at, say, six and figure out what to do for dinner." She went into his bedroom and returned with a small list of supplies in her hand. "I'll see you later," she said kissing him and walking out the door.

Sean checked the messages on his answering machine. The first was Fulsonmayer. He called to let Sean know that he had initiated a meeting with the Ad Board regarding Gustav. He would keep Sean updated as he learned more.

The second was Courtney Hillerman. Vivacious as ever, she wanted to meet Sean for coffee at four-thirty. Sean looked at his watch. That was in fifteen minutes. He pictured her on the other end of the phone, brushing her long blonde hair seductively over her shoulder. She went on to say that she would be out for the rest of the day and that she would meet him at the coffee shop in the Square.

Sean's heart sank. He couldn't stand her up without giving her any notice. He grabbed a few of the books from his class, put on his jacket and headed out to meet his young student.

THE nervous man fidgeted with his car keys as he waited for his accomplice's arrival. The shopping center parking lot was busy. He thought it was a terrible place for a meeting.

A car parked in the space next to him. The driver rolled down the window.

"You're late," the nervous man said.

"Here it is," the driver replied, handing him a paper bag.

The man stopped fidgeting with his keys and took the bag. He looked inside. "That's a syringe."

"No shit," the driver mocked him.

"What am I supposed to do with this?"

"Do what I told you on the phone."

"But nobody said anything about murder," the nervous man protested.

"And nobody is saying anything about murder now. Leave the cap on the needle."

The man grew more agitated. "Is this blood?" he asked, tapping the syringe.

"That's not your concern."

"Listen, I'm really not comfortable with this. I can't kill anyone."

"If that should become an issue, I'll find someone else. I told you what to do. Either you do it or you don't. I thought you said you needed the money."

"I do."

"Then stop your bitching and do what I said," the driver replied before rolling up the window and driving away.

SEAN arrived at the coffee shop located in the atrium of a small shopping plaza. He didn't see Courtney through the window. Maybe he was lucky and she had forgotten.

He went inside to get a better look at each of the tables. No Courtney. He turned to leave, walking past the counter.

"Hey, are you Sean?" the goateed server asked.

"Yes," Sean answered, somewhat taken by surprise.

"This is for you," the server said, handing Sean a folded piece of paper. "A cute blonde left it for you."

"Thanks." Sean opened the note. Courtney was waiting for him at the restaurant above the coffee shop. Sean sighed, growing angry. He needed to handle the situation sensitively.

He climbed the stairs to the second floor and found an Indian restaurant. He walked through the glass doors into the tastefully decorated restaurant. He looked at the bar. A skinny man in a suit sat alone at the far end of the bar, smoking a cigarette and sipping at a martini.

"Can I help you?" the hostess asked.

"I think I'm supposed to meet someone here. A young blonde woman."

"Oh, yes, I forgot. Please follow me."

Sean followed the hostess into the unusually dark dining area. Dark burgundy curtains covered the windows, drowning any sunlight that hoped to get in. Candles cast a warm glow over every table. Sean struggled to see in the dim lighting. The hostess led him past a small group of people at a boisterous table. They all laughed loudly. One of the men toted a camera, snapping countless photos of the others. The flash caught Sean in the eyes, blinding him.

"Here's your table, sir," the hostess said.

"Thank you," Sean said still blinking. When his eyes finally adjusted, he saw Courtney sitting on the other side of the table. She wore a red spaghetti stringed evening gown. He placed his books on the floor underneath his chair before sitting down.

"Thanks for coming Sean," Courtney said, her lips moist with lipstick.

"Courtney—"

"No, I'm not going to hear any of it. This is just a meeting between a teacher and his student. There's nothing wrong with that."

"Everything's wrong with that. Teachers don't meet students in candlelit restaurants. And students don't wear evening gowns when they need help with an assignment."

Courtney leaned closer, across the table. Sean couldn't help noticing that she wasn't wearing a bra. His hand sat on the table. She took it. He pulled away, but she held tightly.

"Just relax. I've already ordered dinner. If you don't enjoy spending time with me, I promise to forget all about it." She released his hand and sat back.

Sean sat for a moment not saying a word. He remembered how crushed and embarrassed he was when his professor rejected his errant advances. He decided to go along with dinner and then set her straight. After that, there would be no question in her mind. Their dinners arrived shortly.

Sean let Courtney carry the conversation. He gave her simple answers when she asked questions. When he took the teaching assistant position, he never imagined having the opportunity to become involved with a student. That only happened in TV mini-series. But here he was, finding himself tempted by the freshman sitting across the table from him.

When the check arrived, Sean reached for his wallet, but Courtney insisted on paying. Sean grabbed his books and jacket and followed Courtney out to the street. They walked in the direction of Sean's apartment.

"That wasn't so bad, was it?" Courtney said.

"Courtney, I'm your teacher. You're a bright, friendly and attractive young woman. You don't need me. You should have no trouble finding a boyfriend on this campus."

"I have a boyfriend," she said matter-of-factly.

"You have a boyfriend?"

"Yes."

"So what are you doing taking me, your teacher, out for dinner?"

"I just want to have a good time with you."

Sean took a deep breath. "Listen Courtney. This isn't going to happen. I'm sorry," he said, waiting for her response.

She bit her lower lip. "That's fine. You can't blame me for trying. I thought that we could be good together."

"Maybe under different circumstances."

"Can I at least have a hug?" she asked, stepping closer.

No harm in a hug, he thought. "I guess so."

She stepped forward. Sean could smell her sweet perfume. He looped his arms around her, his hands resting on the smooth skin of her back. When he let go, she looked up at him and kissed him on the lips. "I'll see you in class," she said, turning and walking away.

Sean stood paralyzed for a moment. He was flattered. He also thought that he'd handled the tempting situation admirably. He looked at his watch. "Damn," he said. He was late to meet Sam.

He hurried back to his apartment. Sam was walking out of his bedroom, carrying a magazine. She sat on the couch. "Sorry I'm late Sam."

"Don't be. I just got back myself."

Sean took a seat next to her. "You smell like Indian food. You've already eaten, haven't you?" she laughed. "Just couldn't wait."

Sean shook his head. He told her about Courtney and her ploy to get him to have dinner with her.

"So there's nothing going on between you?" Sam asked.

"No."

"And she took it well when you told her that there wouldn't be anything between you?"

"She seemed to."

"Then you did a good job."

"I'm sorry about dinner. If you still want to go grab a bite to eat, I'll come with. Or if you want me to put something together here, that's no problem either."

"I'll just go get a sandwich down in the Square," she said. "Care to join me?"

"Sure."

BACK in the Square, Sean sat at a table near the window of a cafe. Sam arrived with a large sandwich and two drinks. She handed one to Sean.

"Thanks," he said. He stood and pulled out her chair for her.

"That's gentlemanly of you. Thank you."

"I saw my brother do it once. I've done it ever since."

"He taught you well," she said. "I almost forgot to mention

that I saw Professor Fulsonmayer when I was running my errands this afternoon."

"What did he have to say?"

"He said that Needham was back from the specialist and that he had some bad news. It turns out that he does have schistosomiasis."

"Fulsonmayer gave me the impression that schistosomiasis was no big deal," Sean said.

"If you catch it in its early stages, it isn't. They're going to run more tests to determine just how advanced it is. They're afraid it's made its way to his liver."

"And if it has?"

"It's hard to say. The infection is rarely life threatening, but it does happen. And then there's the possibility of liver failure, which you know from your hepatitis research is not good."

Sean sat without replying, playing with the straw from his soda. "He looked fine the other night."

Sam nodded. "He looked fine, but he said a few things that weren't like him. I think that Fulsonmayer noticed too. I'm sure he'll be fine. It's just like a doctor to wait until the last possible moment before seeking treatment. And before I forget, Fulsonmayer also wanted to know if I would help you with your draft report. He said that you've been dragging your feet."

"And you said?"

"I said that although you're difficult to work with, I'd help you."

"Thanks," Sean smiled. "So now that you've got me here, why don't you give me your speech on how it's just not meant to be."

"I don't have any speech, Sean."

"But that's what you wanted to talk about, isn't it?"

"I don't want to talk about how we're not meant to be. I just want to talk about the inevitable."

"Which is?"

"My going back to Africa."

"When's that?"

"I'll to try to stay for as long as I can, but I think that I can only stretch it into another week at most."

"At some point, we're going to have to talk about you leaving, but I'd rather put that conversation off for a while.

Talking about the inevitable isn't going to change things, so why don't we just save it for later?"

"If that's what you want."

Sean took her hand. "I love spending time with you. I just don't want to spoil the little that we have."

"I don't want you to think that I'm running away."

"That's not who you are. I know that."

When Sam had finished her sandwich, Sean helped her on with her coat. "Let's go for a walk," he said.

Holding hands, they walked into Harvard Yard. It had grown dark. Lights glowed from all of the ancient dorm windows. A stereo played in one of the rooms, the song muffled as it floated to the sidewalks below. They strolled slowly to the cascading steps of the enormous Widner Library. They sat off in the shadow cast by one of the pillars adorning the massive library's façade. The moon drifted silently through the clouds high above the white steeple of Memorial Church. They stayed on the steps for an hour, holding each other close in the cool night.

RETURNING to his apartment, Sean played the solitary message on his answering machine. It was an excited Ian, saying that he too had spoken with Detective Kwitkowski from the Chicago Police Department.

Both Sean and Sam changed into more comfortable clothes. Sean grabbed a comforter and some pillows. He tossed them on the couch. There, the two cuddled, growing sleepy while surfing through the local news and a few of the late shows. Awkwardness resurfaced as Sam stood to go to bed.

She looked at Sean. "Do you want your bed tonight?"

"No, you take it. I've been doing fine out here. Besides, I'm already set up with blankets and pillows."

"You're sure?" Sam asked.

He nodded.

Sam leaned down and kissed him. "Thanks for a wonderful day."

He smiled, "Goodnight."

Sam turned off the TV and the living room light as she strolled slowly to Sean's bedroom. She closed the door. He could hear her rustling through her suitcase looking for her nightshirt. He heard her turn off the light and climb into bed. He quickly dozed off.

The apartment grew silent. The clock in the kitchen ticked softly, measuring the advancing hours of night. Even the street outside was quiet.

The sound of Sam's scream made Sean jump upright on the couch. He sat still, his heart beating out of his chest. He listened intently. The apartment was silent. Was it a dream?

"Sean get in here!" Sam yelled.

He jumped from the couch in the darkness, tripping over the leg of the coffee table. When he reached his bedroom, the light was already on. Sam was standing at the side of the bed looking at the pillow. Sean stood in the doorway.

"What's wrong?"

"Look," she said, motioning for him to step forward.

Stepping to her side, he saw it. The small syringe rested beside the pillow. It's plunger was drawn back, the body filled with a deep red liquid.

"Is that blood?" Sean asked.

"I'm not sure, but it looks like it."

"And it's not yours?"

"No, it's not mine." Sam leaned to pick it up.

"Well don't touch it."

"Don't worry. The cap's on the needle," she said, holding it up to the light.

Sean stood with his hands on his waist, shaking his head. Sam turned to look at him. She caught his eye.

"That's a fucking syringe," Sean said calmly. "Someone broke into my apartment and put a syringe, with what looks like blood in it, on my pillow. That's not funny."

"Let's call the police," Sam said.

Sean nodded. "I'm not sure what good it'll do, after all, somebody assaulted me with a brick and they called it vandalism."

In ten minutes Sergeant Lyndon from the campus police arrived, accompanied by a unit from the Cambridge Police Department. Lyndon looked tired. His posture no longer had the rigidity of a board.

"What's the trouble Mr. Graham?" he asked.

"Someone broke into my apartment and left this syringe on my bed."

Lyndon took the syringe in his meaty black hand, dropping it into a plastic evidence bag. The two men from the Cambridge Police Department were busy examining the door frame, the windows and the bed. The skinnier of the two approached Lyndon. He spoke in a muffled voice. Lyndon nodded as the skinny officer and his partner left the apartment.

"Well Mr. Graham, there is no sign of forced entry. So whoever left this needle used a key to get in here, or climbed in through an open window. You sure this isn't just a prank? Maybe Gustav again?"

Sean shook his head. "Are you kidding me? Would it be more your speed if it was a prank? You campus cops are a joke. Let me guess, you've had a tough night breaking up keg parties."

"Don't you get smart with me, young man," Lyndon said.

"I'm not, I'd just like some answers this time."

"And you'll get them," Lyndon said as he turned to leave. Sean closed the door behind him.

Sean turned to Sam, "I told you they were incompetent."

"I know, but at least we did it by the book."

Sean nodded.

"I'm surprised that you're not freaking out," Sam said. "Someone broke into your apartment and left a syringe on your bed."

"Don't think that it doesn't bother me. It does. But who knows, maybe Lyndon's right. It might be a prank or something. I mean the cap was on the needle, so it wasn't meant to do any real harm. I'd bet it was Gustav again."

"Breaking into your apartment?"

"It's possible," Sean said, walking Sam into the bedroom. "Are you alright?"

"I'm fine."

"Let's get some sleep. Hopefully Lyndon will stumble on some answers."

Sean returned to the couch but failed to fall asleep. When the sun began to peek through the window, he groaned. He hadn't slept a wink. He pulled a pillow over his head attempting to salvage at least a few minutes of sleep.

SEAN rose two hours later to the smell of coffee and the sound of eggs frying on the stove. Sam looked over the couch and saw that he was awake. "Good morning. I made some breakfast."

"How long have you been up?"

"About an hour. I want to get a jump on the day. From what Fulsonmayer said, we've got a lot of work to do."

Sean rubbed his eyes. "What are you talking about?"

"The draft you're working on. We'll work on it all day."

"Oh no we're not. I'm going to figure out what's going on with my life. But I'd be happy to let you work on the draft."

Sam hit him over the head with a pillow. "There's nothing you can do until we hear from the police. So unless you have some leads to give to them, I suggest that we keep pushing forward with the responsibilities in your life."

Sean knew she was right. "So how did you do the eggs?"

"Sunny side up."

He grimaced.

"What?" Sam asked.

"I don't like runny yolks. I like my eggs scrambled."

"Tough. When you make breakfast, you can make your eggs any way you like them. Now go take your shower so we can eat. We're on a tight schedule today. I'm going to show you how this journal submission business is done."

"Yes ma'am," Sean said, heading to the bathroom.

9

"CHANGE of plans," Sam said to Sean as he cleaned the breakfast dishes. "I have to run up to the University Press to see if I can buy a book that's out of print. So you head to the library and get started on Fulsonmayer's report. I'll meet you there when I'm finished."

"You're not trying to get out of helping me, are you?"

"Not at all," she replied. "But I really need this book." She grabbed her coat and headed for the door. So I'll see you at your carrel in about two hours."

"Do you know where my carrel is?" Sean asked.

"No, but I'll find it."

"Sounds like a plan. Thanks for breakfast."

Half an hour later, Sean passed a dozing Ms. Pierce as he entered the library. He descended the carpeted stairs to the lower level and walked to his desk. He dropped his bag on the floor and immediately studied the desk for any sign of visitors. The tiny mark he had etched into the desk was covered by the corner of a book. His first thought was that someone had been through his research materials. Then he noticed the janitor dusting a desk on the other side of the library.

Relieved, he sat down and began to review his research notes. Fulsonmayer had told him to have the draft ready for the following day. Possible, but unlikely, he thought.

He took out his laptop, placed it on the desk and began typing. An hour later he read through what he'd just written. "Awful," he muttered, before reluctantly erasing the file and starting over.

NEEDHAM sat comfortably in his favorite reading chair. While at his home in Brookline, he made a habit of reading the morning paper, cover to cover, while lounging in the plush, high-backed chair.

The Boston Globe sat folded on the reading table beside a cup of tea.

"I assure you, I'm fine. I just have to wait on the test results before I'm given a clean bill of health. Are you sure I can't get you a cup of tea?" Needham asked his guest.

"No thank you."

"So how is my friend Sean getting on?" Needham asked, squeezing the tea bag with his spoon.

"He's usually a pretty cool character, but he's becoming a bit paranoid."

Needham laughed. "Paranoid?"

"A brick through the window, a break in at his apartment, and a dead drunk in Chicago will do that to you."

"Yes, I suppose it would." Needham blew on his tea before taking a sip. "The way he spoke to me the other night, I got the feeling that he doesn't trust me. Do you have any idea why?"

"No, but I imagine that he's keeping a lot of his thoughts to himself."

Needham smiled. "Well don't let him withdraw from everyone. He's a bright kid. Make sure he doesn't get tangled in his own webs."

SAM arrived at Tozzer library to find Sean battling with writer's block. She placed a small paper bag on his desk.

"What's this?" Sean asked.

"It's a blueberry muffin."

"You're not supposed to bring food in here. If Ms. Pierce sees this, she'll kill me," he said.

"Don't worry. Security around here doesn't exactly rival Fort Knox." Sam pulled a chair up to Sean's desk.

"So did you get the book?" Sean asked.

"Unfortunately no."

"So what have you been doing for the last two hours?"

"Finding you the world's greatest blueberry muffin," she said kissing him on the cheek. "So how's the writing going?"

"Very slowly."

"What do you have so far?"

"A bunch of garbage," he answered.

"Why don't you let me be the judge of that?"

Sean handed her the portions of the draft he had completed. Sam took several minutes reading it. When she had finished, she turned to Sean with a slight grimace. "It needs some work."

Sean sighed. "Like I said—garbage."

"Tell you what. Let's gather all of your research material and move over there," she said pointing to a large table in the corner. "We'll set up a strategy and then forge ahead."

"Fulsonmayer's going to kill me."

"It's not that bad. We'll get it sparkling in no time. Trust me."

HAVING worked without a break until five in the afternoon, Sean napped with his head on the table. Sam was busy reviewing the latest revisions he had made. She nudged him on the shoulder. "Where did you put the data analysis section?" she asked him.

"In the folder," he answered without raising his head.

She picked up one of the several folders that were sprawled across the table. When she opened it, she found the photocopy with the geographical names that Sean had highlighted. She smiled. "I see that you read the syphilis study I told you about," she said.

Confused, Sean picked his head up and looked at her. "To be honest I only skimmed it, but what are you talking about?"

She pulled the photocopied table from the folder and handed it to him. "I'm not sure what this table is, but all of the names you highlighted are towns from my syphilis project."

"What?"

"Are you awake? I said—"

"Yeah, I heard you," Sean said, snatching the photocopied table from her. He riffled through its several pages. He stared at Sam. "All of these highlighted names are of towns from your syphilis project?"

"For the third time, yes."

"What exactly did you do to the participants?"

"As you know, we worked only with prostitutes—"

Sean interrupted, "Why only prostitutes?"

"Because, all of the towns in the study are located along major trucking routes. From the Atlantic to the Indian Ocean, and then again in Egypt. Prostitutes that had syphilis were guaranteed to spread the disease to countless others. A trucker could catch the disease on the west coast of Africa, and by sleeping with prostitutes on his way east, spread it to every major town he hit, until he reached the Indian Ocean. And then the cycle continues: the prostitute then gives it to another trucker who gives it to another prostitute. We found that about half of the truckers paid in drugs like heroin, so god only knows what else they were spreading. Perhaps the worst part of the cycle is that the trucker eventually brings these diseases home to his wife. So on and so on."

Sean didn't say anything. He continued to study the table.

"You have to admit," Sam said, "targeting the prostitutes was rather clever. We knew that they were the biggest threats to spread the disease. If we could treat them, and then get them to use protection, we had a good chance of curbing the disease's spread."

Sean kept flipping through the table, concentrating on the highlighted names. "Sam, what did the treatment involve?"

"Well among other things, we gave the women penicillin shots."

"Penicillin shots? You're certain it was penicillin?"

"Everyone got either penicillin or the synthetic equivalent. What's that table?" she asked. "It's not from the paper we submitted."

"This table was prepared by the CDC. It's a locational timeline for the first known hep C cases worldwide. I highlighted the names on the table because I couldn't remember where I'd seen them before. They're all from your syphilis project."

"So?"

"Maybe it's nothing, but the towns you and Needham visited are not only among the first in their respective regions where people died from HCV infections, they're among the first in the world."

"Let me look at that," Sam said, taking the pages from Sean. She read silently, flipping through the pages, following the names and dates with her finger. "That's just a coincidence. It logically follows that along a major freight route, hepatitis C would surface in many of the towns."

Sean shook his head. "Maybe it's a coincidence, maybe not. Think about what you said about the spread of syphilis. All there had to be was a single prostitute with the disease. If she gave it to a trucker who drove down a highway to another town and gave it to another prostitute, the disease would spread exponentially. Now instead of syphilis, think HCV, spread by high-risk sex—prostitution qualifies; and IV drug use—you just said that drugs were often the only payment. Wait here," Sean said disappearing into the book stacks. He returned with the book he had photocopied the table from. He opened it to a page of maps he'd previously seen.

"Look," he said pointing to the map. "Here are the highways that the towns in your study are located on. This first map is from 1982, before you did your syphilis project. Look along the highway. There are no known HCV, then called Non-A, Non-B, cases along the highways on this map." He turned the page, revealing another map. "Now look here. This map is from 1985, from after your study. These are the highways, and look how prevalent the virus is along them." He flipped to another map. "This is the same region in 1995. No other place in the world shows this type of density for HCV cases. You're telling me that's a coincidence?"

Sam was transfixed by the two maps. She turned back and forth between them, not saying a word.

"Sam," Sean said.

She didn't respond.

"Sam, what if it's not a coincidence? Not that I'd know where to begin to prove it."

"It is," she said flatly.

"There's—"

She wasn't listening to him. "I mean, we gave them penicillin. It was for their syphilis. They were sick. We were there to help them. It was just penicillin. They needed—"

"Sam—" Sean began.

"What? What are you suggesting?" she barked.

"I'm not suggesting anything. I just think it might be possible—"

"Are you listening to yourself? You can't be serious."

Sean didn't respond.

"I have to go," Sam said stepping away from the table. She put her coat on.

"Where?"

"I just remembered, I have a dinner meeting in Boston tonight."

"You never mentioned it before," Sean said.

"That's because I just remembered."

"What about the maps and the syphilis?"

"Sean, it's a coincidence. Drop it."

"So you're just dismissing everything I just said."

She took a deep breath and forced a smile. "I've been doing this for a long time. I know what I'm talking about. You're getting worked up over nothing. Trust me," she answered, leaving him at the table.

Sean sat staring at the map and the highlighted table for another half hour. Part of him said to forget about it all, that he was being irrational. But another part of him said to keep looking for answers. When another hour passed without any progress, Sean packed his bag and left the library.

SAM arrived back at Sean's apartment at eleven PM. Sean was sitting at his computer when she walked through the door.

"How was your meeting?" Sean asked.

"They're all the same. I kiss their asses. They give me money."

"So it was a casual dinner," Sean said, noticing that Sam still wore the khaki pants she had worn to the library.

"You could say that. Is something wrong?" She took off her coat and walked over to his desk.

He didn't answer.

"Is it about this afternoon?" She could tell by his expression that it was. "I'm sorry I brushed off what you said. I just got a bit frazzled when I remembered my meeting. I'm not an expert on the history of the spread of HCV, but I'll do a little research tomorrow to prove to you that my syphilis project is not the origin for the global spread of hepatitis C." She stood behind him, rubbing his shoulders. "I think you're still a bit stressed out with all that's been going on. Your personal life is getting tangled in your work, and it's getting to you. I know you don't trust Needham with the AWOL serum, but you have to trust me on this syphilis thing." She leaned down and kissed his cheek.

Sean spoke to her without turning from the computer. "I've just been having a really difficult time balancing the things that are going on in my life. And I know that I'm a bit paranoid. I find myself looking over my shoulder all the time.

I come home to my apartment and expect something crazy to happen. But you'll be glad to know that I'm not checking under my bed anymore."

"That's a start," Sam said with a smile.

"And I know that I'm making absurd connections based on coincidences. The things I think up sound right in my head, but when they come out, I realize how crazy they are. By the way, I'm having a deadbolt lock installed tomorrow." He turned to her and pulled her onto his lap. She kissed him softly.

"I know you're under a lot of stress, and you're justified in being a bit paranoid. After all, somebody did break into this apartment. On a happier note, I think I have some news that might cheer you up."

"I could use some."

"The company I had dinner with tonight owns a place on Nantucket and they said I can have it for the weekend. What do you think?"

"Am I invited?"

She gave him a long kiss.

"I'm assuming that means yes," he said, picking her up and carrying her to the couch.

He laid her on her back, crawling on top of her. He kissed her neck. Her hands found their way under his shirt. She pulled it off, tossing it to the floor. His fingers inched their way down from her shoulders to her waist. He began unbuttoning her blouse, still kissing her neck. He took the blouse off, gently running his hands across her smooth stomach. He found the hook to her bra and began fumbling with it. She giggled as he kissed her ear.

"Need some help?" she said sitting up. The phone rang. Both sat motionless for a second. "You're not getting that," she said, continuing to kiss him.

He smiled and began kissing her again as she unhooked her bra, letting it fall slowly from her breasts. Sean moved down from Sam's neck, kissing her tenderly. He could feel her heart pounding.

The answering machine picked up and Ian's voice echoed throughout the room, "Hello. Hellllloooo. Hello? Sean, I'm in the Square and I know you're there because I can see your apartment from here, and the lights are on. As you currently have an oh so lovely houseguest, I figured it best to call before dropping in ..."

"He figured right," Sam said. Sean continued to kiss her.

"... Anyhow, I'm comin' up so we can figure out what to do tomorrow for your birthday. I know, you thought I forgot. You have no faith. I'll be there in a minute, so you better get dressed. That is, if you finally got up the nerve to kiss her."

Sam grabbed Sean by the back of his neck, tilting his head up to look him in the eye. "Your birthday's tomorrow? When were you planning to tell me?"

"I don't know. I'm not much into celebrating my birthday," he said sitting up. He put on his shirt. "Can we not make a big deal out of it? Please."

Sam gathered her blouse and bra and went into the bedroom. She came back wearing a navy blue shirt with "Berkeley" written across the front in gold letters. "I won't make a big deal of it, but we have to do something."

"Leave it to Ian, he loves birthdays."

As promised, Ian arrived almost immediately.

"I knew you were home," he said with a mischievous grin. He walked into the kitchen returning with a beer from the refrigerator.

Sean and Sam sat on the couch, as Ian paced restlessly before them. "Okay, so for your birthday tomorrow, twenty-five, that's pretty big. I was thinking that—wait—business first, then pleasure."

"What are you talking about?" Sean asked.

"First, I tracked the letter we sent to Claris. He got it."

"Great."

"I also did a little more sniffing around, trying to find out who this guy is—"

"Wait a minute," Sam said. "Claris, as in Barnard Claris?"

"That's right," Sean said. "You know who he is?"

"Only vaguely. All I know is that he worked with the CDC on the LA hepatitis cases. What did you send him?"

"Some questions about his involvement in the LA research."

"How did you find him?" Sam asked. "I only ask because I remember that he sort of fell off the face of the earth several years back."

Ian smiled, proud of his work. "He's a registered voter. Voter registrations are public records—records that contain mailing addresses. He's in American Samoa." Seeing that Sam had no further questions, Ian continued. "I also found a few articles that mentioned him. This guy is either super-wealthy or well connected, or both. About ten years ago, he sold a huge chunk of land in Samoa to Star-Kist, of tuna fame."

"So how does that make him connected?" Sean asked.

Again, Ian smiled. "While American Samoa is an American territory, it remains unincorporated and technically unorganized."

"Unorganized?" Sean said.

"It means that while they're represented in, and adhere to much of mainland American government practice, their government is based on ours, but it's not identical. In other words, their government mixes some of our laws with some of its people's traditional Polynesian laws and customs."

"Such as?" Sean interrupted.

"Such as land ownership. More than ninety percent of the land on American Samoa is communally owned. It's against the law for anyone to transfer property ownership to any non-Samoan. Claris, I'm fairly certain, is not Samoan, yet he sold some enormous amount of land to Star-Kist. My question is this: how did he come to own the land in the first place? The way I see it, he either knows the right people, or he bribed local officials into looking the other way. In any event, he made a hefty profit from his deal with Star-Kist. If nothing else, he's a rich man with powerful resources."

Sean was impressed by Ian's report. "Sam, you're in the presence of a research genius," he said.

"Now for the birthday," Ian said.

"What do you have planned?" Sam asked.

Ian took up his excited pacing again. "Okay, hear me out. I don't want any input until I'm finished."

"Oh no," Sean mumbled.

"What did I just say? Not a word. Allow me to preface my idea, stating that we currently find ourselves in one of the most historic and beautiful cities in the continental United States. Would you agree?" he asked, turning to his audience.

Both Sean and Sam nodded, not saying a word.

"Good. Now Sam, I'm not sure about you, but I know that neither Sean nor myself has ever fully ventured around the area to learn what any of that history may be. Have you experienced, first hand, all of this great city's patriotic legacy?"

Sam shook her head.

"Good. So here's what I'm thinking. Every time I walk the few blocks from my apartment to the firm, I see these monstrous amphibious machines roll by—they're part bus, part boat. And best of all, they're for tourists! Don't roll your eyes Sean. They're called duck boats or something like that, and they take you on a tour of the city, both on the streets and then up and down the river. How excellent is that? So what I was thinking was that we could have dinner, grab a few drinks, and partake of the historical significance of our fine city, all in the relative comfort of a semi-aquatic vessel."

Sean was mildly relieved by the simplicity of Ian's idea.

Sam laughed. "I think the duck boat sounds like fun."

"Thank you, I too thought it was a good idea."

"Then duck boat it is," Sean announced.

Sam yawned. "I think it's time for me to head to bed. It's been a long day. So if you gentlemen don't mind, I'm going to call it a night." She left Ian and Sean sitting in the living room.

"Any word on the syringe?" Ian asked.

"Not yet. I'm sure I won't hear anything for a while."

"When are you getting the deadbolt put on the door?"

"Tomorrow. I shouldn't even bother. When Fulsonmayer finds out that I'm not done with my draft, he's going to kick me out of the program."

"Just tell him it's your birthday. Nobody can yell at you on your birthday. It's like a universal law or something."

"The only wish I'll have tomorrow, other than that Fulsonmayer doesn't bite my head off, is that I can lose all of this paranoia. This afternoon, I practically accused Sam of purposely spreading hepatitis." Sean said, reflecting on their discussion. "In fact, I did accuse of her spreading hepatitis."

"She has hepatitis?" Ian said, shocked.

"No, you idiot."

"Then where on god's green earth did you come up with that idea?"

Sean explained the syphilis project, the highlighted town names, and the CDC maps. "I was out of line. I'm glad she's still talking to me."

"I gather from the fact that you were screening calls, that

she was doing more than simply talking to you," Ian jabbed.

"That's it, get out of here," Sean said, leading him to the door. "Visiting hours are over."

"But I didn't even get any details." Sean pushed him out the door. "Goodnight," Ian said as Sean closed the door.

Sean put his ear up to his bedroom door. He could hear Sam's breathing. She was already asleep. He stood in the hallway, not knowing if he should try to revitalize their pre-Ian activities, or just retire to the couch. His lack of confidence got the best of him and he prepared the couch for another uncomfortable night.

TWO blocks away, Ian walked to one of the cab stands in Harvard Square. He passed a sports bar on his way.

"See that guy. That's the motherfucker's buddy. I've seen them together before. I oughta' kick his ass too," Gustav said to his friend as he finished his beer. He lifted the pitcher and poured another into his plastic cup.

"So what happens at the Ad Board meeting on Monday?"

"I get to tell my side of the story," Gustav said, scratching his two day old stubble.

"Do you think you're ready?"

"Oh, I'm ready. They're going to love me."

"I don't know why you're screwing around with this guy," said Gustav's fellow drinker.

"I have my reasons."

"They'd better be good, because you might get kicked out of school because of this."

Gustav took another gulp of beer. "After this Ad Board meeting, I may be gone, but I'm taking Sean Graham down with me."

SAM left early the next morning, before Sean woke. When the phone rang at half past eight, Sean picked it up on the second ring.

"Sean, it's Valerie Chapeau. How are you doing?"

"I'm fine. How are you?"

"Just wonderful. Hope I'm not calling too early."

Sean was annoyed with her high energy level. She sounded like she'd had too much coffee. "It's not too early. I've been up for a while," he lied.

"I was just calling to find out how things are going. Any

luck with your search for the missing serum?"

"No. Just a lot of dead ends. I'm hoping that a man named Barnard Claris can help."

"Claris? How did you find him?"

"Why is everyone so surprised that we found this guy?"

"Well, I remember him from Needham's LA team. He was climbing his way up the CDC's ladder when he suddenly went missing. Where is he?"

"American Samoa. I sent him a letter and I'm waiting to hear what he has to say in response."

Chapeau was silent for a moment. When she spoke, she chose her words carefully. "Well, not to disparage the man, but I wouldn't take anything he might have to say as the gods' honest truth."

"I didn't intend to, but why shouldn't I?"

"When he disappeared, the rumor that went around was that he'd had a bit of a breakdown. That's why he disappeared."

"That may be the case, but nevertheless, I'm still interested in what he might have to say."

"How are your classes going? Is that hockey player still pestering you?"

Sean was taken aback by the question. "How'd you know that he was a hockey player?"

There was silence on the other end of the line. "You must have mentioned it when we last spoke. Unless I read it in the paper. You know, I think that's what it was. My husband played hockey at Brown and there was a big article on Ivy League hockey that he showed me. There was a player profile on that Gustav boy. He's a big pro prospect. I remember pointing it out to my husband."

"The kid's gotten into my head. He has me making crazy paranoid accusations aimed at my friends. I went so far as to say that my friend intentionally spread HCV across the African continent," Sean admitted in an embarrassed tone.

Chapeau laughed. "I'm going to assume that you don't need me to tell you how ridiculous that is."

"No, I already know. It was just a side effect of my paranoia. Any more leads from your side?" Sean asked.

"Sorry, nothing that I can think of."

"SISS must have had a records manager, someone who kept track of incoming and outgoing shipments. I would think that that person might be of some help."

"Let me think for a moment. Dr. Cameron was responsible for most of the lab's paperwork. But I think she did things like grant applications, not shipping invoices. I can't really remember."

"Do you have her number?"

"No. We lost touch a long time ago."

"What was Dr. Cameron's first name?"

"Olivia."

"Thanks," Sean said writing the name down. "I'll see what I can come up with."

"Let me offer you a bit of advice before you go driving yourself crazy over this."

"I'm all ears."

"Why don't you see if you can get away for a while. It'll help you regain your perspective."

"As luck would have it, I'm heading down to Nantucket for the weekend," he said.

"That sounds wonderful."

"It's a much needed vacation. Dr. Chapeau, I don't mean to be rude, but I have a meeting with Professor Fulsonmayer that I have to go prepare for."

"Oh, I'm sorry. I didn't mean to hold you up. Hope everything's coming along well. Let me know if anything else turns up."

"I will," Sean said, hanging up the phone.

AN hour later, Sean wandered through the Peabody Museum, home to Harvard's anthropology curiosities as well as the department's faculty offices. Fifteen minutes early for his meeting with Fulsonmayer, he meandered through rare collections of poison darts and shell necklaces. He thought about the people that had brought back the displayed artifacts. Like Fulsonmayer, they were real life adventurers. They traveled to uncharted lands, making contact with people no one in the outside world had ever seen. When they returned, they brought with them small trinkets from lost worlds: proof of their exploits. Without the concrete proof, nobody would believe the stories the adventurers had to tell. The museum's exhibits were full of tangible evidence of people and places whose existence was all but invisible to the developed world.

"Proof," Sean found himself whispering. All of his wild conjectures missed the essential element of proof. He thought about the theories he'd contrived and the accusations he'd made. He felt foolish, and Fulsonmayer was about to nail home the point. He began to realize the ramifications of the absurd tangents he'd chased in the past weeks. He had shirked his responsibilities in pursuit of phantoms. And now, Fulsonmayer's draft was incomplete, and he had nothing to show for his other overzealous efforts.

At the prescribed time, he made his way to Fulsonmayer's office. The professor sat behind his desk, buried behind a think stack of paperwork. "Have a seat," Fulsonmayer said, without looking up. "Be with you in a moment."

Sean sat across from him, in front of the large cluttered desk. He reached into his bag, hesitantly withdrawing a folder. In it, sat the unfinished draft of the lion project report, not yet ready for viewing by Fulsonmayer's eager eyes.

"I hope you have good news for me Sean. It's only nine-thirty and my day's already headed down the drain."

Sean's heart sank even lower.

"So let's see the draft," Fulsonmayer said, extending his open hand. Sean gave him the folder.

Fulsonmayer weighed it, waving it up and down with his hand. "A bit scant, wouldn't you agree?"

Sean answered with a slight nod.

The professor uncapped a red pen, opened the folder and began reading. His eyes raced down the pages, the pen leaving broad red strokes in its wake. His stare was fixed on the pages, not once looking up at Sean. As Fulsonmayer read, an antique clock counted the minutes aloud, its hands migrating a quarter of the way around the face.

When he arrived at the last page, a perplexed look crossed his face. He flipped back a few pages, thinking he might have missed something. He looked at Sean over the glasses perched on the end of his nose. "Did you forget to give me a few pages?"

"No, that's all I have."

"But you don't even have a conclusion."

"I know. I've just been bogged down."

"Bogged down?" Fulsonmayer said, tossing his glasses on the desk. He pinched the bridge of his nose between his thumb and index finger. "Sean, we agreed that you would have this done on time. I gave you one extension already, and it's still not finished. And what you do have isn't exactly the greatest piece of writing."

Sean sat in the leather chair without offering a defense. He knew it was all true.

"Damn it, Sean. This isn't a term paper we're talking about here. My career is at stake. I humored you on all of your hepatitis C goose hunts because you said that you were making progress with my work. I'm giving you one last chance with this draft. You have until Monday to write a pristine copy. It better be perfect, because you won't get another chance." Fulsonmayer handed the folder back to Sean. "Am I making myself clear?"

Sean nodded.

"Then excuse yourself. I have a lot of work to get through," Fulsonmayer said putting on his glasses.

Sean stood and walked to the door.

"One other thing," Fulsonmayer called after him. "I thought you might want to know that that Gustav kid goes before the Ad Board on Monday. I'm fairly certain that at the minimum, he'll be asked to take a leave of absence for the year." As he finished his sentence, he had already turned his attention from Sean.

WHEN Sean reached the street in front of the Peabody Museum, he took a seat under a tree. He sat in the brown grass, leaning back against the trunk. A squirrel walked cautiously by him, its attention focused elsewhere. A small object hit Sean in the back with a weak thud. In seconds, another came. Sean turned to see what was hitting him.

"So sorry Sean," Chester Hamilton said, dipping his hand into a paper bag. "Would you like some nuts?"

"No thank you professor."

"Why are you sitting under that tree? Come with me into the courtyard behind the museum. There's a bench back there that we can sit on. Plenty of hungry squirrels too."

Sean stood and accompanied Hamilton, realizing that "no" would be an unacceptable answer for the heavily wrinkled professor.

They walked slowly around the museum, into the protected courtyard. Sean helped ease Hamilton onto the concrete bench. Once comfortably situated, Hamilton rested his well-traveled cane against his leg. Sean took a seat next to him. Hamilton reached into the paper bag, handing Sean some nuts.

"Go ahead," he said. "Throw some to the squirrels."

Sean lackadaisically tossed some nuts ten feet away. Hamilton promptly whacked him on the knee with his cane.

"Ow."

"Now why would you go throwing the nuts so far away? The squirrels will never come up to you from there." He dropped a few nuts right at their feet. Two squirrels apprehensively approached the nuts. Once retrieved, the squirrels scurried off into a nearby bush.

"Of course you're aware that those things have rabies," Sean said.

Hamilton shook his head as he dropped more nuts. "Young Sean Graham, must you concentrate on the negative side of the equation? I know you're not a pessimist, but it seems that whenever you venture into uncharted water, you tend to look at the things that might go wrong, rather than at the excitement inherent in something new. Tell me, how is your research proceeding?"

Sean related all that had transpired since their last meeting. Hamilton chuckled.

"Poor Richard Fulsonmayer. Always so focused. He's like a horse running with blinders on. He has to rely on a jockey to get him from point A to point B."

Sean laughed at the analogy.

Hamilton continued, "Don't you worry about Richard. I know that's a difficult thing to do, but there are more important things to life than striving blindly toward a goal. When we shelter ourselves from the outside world, we miss out on life. If you get the draft done and he likes it, wonderful. If not, don't fret it. Your life shouldn't be about making a name for someone else."

Sean nodded.

"And as for your friend's syphilis project in Africa, why did you dismiss it as coincidental with the spread of hepatitis C?"

Sean shrugged. "It just seemed ridiculous: a man that was on his way to leading the World Health Organization was spreading HCV in Africa?"

Hamilton gnawed on a nut. “And why is that ridiculous?”

“When I took a step back and looked at everything, I realized what I was saying. This man is the top dog in the field of public health. He’s the leading thinker in the war against AIDS.”

“What better way to cover up evil than by doing some good?”

“I’m not sure I understand you,” Sean said.

“I’m not saying that it happened, but what if it is as you said, that he intentionally spread HCV across Africa? If he knew its origins, that knowledge alone would give him a head start on his competition for the high seat at the WHO. Theoretically, he could have known the origins of the disease and then fed others viable alternatives, covering up his trail. Tell me this,” Hamilton said. “Why do you let these questions about the origins of hepatitis C keep creeping into your life? It seems like you would rather ignore it all, and move on with your work. Why haven’t you just forgotten about it?”

Sean kicked a nut to squirrel. “That’s a good question. I think I just want to be respected for my work. I think I’m asking legitimate questions of people, but they keep dismissing me because I’m only a student. After everyone said my questions were ludicrous, Needham himself tells me that I was correct in asking them. There’s legitimacy to my questions, it just seems like everyone dodges them by saying that they’re ridiculous. It really gets to me.”

Hamilton patted Sean on the knee. “That’s what I wanted to hear you say. There is legitimacy to your questions. You don’t have to wait to be told that by someone you consider to be an authority. You’re a bright young man. So why stop with the easy questions? Don’t be afraid to rock the boat. Why not push Needham on this HCV issue?”

Sean shook his head. “I don’t know, he’s a very well respected man, and I’m not sure that he’s even capable of that type of evil.”

“I’m not saying that he is.” Hamilton paused, rubbing the elephant’s head atop his cane. He scattered a few nuts on the ground. “Once upon a time, there was a group of medicine men in a remote village on the other side of the world. It came to pass that a disease made its way into the village and began to wreak havoc among the population.

The medicine men toiled day and night until they found a cure for the disease. They rejoiced and celebrated their discovery. Before they dispatched the cure, however, one of the medicine men had an idea.

"For the betterment of their primitive science, he proposed that the cure be given only to the productive members of the village. He wanted to allow the less productive members of the village to live out their lives without the benefits of the treatment, so the medicine men could study the long-term effects of the disease when left untreated. After considerable debate around the traditional village fire, all of the medicine men consented. The productive members of the village were given the cure, while it was withheld from the others. Eventually, many of the people without the cure died from the disease; all in the name of primitive science."

Sean looked at Hamilton. "I'm not sure what the point of the story was."

"Should we have expected anything more from the primitive medicine men, simply hoping to better their science?" he asked Sean.

"I would hope that the medicine men could see the moral and ethical problems with their experiment, but then again, they live in a culture completely different from our own."

Hamilton smiled, tapping his cane on Sean's shoe. "Those primitive medicine men, they were Americans. What I just described to you was a forty-year-long experiment that took place in the United States. Ironically, it's called the Tuskegee Syphilis Incident."

"What?"

"In 1932 the US Public Health Service initiated a study to examine the natural course of untreated syphilis in black men. For the most part, they were uneducated sharecroppers that weren't even told that they had syphilis. Instead, they were told that they had 'bad blood'. They weren't told that the disease could be contracted through sexual intercourse, and when penicillin became available in the forties, the men were denied treatment. About one hundred of the men eventually died from the disease. The study ended in 1972 when it was exposed by *The Washington Star.*1972," Hamilton said, running his hands through his wiry white hair. "That's not too long ago."

The old professor emptied the crumbs from the bag onto

the ground. He slowly made his way to his feet. "So if you think that barbaric acts are reserved for tribal men sitting around the ceremonial village fire, think again. Take off your blinders. It's time you ran your own course."

SEAN remained on the concrete bench long after Hamilton had wandered off. The professor was well intentioned, but he was adding more turns to a labyrinth that Sean could already barely navigate. Sean had just recently convinced himself to forget about Tran, the serum and the HCV. None of it concerned him. Then Hamilton came along goading him to push forward, to take the reigns. Sean reminded himself that Fulsonmayer was pissed off and was right to be so. He gave Sean an ultimatum, and Sean planned to see to it that he delivered on it.

With much effort, Sean forced his conversation with Hamilton out of his mind. He looked at his watch: 10:15. Sam was busy with meetings all morning. He was supposed to meet her back at his apartment at noon. Wasting no time, he walked to the Tozzer library, planning on working for the next hour and a half.

After greeting the dozing librarian, he descended the stairs and rounded the stacks leading to his carrel. He was surprised to hear noise coming from the area of his desk. Tucked into a poorly lit corner of the basement, none of the desks around his were ever used. He walked quietly down the row of desks, growing more confident that somebody was at his desk. His approach was silent; his shoes muffled by the brown carpet. When he was near enough, he peered around the corner of the cubicle.

"Sam?" he said surprised.

She jumped. "My god, Sean. You scared me half to death."

"What are you doing here?"

"I was getting a jump on collecting materials to help you finish your draft. But maybe I'm being premature. How did the meeting with Fulsonmayer go?"

Sean looked at the papers on his desk. They were from his HCV research, not from the draft. He answered Sam without looking at her, "He wasn't happy, and he's given me until Monday to give him a perfect draft." He looked her in the eyes. "I thought you said that you'd be in meetings all morning."

"I had one meeting, and the other canceled. Lucky me," she said smiling. "I almost forgot. Happy birthday." She kissed him on the cheek.

"Thanks."

Sam pulled a folder from her bag and handed it to Sean. "I thought about yesterday and I realized that I kind of blew you off about my syphilis project. I pulled together this material for you, hoping that it'll put the issue to rest. Those are four or five different reports, each claiming to have found the smoking gun that caused the hepatitis C pandemic."

Sean pulled another seat to his desk and sat next to Sam. He began silently reading the documents in the folder.

They addressed a wide range of topics, from blood letting of baboons to the tattooing practices of aborigines. Each document hypothesized an origin for HCV.

When Sean had finished reading, he closed the folder and tossed it on the desk. "Why are you showing me these?" he asked.

"To prove to you that I had nothing to do with the spread of hepatitis C. You can imagine that your thinking I was somehow involved in the spread of HCV casts a rather large wrinkle in our relationship."

"I told you, I don't think that you had anything to do with it. Each one of these presents a theory on how the disease spread, but then admits that nobody knows the disease's origin. So although I know you had nothing to do with the spread of HCV, these documents don't exactly vindicate you."

Sam simply nodded. "I just wanted you to believe me."

"I do," Sean said, collecting some books from his desk. "Let's go grab some lunch."

TREVOR Matthews sat down on the curb in front of the international terminal at Logan International Airport in Boston. After what felt like weeks, he had finally reached his destination.

A cab driver walked over to Matthews. "Are you alright buddy? You don't look so good."

Matthews looked up at the man and nodded slowly. "I'm fine, thanks. I'm just tired from my flights."

The man shrugged and walked away.

After several months of living a near solitary life in the

rain forest, the fast pace of the American airport flustered Matthews. A sensation of vertigo took control of his body, forcing him to sit on the ground.

After fifteen minutes of staring blankly at the pavement, he was able to muster the energy to stand and hail a cab.

He stumbled into the back seat.

"Where to?" the driver asked.

"Harvard Square."

10

AS Sean and Sam walked across the campus, it was apparent that midterms were approaching. Usually bustling with activity, the Yard was peaceful. No Frisbees or footballs floated through the air. Students sat silently under trees reading books and highlighting lecture notes.

When they arrived at Sean's building, the superintendent gave Sean the key to the new deadbolt lock. Sean smiled at the added security.

He checked the messages on his answering machine. There were two. Pete called to wish him a happy birthday and to pass along greetings from their father. The other was Ian calling from the law firm. He asked Sean to call him back.

Sam had disappeared into the bedroom, giving Sean the opportunity to return Ian's call.

"I've got great news," Ian said as soon as he heard Sean's voice.

"Lay it on me."

"The senior litigation partner is taking me out for dinner tonight."

"I thought we were going out tonight," Sean said.

"I know, and if you still want to, I'll cancel with the partner, but this is huge."

"No, we can do the duck boats another time."

"I'm sorry. I promise we'll celebrate some time soon. It's just that this guy never takes anyone out, and now he's invited me to dinner."

"What did you do?" Sean asked.

"There's this patent infringement case we're working on. At the center of the case is this tiny valve that has some minute function in pumps used at water reclamation plants."

"The exciting world of corporate litigation—one nonstop thrill-ride," Sean said, faking a yawn.

"It pays the bills. Anyhow, to make a long story short,

nobody could find any information about this valve anywhere; the thing's ancient. But this morning, I found everything we needed to know. We have enough to get the complaint against our client dismissed. Let's just say that this client has deep pockets, and the partners are very, very happy with the results."

"How is it that you can find stuff that nobody else can?" Sean asked.

"Sometimes you have to pretend to be someone you're not."

"So you lie?"

"Not exactly, I like to think of it as being persuasive. It's amazing what people will believe if you say things with confidence and authority."

"So what you're telling me is that you're selling your soul to this partner instead of riding the duck boat with me?"

"Is Sam going to be there?" Ian asked.

"Of course."

"I'll come if she wears that black skirt," Ian teased Sean.

"Good-bye Ian."

"I'll talk to you later. Happy Birthday."

"Oh, Ian, one more thing."

"Yes?"

"Dr. Olivia Cameron—she used to work at SISS. Can you find me a phone number?"

"I'll do my best."

"Thanks."

"Talk to you later," Ian said.

Sean hung up the phone. He walked to the bedroom and found Sam napping. He sat down on the bed next to her. She opened her eyes and smiled.

"Looks like it'll just be the two of us for my birthday," Sean said. "Ian has to celebrate a big victory for the law firm."

"That's too bad," Sam said, sitting up and stretching. "But that also means that we can take off for Nantucket right now."

"Right now? I have a ton of writing to do for Fulsonmayer."

"And what better place to do it than on an island, far from all distractions? Pack everything you need. We'll hit the road and be there in a few hours. Don't even bring your computer. I've seen the way you type. It'll go faster if you write everything out and then type it all when we get back Sunday night. Come on, no excuses." She stood and began packing a small duffel bag with clothes. When she finished, she turned to Sean who still sat idle on the bed. "I'm ready. Now hurry up."

"Fine. I'll pack. Could you do me a favor and grab my mail downstairs?"

"Certainly," she said taking the keys to his mailbox. She left the apartment as Sean packed one bag with clothes and another with books.

He was still packing in his bedroom when he heard Sam return with his mail. He heard her rummaging through the refrigerator. He arrived in the kitchen in time to see Sam knock over her glass of fruit punch with her elbow. The wave of red liquid raced across the counter and onto the neatly stacked pile of mail. Sean lunged for the pile but was too late.

"I'm so sorry," Sam said, hastily wiping up the punch with a handful of paper towels.

Sean fanned the letters over the sink. "Don't worry about it. I was able to salvage the Victoria's Secret catalog."

Sam managed a small laugh.

Sean looked at the soaked mail. "Damn," he whispered, his attention focused on an envelope.

"Who's it from?"

"Mason," he answered, opening the envelope carefully. He accidentally tore the waterlogged letter in half. The words were written in ink and for the most part were illegible, as the red juice had already saturated the paper. "I can't read any of this." He blew on the paper, trying to dry it.

Sam carefully took the letter from Sean, holding it between her thumb and index finger. She examined what remained of it. Beads of red juice dripped from its bottom.

"I can't make any of it out either," she said.

"Words from beyond the grave silenced," Sean said shaking his head.

"Sean, I'm so sorry. I shouldn't have had the juice next to your mail."

"Forget about it," he said, realizing how awful she felt. "Let's just get out of here."

They gathered their bags and headed to Sean's car. Sam had just put her seat belt on when she grabbed Sean's hand, startling him. "What is it?" he asked.

"Your present. I forgot it upstairs."

"It can wait until Sunday," Sean said.

"It certainly cannot. Give me your keys."

Sean stopped the car and handed Sam the keys. "Don't forget the deadbolt," he said as she ran from the car.

She returned shortly with a small bag in her hand. She placed it in the back seat. "No peeking," she said, kissing him on the cheek.

AFTER a brief lunch on the road, and a couple hours of driving, the two arrived at Hyannis on the southern exposure of Cape Cod. From the small touristy town, they caught the last ferry of the day to Nantucket. Sean sat at a table beside a window in the protected cabin of the large boat. The rhythmic humming of the engine caused the table to vibrate. Sean was nervous about completing Fulsonmayer's draft.

Sam tapped at the window from outside. She smiled at Sean when he looked up. The day had grown ominously gray and cold. The dark clouds of a thunderstorm steamed ahead from the west. Sam wore faded blue jeans and Sean's cream colored Irish knit sweater with the cuffs rolled into thick bands at her wrists. The wind off the water blew her hair back from her face. Sean had trouble taking his eyes off of her.

Out on the deck, Sam walked to the railing of the ferry, staring down at the water as it rushed by in the boat's wake. Gulls floated effortlessly above the ferry, riding the boat's strong draft. As the sun began to fall into the land to the west, the island of Martha's Vineyard melted into the water off the right side of the boat.

THE cellphone rang. Santiago removed it from the pocket of his New England Patriots sweatshirt. "Go ahead."

"What's new?" Claris asked.

"Yesterday Graham received a letter from a James Mason in Chicago, a phone bill, a credit card offer and a Victoria's Secret catalog."

"Mason?"

"Yeah, James Mason."

"I don't suppose you got a look at it."

"No," Santiago said.

"Mason's someone we'll have to look into."

"I've already started the ball rolling."

"Did you get a look at the phone bill?"

"No. Tenants were walking in and out of the entryway."

"Where's he now?"

"We're on a ferry to Nantucket. The kid's working away inside, and the woman's out on the deck," Santiago said, adjusting his Red Sox cap. He peeked around the corner at Sam. "Give me a call tomorrow and I'll fill you in on anything that goes down out here."

"Just remember this isn't a vacation," Claris said hanging up the phone.

AN hour after sunset, the ferry docked on the sandy, weather beaten island of Nantucket. Sam pulled the directions to the house from her bag, reading them to Sean as he guided the small white Ford around the tight turns of the narrow road. It began drizzling just as they turned off of the road onto a sandy drive. Winding their way on the heavily wooded path, they eventually broke into a clearing. The beach house and its recently shorn lawn sat enclosed by a waist-high stone wall. Sean parked the car at the side of the house. The rain grew heavy.

"You didn't think to bring an umbrella, did you?" Sam asked.

"Unfortunately, no. We'll have to make a run for it."

They grabbed everything they could hold and ran to the front door. After a bit of coaxing, Sam got the door open. They searched for the lights in the nearly pitch-black house. Sean found the switch by the door. He clicked it up and down. The house remained dark. Lightning lit the room for an instant before it returned to black.

"The electricity is out," Sean said. "I'll get my flashlight from the car." After retrieving the flashlight, he returned to find Sam with a candle lit in the kitchen. Together they found more candles and placed them around the house.

"Look," Sam said, holding a basket of fruits and jams. "The foundation left it for us."

"You really must have impressed them."

They left the basket in the kitchen and explored the house by candlelight. The walls on the ocean side of the house had enormous floor-to-ceiling windows. The floors were all hardwood with beautiful area rugs decorating the various rooms. Decorations were minimal, adding to the spacious feeling of the house. Ascending the stairs, they found the master bedroom. It also looked out onto the ocean. Sam opened a set of sliding doors leading out onto a large balcony.

"Too bad it's raining. This balcony has an incredible view," she said, stepping out onto the moderately protected terrace. Large waves crashed on the beach below. The wind whipped through the tall grasses out on the dunes.

Sean placed his candle on the nightstand next to the bed. He met Sam in the cool air and rain on the balcony. From behind her, he wrapped his arms around her waist, pulling her close to him. The wind shifted, blowing large raindrops onto them. Within seconds they were soaked. Sean pulled her wet hair from her neck and began kissing her forcefully from behind. She reached back without turning around, grabbing the back of his neck in her hand.

A loud thunderclap erupted overhead, shaking the house. Sam turned and faced Sean, kissing him passionately. She pushed him backward out of the rain, not stopping until he fell onto the bed. She stood over him at the side of the bed. She removed the water-logged sweater, dropping it to her feet. Sean sat up on the edge of the bed, kissing her bare stomach. Finding the hook to her bra, he unfastened it, letting it fall to the floor. She removed his shirt, and pushed him onto his back. Soon they were lying together naked. Sean pulled her to his side, her chest against his. The candle flickered as the cool wind and misty rain blew through the open door. He rubbed his hand gently up and down her back. He could feel the goose bumps on her skin.

"Do you want me to close the door?" he asked.

"No, I like the breeze. And you're so warm. Let's just crawl under the covers."

Sam slid under the comforter. Sean followed, lying on top of her. He began softly kissing her. She slowly rubbed her face against his, absorbing the warmth of his skin.

"There were more than a few times in the Serengeti that I imagined something like this happening," Sam whispered.

A small smile crossed his face. "I can admit that the thought crossed my mind a few times too."

GAINING access to Sean's apartment wasn't a problem. Not

even the new deadbolt would have been much of a deterrent. What was surprising, however, was that the deadbolt hadn't been locked.

The clandestine visitor produced the key to the door and walked into Sean's apartment. A tiny flashlight lit the path to Sean's desk, tucked into the bay window of his apartment. With the flick of a switch and a faint whir, Sean's computer came to life. It immersed the apartment in a dull bluish light. As the computer ran through its systems checks, the intruder walked calmly to the refrigerator, opened it and poured a glass of fruit punch.

After returning to the computer, the hacker began searching all of Sean's files. An hour later, he had examined all of the databases. He found nothing noteworthy. Sean's visitor picked up the phone.

"There's nothing on the computer."

"Are you sure?"

"I'm not a pro with this stuff, but I searched the entire thing."

"Just to be sure, take the computer, and mess the place up a bit. Make it look like a robbery. Take the CD player if he has one."

The dark clothed intruder found some small electronic equipment and tossed it into a bag. Seeing the picture of Sean and Pete fishing in Montana, the interloper placed it on the floor, and stepped on it, shattering the glass. In seconds, the apartment was empty again, the night's events forty-eight hours from being discovered.

EARLY the next morning, Sean rose from bed without waking Sam. He walked quietly down to the kitchen. He was amazed by the house, now that he could actually see it in the light of day. He stepped out the back door of the house and walked through the dunes down to the water. The sun unsuccessfully attempted to break through the overcast sky. A strong wind blew up from the south. He pulled the Detroit Tigers cap snug onto his head and began his run down the beach. Foot high waves broke on the beach, leaving foamy traces on the sand before retreating to the cold Atlantic.

Sean ran with a slight grin on his face. He passed a warmly dressed middle-aged couple walking hand in hand in the opposite direction.

Twenty minutes into his run, his thoughts turned to the draft report. Since his return to school, Sean felt that he'd let Fulsonmayer down. On Monday he would give Fulsonmayer an excellent draft, thereby redeeming himself in the professor's eyes. Everything would be back to normal.

When he arrived back at the house, he climbed the stairs to the master bedroom. He could hear Sam stepping into the shower. He quietly disrobed and entered the steamy bathroom. Sam caught a glimpse of him as he pulled back the shower curtain. She jumped, but was happily surprised. "You scared me. Haven't you seen *Psycho*? Don't sneak up on me like that," she said, pulling him under the showerhead.

"I just wanted to surprise you."

She began kissing his neck. "I never would've believed that you had it in you."

BY mid-morning, Sean had built up a full head of steam and was deeply entrenched in the draft for Fulsonmayer. He addressed all of the comments that Fulsonmayer had made on the earlier version. He wrote pages of tedious notes on a yellow legal pad.

Sam entered the kitchen. "I'm running to town for some bagels. Do you want anything?"

"Actually, I'll come with you. I need to get some cash at the ATM," Sean said, beginning to stand up. Sam pushed him back into his seat.

"Oh no you don't," she said. "You keep plugging away. I'll get the cash for you."

"And how do you propose to do that?"

"You give me your ATM card."

Sean hesitated before answering. Sam jokingly tapped him on the head. "What?" she asked. "You're going to wait until after we sleep together not to trust me?"

"No. I trust you." He wrote down his PIN number and handed it to her. "Just don't lose it."

Sam took the piece of paper. "How much money do you need?" she asked.

"Don't laugh when I tell you."

"Why would I laugh?"

Sean hesitated. "Five hundred."

"Five hundred dollars! You're kidding me. Why do you need that much cash?"

"I have this thing about banks."

"What kind of thing?"

"I can't stand them. So I keep a large reserve of cash at my place. That way I can avoid the bank for a few weeks."

"But five hundred bucks? Isn't there a limit on the amount you can withdraw from an ATM?" Sam asked.

"There usually is, but I had them lift the restriction on my card. Now it's unlimited."

"So you're sure you want that much money?"

Sean nodded.

"Okay. I'll see you in a bit," she said, as she walked out the door.

Forty-five minutes later she returned. The smell of the warm bagels found its way to Sean sitting on the porch. Sam brought him the bagels and a glass of orange juice. She handed him a thick white envelope full of twenty dollar bills.

"Thanks," he said.

"Who's that?" Sam asked, pointing to a man down on the beach.

"I have no idea. He's been milling about for a half hour. I think he's treasure hunting."

Sam turned her attention back to Sean. "How's it going?"

"You were right. I write a lot faster without my computer." He handed her the legal pad. She flipped through its pages.

"Let me know when you want my comments," she said. "Do you realize that we got so caught up last night that I forgot to give you your present?"

He pulled Sam onto his lap. "I thought that was my present." He kissed her.

She jabbed him lightly in the stomach. "I'm not that kind of girl." She hopped off his lap. "I'll be right back." She left him and returned with a small wrapped package. She handed it to him, kissing him on the cheek.

"Should I open it now?" he asked a bit shyly.

"Of course."

He tore open the wrapping paper, revealing a small poster tube. Inside the tube he found a cloth mural depicting scenes from life in East Africa. Around the border of the mural were words written in Swahili.

"It's beautiful," Sean said.

"Can you read any of it?"

He examined the writing. "There's something about rain and death. That's all I can understand."

"It's called a *batik* and this one teaches the value of perseverance. The pictures tell the story of the cycle of life and death on the African plains. There are times of plentiful rains, and times of droughts," she said, pointing to different scenes on the mural. "The story teaches that the true spirit of man isn't measured in times of plenty, but rather, in times of hardship. Anyone can survive during moderate years. It's the years of adversity that test the will. And during these times, the best resource man possesses is that of perseverance. As long as perseverance remains, man can survive."

"I love it," Sean said, standing to hug Sam. "Thank you very much."

Sean spent the remainder of the weekend writing. As soon as he'd finished a section of the draft, Sam would edit the writing and return it to him. By Saturday night, the draft was in solid shape. They took the night off, eating a candlelight dinner on the porch overlooking the ocean. That night, the clouds finally pushed off into the Atlantic. Sam and Sean took advantage of the moonlit sky, walking for an hour along the beach. When they arrived back at the house, Sean stripped to his boxers and raced into the water. Sam followed. They swam briefly in the chilly ocean before calling it a night.

After working all of Sunday morning on the draft, both Sean and Sam were satisfied with the finished product. All that remained was for Sean to transfer the handwritten notes into his computer when he returned to Cambridge.

Reluctant to leave after the great weekend, they caught an afternoon ferry back to Cape Cod. Sam napped on the car ride back north to Boston. Sean sped the entire time, anxious to get the draft typed and presentable.

STEPPING into his apartment alone, Sean stood in disbelief at the sight of his desk. Papers were strewn across the floor, his laptop and portable CD player were missing, and his favorite photo of his brother was smashed. He fell limp onto the couch. He dropped his head into his hands, emotionally exhausted.

Sam had gone to the Square for a coffee. Sean heard her enter the apartment. "Oh my god," she said softly.

Sean mumbled something through his hands.

"What?" Sam asked.

He spoke without looking at her. "You didn't lock the door."

Sam stood quietly for a moment. "I'm pretty sure I did, but maybe, well—"

"Don't. Just forget about it." He picked up his bag and put his coat on. "Can you call the police? I can't deal with this. Not now. I'm going to the computer lab to type this draft." He walked past Sam and out the door.

TWO hours later Sean returned to his apartment. Sam sat on the couch reading a magazine. She had cleaned the mess by his desk. He walked over to the couch and placed a brown paper bag on the coffee table.

"What's this?" Sam asked.

"A flavorful offering of apologies," he said, pulling a pint of chocolate chip cookie dough ice cream from the bag. He handed her a plastic spoon. "I'm sorry I just left. I couldn't handle it. All I wanted to do was get the draft done."

Sam took a scoop of ice cream. "You don't have to apologize. I understand. Sergeant Lyndon came by to examine the apartment. They took some photos and asked a bunch of questions. They asked how the burglar got past the new deadbolt and I had to admit that I forgot to lock it. I'm so sorry Sean."

He shrugged. "Nothing that they took was irreplaceable. I just hope I can find the negative for this picture of Pete and me," he said picking up the crushed photo. "I imagine that Lyndon gave you the 'no leads' speech."

Sam nodded.

"Figures. Maybe the needle was some sort of prank, but not this time," Sean said, looking at the spot on his desk where his laptop would have been. Well, at least the draft's done." He handed Sam a folder with the draft inside of it. She flipped through its pages.

"It looks great."

"Let's just hope Fulsonmayer agrees." Sean took the folder and placed it into his bag.

"Oh, your father called while you were out."

Sean frowned. "What did he have to say?"

"He's in town tomorrow on business and wants to take you out for dinner."

"Wonderful," Sean sighed.

"He's calling back tomorrow to iron out plans."

"I can't wait." Sean took a gigantic scoop of ice cream and with an exaggerated motion, shoved it into his mouth. "Let's go rent a movie."

They returned half an hour later with another foreign film. "I'll make you cultured yet," Sam had proclaimed at the movie store. But within twenty minutes, they were both sound asleep on the couch.

Ian called at eleven PM waking them. Sam got up and groggily wandered to the bedroom. Sean told Ian about the latest break in.

"They stole your laptop?" Ian asked.

"Uh-huh."

"I thought you were working on the draft for Fulsonmayer this weekend. How did you write the draft without your computer?"

"Sam suggested that I write it all down freehand, then type it later. At the time, I thought it was a good idea. Now, well, as they say, hindsight is twenty-twenty."

"Aside from the burglary, how was the weekend?" Ian asked.

"It was great."

"Romantic?"

"You could say that."

Ian was silent as he waited for Sean to elaborate. "That's all you're going to say?"

"Yep, that's all I'm going to say."

"No details?"

"A gentleman doesn't kiss and tell."

Ian laughed. "Since when. You told me all about Katie Regent."

"I've done a little growing up since then."

"Fine. Then I'll have to tell you all about my dinner with the senior partner."

"How did it go?" Sean asked.

"He threw another fifteen grand on the signing bonus if I work for him."

"That's a lot of cash."

"I know."

"More than you'd make in New York."

"I know, and I'd be able to help my parents finally pay off

their second mortgage. And best of all, I'd get to stay here in crime free Boston."

"Not totally crime free," Sean added.

"I guess not," Ian admitted. "Tell me one thing. How the hell does one get past a deadbolt?"

"It's not too difficult when it's not locked."

"You got a deadbolt and forgot to lock it?"

"Sam forgot to lock it."

Ian paused before speaking again. "Is she right there?" he asked.

"No, she went to bed."

"I know you're going to bite my head off, but hear me out."

"Fine."

"First of all, you know I like Sam," Ian began.

"I was under that impression."

"Well you've told me all of your crazy stories about Tran and HCV, and believe it or not, I was listening."

"That's good to know."

"Tell me this: how well do you know her?"

"Very well. I lived with her for eight months. Don't say it, Ian. I know she's not a man."

Ian laughed. "I wasn't going to say that." He paused. "It's just that ... forget it."

"Let's go, out with it."

"No really, forget about it," Ian said.

"Say what's on your mind."

Ian hesitated, "I'm not making any accusations, but don't you find it odd that she's tied to everything that's happened to you and your apartment. Not to mention that she came back to the states unexpectedly, months before she was scheduled to."

"She has meetings in Boston."

"Has she ever brought home any material from these meetings? You know, those bulky folders they leave on all of the chairs."

"Not that I've noticed," Sean admitted. "But she was with me all weekend. How do you explain the break in?"

"I'd imagine it's a lot easier to break into an apartment without the deadbolt locked. And then there's the needle on the pillow. What did the cops say? No signs of forced entry. She could have put that needle there right before she called you into the room."

"You're being an asshole. What's your point? Besides, she wasn't even in town for the brick tossing fiasco."

"Maybe she was."

"I'm not listening to this anymore. When you're ready to be my friend, give me a call."

"I'm sorry. I like Sam, I just want you to look at all of the possibilities involved here. It all just seemed a bit too coincidental to me. Whatever it is, I think you touched a nerve with someone."

"I really don't care anymore. Tomorrow I hand my draft report in to Fulsonmayer and move on with my life."

"Are we still on for duck boats?" Ian asked.

"Another time. My dad's in town on business. Unfortunately I have to do dinner with him. Let's catch a movie afterward."

"Sounds like a plan. Oh, by the way, I found nothing on your Dr. Olivia Cameron. No phone number, no address. If you want, I'll keep trying."

"No. Don't worry about it. It was probably a dead end anyway. Thanks for trying. I'll call you tomorrow." Sean hung up the phone, somewhat angry with Ian. He thought about what his friend said about Sam. While the possibility was there, he convinced himself that she wasn't involved in any of it. After double-checking the deadbolt lock, he went to the bedroom and crawled into bed with her.

IAN was restless after speaking with Sean. There was something about Sam that didn't sit well with him, but he couldn't put his finger on it. His mind wandered aimlessly, conjuring up ridiculous scenarios and conspiracies, each with Sam as the focal point. He walked to his refrigerator, longing for a glass of chocolate milk, something his mother had always given him to calm his nerves when he was young. He poured the milk into a tall glass. He took the Hershey's Chocolate Syrup from the shelf, uncapped it, and held it over the glass. After a vigorous shaking, only two small globs of chocolate fell into the milk. "You've got to be kidding me," he mumbled.

He put the glass in the refrigerator and left his apartment. As he walked out onto the steps of the building, he passed a young woman. She had sandy blonde hair and deep green eyes. She was very attractive. "Can you hold the door?" she asked, smiling at him.

He'd never seen her before in the building. He wanted to talk to her, but couldn't think of anything to say. "Can I help you?"

"No, I don't think so."

"Well I can't just let you into the building without knowing who you're visiting."

"I'm not visiting anyone. I just moved in today. I rented the small studio on the fourth floor."

Ian took a step toward her, extending his hand. "Oh. I'm Ian Nielson, I live across the hall from you."

She shook his hand and smiled. "Nice to meet you, Ian. I'm Jessica Weston. I wish we'd met earlier. I could've used a pair of strong arms to help me move in this afternoon."

"I'm just happy to see that we got a little young blood into this building. We're the only two that are under fifty."

She smiled. "Then I guess it's a fairly quiet place."

Ian nodded. "That's a pretty accent you have there. Let me guess, you're from Tennessee, and you've moved to Boston to get away from all of the tobacco farmers."

"Not exactly. My folks live about fifty miles outside of Athens, Georgia. I'm up here in my first year at Suffolk University Law School."

"That's great. I'm a law student over at Harvard. We can help each other study."

"I'm sure I'll need all the help I can get."

Ian had to stop himself from smiling too broadly. A beautiful southern belle law student living across the hall from him.

"Ian, it was a pleasure meeting you, but I've had a truly busy day, and I need to get some sleep, so if you'd be so kind as to excuse me."

"Sorry to have kept you so long. I guess I'll see you around. Goodnight."

"Goodnight," she said, flashing a smile of the whitest teeth he'd ever seen.

Ian watched her disappear up the stairway, then turned and with a spring in his step, walked up the street in search of chocolate syrup.

When he returned to the fourth floor of his apartment building he was surprised to see Jessica sitting in the hallway, leaning against her door.

"Hi, Ian," she said when she saw him. "Can you help me with these keys? I can't get any of them to work. I had trouble getting in all day, but I couldn't get a hold of the landlady. I think this is the right key. You have to jiggle it a lot."

Ian laughed. "The landlady's never around. She can sense when there's a problem with the building." He took the keys, trying all of them. A few went into the keyhole, but didn't work. "Tell you what. Why don't you come into my apartment, give the landlady a call, and help me eat some ice cream while you wait."

"Do you mind? It's really late."

"Not at all."

"And my parents told me that I had to watch out for men 'up north'. I can't wait to tell them that you live across the hall from me. They'll be so relieved."

Ian smiled and showed her into his apartment. "The phone is next to the couch," he said, walking into the kitchen. "Her number is on the speed dial."

Jessica dialed the number. "There's no answer," she said in a dejected tone.

Ian placed a bowl with a mound of chocolate syrup covered ice cream in front of her. "No worries. She probably just ran out to get her fix of crack. When you're done with the ice cream, you can try again, and if she's still not in you can crash here."

"That's really sweet of you. This has been such a crazy week, and you've managed to save me from the brink."

"Other than the key, what else is going on?"

"The law school just finished putting all of us first years through a hectic orientation period. It was lecture after lecture on the evils of plagiarism and the righteousness of law. Yuck!"

"I remember it well. Any assignments yet?"

She nodded, "I have to research bank foreclosures. I guess they're starting us with the less glamorous side of the law. I'm excited to get started, but it's going to be tough. I have to go home to Athens for a few days to move the rest of my stuff up here."

"Bank foreclosures. I wrote a mock brief this year that dealt with a bank foreclosing on a home loan. If you'd like, you could take a look at it. There's probably some relevant case law in it for you. If anything, it'll be a start."

"I don't want to trouble you anymore than I already have," Jessica said.

Ian smiled. “It’s no trouble. Give me a second,” he said walking over to the file cabinet next to his desk.

Jessica looked around the apartment. “So you’re not seeing anyone, are you?”

Ian looked up from the cabinet. “Why do you say that?”

“Because there’s not a single picture of a girl in sight.”

“So?”

“So, if I had a boyfriend, you can be sure that he’d have pictures of me plastered all over his apartment if he wanted to remain my boyfriend.”

Ian laughed. “Good observation. I’m single,” he said walking over to her and handing her the graded paper.

He watched her as she read through his work. When she’d finished, she looked up at him.

“I’m a novice at all of this law stuff, but it looks great to me,” she said.

“Keep it until you’re done.”

“I can see that having you across the hall will be great for my GPA.”

Ian smiled. Jessica picked up the phone to call the landlady.

“Don’t bother,” Ian said. “She’ll never answer this late. The couch pulls out into a bed. You can stay here tonight. We’ll give her hell in the morning.”

“I can’t stay here,” she said unconvincingly.

“Well you’re not sleeping out in the hall. If you want, you can call one of your friends so that someone knows where you are. It won’t hurt my feelings.”

“You’re sure you don’t mind?”

“Of course not. Tell you what,” he said, “if you let me take you to dinner tomorrow night, we can discuss your assignment.”

“I wish I could, but like I said, I’m on a plane at noon tomorrow and I won’t be back for a few days. Thank god I’m not going to miss any classes.”

“That’s right, I forgot. Then we’ll talk at breakfast over my world famous crepes.”

“I’d like that,” she said with a warm smile.

THE following morning, Ankur Gustav looked as distinguished as a crooked-nosed, two hundred twenty-five pound hockey player could look. Dressed in his best navy blue suit, he sat attentively with his faculty advisor. The Ad Board wasn't what he expected. He was prepared to face a committee of perhaps ten faculty members and administrators. He had imagined the panel would consist of eight gray haired, WASPy men with a token woman and a minority. Instead he found himself in a large lecture hall on the ground floor of Emerson Hall. Several people filed in.

All interested branches of the university were represented by what Gustav estimated to be about two dozen people. The only person Gustav could place was the Dean of Students, Simon Blackwell. The portly, bow-tied dean presided over the Ad Board proceedings.

When all of the members of the Board were present, Blackwell called the meeting to order.

Gustav and his faculty advisor took their places at the front of the auditorium, facing the members of the disciplinary committee who were spread out in the seats of the lecture hall.

Dean Blackwell addressed Gustav, reading from a piece of paper. His voice echoed around the large room. "Mr. Gustav, you've been brought before this session of the Ad Board amid allegations that you have on multiple occasions acted in a manner inconsistent with the expectations placed on a Harvard student. Specifically, Mr. Sean Graham, a candidate for a master's degree in the fields of public health and anthropology, and a teaching fellow for the same disciplines, claims that you have on multiple occasions threatened him with physical violence." Blackwell finished reading, looking up at Gustav.

The dean continued, his eyes fixed on Gustav. "The allegations that Mr. Graham has made are of a very serious nature. The disciplinary committee of this Ad Board has prepared a recommendation that will be executed directly, unless there should be any extenuating circumstances that should be brought to the floor. Though it is not customary in these proceedings, I would like to hear what you have to say. Prior to opening the floor to your rebuttal, Mr. Gustav, a word of caution. I'm sure that your advisor, Dr. Yanovich, has explained to you that this committee frowns heavily upon students presenting false claims for the purpose of exoneration."

Gustav nodded.

"Very well. The floor is yours."

Gustav cleared his throat. "I deny any wrongdoing whatsoever. At no time did I threaten Mr. Graham, or even so much as cast a malevolent look in his direction. Mr. Graham brought these charges against me in an effort to silence me."

"Silence you from what?" asked Blackwell.

Gustav pulled a manila folder from his bag. Whispers went around the large room. Many members of the Ad Board thrived on controversy; the mysterious manila envelope more than qualified.

"The contents of this folder should tell you everything," Gustav said, crossing the carpeted floor to the seated Blackwell. He handed the stout dean the envelope.

Blackwell adjusted his glasses before opening it. The room fell silent. He examined the folder's contents. When he finished, he placed the material back into the envelope and sealed it.

Blackwell addressed the other Board members, "Remarkably, Mr. Gustav has succeeded in producing sufficient evidence of extenuating circumstances to merit further review by this Ad Board. We will reconvene at a day and time to be determined. I thank you for your attendance. This session of the Ad Board is continued for further review." The small gathering slowly shuffled out of the room, speculating in hushed voices over the nature of the envelope's contents.

Gustav collected his belongings with a wide smile across his face. Not only had he dodged a bullet, but he managed to redirect it at Sean Graham.

SEAN rose at nine o'clock, unaware that Gustav had already gone before the Ad Board. Sam was nowhere to be found. He walked sleepily to the kitchen and prepared some coffee. The juice stained letter from Mason sat on the counter. He picked it up, trying to read it again. It was even more difficult now that the letter was fixed in a wrinkled and smeared state. He gave up on the letter, tossing it back on the counter.

After eating breakfast and showering, Sean sat down at his desk. He took the draft report out of the folder. He proofread it three more times. It looked about as close to perfect as it would get.

He walked across campus with a pang of nervousness that he hadn't felt since opening the letter from Georgetown telling him whether he had been admitted or not. He wandered slowly through Harvard Square, glancing in all of the shop windows. He looked at his watch. He had plenty of time before his meeting with Fulsonmayer. He stopped in a music store to look at compact discs, then remembered that his CD player had been stolen. Looking for another means to kill time, he stopped at a coffee shop, wisely choosing a decaffeinated blend.

The air was brisk and people around the Square seemed to be particularly rushed. Sean sat at a table outside of the coffee shop and watched the circus-like atmosphere. At the next table, two elderly men played a lazy game of chess. A cardboard sign hanging from their table read "$2 To Challenge a Certified Chess Master." Sean wondered how one became certified as a chess master.

With ten minutes until his meeting, Sean threw out the remainder of his coffee and began walking. He had just entered the black iron gates of Harvard Yard when he realized that he forgot his wallet at the coffee shop. He wheeled around, running back through the gate.

Racing around the blind corner, he ran straight into a lean Hispanic man in full Harvard tourist garb, knocking him over.

"I'm so sorry," Sean said, offering the man a hand up.

"No, no. It was my fault," the man said, brushing the dirt from his pants. He began to walk away. Instinctively, and without knowing why, Sean grabbed his arm.

"Hold on," Sean said.

The man turned to face him. "What's the problem?"

"You've been following me. I saw you every place I've been this morning."

"I think you're mistaken," the man said, beginning to turn. Sean held tight.

"No, I'm not. I noticed all of that ridiculous Harvard-wear. Who the hell are you?"

"Sir, I'm quite sure you are mistaken. Take a look around you. Dozens of people are wearing these same clothes. Now take your hands off of me before I call the police."

Sean let him go. The man quickly walked away from the Yard and hailed a cab. Sean watched as the cab pulled away and headed down Massachusetts Avenue.

After the cab disappeared, Sean returned to the coffee shop. The cashier anticipated his arrival. She handed the wallet to him as soon as he walked in. Sean shook his head as he reentered the Yard. The short hiatus from his paranoia was over.

"SO where are you going?" the cabbie asked.

"Just drive for a minute," Santiago said, sweating heavily in the back seat.

"Suit yourself," the cabbie replied. He looked into the rearview mirror. He saw Santiago trying to regain his composure. "You're sweating like a cow. You just rob a bank or something?"

Santiago didn't answer. He pulled his sweatshirt up, wiping the perspiration from his face. The cabbie saw the shiny revolver tucked into the waist of Santiago's pants. Catching the driver's eyes in the mirror, Santiago recognized the frightened look. He knew the cabbie had seen his gun.

"Let me out here," Santiago barked.

The cabbie promptly swerved to the curb.

Santiago stepped out of the car, peeking back in the window. "Get lost," he said.

TREVOR Matthews had watched from outside the coffee shop as the cashier handed Sean his wallet. Matthews had been following Sean's every move since his arrival from Kinshasa. He couldn't figure out who the other guy following Sean was, or what he wanted.

Matthews had a close run in with Santiago on the day he began tailing Sean. Sean had been in Harvard Square purchasing a newspaper. As Sean left the newsstand, Santiago gruffly shoved Matthews out of his way trying to keep Sean in his sight. Matthews hadn't thought much of the incident until he realized that Santiago was following Sean. It worried him. He desperately wanted to avoid confrontation.

After Sean entered Harvard Yard, Matthews fell into pace twenty yards behind him. He wanted to make contact with Sean, but the guy who vanished in the cab had always been too close. Now, he was gone, leaving Matthews as Sean's lone shadow. This might be the only chance, Matthews thought. But in approaching Sean now, his anonymity would be lost. Sean wouldn't accept the word of a complete stranger without asking several questions of his own.

Matthews wanted his involvement with Sean to be as minimal as possible. There had to be a better way of getting Sean to move in the right direction. Matthews struggled to come up with a plan—he wasn't accustomed to such covert activities. He began to quicken his pace, slowly catching up to Sean. As Matthews drew near, Sean turned and jogged up the steps of the Peabody Museum, disappearing behind its heavy doors.

Matthews stood on the sidewalk with arms akimbo, staring at the door. He had hesitated too long. He would have to regroup and try again. But the next time, he knew that the other shadow would be back, watching Sean's every move.

ASCENDING the stairs to Fulsonmayer's office, Sean passed the Dean of Students, Simon Blackwell. Blackwell walked by without saying a word.

Sean greeted Fulsonmayer's secretary, trying to appear calm. "Good morning, Nancy. Is Professor Fulsonmayer in?"

"Yes, he's expecting you, go right in." She looked at Sean and smiled, but her eyes betrayed her thoughts. The same forced optimistic look the doctor gives you before revealing just how bad the test results are.

Sean felt sick to his stomach. But it should all change as soon as Fulsonmayer sees how good the draft is, he thought. Entering the professor's office Sean again played the cheerful, confident student. "Good morning Professor Fulsonmayer."

"Have a seat Sean," he said gesturing to the chair in front of his desk. Fulsonmayer sat in his worn leather chair, his desk empty except for a manila envelope. He ran his fingers slowly across it.

"It took a lot of sweat and tears, but I think you'll be pleasantly surprised." Sean handed the folder to Fulsonmayer, who weighed it in his hands.

"A bit more beef to it."

Sean smiled. "It's all there this time, I assure you."

"I hope so," Fulsonmayer said. He opened the folder,

retrieved a red pen from his desk, and began reading. The way Fulsonmayer sat reading intently without glancing at him, reminded Sean of high school.

Sean always dreaded bringing home a paper that had just been graded by a teacher. His father would arrive home from work late at night. After watching the stock market report he would call Sean into his study. "So let's see this paper," his father would say, his tie still tight around his neck.

Sean would nervously hand it to him and take a seat opposite his father. When he finished reading the paper, his father would make his criticisms of both Sean's writing and the teacher's comments. Only on the rarest of occasions was there praise, and even then it was mild: "A strong, yet poorly assembled argument." Sean hated sitting in his father's study. Its walls were lined with his private library of legal journals and reporters. The room represented everything Sean hated about his father. The dark antique furniture, the degrees and awards. Everything revolved around his job. Nowhere in the study was there a single picture of Pete or Sean.

Sitting across the desk from Fulsonmayer, Sean shook his head slightly at the memory. The professor's red marks were less frequent this time around. Small notes here and there, instead of the broad X's across entire pages. Fulsonmayer finished reading and placed the draft on his desk.

"That's good work, Sean. Needs only minor changes."

Hearing Fulsonmayer's words, a calming sensation ran through Sean's body. "No problem, I can get those back to you by five o'clock."

Fulsonmayer shifted uncomfortably in his chair. "They're mostly clerical, I'll just have Nancy enter the changes."

"Are you sure?" Sean asked.

"It won't be a problem."

"Okay," Sean said, shrugging his shoulders.

Fulsonmayer pushed the folder with the draft inside to the edge of his desk. Again he ran his fingers over the manila envelope. "We need to talk."

Sean nodded, not knowing how to respond.

"I want you to be honest with me," Fulsonmayer began. "Are you engaged in any activities that would be frowned upon by the university?"

Sean shook his head, "No."

"You're certain?"

"Yes, I'm positive."

Fulsonmayer opened the manila envelope and slid its contents across the desk to Sean. Sean leaned forward and looked at the small pile, not taking it off the desk.

The first thing he saw was an 8x10 inch black and white photograph of himself sitting across a candlelit table from a scantily dressed Courtney Hillerman. She held his hand in her own.

Sean felt his body go into an instant cold sweat. He was shocked. He flipped through the next photos, more of the dinner, one of Sean drinking wine. The last was taken on the street in front of his apartment. Taken from behind Courtney, it showed the two embracing in a kiss.

"Would you like to explain yourself?" Fulsonmayer asked.

Sean stared blankly at the pictures. "Where the ... who, where did you get these pictures?"

"Dean Blackwell just stopped by my office—"

"Well they're not real," Sean began. Fulsonmayer's brow grew rigid. He liked Sean, but wouldn't tolerate lies. Sean continued, "Well of course they're real photos, but I was set up. I assure you that there's nothing going on between me and Courtney Hillerman."

Fulsonmayer collected the photos into the envelope again. "Don't waste your breath on me, Sean. You'll need everything you've got when you go before the Ad Board. Dean Blackwell will be calling you with the date. As of this morning, he suspended you from your teaching responsibilities until further notice. He also asked me to advise you not to have any contact with Miss Hillerman until after the Ad Board proceedings are over."

Sean stared at the envelope.

Fulsonmayer stood and walked around the desk. "I think you need some time to think this over," he said, leading Sean to the door. "When the time comes, and you take the floor in front of the Ad Board, do yourself a favor—don't lie."

Fulsonmayer closed the door behind Sean. Nancy, who had been painting her nails, quickly picked up the phone and made a call, not looking at Sean. He walked in a daze out of Peabody Museum. So far, the day had not gone at all according to plan.

BACK at his apartment, Sean found a single message on his answering machine. It was Sergeant Lyndon from the campus police. Sean groaned. He sat on the couch and returned the call.

"Harvard University Police, is this an emergency?" a woman said on the other end.

"No it's not. May I speak with Sergeant Lyndon please?" Sean asked.

"One moment." The switchboard operator transferred the call.

"This is Lyndon."

"Sergeant Lyndon, this is Sean Graham returning your call."

Lyndon let out a chuckle on the other end. "Yes, Mr. Graham, I've eagerly anticipated your call. First, with regard to the needle from your apartment, our lab sent the results back this morning. Not blood, not lethal. It was red food color mixed with a gelatinous corn starch solution. And second, we received word about Ankur Gustav's Ad Board meeting. Seems he produced some rather incriminating evidence against you. At Dean Blackwell's request, we're reviewing all of the police reports you've recently filed."

Sean was silent.

"Do you remember those police statements you signed? You did so under the penalties of perjury. All of those breakings and enterings with no sign of forced entry. This should be an open and shut case. I'd look into hiring an attorney, if I were you. And as if it wasn't bad enough that you were trying to frame Gustav, you were taking liberties with his woman as well. That's downright awful. We're going to nail you on this Graham. Count on it."

Lyndon hung up the phone, leaving Sean sitting with the phone to his ear. Finally, he hung up. Courtney and Gustav?

Sean picked up the phone and called Ian at his apartment. No answer. He called the law firm.

"Ian Nielson."

"Ian, I think I'm in a bit of trouble."

"Why?"

"The dean is convening an Ad Board proceeding against me. They set me up."

"Whoa. Slow down. Start from the beginning. Gustav's

Ad Board meeting was today. What happened?"

Sean took a deep breath and explained everything. When he finished, Ian's reaction came in a single word. "Outlandish."

"They suspended me from teaching. This could mean my career. This is what I want to do with my life, and now I might lose it all. I've worked too hard to let this happen."

"Take it easy. Nothing's happened yet. We'll figure something out. I promise."

"I'm not rolling over."

"Listen, I don't mean to be rude, but I'm late for a meeting. I'll stop by after work."

"Alright, I'll see you then."

"Hang in there," Ian said as he hung up the phone.

Sean sat comatose on the couch. He feared that the manufactured scandal could wreck any career he'd hoped for. If he was kicked out of school for fooling around with a student, no school would even consider him as a candidate for any graduate programs.

He managed to calm himself. He poured a drink from the refrigerator and sat in front of the television. A conversation he once had with his brother kept replaying itself in his head. About six months after Pete learned he was HIV positive, the brothers spent a weekend together in New York. At the time, Sean still hadn't adjusted to Pete's illness. One evening at dinner, Sean sat restlessly fidgeting across the table from Pete.

"What's on your mind?" Pete asked.

"Nothing," Sean replied.

"You can't bullshit me."

Sean shrugged. "Aren't you worried about getting sick?"

Pete drank some wine before answering. "The concern is always there, but I've managed to push it into the back of my head. I figure that my worrying about it does little more than drive me crazy—so why worry? If I'm going to get sick, I'm going to get sick. Worrying about it will only make me miserable now, when I'm relatively healthy. There are some things that are completely out of our control. It's a waste of energy giving them too much thought. It's like flying. Why worry about crashing? If you're going to crash, it's totally out of your hands."

Sitting in front of the TV in his apartment, Sean knew

that his brother was right. Some things were out of his control. There really was no sense worrying about Gustav or Courtney or the ominous Ad Board. He would do his best to prepare himself, then deal with the problem at the appropriate time. All of the worrying in the world wouldn't help his cause. He surfed the channels, not really watching any of the programs.

Sam entered the apartment and found Sean lounging on the couch. She had a concerned look on her face.

"What's wrong?" Sean asked.

She sat next to him on the couch. "I just visited Needham."

"So how's he doing?"

"Not good. He's a bit out of it. I'm not sure if he's losing it, or if it's just a side effect of the drugs they're giving him. His doctor's found some evidence of the parasites in his liver. They're running more tests, but it doesn't look too good. He's fairly sick."

"Where did you see him?"

"Down at Mass General." She sighed. "He looks awful, not at all like he did the other night at dinner. But he convinced his doctors to let him go home in the morning."

"So it's pretty serious?"

She nodded. "How was your day?" she asked, attempting to find a brighter subject.

He laughed. "Apparently not as bad as it could have been."

"How so?"

He explained about Gustav, Courtney, the photos and the Ad Board.

"You don't seem too concerned," Sam said.

"I'm already past the freak out stage. Ian took the brunt of it. I know this is bad, but it could be worse."

"I guess so," Sam agreed. "But I think I'd be pulling my hair out."

"I'm just trying not to think about it right now. In fact, I'm going to call Ian and make sure he can still go to this movie tonight. We still haven't celebrated my birthday."

"Are you sure you don't want to talk about the Ad Board?" she asked.

"I'm positive. Thanks for your concern, but I'll be fine."

She smiled. "Well then I'm going to take a nap, if you don't mind. An early morning of meetings and the visit to the hospital have wiped me out."

"Go ahead, I have some things to do."

Sam stood and kissed him on the forehead before retiring to the bedroom. Sean picked up the phone and called Ian. He got Ian's voicemail.

Sean left a message: "Ian, I'm running out for a while, and then I'm having dinner with my father at The Bridgetender. Anyhow, I want to make sure that you don't cancel on me again. I won't be back at the apartment before we meet, but if you can't make it for some reason, leave a message on my machine. I won't be here, but Sam will. She never picks up the phone, but if you yell to her while the machine's recording, I'm sure she will. I'll call you or her to find out what the plan is. Talk to you later." He hung up the phone.

He went to his room. Sam was already asleep. He left his apartment, the only thing on his mind was the dinner with his father. He dreaded the encounter. At twenty-five years old, he'd yet to learn how best to deal with his father.

NORMALLY active at the law firm's meetings, Ian sat silent at the large table. Instead of vocally participating, he day-dreamed as the attorneys brainstormed around him. His mind wandered between seductive thoughts of Jessica and his concern for his friend. How had Sean gotten himself into so much trouble? Although he couldn't pinpoint any specific answers, Ian had a hunch about the answer. One thing he had learned in law school was to trust a hunch. Sam was somehow involved. Ian had floated the idea by Sean, but he wasn't even remotely receptive. Ian let the subject drop for his friend's sake, but he still believed it. So while the lawyers talked about the importance of winning temporary restraining orders and summary judgments, Ian kept trying to place Sam into the puzzle that Sean's life had become.

When the meeting finally let out, and the associates and partners all raced to their desks, Ian retreated to his own office. He closed the door and checked his voicemail. He listened to Sean's message. It confused him so he played it over. Sean wouldn't be there, but Sam would. She wouldn't pick up the phone, but would screen the calls on the answering machine.

Ian came up with an idea. Whether it worked or not, Sean would be livid.

11

CLARIS sat on his usual bench in the government square of the tropical island town. The heat was suffocating. He had just finished reading *The New York Times* on his computer for the first time in a number of days. In his opinion, other than those in his own life, there were no significant happenings in the world. He finished his mango, wiping his sticky hands in the grass.

He disconnected the cellphone from the computer and dialed Santiago. The PI picked up immediately.

"Santiago, this is Salieri," Claris said, wiping the sweat from his forehead.

"Who else would it be?" Santiago said, a bit annoyed.

"What's happening there?"

"The shit has officially hit the fan. Your boy Graham might get his ass kicked out of school."

"What?"

"I don't have all the details yet, but apparently he was a little too touchy feely with one of his students. From what I understand, there's a hockey player who was facing expulsion. He offered some kind of plea bargain to the school's administration. What he gave them was some photos of Graham wining and dining a female student of his."

"That could throw things off schedule," Claris said.

"Schedule? What schedule?"

Claris shook his head. "Don't think that just because I'm on the other side of the world that I can't orchestrate things the way I see fit."

"Whatever," Santiago said. He thought that Claris was a head case. But he paid well, so Santiago was more tolerant.

"It's time we got the ball rolling. No more screwing around. Listen to me closely. I don't want you to deviate in the least from this plan."

Santiago took a pen and pad of paper from his jacket. He scribbled notes on what Claris told him. When Claris finished, Santiago capped the pen. "You're sure this is what you want?" Santiago asked. "It seems risky."

"Just get it done," Claris said hanging up the phone.

THE ringing telephone woke Sam from her nap. After a few rings, the answering machine switched on. Sam recognized Ian's voice as he left the message.

"Sean, I've got some big news. I know you want to put it all behind you, but I found another player in the Tran puzzle. He wants to meet with us this evening. This is breakthrough information. Come alone. Meet us in the basement level of the Harvard Bookstore at six thirty. He said he'd leave if we didn't come alone. And if he leaves, he said he's gone for good. This is a one shot deal. Be on time. See you there," Ian said. The answering machine rewound itself.

Sam replayed the message. Who was this new player? She looked at her watch. The meeting wasn't for a while yet. She picked up the phone and made a call.

TRYING to relax before dinner with his father, Sean found a quiet tree in Harvard Yard and began reading a book he had assigned to his class. He was fifteen pages into the dry ethnography when he realized that someone was standing over him.

"Hi, Sean," said his student, Michael Rubicon. Sean looked up to see Rubicon carrying a boatload of text books.

"How are you, Michael?" Sean asked.

"Better than you, I suppose," he replied, taking a seat next to Sean.

"What's that supposed to mean?"

"There's no sense pretending. It'll be all across campus tomorrow. I know all about the photos. I work for the school paper. Someone leaked copies of the photos to the editorial staff. They're busy writing the copy as we speak."

"So tell me, Jimmy Olsen, what's the scoop?"

"It's not looking good for you. The only positive thing is that they aren't printing names yet. They won't until after the Ad Board has reached its decision. They don't want to face a libel suit."

"Great," Sean muttered.

Rubicon looked anxiously around the Yard. He staggered

to his feet. "I feel bad because all of this could have been avoided."

Sean shrugged. "No kidding. I should never have agreed to that dinner."

"That's not what I meant. You were going down from the beginning."

Sean looked at Rubicon, waiting for him to elaborate. He didn't.

"I have to go. I'm sorry all of this is happening to you. You're a great teacher."

"Thanks. I hope the Ad Board sees it the same way."

Rubicon slowly shook his head. "Not likely. *Bonne chance*," he said.

"What?"

"It's French. It means 'good luck,'" he said turning and quickly walking away.

"Right, I forgot you're a linguistics major," Sean mumbled to himself.

THE Bridgetender was located a few blocks outside of Harvard Square. It was a trendy bar & grill offering decent yet overpriced fare. Most of the entrees were just out of the college students' budgets. The result was that it was a favorite destination for students with visiting parents in town.

Part brewery, part restaurant, The Bridgetender was heavily decorated with Harvard Memorabilia. Crimson colored pennants hung from the rafters. Banners listing the school's Ivy League athletic titles covered large sections of the walls. Reproduced photos of Harvard sports stars from centuries past sat behind the bar.

Sean walked down the stairs from the street and into the restaurant. He saw his father chatting with an attractive bartender. He walked along the bar and joined them.

"You're late again," his father said, winking at the bartender.

"Give him a break, he's cute," she said.

Sean blushed at the comment.

"Our table's ready. Let's eat," Martin Graham said to his son. After picking up his glass of Scotch, he left a five-dollar tip on the bar.

Sean's father wore a business suit, while Sean wore a

navy blue polo shirt and blue jeans. They sat at a table under a banner announcing the Harvard football team's 7-6 win over Oregon in the 1919 Rose Bowl.

"Do you even own a suit anymore?" the elder Graham asked his son.

"Yes, I own a suit, but there's a time and a place and this is neither."

"So I came here with the intention of giving you some news, but apparently there's some news that you'd like to share with me," Martin Graham said before finishing his Scotch.

"I'm not sure what you're referring to."

"Don't play dumb with me, young man. I called the dean of the Law School this morning to ask if he wanted to play golf. He said that under the circumstances, he thought it better if he took a rain check. I asked him the reason, and he suggested that I speak with you. So pray tell me why my former classmate shunned my offer."

Sean considered how best to tell his father what had transpired that morning. When he decided the brutal truth was the best route, it just poured out. "The administration is currently contemplating whether or not they should expel me."

His father sat motionless, with a confused look on his face. "What the hell are you talking about?"

"Well, someone gave the Dean of Students some photos that made it look like I'm romantically involved with one of my students. Obviously, the practice is strictly forbidden. I'm not going to bother to attempt to explain my innocence or the actual circumstances surrounding the matter, because, supportive father that you are, you'd never believe me. Any questions?"

His father sat speechless.

Sean continued, "I've come to realize that my entire life, I've been trying to gain your approval. I've always wanted you to be proud of me. And no matter what I did, it was never enough."

"What on earth has gotten into you?"

Sean ignored the question. "Why do you think that I went to Georgetown? I got into three schools on the West Coast but I chose to go to Georgetown because you went there. I thought that maybe you'd be proud of me. Do you remember what you said to me when I read you the admittance letter? Not 'congratulations.' Not 'good job.' No, you looked at me and without even a pat on the back said, 'You damn well better have gotten into that school. I've given them plenty of my hard earned money.' I'm finished trying to live my life concerned about how you'll react. I've busted my ass for the past several years without any support from you."

"I know that at times my job has taken me away from you boys, but how could you say that I'm not a supportive father?"

Sean had started out strong and wasn't about to pull any punches. "Supportive? Your idea of supportive is dishing out a well deserved tongue lashing. 'It's for your own good. It'll make you a stronger man.'" Sean said, imitating his father's voice. "I can't imagine a less supportive person than you. Never a word of encouragement or congratulations. Do you know how awful it was growing up? I'm sure you don't remember this, but when I played baseball in junior high, my team was terrible. We didn't win a game over two years. Then finally, our last game ever, we won. We went nuts. You'd think we just won the World Series. All of my friends ran into the stands to be with their mothers and fathers. I remember my friend Billy. His dad kept tossing him into the air. Over and over again. I sat alone in the dugout. By then I'd learned not to cry. It should've been a happy memory. Shit, we won our only game. Instead, I dread thinking about it." There was no emotion in Sean's voice. He was lost in the memory.

His father sat stunned by his son's outburst. The litigator in him came out. Instead of quietly letting the moment pass, he launched into his rebuttal. "I made it to as many games as I could. I have a tough job. You know that. I remember one of Pete's hockey games in high school. You and I sat together in the stands. Do you remember that? He scored the winning goal of the conference championship."

"Yes, I remember that. Pete split two defenders by playing the puck off of one of their skates, then went five-hole on the goalie. It was one of the greatest shots ever. On the car ride home, you wouldn't stop riding Pete about hot dogging. 'You could have cost your team the title show-boating like that,' you said. I don't want to rain on your parade, but that's not what one generally calls being supportive."

"Sean, I don't think you realize just how tough it was raising you boys without the help of your mother."

Sean interrupted him. "Don't even bring her into this. Can't you just accept your mistakes? I used to hate her. I used to wonder how she could just up and leave. Do you know why she left? Because you sold her such a raw deal when you got married. Sure you got the nice house out in the suburbs right after you got married. But she didn't fit in with all of the lazy-ass country club wives whose idea of an exciting life was sleeping with the club tennis pro. She wanted to live life as a participant, doing things that mattered to her, not just as a supporting cast member in your life. I hated her when she left, but now I realize that leaving was something she had to do. I can't say that I admire her choices, but I think that I can at least understand them."

The waitress arrived at the table. Sean's father waved her off. He straightened his tie. "Well, I see that we've covered your adolescence rather thoroughly then. It's good to know that I've done such a remarkable job raising my boys. One's a drug addict dying from HIV, and the other is getting kicked out of the nation's finest school for playing patty-cake with one of his students."

"Say what you want about me, but don't bring Pete into this," Sean interrupted.

His father ignored him. "I built my own law firm, and now it's one of the most successful firms in Manhattan. I did that for you and your brother, so that you could have anything you wanted. Cars, boats, whatever."

"What we needed was a father."

"Wonderful. Anyhow, it would appear as though my visit couldn't be better timed. The news that I have for you, is that in accordance with its original parameters, having turned twenty-five years old, your trust fund is now open to you. The money was wired into your account this morning. As I'm sure you can imagine, this is quite the substantial amount of money. Do with it what you choose. You will not get another cent from me."

"I don't want your money."

"Then burn it. Give it to a bum on the street. I don't care. You're on your own now."

Sean took a few deep breaths, calming himself. He stood from the table. He spoke in a calm voice, "Listen. I'm really on edge with all the things going on in my life right now. I'm sorry that I blew up on you, but I meant most of what I said. I have to leave, but I'd like to get together again and try to talk things out. I'll see you later." Before his father could reply, he walked away from the table.

Martin Graham remained under the Rose Bowl banner, staring blankly ahead. The waitress passed without looking.

As Sean neared the hostess, she stopped him.

"Are you Sean Graham?" she asked.

"Yes, I am."

"Great description your friend gave me. This is for you," she said handing him a note.

He thanked her and climbed the stairs to the street. It was chilly outside. He read the note from Ian and looked at his watch. Ian would be expecting him.

SEAN entered the recently renovated Harvard Bookstore and headed directly to the store's coffee shop. Added to the store as a marketing ploy, the cafe sat on a terrace, overlooking the establishment's lower level. Caffeine-high students busily typing midterm papers on laptops occupied the majority of the terrace tables. Ian sat alone at a small table, partially hidden behind a newspaper. Sean walked over to him. "So what's so important that you leave a cryptic little note for me at The Bridgetender?" Sean asked.

Ian peered around the paper. "Would you just sit down," he said. He handed Sean the automotive section.

"What are you doing?"

"I'll tell you in a minute, just open up that paper and hide your face."

Sean complied. "Is this some kind of sting or something?"

"You could say that. Now just be quiet."

Ian had chosen a table overlooking the lower level of the bookstore. Only seven or eight people browsed through the shelves.

"I hope you're not stalking some poor woman," Sean said through his newspaper. "Because your being hard up for a date is no reason to start—"

"Shut up already. We're not stalking anyone," Ian said.

"Then what the—"

"There she is," Ian interrupted, looking down to the lower level. "I knew it."

Sean cautiously peeked around the side of his newspaper. He scanned the floor below. An old woman. A young father with his son. "Sam?" Sean said, spotting her alone in the shelves below. "What's going on here?"

"Just a second," Ian said.

Below them, Sam slowly made her way around the large selection of books, now and then pretending that a title caught her eye. She wore a baseball cap with her hair pulled into a pony tail. She looked around suspiciously.

"Ian, tell me what's going on."

"This afternoon, I called your apartment and left ..." he paused. "Who the hell is that?"

A man in a leather jacket and a Greek fisherman's cap approached Sam. They exchanged a few words. He then took her by the arm and led her to the corner of the store, behind a large bookshelf.

"Who the hell is that?" Sean asked.

Ian was shocked. "I have no idea."

"Well I'm going down there."

Ian grabbed his arm. "You can't. Are you going to tell her that you're spying on her? She's fine. We're in a bookstore and there are plenty of other people down there. Nothing's going to happen."

Sean sat back down. "Is that what we're doing here? Spying on Sam?"

Ian kept his eye on the bookshelf. "In a way, yes."

"Keep talking."

"I knew you weren't at your apartment, and that Sam was. So I left a message saying that I'd found another person from this Tran thing, and that he wanted to meet with us. Here. I specifically said to come alone, or we would risk blowing the whole thing. Sam obviously heard the message and decided to take the risk of losing this guy. Or maybe she wanted to scare him off. Or maybe she was here to spy on you."

"Why would she do that?"

"That's a good question, but any way you paint it, she's here."

Sean peeked at the bookshelf again. He could see the top of both Sam's and the man's hats. "So who is this guy down there?" Sean asked.

"I have no clue. Maybe an old friend."

"Do you really believe that?"

"Maybe. How many people let strangers take them by the arm and lead them into secluded corners of bookstores. Maybe she knows this guy."

"But how many long lost friends don't just have their reunion out in the open?" Sean asked.

"Maybe they're more than friends. You know, lovers." Ian laughed.

"Shut up. Just keep your eye on them."

Sean and Ian watched the lower level intently. Finally, Sam reappeared from the corner. She looked around for a second and then left the store in a hurry. The man wandered about the shelves for a few more minutes before heading to the door.

"Let's go," Sean said, putting on his jacket.

"Where are we going?"

"To find out what just happened," Sean answered.

"But you can't say anything about this."

"I'll just ask how her day went. And what she's been up to."

"And when she asks you about the message on your answering machine?"

"I'll say that I was at dinner with my father, and that I never got the message."

"Then how do you explain walking in the door with me?" Ian asked.

"She knows we had plans to go to a movie tonight. We'll say that we just met each other in the Square."

"Sounds good enough for me," Ian said as they left the bookstore.

WHEN Sean and Ian arrived back at Sean's apartment, Sam was in the bedroom. Sean quickly hit the button on the answering machine. Ian's message ended as Sam entered the room.

Sam walked over and hugged Sean. "Has your day gotten any better since this afternoon?" she asked.

"Yes and no. I had a bit of a blowup at my father before dinner. He didn't take it well. I think I might have been a bit too harsh."

Sean hadn't told Ian about his argument with his father. For the past several years, Ian had seen Sean's interactions with the elder Graham. He was glad that Sean finally stood up to him.

Sam frowned. "Whatever you say to him, you have to remember that he's your father."

"I know what you're thinking," Sean said. "Don't worry, I tried to soften the blow before leaving."

Sam rubbed his neck. "So what was that message all about, Ian? I was here when you left it. If you don't mind my asking, who is this mystery man?"

She put Ian on the spot. He searched for an answer. "He called and canceled the rendezvous. He said he'd set up another date if he felt so inclined."

"What does he have to offer?" Sam asked.

"I'm not really sure."

Sam shrugged. "Doesn't sound like too much of a star witness to me."

Ian only nodded. He wanted to launch into a rebuttal accusing her of spying on Sean, but refrained. "Only time will tell." Ian looked at Sean as if to prompt him to question Sam.

Sean caught the look. "How about you?" he asked. "What have you been up to?"

Sean and Ian eagerly awaited her response. "Nothing really. I took a walk around the campus. That's about it," she said.

Sean didn't know how to dig any further without prying too much. "Are you coming to the movie with us?" he asked.

"No, I don't think so. I'm really tired, and I'm afraid that I'd just fall asleep if I were to go with you. But thanks for the invite."

Ian stood up. "Then I think we should get going," he said, heading for the door. "I hate to miss the previews."

Sean followed him to the door. He turned and looked at Sam. "You're sure you don't want to come along?"

She nodded.

"Then we'll see you later," he said walking out the door.

LEAVING the apartment, Sean and Ian passed Santiago, who stood at a bus stop, looking as though he were patiently awaiting the arrival of his ride home. The PI watched as they passed, then fell into stride when they were far enough away.

When they had walked a few blocks from Sean's apartment, Ian stepped in front of Sean, pushing him against the wall. "She's bad news," he said.

Sean pushed Ian back. "Quit fucking around. Something might be going on, but I'm not jumping to any conclusions. Who knows who that guy was? I thought that they were supposed to teach you constitutional law during your first year. You seem to have forgotten that minor 'innocent until proven guilty' thing."

"Take off the rose colored glasses Sean. She's in on it."

"In on what? We don't even know if there's an *it* to be in on." Sean continued walking toward the theater. "And why are we walking to the movie theater? We're an hour early."

"I just wanted to get out of there," Ian said. He stopped in front of one of the college bars. "We can kill the time in here. Let me buy you a birthday drink."

"That's the first positive thing I've heard out of your mouth today," Sean said, walking through the door into the smoky bar. The place was fairly crowded for a weeknight. The two pushed their way through the mostly underaged patrons, to a table at the back of the bar.

A waitress quickly arrived at their table. "What can I get you?" she asked haughtily.

"I'll have a Sierra Nevada," Ian answered.

"And I'll have a Guinness," Sean said.

Ian grimaced. "You don't actually like that syrup, do you? You're all about the image."

"Real men drink Guinness."

"So what's your excuse?"

"Very funny. Perhaps you'd like mommy to order you a chocolate milk?"

Ian nodded, playing along. "I've tried before. They don't have Hershey's here." Ian began to say something, but Sean stopped him.

"I don't want to talk about Sam," he said.

"I had no intention of talking about Sam," Ian replied. "I'd like to talk about my love interest for a change."

"So how is Sarah?"

"Not Sarah," Ian said.

"Not Sarah? That's already over?"

"She came into the office the other day with a large rock on her finger. Seems the boyfriend popped the question. Now she's completely ignoring me."

"So who then?"

"Her name is Jessica Weston. She's a debutante from Georgia, and man is she hot."

"Yeah, right. They're always hot."

"I don't make the news, I just report it."

"So how did you come to meet Miss Georgia?"

"She came calling at my door one late night, lost in the big city, looking for a strong shoulder to lean on."

"You're full of shit."

"She moved into the apartment across the hall from me. She couldn't get her keys to work last night so I let her crash in my place."

"Oh, how nice of you. You let her crash in your place. And I suppose she slept on the couch."

"She did."

"Little did she know that you broke a toothpick in her lock."

"I did no such thing, but that's a good idea. I'll have to remember it. Anyhow, she's a really nice girl. She just started her first year over at Suffolk Law."

"So why didn't you invite her out tonight?"

"I did, but she had to go back to the farm to pick up the rest of her belongings."

Sean laughed. "The farm? Is she burly?"

"Not at all."

"Yeah right."

"I'm telling you, she's hot. Her father probably chased boys off with a shotgun."

The waitress arrived with their beers. Sean raised his glass. "To farm girls from the south."

"I'll drink to that," Ian said, touching his glass to Sean's.

Sean had just finished his second beer when Ankur Gustav walked in the door, followed by Courtney.

"Well look who we have here," Sean said, looking over Ian's shoulder. Ian turned to the door.

"Who's that?"

"That's the couple that set me up," Sean said, standing from the table.

Ian took hold of his friend's arm. "Sit down Sean, that guy is huge."

"*Et tu, Brute*?" Sean said, pulling his arm free.

"What are you going to do? Bite his ankle?" Ian called to Sean as he walked away.

From the end of the bar, Santiago watched as Sean approached the hockey player. He wanted to move closer to hear their exchange, but didn't want to chance Sean spotting him again.

Gustav and Courtney stood at the bar waiting for the bartender to pour their drinks.

"So nice to see you here," Sean said when he reached them.

Gustav turned and faced him. Courtney hid behind her boyfriend's hulking frame.

"What the hell do you want?" Gustav asked.

"Why'd you do it?"

"Fuck off," Gustav said. "I told you I'd play hockey this year. And as for you, you got what you had coming. You shouldn't mess around in other people's business. Besides, you were trying to get it on with my girlfriend. I have pictures," he laughed.

Sean stepped around Gustav and stared at Courtney. "What's your excuse?" he asked.

She didn't answer.

"I asked you a question," Sean said, taking her by the sleeve.

Gustav grabbed Sean by the neck. He punched Sean squarely in the stomach with his free hand. Sean doubled over in pain. Ian grabbed his friend, leading him to the door.

"You want some too?" Gustav said to Ian.

Ian ignored him, helping Sean outside.

Santiago finished his beer and walked slowly past Gustav, memorizing his face.

Outside, Sean caught his breath. "That really hurt," he said to Ian.

"Next time, think before you go confronting a guy three times your size."

"I thought I could handle it," Sean said.

"That was the alcohol." Ian looked at Sean leaning against the wall. "Let me take you home," he said.

"No way. We're going to see this movie. I've waited a long time for this sequel, and I'm not going to miss it now." Sean stood up and began walking toward the theater. Ian shook his head and followed.

After buying tickets, Sean stopped at a pay phone before

entering the theater. "Do you have any change?" he asked Ian.

"Who are you calling?"

"Sam. She can still make it, if she wants."

"You're unbelievable."

"Just give me the change," Sean said, hand outstretched.

Ian handed him some coins. Sean dialed his apartment. There was no answer. He left a message in the event that Sam was screening the calls.

"She's not picking up," Sean said.

"Then let's go. I don't want to miss the previews."

Sean followed Ian into the cold theater. They found seats just as the first preview hit the screen.

SANTIAGO waited outside the theater. He asked the ticket seller what time the movie would be over. He checked his watch as he walked away. He would be ready when they reappeared.

He found a bench on a relatively quiet side street off of Harvard Square and took out the cellphone. He dialed the number to his shoe box office in San Diego.

Whenever he anticipated being away from the office for more than a week, he had Doris—his sometimes girlfriend—man the office. To his surprise, she answered the phone. "Santiago and Associates."

"Good for you baby, you're actually there," he said.

"You can't call me baby while I'm on duty. It's harassment."

"Calling you 'baby' does not qualify as harassment."

"Just watch your mouth."

"Whatever you say baby. Did anyone call today? And if you tell me that sonofabitch Marcello called about the rent, I'll fly back there tonight and kick his ass. That ceiling fan was broken when we moved in there a year ago. Did you remember to tell him that?"

"He didn't call," Doris assured him. "Geez, settle down tiger."

"Any messages?"

"A process server left a summons for you today. He asked if I was an officer of your company and I said that I supposed I was. Then he threw this envelope at me and said I was served. Can he do that?"

"I guess so. Did you open the envelope?"

"Yeah. Remember that Mexican you brought in for jumping bail about two months ago? Manuel Guerrerro."

"Sure, drug running illegal. What about him?"

"You busted him at his brother's place, right?"

"Yeah, we got into a big tussle. Broke a lot of stuff in the place. Why?"

"His brother is suing you for all of the damage you caused."

"He's suing me? How the hell can he sue me? He's an illegal too. What happened to the rights of the people who are actually supposed to be living here. I'm a tax paying citizen. I'm a registered voter—"

"And now you're a defendant."

"I can't believe this."

"You're lucky he's not suing you for the broken arm you gave him."

"Bail enforcement officers have rights too. I was acting within my stated legal authority," Santiago said.

"Well, as an officer of Santiago and Associates, I advise you to get yourself a good lawyer, and not your friend Seth. He's a dirt bag. Besides, he's always touching me."

"I'll wait 'til I get back there to deal with that. I think things out here are about to get messy."

HALF a block away from the movie theater, the shiny black car sat idling at the curb. When Ian and Sean emerged from the theater, the driver snapped to attention. There was only one chance. Keeping the headlights off, the driver put the car in gear and slowly pulled away from the curb. The car crept down the street in darkness, following Sean and Ian from a short distance.

A group of students leaving the movie theater walked into the street in front of the car. A skinny Japanese guy tapped the hood of the car as he walked in front of it. "Headlights would be nice," he said to the driver. The driver ignored the comment, straining to keep Sean and Ian in sight.

"So what did you think?" Ian asked.

"It was nowhere near as good as the original. It had some decent effects, but the plot was awful."

The two continued down the sidewalk, oblivious to their stalker a block behind them. The driver accelerated to keep them in sight.

"Are you taking the T or a cab home?" Sean asked.

"The T I guess," Ian said reaching into his pocket for change. "Except you used all of my change when you called Sam."

"I have a token," Sean said, opening his wallet.

They began to cross the street. The car down the block made its move, speeding quickly toward them.

"Here," Sean said handing the token to Ian. He dropped it. The token bounced off Sean's shoe and back toward the curb. Sean took a step back to retrieve the token at the instant that the black car smashed into Ian, sending him careening off the windshield and onto the pavement.

A woman on the sidewalk screamed as the car screeched around the corner. Sean only heard the crash. He turned quickly around, token in hand. At first, he didn't see Ian. He took another step into the street. Ian lay face down in a heap next to a parked car. Shattered pieces of black bumper and headlight littered the street.

"Holy shit!" Sean shouted, running over to Ian. "Somebody call 911." Ian wasn't moving. His head bled badly. Sean could hear his friend's labored breathing, but he was unconscious. "It's going to be okay, Ian. Help's on the way."

A woman ran over to Sean. She almost vomited at the sight of the blood flowing from Ian's head. "The ambulance is on the way," she said. "That car didn't even slow down."

Sean held Ian's hand. "Hang in there, Ian. Help's on the way."

FIVE minutes later, cellphone in hand, Santiago scanned the scene from a safe distance. Several police cars blocked off both ends of the small street. A yellow police line was strung between parking meters, keeping people on the sidewalk, away from any potential evidence. Several uniformed policemen collected evidence from the scene, carefully bagging shattered pieces that had fallen from the car. Santiago watched as two officers made marks on the street with the aid of a tape measure. He walked closer to the paramedics. "They're loading him into the ambulance as we speak," he said.

"How bad is he?" Claris asked.

"He's still unconscious, they got his neck immobilized, and his head's heavily bandaged."

"What about Graham?"

"Not a scratch on him. Looked like he ducked out of the way just in time. I gotta' go. Cops are starting to ask witnesses questions. I want to hear what they say. Call me later."

AT two-thirty in the morning, Sean finished his fourth cup of coffee. His concentration faded. He had trouble focusing his eyes. He didn't notice Sam until she stood directly in front of him. She bent down and gave him a hug. "How's he doing?"

"The doctor said that I could see him in about five minutes. They've been running all types of tests, checking for internal bleeding and a bunch of other things. The doctor thinks that he's going to be fine. I guess he has a concussion, but so far that's it, other than the gash on his forehead from hitting the windshield."

"So he's going to be fine," Sam said.

"Looks like it. His doctor also said something about a possible sprained knee, but that's nothing."

"I'm so relieved to hear that he'll be alright."

"Where were you when I called?" Sean asked.

"I was in bed. I didn't hear the phone. The second time you called, I looked at the clock and saw how late it was. I got worried, so I listened to the messages and came as quickly as I could."

Sean hugged her again. "I'm glad you're here."

A nurse walked out of Ian's room. "Mr. Graham, you can see your friend now."

Sean stood up, holding Sam's hand. She stopped him. "Maybe you should see him alone," she said.

Sean nodded and walked into the room. Ian was lying in bed. The doctor spoke as he stood over Ian. "So we'll keep you here tonight for observations, just to keep an eye on you. But like I said, this is just a precautionary measure. All of your tests came back fine. The concussion didn't look too bad. If you need anything, give one of the nurses a holler," he said patting Ian on the shoulder.

"Thanks doc," Ian said, as the doctor disappeared out the door.

Sean apprehensively walked over to the bedside. Ian saw his friend's demeanor. "So the cowboy said to his horse,

'Why the long face?'" Ian joked.

"Shut up. You scared me to death, lying all bloody on the street."

"But I'm fine," Ian assured him. "Except for these. There's thirteen of them," he said, pointing to the stitches in his forehead.

"Have you called your parents?" Sean asked.

"Just got off the phone with them. They asked the poor doctor ten minutes of questions before I finally kicked them off the line. You know what my mom asked me?"

"What?"

"If I looked both ways before crossing the street. And you know what? I swear that I did, but I never saw the car coming."

"I didn't either, but some witnesses said that they saw the car without its lights on," Sean said.

"Did anyone get the license plate number?"

"I don't think so. But someone who saw the car take off said that the grille was pretty smashed up. The police said that if the driver doesn't have it repaired quickly, that it wouldn't be too difficult to locate. That is, assuming it's from the area."

"There's no reason to believe that it is from the area, is there?"

Sean shook his head. "What kind of person hits someone, and drives away? You could have been killed."

"That's probably why they drove away. If I died, they'd be facing involuntary manslaughter or something along those lines," Ian said.

"Yeah, but if it was an accident, they probably wouldn't serve any time. Anyhow, the police said they'd be calling me as soon as they had any more news."

Sean sat in the chair next to the bed. "Sam's out in the hall. I think that she'd like to see you," he said.

Ian took a few seconds before responding. "No offense, but I'd rather not see her right now. Can you just tell her that I'm not feeling well and that I appreciate her stopping by?"

"Ian, she came all the way down here at two in the morning."

"I realize that, but I'm not in the mood to see her."

"Why not? Is it about the bookstore?" Sean asked.

"Yes, it's about the bookstore, and everything else, for

that matter. Maybe I'm wrong, god knows it wouldn't be the first time, but there's something sketchy about her. And I wouldn't be saying this to you if I thought it were something small. That's not what friends do."

"What do you mean?"

"I mean that friends aren't supposed to question each others' girlfriends—ever. And I am now. That's how strongly I feel about this. There have been plenty of girlfriends of yours that I thought were garbage, but I never said a word."

Sean laughed. "Like who?"

"Well, Katie Regent for one."

"What was wrong with her?"

"Oh, I don't know, maybe the fact that she's the biggest snob I've ever met."

"Well I can't wait to see your farm girl when she gets back wearing her brand new Oshkosh B'gosh overalls."

"I'm serious about Sam. And I hope I'm wrong and I hope you make me eat my words. But she's hiding something from you. I'm not sure what, but she's hiding something."

"Ian, I know you're trying to look out for me, and that's why I'm not going to stuff that pillow down your throat. But you're wrong about her. There's no way for me to prove it, but I know you're wrong."

"I hope so," Ian said groggily.

"I'm going to take off. Get some rest. I'll pick you up tomorrow if they let you go," Sean said walking to the door.

"Thanks. I'll see you then."

BACK at Sean's apartment, Sam changed into an oversized T-shirt and crawled into bed. Sean sat on the edge of the bed, wide awake from the coffee he had at the hospital. Sam rubbed his back.

"Why so quiet?" she asked him.

He shrugged. "I'm just tired, and I know that there's no way I could ever fall asleep right now."

"So lie down and talk to me."

Sean undressed down to his T-shirt and boxers. Once he reclined on the pillows, Sam rested her head on this chest. He quietly ran his hands through her hair.

"What's wrong?" she asked.

"Nothing's wrong. I told you, I'm just a bit out of it right now."

"I know there's something that you're not telling me. It has something to do with Ian." She placed her hand under his shirt and slowly rubbed his chest. "If it's something you don't want to talk about, just say so. But if there's something wrong, maybe I can help."

Sean thought before answering her. He kissed her forehead. "Sam, I'm not sure why, but Ian doesn't trust you. Maybe trust is the wrong word, but that's what he said."

Sam continued to rub his chest. "Trust me with what?" she asked calmly.

"I don't know exactly. I think he's under the impression that you're somehow involved in the Tran thing. The other day, he rattled off a bunch of reasons why he thought you were mixed up in some conspiracy with the missing serum. I told him that he's been watching too many movies."

Sean felt Sam laugh. "So is this an issue for you?" she asked.

"Is what an issue?"

"That your friend doesn't trust me."

"Only in that I'm close to both of you, and nobody likes to see their friends at odds."

"But is trust a problem between us?" she asked.

"Not at all," Sean answered sincerely. "I trust you one hundred percent."

Sam looked up at Sean and kissed him. She got out of bed and turned off the bedroom light. She returned to the bed and crawled under the covers. "Come under here with me," she said.

He joined her, starting to kiss her neck. "Have I told you how badly I'm falling for you?" he asked her.

"Not today."

"Well words don't do justice."

"I want to fall asleep in your arms."

"I'm sure I can arrange that," he said pulling her close. She smiled and kissed him goodnight.

12

EARLY the next morning, Gayle Needham showed Richard Fulsonmayer into the study of the Needham house in the suburb of Brookline.

"Larry will be down in a moment. What time did he ask you to be here?" Gayle asked, pouring her guest a cup of coffee.

"Eight-thirty, so here I am," Fulsonmayer replied.

She shook her head. "I asked him if I needed to wake him when I got up this morning. He said 'no'. I'm starting to get very concerned, Richard."

"What have his doctors told you?"

"The schistosomiasis is in an advanced state. I guess that it's not unusual to see cognitive abnormalities when the parasite has gone so long before it's finally caught. But they're not as worried about the neurological effects so much as the damage to his liver. The early lab results aren't promising. We're supposed to get the results from the latest battery of tests either tomorrow or the following day."

"Has he shown any signs of neurological problems?"

She nodded. "Too many. Recently he's been forgetting things. He's been very moody, ranting about anything and everything under the sun. You know Larry, that's just not like him. His words are usually so well thought out. Now, he just blurts out whatever comes to mind."

"But the neurological effects can be treated, right?" Fulsonmayer asked, before taking a sip of his coffee.

"Yes. His doctors have him on several drugs. They said that in most cases that are this advanced, a complete neurological recovery is still expected. It's the liver that we're all concerned about. If these latest tests come back revealing bad news, well ... you know, I'd rather not think about it."

Fulsonmayer patted her hand. "He's going to be fine."

"Who's going to be fine?" Larry Needham asked, entering the room in his robe.

"Larry, you could have at least put on some clothes," his wife said.

"At this early hour? Nonsense. Would you mind excusing us, darling? We have some important business to discuss."

She stood up, looking at Fulsonmayer. "I'll be in the next room if you need me."

Fulsonmayer smiled at her as she left the room.

"So why the early morning visit, Richard?" Needham asked.

"Last night you asked me to stop by. You said that it was rather important."

Needham took a seat next to his friend, a confused look on his face. The electricity was gone from his blue eyes. "What was so important?"

"I'm not sure," Fulsonmayer responded. "How have you been feeling?"

"So, so. My doctors are concerned about my liver. As if that's not enough, they said that I'll be having some difficulty concentrating as well."

"And are you?"

Needham nodded, a hint of embarrassment crossing his face. "I don't always know when I'm in the middle of what Gayle calls 'a spell of the crazies', but when it's over, I know it's happened."

"Do you remember why you asked me over?" Fulsonmayer inquired.

"I do now," he said, pouring himself a cup of coffee. "I was wondering if I could ask a favor of you."

"Absolutely."

"A favor that I can't necessarily explain at the moment," Needham added, stirring a spoonful of sugar into his coffee.

AN hour after Fulsonmayer left the Needhams' Brookline home, Sean sat in Needham's study waiting for the doctor to return. The doctor's wife brought Sean a cup of coffee.

"It's been a busy morning," she said. "Richard Fulsonmayer stopped by earlier. Do your visits have anything to do with each other?"

Sean wondered if Fulsonmayer told Needham about the Ad Board situation. "No, I'm sure they don't. I just wanted to apologize to your husband for my questions the other night at the Fulsonmayers. I'm not sure what got into me."

She smiled at Sean. "I'll go get Larry," she said leaving the room.

Sean looked at the pictures around Needham's study. There was a faded black and white wedding portrait of what Sean figured to be Needham's parents. The couple wore serious looks on their faces. There were several family portraits on the walls. The Needhams had two children: a boy and a girl. In the most recent photo the children looked to be teenagers.

"They're both off at prep school studying hard to get into college," Needham said entering the room. "I'm really proud of them. Brad is the captain of his lacrosse team, and Heather is the captain of the soccer team. She already has twelve goals this season. She needs just eight more to break the career record at the school."

Sean stood and shook hands with Needham. Sam was right, he looked a bit pale, and his eyes weren't as sharp. "So what brings you by Sean?" Needham asked.

"I just wanted to say that I'm sorry if I was a bit out of line the other night."

Needham smiled. "Nonsense. You and I are searching for the same thing: truth. Every once in a while we get a little sidetracked. It happens to everyone. The important thing is that when you stray off course, that you readjust quickly, wasting as little time as possible."

"I've tried to do that," Sean said.

"So what's come of the serum mystery?" Needham asked.

"I've dropped it. I wasn't getting anywhere with it, and it started to affect my other work."

"So no new leads?"

"No. It's a thing of the past," Sean answered. But Needham didn't appear to be listening anymore. His attention was focused out the window. Two minutes passed; neither said a word. Sean sat uncomfortably, not knowing what to say. The room was silent. Sean could hear a dog barking somewhere outside the house. After a while, Sean spoke again, "So Dr. Needham, how are you feeling?"

Needham didn't respond. He continued to stare out the window. His eyes fixed in a vacant gaze.

Sean grew uncomfortable. Finally Needham turned back to Sean. But something in his eyes told Sean that Needham wasn't recognizing him. After a moment, Needham spoke.

"Gayle, why so many questions about that damn serum? It all happened so long ago," he said.

Sean looked around the room to see if somehow Needham's wife had entered without him noticing. She hadn't. "Excuse me?" Sean said.

"Gayle, I want to know why they're asking so many questions about that serum."

Sean didn't say anything.

"And that lab," Needham continued, "Its closing was a coincidence? I should think not."

"Excuse me?" Sean said, completely confused.

"Did you see Nixon's farewell speech last night?" Needham asked.

"Was it on PBS?"

"Of course not, it was live," Needham answered.

Sean desperately hoped that Needham's wife would enter, putting an end to the bizarre conversation.

"And as for Watergate. That whole mess could've been cleaned up with a simple fire. Fire washes the slate clean." Needham finished talking and sat quietly staring out the window again.

Sean stood and walked past Needham into the kitchen. "Mrs. Needham, I think your husband's not feeling well," Sean said.

"Is he confused again?"

"I think so."

"I'll go take care of him," she said. "Would you mind showing yourself out?"

"Not at all. Please tell him that I hope he feels better."

"I certainly will," she said before walking into the study.

Sean walked out to the street. He wiped the perspiration from his forehead. The conversation had made him uncomfortable.

IAN changed into the clean clothes that Sean had brought him. He was glad to leave the hospital. "So what did Needham say that's got you so worked up," he asked.

Sean sat on a cabinet, his foot tapping against the wooden door. "He was babbling about the lion serum."

Ian stopped packing his small gym bag and looked at Sean. "I thought you weren't going to bring that up anymore."

"I wasn't. I didn't. Needham did."

"Without your coaxing?"

"Not even a hint," Sean replied.

"So what did he say?"

"He thought I was his wife, and he asked why so many people were asking about the serum."

"What do you mean that he thought you were his wife?" Ian asked, tossing his white T-shirt into the bag. It had a large blood stain across the chest. "A nice souvenir," he mumbled.

Sean nodded. "It's the schistosomiasis. It affects his brain."

"So what else did he say about the serum?"

"Nothing. But he also said something about a lab closing, that it wasn't a coincidence. I'm not sure if he was referring to the SISS lab or not."

"Sounds like he's gone crazy."

"That was the sane part of our conversation. Before I left, he started telling me how he saw Richard Nixon's farewell speech last night."

"So?"

"So he said it was live."

Ian laughed. "Oh. That's different."

"I know."

Ian zipped the bag and walked to the door. He had a slight limp. "Well I'm ready. Let's get out of here."

After they pulled out of the parking garage, Ian turned to Sean, "So have you given any more thought to what I said about Sam?"

"I have, and you're wrong."

Ian shrugged his shoulders, "Okay. That's the last you'll hear of it from me."

"Sure it is."

AFTER dropping Ian at his apartment, Sean went home. Sam was busy writing at his desk. She looked up when he walked in. "How are they doing?"

"They?" Sean asked.

"You saw Needham and Ian, right?"

"Oh yeah. I just dropped Ian off. He has a bit of a limp, but I'm sure he'll be fine. Needham, on the other hand, was in outer space. He seemed fine for a while, but then he started to babble incoherently."

"Maybe I should stop by their house and see if there's anything I can do."

"I'd wait until tomorrow. You'd be the third visitor of the day, and he already seemed like he needed a rest."

"You're probably right," Sam said. "So what are you up to today?"

"When I spoke with Fulsonmayer yesterday, he asked me to stop by this morning to discuss how to approach this Ad Board thing. He said that he'd be my faculty advisor for the proceedings."

"Have they given you a date for the meeting yet?" Sam asked.

"No. I'll ask him about that when I'm over there." Sean took a seat on the couch. "I'm really not looking forward to it, but I'll be glad when it's over."

"It's going to be fine. I really don't think that you have anything to worry about."

Sean nodded. "So what are your plans for the afternoon?"

"I have a few errands to run. I have to pick up some camping supplies."

"For the bush?"

Sam nodded. "Do you think that I could borrow your car?"

"Of course. I'm just staying here on campus," Sean said. He tossed her the keys.

"Thanks. I'll see you later this afternoon," Sam said as she left.

Sean checked his watch. He wanted to meet with Fulsonmayer before the professor's classes began for the day. He was eager to get the Ad Board proceedings behind him.

IAN stared at his bathroom mirror. The area around the stitches in his forehead was swollen and purple in color. He still had a headache. He opened the medicine cabinet and found that he was out of Tylenol.

After searching the rest of his apartment, he grabbed his jacket and headed out the door. In the hallway, he found Mrs. Webster his landlady talking to a wrinkled gray haired man.

Mrs. Webster turned to Ian. "Oh, Mr. Nielson, I'd like you to meet Mr. Anthony Sorrano. He's a new tenant."

Ian shook Sorrano's hand. "It's nice to meet you. Which apartment are you moving into?"

Sorrano pointed to the door opposite Ian's. "Why I'm moving into this here studio across from you. It's a bit small, but I don't have many belongings. And kind Mrs. Webster here has said that I can keep my cat Confucius with me. I'm sure you'll get to know Confucius, she's—"

"What do you mean the studio across from me?" Ian interrupted.

"Why this one right here," Sorrano said, again pointing to the door.

Ian turned his attention to Mrs. Webster. "But what about Jessica?"

"Jessica who?" she inquired.

"Jessica Weston, the law student. You know, really pretty girl, with a southern accent."

Mrs. Webster shook her head, "I have no idea who you're talking about."

"She already rented that studio," Ian insisted.

The landlady noticed Ian's stitches. "What happened to your head?"

"Car accident, it's nothing. So Jessica already moved out?"

"Mr. Nielson, I'm sorry but I have no idea what you're talking about. Maybe you should see a doctor about your head. Now if you'll excuse us, I was just letting Mr. Sorrano into his apartment," she said, turning her back to Ian.

"So you're sure you don't know who—"

"Mr. Nielson, if you don't mind," Mrs. Webster said without looking at him.

Ian began down the stairs. He had forgotten why he left his apartment. As he rubbed his hands over the stitches again, he remembered the Tylenol.

Walking to the store, he tried to recall his entire interaction with the attractive law student. He remembered that she was returning to her parents place in rural Georgia. There had to be some mistake. After he bought the pills, he returned to his apartment. When he checked his mailbox, he learned that the mistake had been his own.

In his mailbox, he found a manila envelope. His name was written across the front in large black letters. He opened the envelope. What he found inside shocked him. He stuffed the contents back in the envelope and ran up the stairs to the privacy of his apartment. Once inside he locked the door behind him. His head pounded from the run upstairs. He dropped the envelope on his dining room table before heading to the kitchen and taking two tablets.

He sat down at the table and opened the envelope again. He removed the document and placed it on the table. He paged through it. It looked very official. On the last page, he found what he dreaded: his signature.

He flipped to the front again, reading the caption at the top of the page. "WILKES COUNTY SUPERIOR COURT. LEE and GLADYS WESTON, Plaintiffs V. HOMESTEAD SAVINGS BANK OF RAYLE, GEORGIA, Defendant." Below the caption of the document he read the crooked stamped message: "RECEIVED BY INTAKE CLERK #09. CASE #WCSC 1929.4-CS."

Ian slowly lowered his head to the table. The document was almost a carbon copy of the assignment he had submitted in class. The same document that he'd given to Jessica Weston to borrow. Apparently she had filed the paper, with the addition of a few essential facts, in the Wilkes County court in Georgia. Everything about the document looked real. Even his signature looked about right. Ian would have believed it was his own if he weren't certain that he had not signed it.

"What was she thinking?" Ian muttered to the table. He knew that if anyone found out that he had filed the document under a false bar association number, it would be the end of his career. Practicing law without a license was a serious offense.

After the initial shock had passed, Ian began to think clearly. Was the document real? Where was Jessica Weston?

He picked up the phone and called information. In five minutes he had scribbled down several phone numbers on a yellow legal pad. He dialed the first.

"Wilkes County Superior Court. This is the intake room," said a pleasant sounding woman on the other end.

"Hello. My office recently filed a law suit with your court, and we haven't received any hearing dates. I'm just wondering if it's made its way to the judge yet," Ian said as calmly as possible.

"Can you give me the case number?"

"Sure," Ian said reading it to her from the document.

"Okay. Just a moment," the woman said, placing the phone on her desk. Ian could hear her opening file cabinet drawers. She returned to the phone. "Alright, I found it. Westons versus Homestead Savings Bank. No, it hasn't reached the judge yet. It's been assigned to Judge Reynolds. He's out of town for another week, so the case won't get to his desk for a while. Did you want me to see if I could get it assigned to another judge?"

"No, no," Ian snapped. "Thank you. That's just fine. Thank you for your time. I appreciate it," Ian said before hanging up the phone.

She had really filed it. The good news was that no judge had seen it yet. He had some time to figure out how to get it back.

He dialed the next number on his list. After several rings, a woman answered the phone.

"Hello," she said.

"Hello, this is John Williamson with Homestead Savings. May I speak with Gladys or Lee Weston," Ian said.

"This is Gladys Weston. Are you calling about the foreclosure?"

Damn, Ian thought, the bank really was foreclosing on the Westons. "Um, no ma'am, I'm calling with regard to an inquiry that your daughter made at our bank. Does she currently live at your residence?"

The other end of the line was silent.

"Hello? Mrs. Weston?" Ian said.

"I'm here."

"Does your daughter—"

"I'm sorry, but we don't have any children."

"But a Jessica Weston gave us your—"

"Sir, I think that I would recall giving birth to any children, and I'm quite certain that I have not. Now, good day," she said before returning the phone to its cradle.

Ian sat holding the phone for a second before he hung it up. "What the hell is going on?" he said. Whoever Jessica Weston was, she had done plenty of research to put Ian in the spot he was in. He flipped through the document again. No additional clues. He turned the envelope upside-down and shook it. A small piece of paper fell out. He unfolded it and read:

THIS ALL GOES AWAY IF YOU DISAPPEAR FOR A

WHILE. WE KNOW HOW IMPORTANT YOUR CAREER IS. YOU'LL FINALLY BE ABLE TO HELP MOM AND DAD GET OUT OF DEBT. DON'T BLOW IT NOW. WE'LL BE IN TOUCH. AS FOR AUTHORITIES, WE'RE SURE YOU KNOW WHAT NOT TO DO. CAR ACCIDENTS AREN'T THAT UNCOMMON.

Ian placed the small typewritten note on the table. He read it again. The accident was intentional? He placed the document and the note into the envelope and went into his bedroom. He packed a suitcase with a few essentials.

When he'd finished, he picked up the phone and made one last call. "Hi, I need to purchase a plane ticket for this afternoon."

THE lunch hour neared. Harvard Square was crowded. Sam stood nervously in front of Northeastern America Bank. She had waited patiently, but grew concerned. Finally he approached.

"I don't think that I can do this," she said.

"You said that we could trust you. Now all you have to do is prove it."

Sam shook her head. "So this is it. I won't have to do anything else."

"We'll see. This will be all for now. But I can't give you any guarantees."

Sam looked at the piece of paper in her hand. She read the number scrawled on it. The conversation over, she turned to the task at hand.

BEFORE Sean entered the Peabody Museum to meet with Fulsonmayer, he looked over his shoulder one last time. The entire morning, he had the feeling that he was being watched. Paranoia.

Fulsonmayer's secretary ushered Sean into the professor's office. "Sean Graham is here to see you," she announced.

Fulsonmayer didn't look up from his work. "Have a seat Sean."

Sean complied.

"What can I do for you?" Fulsonmayer asked.

"Yesterday when we spoke, you'd asked that I stop by. I was hoping that we could go over the Ad Board process if you're not too busy. I'm wondering what I should be doing to prepare myself."

"The first thing that you have to do is find yourself a faculty advisor. Then discuss your options with that person," Fulsonmayer said, still concentrating on his work.

"I thought that you were going to be my advisor. Yesterday on the phone—"

Fulsonmayer dropped his pen in an exaggerated manner. He peered over his glasses at Sean. "I know what I said yesterday on the phone, but I thought about it, and in light of your performance of late, I think that you'd be better off finding someone else. I still have a lot of work to do if I'm going to get this project published. I'm sure you can understand that I can't become entangled in a scandal right now. This might be my last chance at tenure."

Sean nodded. "I see."

"Nothing personal."

"What about my classes?"

"I told you before, you've been relieved of your teaching responsibilities pending the findings of the Ad Board."

"So all I can do is wait."

"That's right," Fulsonmayer said. "Now, if you don't mind, I have a lot of material to review before my lecture today."

Sean took his cue and left the office. On the street in front of the museum, he saw Chester Hamilton walking even slower than normal, intently staring at the ground. Sean walked over to the professor.

"Did you lose something Professor Hamilton?" he asked.

Hamilton turned to see who was talking. "Hello Sean. Yes, I lost a pin of mine. It was given to me by my wife just before she passed away. It's very special to me."

"When did you lose it?" Sean asked.

"Some time this morning during my walk."

"You're sure you were wearing it?"

"I'm certain. I never leave home without it."

"When did you realize that you'd lost it?"

"Oh, about two hours ago. I've been retracing every step I took."

"You've already been looking for two hours?"

"Well the way I saw it, I'd either have to look for it, or pray to St. Anthony to help me find it. I already gave St.

Anthony a shot. So far he hasn't been of much help, so now I'm playing the roll of bloodhound."

"Good luck," Sean said.

"I only have about a mile to go to finish retracing my steps back to my house. It shouldn't take too much longer. Maybe a few hours."

"Professor Hamilton, I don't want to sound too pessimistic—"

"But?"

"—but you're looking for a needle in a haystack."

Hamilton laughed. He continued to walk slowly down the sidewalk. "When I lived in the rainforest I learned how to track every type of animal, no matter how small. Retracing my own steps won't be a problem. It just takes patience. If you're patient and concentrate enough, you can find anything. Retrace one small step at a time."

Sean took note of Hamilton's comment.

"Sean, you wouldn't happen to have any free time would you?"

"Sorry Professor Hamilton, I'd love to help, but you just reminded me that I have to go somewhere," Sean said, quickening his pace and leaving Hamilton hunting along an invisible path.

SANTIAGO ate lunch at a table in front of a deli in Harvard Square. As soon as the cellphone rang, he knew that it would be a tough conversation. "Go ahead."

"What's he up to?" Claris asked.

Santiago took a deep breath, "I'm not really sure."

"What do you mean, you're not sure?"

"I lost him. I was with him this morning. He visited Needham, picked up his buddy from the hospital and returned home. After that, I'm not really sure. I wouldn't be concerned. He'll turn up."

"I'm paying you to keep an eye on him. Telling me not to worry, that 'he'll turn up' isn't worth too much to me," Claris barked.

"Listen. You said to contact the girl, and I did. I can't be in two places at once."

Claris knew Santiago was right. "So is she with us?"

"As far as I can tell she is. She's done everything I've asked."

"Then get your ass in gear and find Sean Graham," Claris said. He hung up the phone and took another sip of lemonade.

AFTER several hours on a plane and an enormous hassle at the rental car counter, Sean drove along a deserted street in a long since forgotten industrial park. He pulled the car to the curb and looked at his map. After pinpointing his location, he realized that the address he sought was two blocks further. Abandoned warehouses lined both sides of the street. Tall weeds sprouted from the cracks in the pavement.

When Sean found what he thought to be his destination, he pulled into the parking lot. He walked to the front of the building, looking for an address or any sign identifying the rundown property. Behind a large overgrown bush he found what he'd been looking for. The mounted lettering was gone, but the years of southern California sun had caused the bricks to fade around the now missing letters. Sean had found the Sierra Institute for Serological Studies.

The glass doors that once sat at the entrance of the lab had been replaced by thick sheets of wood, nailed shut to the outside world. Sean walked around the perimeter of the lab looking for a way in. He pushed his way through the thick bushes and weeds, searching for a window to climb through. The building had none. He made his way around to the back of the building where he found the freight entrance. There he found a set of double doors. A thick chain held the handles of the doors together. Looking at the chain, he saw that it lacked a lock. He loosened the chain. When it wouldn't unravel any further, he opened the doors. He got them wide enough apart to where he could squeeze through.

He looked into the building. It was dark inside. Sections of the roof had deteriorated and some sunlight broke through. He grabbed a brick and wedged it in the door. Pulling the doors apart again, he squeezed into the lab.

During the flight to Los Angeles, Sean had plenty of time to debate his sanity. Somewhere over Arizona he convinced himself that he was doing the right thing. Relieved of his teaching responsibilities, he had no pressing commitments at home, and no matter how hard he tried to convince himself otherwise, he still wanted answers about the missing serum. Following Chester Hamilton's lead, Sean began retracing the serum's steps back to the beginning—the lab.

The idea of returning to the origin had seemed like a good idea. Sean wasn't sitting around his apartment anymore, just waiting for someone to call with more news that would change his life. He felt like he was finally taking control of the process—acting instead of reacting. As he waited for his eyes to adjust to the dark interior of the lab, however, he began to think that the idea had been reasonable only in theory.

Sean stood in the large room that had once been the holding area for the lab's animals. A few rusty cages sat scattered across the floor. There was a faint scent that Sean immediately recognized. The building smelled like an old campfire. Sean followed the walls of the room to the high ceiling. As sunlight filtered through the holes in the roof, Sean could see that a fire had left sooty stains on the once white walls.

He walked slowly around the large room, not certain what he was looking for. Every step echoed around the vast empty chamber. He spotted a door on the far wall. It had a small square window on it. He walked to the door and opened it. It revealed a long corridor, but almost no light made it past the holding area. It was too dark to go any further. As Sean stood looking down the corridor, he heard the door open behind him. He spun around. The powerful beam of a flashlight shined in his face. He squinted, but couldn't see past the bright light.

"Hold it right there," the man with the flashlight ordered. "Put your hands up."

Sean complied with the command. "Who are you?" Sean asked.

The man took a few steps closer. "I'm Officer Mills with the Mira Loma Police Department, and you are trespassing on private property." As Mills drew closer, Sean saw his hand on the holstered gun.

Sean kept his hands above his head. "I wasn't aware that I was trespassing," he said.

"So you saw the chain on the door as an invitation more than anything else?"

"You have a point," Sean said.

"I'm glad you think so. Now please turn around and place

your hands above your head against the wall."

Sean did as directed. Mills frisked Sean. "Who are you and what are you doing here?" he said.

"My name is Sean Graham. I'm a student and I'm researching a project that involved this lab. I came from Boston just to see this place firsthand."

"If that's not a load of shit."

"I swear it's the truth," Sean said, still facing the wall. "My identification is in my wallet. See for yourself."

Mills took Sean's wallet from his pocket. He found Sean's school ID. "What did you say you were researching?"

"I'm just here to learn more about this place."

"So you flew out here from the East Coast just to see an abandoned building?"

"I need the grade," Sean said.

Mills recognized that Sean didn't pose a threat. "Okay. You can take your hands down."

Sean turned around. Mills returned his wallet. Sean saw the police officer clearly for the first time. He was a short and stocky man of about fifty. Curly brown hair protruded from beneath his navy blue uniform cap. "So what interests you about this lab?" Mills asked.

"The research that they performed here," Sean answered.

"But what good did coming out here do? Didn't you know that they had a fire here?"

"No."

"This entire industrial complex has been deserted since the late eighties."

"It looked like a ghost town driving in here."

"That's why it was so easy spotting your car. Nobody ever comes to this area anymore. The town's mayor is trying get all of these factories and warehouses torn down to make some room for condos and a park. I saw the plan. It looked really nice. Of course we'd need to bring more jobs into the area. All of these places were hard hit by the recession back in the eighties. Now, like you said, it's a ghost town."

"When was the fire?" Sean asked, seeing that Mills was a fountain of information.

"Let me see. Must have been eighty-two or three. I remember this place was in trouble. Something about not getting federal funding. The fire really gutted this place. Everything was destroyed. I mean everything. When the fire hit, we all suspected arson, with the lab's money trouble and all. Most of the scientists here had already left. Come to think of it, there's only one that's still in the area—Dr. Paton.Very nice lady. She helped me with the arson investigation paperwork."

Mills began to walk to the exit. Sean followed, sensing that Mills was declaring the visit over.

"Do you know where Dr. Paton works now?" Sean asked.

"Sure, she runs an animal clinic over on Sepulveda Boulevard. Can't miss it."

Sean exited the building in front of Mills. He squinted in the bright sunlight. Mills pulled the chain tight around the door handles. "I'll have to get a lock for this chain."

The two men walked back to the parking lot. Sean climbed into his rental car. Mills walked over to his window. "Have a nice day Mr. Graham, but don't let me catch you trespassing again. I'll have to bring you in if I do," he said with a tip of his cap.

"WHERE are you?" Sam asked.

"I can't say right now," Sean answered. "But I have one more thing to do before I come home. It might be too late to catch a flight today, so I might be back in the morning."

"What's with the secrecy?"

"It's nothing really. Don't make anything out of it."

"I wouldn't except that Ian's doing the same thing," Sam replied.

Sean read his map as he stood talking on the pay phone. He found Sepulveda Boulevard. "What do you mean Ian's doing the same thing?"

"He left a message on your machine saying to call him at one-seven-two-nine. What's that?"

"One-seven-two-nine? When did he call?"

"About an hour ago. He wanted you to call him from a pay phone. Sean, what's going on?"

"Nothing. I have to go. I'll either see you late tonight or early tomorrow."

"Sean what—"

"I don't have time to explain. I have to go," Sean said hanging up the phone. He checked his watch. It was just after four in the afternoon. If he wanted to catch Paton before she finished work, he couldn't waste time.

Ten minutes later, Sean parked his car across the street from the Sunset Valley Animal Clinic. It was a small white Victorian house with black trim. He thought it looked a bit out of place on a street lined with strip malls. The tiny house looked like it had been transplanted from a rural Vermont town, where kids would play out in front on a tire swing hung from a large elm tree.

Sean entered the clinic's empty waiting room. A pleasant young receptionist greeted him.

"Can I help you?" she asked.

"I'm here to see Dr. Paton," Sean replied.

The receptionist leaned across the desk to look past Sean. A confused look grew on her face. "Did you forget something?"

"Pardon me?" Sean said, also turning to look behind him.

"Your pet. You didn't bring it."

"Oh. I don't have a pet. I'd just like to speak with Dr. Paton if she has the time."

"Please have a seat. I'll let her know you're here. What's your name?"

"Sean Graham."

A few moments later, the receptionist returned and ushered Sean to Dr. Paton's office. She stood from behind her desk to greet Sean. Several family photos decorated the office. Sean counted at least four different dogs in the pictures. Paton's veterinary degree hung on the wall behind the desk.

"Dr. Paton, my name's Sean Graham. Thanks for seeing me."

"No problem," she said. "Please have a seat." She gestured to the chair in front of her desk. Sean guessed that she was in her early forties. She had a very warm smile. Sean imagined that her smile helped calm many frantic pet owners.

"What is it that I can help you with, Mr. Graham?"

Sean had conjured up the story on his trip over from SISS. "I'm writing a paper on arson as a means of cover up for one of my graduate school seminars, and I wondered if I could ask you about your job at the SISS lab."

"That was a while back. Who told you that it was considered an arson?"

"Well that's just it, it was never proven that it was arson, but I interviewed a police officer named Mills who said that it was very likely arson."

"That's right. It was never proven, but arson was certainly suspected."

"Let's, for the moment, assume it was arson that caused the fire. Do you have any idea what the motive would have been? I know that the lab was in financial trouble, because it failed to secure federal grants."

"That was the focus of the police investigation. They figured that it was for the insurance money."

"And you don't agree?" Sean asked.

"I'm not sure. The facility really wasn't worth much. Especially because the recession was on it's way in. If you've been over in that area, you can see that the land isn't worth the cost it would take to bulldoze all of those warehouses. So no, I don't think that it was for the money."

"Why then?"

"I'm not sure."

"Okay. What about possible suspects? I found a person that I thought fit the profile of an arsonist. He had been arrested for stealing things from the lab. Maybe he was out for revenge. His name was Marcus Tran," Sean said, watching closely for Paton's reaction.

"Oh, no. It wasn't Marcus Tran."

"How can you be so sure?"

"Because he died of some liver disease long before the fire."

"Really?" Sean said, doing his best acting job.

"I'll never forget him. They caught him stealing some product from the lab. But like I said, it couldn't have been Tran. No, the police started questioning all of the researchers because many had begun looking elsewhere for jobs. After we didn't secure any federal funding, everyone saw the writing on the wall. It wasn't too long before the lab went under."

"So you too were looking for a job at the time?" Sean asked.

"Not really. I had my mind set on opening this veterinary practice since I moved out here from the Northeast. The SISS job was something that paid me well. I saved a lot of money over the few years that I worked there. But I was also ready to jump ship. Hell, everyone was," she paused, thinking quietly to herself. "Come to think of it, Valerie was the only one who had already taken a position elsewhere. A place called Hydan something-or-other.

"How do you spell that?"

"I think it was H-Y-D-A-N. I can't remember, but it was based in Washington, DC."

Sean straightened in his chair, "Valerie Chapeau?"

"Yes, Valerie Chapeau. She's a good friend of mine. Now she works at a place in Stamford, Connecticut. We talk every Thursday like clockwork," she smiled, thinking about her friend. "Except last week. For some reason she called a few days early."

As Paton spoke, Sean saw the nameplate on her desk for the first time: OLIVIA PATON, D.V.M. Sean looked over her shoulder at the degree on the wall. It had been awarded to Olivia Cameron.

"You got married," Sean said.

"Excuse me?"

"Your maiden name is Cameron."

"Yes it is," Paton answered, still confused. "Why is that important?"

"Oh, it's not. I just remembered reading your name in one of the police files. I didn't realize that you were one and the same." Sean paused for a second. "I think that's all I have to ask you. You've been really helpful. Thank you very much for your time."

Sean shook hands with Paton and showed himself out of the clinic. Chapeau had lied about losing touch with Paton. He needed to find out why.

13

THE red-eye flight wasn't the most appealing option, but Sean had to get back to Boston. He shifted uncomfortably in his window seat. Early into the flight he realized that he probably wouldn't be able to sleep. Remembering Ian's call, he took the airphone from the seat back in front of him. He dialed the number to the small home in rural Pennsylvania. Summoned from her sleep, a woman answered the phone.

"Hello?"

"Hi Mrs. Nielson, this is Sean. How are you?"

"I'm fine. It's so nice to hear from you. We haven't seen you in so long. How's school?" Ian's mother asked.

"It could be better, but I'm getting by."

"I'm sure you're doing just fine."

"By any chance is Ian there?" he asked.

"Yes he is. He surprised us this afternoon when he showed up on our front porch. Let me go get him."

Moments later Ian picked up the phone. He sounded nervous. "Where are you calling from?" he asked.

"Somewhere over the Midwest."

"What?"

"I'm on a plane. I'm heading back from Los Angeles."

"Why were you in LA?"

"Not so fast. What are you doing at home?" Sean asked.

"You're not going to believe this," Ian began. He told Sean how Jessica Weston filed his law school paper in the Wilkes County Court.

"You're kidding me," Sean said. "What happens if anyone finds out?"

"My career is over before I even take the bar exam. That's practicing law without a license." Ian went on to tell Sean about the note accompanying the copy of the law suit. "So whoever this is also knows about the car accident," Ian finished.

"Or caused it."

"Right. Sean, I'm not sure what's going on here, but I'm laying low here for a while."

"What about school?"

"I already spoke to all of my professors. I told them I had a family emergency and that I'd make up all of the work. They understood."

"So now what?" Sean asked.

"I'm not sure on my end, but threatening my family was enough to get me out of Boston. How did you end up in Los Angeles?"

"I was trusting my instincts. I had that strange meeting with Needham this morning. Then I met with Fulsonmayer who turned his back on me. This all has to do with that damn serum."

"I'm not questioning it anymore. I'm at a loss for explanations over here. So what did you find?"

"Local authorities think that somebody intentionally torched the SISS lab. But they lack a suspect or motive."

"Insurance money?"

"That's what the cops figure, but it doesn't make sense. The recession tossed the value of the property into the sewer. Nobody stood to gain anything by burning the building. At least not in monetary terms."

"Files?"

"What do you mean?" Sean asked.

"Were the lab's files lost in the fire?"

"As far as I know, everything was lost," Sean replied.

"Probably wasn't money after all. Think about it. It would be the perfect cover up. SISS didn't get government grants, so they needed money or they would close. By burning the building down, the immediate reaction would be that the arsonist hoped to collect on the insurance—"

"When, in fact, the fire was set to destroy records," Sean said, finishing Ian's thought.

"Exactly."

"If that was the plan, it worked, because that's exactly what the police think."

"Did you learn anything else?" Ian asked.

"Chapeau lied to me about one of the doctors at the lab, a Dr. Paton. Chapeau said that she had fallen out of touch with Paton years ago. I met with this doctor today. Chapeau called her just last week. I'm confronting Chapeau tomorrow."

"Let me know what happens," Ian said.

"And you let me know if the police come up with anything else on the hit and run."

"I will. And Sean, be careful," Ian said.

"Thanks mom." Sean replaced the phone in the seatback in front of him. He stared out the window into the black night sky. After an exhausting day, he was finally able to close his eyes and sleep.

AFTER locking the door to his apartment, Sean tip toed into his bedroom. Sam was sleeping quietly in the bed. He crept to the bedside and kissed her on the cheek. A small smile crossed her face when she woke and saw Sean sitting next to her. "What time is it?" she asked.

"It's a little after three."

"Where have you been?" she asked, still half asleep.

"We'll talk in the morning."

SEAN woke early the next morning. He waited as long as his nerves would let him before calling California. He was surprised when Dr. Paton answered her phone.

"Dr. Paton, this is Sean Graham. I stopped by your office yesterday afternoon. Have I caught you at a bad time?" Sean asked.

"No. I was just a bit surprised to get a call this early. More questions?"

"Just a couple. Do you happen to remember what Marcus Tran stole from the lab?" Sean asked.

"Sure. We know that he stole a few of our test samples, and I believe he also stole syringes and vials."

"What were the test samples?" Sean asked, although he already knew the answer.

"They contained serum from our lion's blood. At least that's what they found at his apartment. For all we know, he could also have stolen urine, semen, feces, anything. You name it. We had it all."

"You had all of those samples?"

"Sure. We had samples on that lion dating back at least a couple of years."

"Is there any way that any of those samples still exist?" Sean asked excitedly.

"Unfortunately no. Everything was destroyed in the fire.

Several animals died too. Hatari the lion was among them."

"I thought he died from exposure to radiation," Sean said.

"No. I'm sure that eventually would have been the case. But no, he died in the fire. Most of the large animals died in the fire. It was terrible. Once we lost our grants, the place was destined to close. It wasn't really popular with the locals. They got their wish when we lost our grants. But then when the fire killed so many animals, well, let's just say that had the building not already burned down, the locals would've torched it."

"Nothing survived the fire?" Sean asked for the final time.

"Nothing," she replied.

"Okay. Thanks," he said, wrapping up the phone call. After he hung up the phone, that feeling came over him again. Sean felt that with the closing of each of his conversations, he finished with more questions than answers.

AFTER Sam rose from her sleep, she joined Sean at the kitchen table for breakfast. After a little prodding, he eventually explained his trip to Los Angeles. Sam listened intently. She took a sip of her coffee before speaking. "I just don't see why you'd waste time and money by going out to LA. You have enough to worry about here."

"I had to go," Sean defended himself.

"Why?"

"Because I've been tossed around like a rag doll here at school. All of these walls have crashed in on me and I started to feel a bit suffocated. Maybe I was foolish to open up this Tran thing again, but I'm finally starting to get some answers. I had a hunch before, but now I'm positive—I'm onto something here."

Sam forced a smile. "I hope you're right. I just don't want you to get so caught up in it that you forget about the Ad Board."

Sean took her hand from across the table. "Thanks for the concern, but I'm going to be okay. Being in LA was pretty exciting. Even if I didn't party with any movie stars, it couldn't have been as dull as things here."

"Needham was rushed to the hospital yesterday afternoon," Sam said flatly.

"What now?"

"It's his liver. They got the tests back. Bad news. They

expect his liver to give any day. I spoke with Mrs. Needham. She quoted the doctors as saying that he had a week at most."

Sean was silent. "Wow."

Sam nodded. "I know, I can't believe it. Schistosomiasis."

"What about a transplant?"

"They put him on the list, but it could take months before his name reaches the top," Sam answered.

"But he's the Director-General of the World Health Organization. Doesn't that mean anything?"

She shook her head. "The list is deaf, dumb and blind. He could be the Pope and it wouldn't get him a liver any faster."

"Have you seen him again?"

"Not yet. I thought about stopping by later this afternoon."

The two didn't say another word for the remainder of breakfast. Finally Sean stood from the table. "I'm going for a run. I'll see you in a bit."

LIKE Santiago, Trevor Matthews had lost Sean the previous day. He had followed Sean as far as Logan Airport, but couldn't afford the same day fare to Los Angeles. Fortunately for Matthews, Sean arrived back at his apartment during one of the late night intervals in which Matthews was actually awake in his rental car parked across the street.

After an early breakfast, Matthews stood in the brisk morning air waiting for Sean to emerge from his apartment building. He knew Sean's general routine, and was dressed in sweatpants and a sweatshirt, ready for Sean's morning jog.

As anticipated, Sean burst out of the building and ran down JFK Street toward the Charles River. Matthews attempted to follow, but within fifteen seconds, Sean's young legs outpaced the middle-aged researcher by two hundred yards. Matthews' already lagging jog slowed to a walk.

When he finally arrived at the Charles, he saw Sean disappear around a bend in the river a quarter mile away. Luckily, he knew Sean's route. Eventually, Sean would cross the river and return on the far bank. Matthews walked in a direction that would intercept Sean's return path. Not knowing where Santiago was, but that he would be watching, Matthews knew that he would have only one shot.

SEAN liked autumn. It was his favorite season for running. The cool air was easy to breath and felt great in his chest.

When he arrived back at his apartment, he reached into the large pouch on the front of his sweatshirt to retrieve his keys. When he pulled them out, a small folded piece of paper fell out onto the floor. He opened the door and scooped up the scrap of paper as he entered the apartment.

He tossed his keys on the kitchen counter and opened the lid of the trash can ready to toss the scrap out. Curious, he opened it. He removed his foot from the lever at the bottom of the garbage can. The lid closed. He stared at the paper. He hadn't written the three words on the note:

HYDAN INTERNATIONAL ENTERPRISES

Sean remembered that Paton had said something about a firm with the word Hydan in it. She said that Chapeau took a job there after leaving SISS. But Sean hadn't brought the sweatshirt to LA. How did the note get there? Then he remembered the staggering jogger he had just encountered. As Sean ran back toward campus, a jogger approached him from the opposite direction. The man seemed to alter his path several times, each time running directly at Sean. At the last instant, Sean sidestepped a substantial collision, suffering only a glancing brush of the man's elbow. Now, he realized that it was all intentional. The jogger had passed the note.

Sean tried to remember the man's face but couldn't.

SANTIAGO managed to corral the jogger into an alley just off of the river. "Who are you?" the PI asked.

Matthews was exhausted from the short jog. "Why don't you tell me who you are?" Matthews replied.

Santiago shoved Matthews into the brick wall of the alley. "I'm giving you one more chance. Who are you and why are you following that kid?"

"I have no idea what you're talking about," Matthews said. He hoped that pleading ignorance would win his freedom.

"Quit fucking around. I know you've been following him. What did you pass him when you bumped into him?"

"I have no idea what you're talking about."

Santiago pulled the revolver from his pocket. He emptied the bullets into his hand and placed them in his pocket. "Is that the story you're sticking with?"

Matthews began to shake. He put his hands out in front of him, as Santiago took a few slow steps closer. He told himself not to be intimidated.

"One last time," Santiago began, "who are you?"

"Listen, it's like I told you. I don't know—" Matthews said. Santiago didn't wait for the answer. He struck Matthews in the head twice with the butt of the revolver, sending Matthews to his knees. He knelt hunched over with his hands protecting his head. The gun opened a large gash just above his eyebrow. Though a large cut, it didn't bleed heavily. Over the next forty-five seconds, Santiago kicked and punched the cowering Matthews, who did little more than pray for the experience to end.

Three hours later, as his plane pulled away from the gate, Matthews swallowed two painkillers. His head and chest throbbed with pain. He was glad to leave Boston. He wasn't sure if Sean Graham would understand the three word message, but Matthews wasn't taking any more risks. One beating was enough.

Trevor Matthews began the long journey back to his research in the jungles outside of Kinshasa. And as the plane left American soil and set out over the Atlantic, he hoped that his trip to the states would prove worthwhile. It was out of his hands now. His hopes fell on Sean Graham.

AFTER breakfast with Sam, Sean headed to the law school library to do research. He couldn't wait on Ian to answer his question about Hydan. For the time being, he was more interested in determining what the message meant, than in finding out who the jogger was that passed it to him.

After searching the law school's databases for an hour, he found what he was looking for. Hydan International Enterprises was incorporated in 1980. That was all of the information that Sean could find. The corporation had no physical address or phone number listed. The database didn't even list an industry for the name. He wrote the word

Hydan across a piece of paper in large letters, underlining it three times. Writing the word larger failed to reveal any of its secrets.

Sean searched the computer for another hour before giving up. As he packed his bag, Michael Rubicon approached him. "Hi Sean," he said.

"Hi Michael. What are you doing here? Don't tell me you're one of those prodigies and you're concurrently enrolled as an undergrad and a law student."

Rubicon smiled. "I like studying here because law students are too busy reading to screw around like all of the undergrads. Everyone here is quiet."

"I know what you mean."

"We missed you in class today. How are things going with the Ad Board?" Rubicon asked.

"As you're no doubt aware, I've been temporarily relieved of my teaching responsibilities," Sean said.

"So you're spending your free time catching up on your old English?"

"What?"

"Your old English. Hydan," Rubicon said, pointing to the large word on Sean's paper, "it's old English. Like the word foot. It came from the old English word *fot* which meant—"

"Hold on a second," Sean interrupted. "Go back to Hydan. What does it mean?"

"It's where we get the verb "to hide". I'm taking this excellent linguistics class called the Origins of English taught by Professor—"

"To hide?"

"That's right," Rubicon said.

"You're sure?"

"Positive."

"Thanks, Michael. I have to run," Sean said, tossing the remainder of his books into his bag and running out of the library.

When he reached the pay phone outside he dialed Ian's number.

"Ian, what's a holding company?" Sean asked, trying to catch his breath.

"What?"

"What's a holding company?"

"Why?"

"Because I found another company that I think is involved in this mess, but it's like the place doesn't exist. At least not that I could find," Sean said.

"It might not exist," Ian said, "at least not physically. What's the name of the company?"

"Hydan International Enterprises."

The name didn't ring any bells. "And where did you come up with it?"

"Some guy passed me a note with the name on it while I was jogging. I've been at the law school trying to find anything out about it."

"Back up a second. Someone passed you a note? Who was he?"

"I don't know. I've never seen him before. I'll figure that out later. So what can you tell me about holding companies?"

"Lots of companies form them for various reasons. It's a relatively easy way to spread money around."

"Ian, do me a favor and see what else you can dig up on Hydan International Enterprises. I'll call you back in a bit," Sean said.

Ian laughed. "You seem to have forgotten that I'm out in the woods here at my parents' house. I don't know how quickly I can get any information."

"You'll figure something out," Sean said.

"By the way, I'm supposed to call the police about the hit and run. They left a message on my answering machine this morning. They probably called you too."

"I'll have to check. Have you figured out what you're going to do about that law suit in Georgia?"

Ian sighed, "Not yet. I don't really feel like finding out if the threat in the note was serious."

"Let me know if there's anything you want me to do."

"I will. Listen, I'm going to return that call to the police. You should probably do the same."

"I will. I'll call you later," Sean said hanging up the phone.

AS Sean stood talking on the pay phone, Santiago watched from a safe distance. His cellphone rang. "Go ahead," he said.

"What did the jogger say?" Claris asked, the concern apparent in his usually steadfast voice.

"He didn't say a thing."

"Did you use your charm to get it out of him?"

"You could say that."

Claris shook his head. "I just don't want the police to get involved. So where is he now?"

"I don't know, but I have a feeling we've seen the last of him."

"Good. What about Graham?"

"I'm watching him as we speak. He's been on a pay phone for quite some time now. I saw him dial the number. I guess Ian is at his parents' house in Pennsylvania."

"So Sean's not in his apartment?" Claris asked.

"That's affirmative."

"Then it's time I left him a message. I don't want him to think that I'm being uncooperative with his investigation. He'll soon be of the impression that I have nothing helpful for him. Keep in touch. Watch him closely."

"Of course," Santiago said.

"By the way. Nice recovery getting your secretary to fly up to LA and pick up the trail after you lost it," Claris said before hanging up.

Santiago shoved the phone into his pocket. "Asshole."

AT four o'clock Sean sat on a hard wooden bench at the Cambridge Police Department Headquarters. Detective Greene had asked him to stop by. Sean remembered Greene from the accident scene. Within seconds of arriving on the chaotic street where the paramedics tended to Ian, Greene had cordoned off the potential crime scene. He was extremely organized and efficient.

From behind a set of glass doors, Greene entered the waiting room. He brought Sean back to his desk. "Have a seat," he said. He had a gruff voice. "Can I offer you anything? Coffee?"

"No thank you," Sean answered.

"How's Mr. Nielson feeling? I left him a message earlier and we've been playing phone tag, so I haven't spoken with him."

"He's okay. He's happy to be out of the hospital."

"I'm sure he is," Greene said. The social aspect of the meeting over, he opened a manila folder and withdrew a few documents. “Here’s what’s new on our end. We found the car. A snazzy new black Lexus.”

“That’s great,” Sean interjected.

“Yes, it is. It was abandoned in a lot up at Fresh Pond. The pieces of the bumper and grille found at the scene match the car. Blood stains recovered from the windshield are from Mr. Nielson. That much we know.”

“This is all good news, right? Yet you don’t sound very optimistic.”

“That’s because the car was reported stolen earlier that day. Car-jacking. The owner was forced out of the car by two teens with a gun. That’s all we have to go on. Unless we can find those kids, we won’t be able to charge anyone with any crime.”

“What are the odds that you’ll find anything?” Sean asked.

Greene shook his head. “Not very good. Ordinarily finding the car is a major break. In this case, it’s not too helpful. The kids were probably out joy-riding when they hit Mr. Nielson. So unless we come up with some more leads, this will be a tough one.”

Sean wanted to tell Greene about the letter Ian had received and how it mentioned the accident. Ian made him promise not to say a word, not even to Sam.

After Greene finished relaying his disheartening news, Sean returned to his apartment. When he walked in the door, he was surprised to see that the dining room table was set for dinner, complete with candles. Walking into the kitchen, he found Sam.

“Sean, I didn’t think you’d be home for a while yet,” she said surprised.

“What’s the occasion?” he asked.

“This might be our last unrushed dinner together for a while. I don’t think I can stay longer than two more days without paying a fee on my plane ticket.”

“I forgot about that. I was getting used to having you around.”

“I know, so was I. But I’ve been away from my work for a good amount of time now, and I have to get back. Besides, you’ve got a lot of things going on here that you have to concentrate on, and I’m sure that I’d be a distraction.”

“A pleasant distraction.”

Sam smiled. “What did the police have to say?”

"The good news is that they found the car. The bad news is that it was stolen earlier in the day. The hopes of finding the driver are nil."

"I'm sorry. But when you consider what could have happened to Ian, finding the driver loses its importance."

"You're right," Sean said. He thought about the note that Ian read to him. "Sam, I'll be right back."

Sean went down to the corner to use the pay phone. He called Ian.

"What's new?" Ian asked.

Sean told him about his meeting with Greene. "I've been thinking, Ian. Greene and the police are ready to write this off as a random hit and run."

"Yeah?"

"I began thinking about the fact that whoever set you up in rural Georgia had to go to great lengths to make everything fall into place. I don't want to make you any more paranoid than you might already be, but these aren't morons you're dealing with."

"I realize that, Sean."

"I'm starting to think that the hit and run wasn't an accident at all. Maybe the car-jacking took place specifically to have a stolen car involved in the accident."

"You're saying that someone tried to kill me."

"Maybe."

"I don't know. Why hit and run?"

"The police have no leads right now, that's why. Listen, that's just food for thought," Sean said.

"Okay. Now I have some news for you. I found some interesting stuff on Hydan International Enterprises."

"Hit me."

"Well the third most interesting thing I found was that Hydan was founded and is currently owned by one Lawrence Needham."

"Needham?"

"Yeah. Are you ready for the second best part?"

"Shoot," Sean said.

"It has two subsidiaries. One is located in American Samoa."

"No shit. So—" Sean interrupted.

"Hold on. That's not the best part. The best part's that the other is a laboratory in Stamford, Connecticut. None other than—"

"New England Integration Laboratories," Sean said, his mouth remaining open.

"You got it."

"Holy shit. How is it that you can find all of this stuff and I can't?"

"You just need to know where to look. Even though Hydan exists only as a PO box, it still has to file all of its regulatory papers with the federal government. Most of that information is open to the public. It's just a matter of looking in the right places."

"You are a research machine."

Ian smiled at the comment. "Now that I've given you all of the answers, why don't you explain to me what this is all about?"

Sean shook his head as if Ian could see. "I'm not sure, but I'm starting to get an idea. I have to run. Thanks again. I'll call you later."

When Sean reentered the apartment, Sam was lighting the candles. "Hope I'm not going overboard," she said.

"Not at all. It's a nice touch. Is there anything I can do?"

"Nope. It's all ready. While you were out, someone called. I didn't hear who it was, so you might want to check your answering machine."

Sean walked over to the machine and played the message. It was the first time that Sean heard Barnard Claris's voice. Sean felt that the message was, for the most part, a polite blow off. That was how Claris wanted it to be received. Sean listened attentively to everything Claris said. None of it was the least bit helpful. Then Claris slipped. Sean replayed the message. He scribbled a few notes on a piece of paper before sitting at the dining room table.

Sam entered the room with a baked lasagna. "You have to tell me the truth about this lasagna. This is only the second time I've made it, and last time it was a total disaster. So be honest," she said, slicing a piece and placing it on Sean's plate.

Sean poured each of them a glass of wine. "It smells wonderful," he said.

"Smell is one thing; taste is another."

As they began eating, Sean picked up the notes he had taken on Claris's message. "Have you ever heard of Double Helix Labs?"

"Sure. We used them all the time."

"Who do you mean by 'we'?"

"I don't know. Pretty much every time I needed any medical supplies prepared for the field I used them. They're kind of like a wholesale pharmacy. I suppose they're just like Merck or Pfizer, but they specialize in relief pharmaceuticals. They prepare large volumes of vaccines for groups like the Red Cross or Doctors Without Borders. Why? Who left that message?"

"That was Barnard Claris calling from American Samoa. Seemed liked a very pleasant man. He said that he really couldn't remember too much about the lion serum."

"Well at least he called you back."

"Yeah."

"So why the questions about Double Helix Labs?"

"Because Claris must have been confused. He said that he remembered Needham returning the serum to Chapeau."

"So?"

"He said that the serum was returned to Double Helix Labs."

Sam was silent for a moment. "It was a long time ago. I'm sure he meant SISS. He probably used Double Helix a lot too. Honest mistake."

Sean nodded. "Yeah, I'm sure you're right." Sean let the subject drop and continued eating dinner. It might have been an honest mistake, but he wasn't going to let it go unchecked.

WHEN Sean woke the next morning, he went immediately to his car. He sat there for a few minutes before starting the engine. His night was a sleepless one. Every time he managed to sleep for a few minutes, he found himself in the middle of a recurring dream. In the dream, he was caught in the middle of the accident he witnessed on the turnpike several days earlier. The dream was silent. Cars were demolished, people were bleeding. Sean could see people screaming, but couldn't hear any words. Every time, he just slowly drove past the wreckage, knowing that he could do nothing to help. The dream had resulted in a couple fitful nights.

Sean took another sip of coffee from his mug. He finally started the car and plotted his course to Stamford, Connecticut. Valerie Chapeau had not returned any of his calls the previous day. Sean would visit her in person.

Two hours after he left Cambridge, Sean parked his car in the lot of New England Integration Laboratories. He had several pointed questions to ask Chapeau and he hoped he could keep his composure while asking them.

He stepped out of his car and walked to the entrance of the building. Nearing the doors, he passed a cream colored Mercury Topaz in a parking space identified by a placard as Chapeau's. He was relieved to know that she was in the office.

Sean approached the security desk. He told the guard he had a meeting with Chapeau.

"And your name is?" the guard asked.

"Lawrence Needham."

The guard picked up the phone and dialed a three-digit extension. "Good morning, Dr. Chapeau. A Lawrence Needham is here to see you." He hung up the phone and turned his attention to Sean. "Here's your visitor's badge. You can wait by that door over there. She'll be right out."

Sean took the badge and waited by the door. He could hear footsteps approaching from the other side. Chapeau opened the door. She was visibly surprised to find Sean on the other side. She looked past him anticipating Needham. "The guard said that Larry Needham was here."

"That's what I told him," Sean said.

"Why on earth would you do that?"

"Because I had a feeling that if you knew it was me, you wouldn't be standing at this door right now."

"That's nonsense. But I'm very busy this morning, Sean. Is there any way we could do this another time?"

"I'm afraid not. I came all the way down here to speak with you in person."

"But, as I said, I'm really rather busy. Maybe—"

"This can't wait," Sean said flatly.

Recognizing that Sean wasn't about to leave, Chapeau escorted him to her office. It was messier than it had been the last time Sean saw it. Chapeau quickly made her way around the desk and placed the documents on it into a manila folder. She tossed the folder onto a stack of papers sitting behind her desk. Sean could see that she was agitated.

"So what's so important that you drove down here to see me without a call?" she asked.

"Well, Dr. Chapeau, I'm not very good with confrontations. I have a tendency to beat around the bush. But on my way down here, I promised myself that I wouldn't do that today. So I'm just going to come right out and tell you what's on my mind," he said, taking a deep breath. "I don't think that you've been very truthful with me."

Chapeau grew immediately defensive. "About what?"

"I made a trip out to California to see the SISS lab for myself. And while I was out there I tracked down an old friend of yours. The same person you lied to me about."

"I have no idea what you're talking about."

"Dr. Paton. Or should I say Dr. Cameron? The person you claimed to have lost touch with years ago. Funny thing is that she recalls having a conversation with you as recently as last week. Why would you lie to me?"

"I ... I just didn't think that she would appreciate your pestering her. She's a very busy lady. She has a large veterinary practice to run. Your crazy questions wouldn't be welcome."

"That's something that you should have let her decide."

"So maybe I was overprotective. She's a friend. That happens sometimes."

"What about Needham? Are you protecting him from something?"

"What are you talking about?"

"You lied about him as well."

"With regard to what?"

"The fact that he got you this job. The fact that his company owns this place. Why all the lies? Did you think that I wouldn't find out about Hydan International Enterprises and its relationship to this lab?" Sean said, noticing for the first time the photo on the book case behind Chapeau.

"Sean, you're reading more into all of this than you should," Chapeau replied, but he wasn't listening. He had turned his attention out her office window to the parking lot.

He pulled his cellphone from his jacket pocket. "I need to make a call," he said, standing from the chair and walking to the corner of the room, out of Chapeau's earshot.

Chapeau sat nervously behind her desk. She began to sweat. She watched as Sean spoke into the cellphone, his back turned to her. When he finished, he placed the phone back into his pocket. He turned slowly and after a second approached her desk.

"If that's all you came here to say, I would appreciate it if you left now. As I told you before, I have a very busy morning ahead of me."

Sean stood in front of the desk. His face was expressionless. "So it wasn't Ian."

"Excuse me?"

"It was supposed to be me."

"I have no idea what you're talking about."

"The accident. I was supposed to get hit by the car. Not Ian."

"What the hell are you—"

"I saw the insurance claims you quickly stuffed away when I walked in here. And that photo on the book case: you and your husband and a brand new black Lexus. When I walked in this morning I saw that car in your parking space. With all the money you're always talking about making, a Mercury Topaz isn't exactly your style. It's a rental, right?" He paused. Chapeau didn't speak. "You tried to kill me."

The sweat was visible on her forehead. "What are you talking about? I'm calling security."

"Go ahead. The Stamford Police are probably on their way. I just called Detective Greene at the Cambridge Police Department. He confirmed that the car from the hit and run was registered to one Valerie Chapeau. That's too much of a coincidence for me. The original charge would have been something along the lines of leaving the scene of an accident and maybe reckless driving. When they find out it was your car and that we know each other, I'm sure the charge will be changed to attempted murder or something like that."

Chapeau stared at Sean, not saying a word.

Sean continued, "I was right all along. This is all about the lion serum. You lied about Paton because you knew she'd tell me all about the lion's files and the arson. You burned that place down as a cover up. But what about Needham? What does he have to do with any of this?"

Chapeau began to cry quietly.

"Where does Needham fit into this?" Sean repeated.

Chapeau picked up the phone and made a quick call. She mumbled a few words into the phone that Sean couldn't hear.

"What about Double Helix Labs and Barnard Claris? What do they have to do with this?" Sean demanded.

Chapeau ignored his questions. She turned to her bookcase and took the photo in her hands. "I'm not saying anything else. My lawyer is on his way. I'm turning myself in."

14

AFTER an exhausting day in Stamford, Sean called Ian from a pay phone with the news.

"So the police just hauled her away?" Ian asked.

Sean nodded. "They asked her to go down to the station to answer a few questions."

"I can't believe that she hit me with her car."

"For what it's worth, I'm pretty sure that she was aiming for me."

"Small consolation. So what now?"

"I need to call this lab that Claris mentioned. I think that it just slipped out when he left the message."

"Tell me that you know what's going on here, because I'm more than a bit concerned," Ian said.

"No idea. Anything new with the Georgia law suit?"

"Nothing. But at least that judge isn't back from vacation yet."

"That's good news, and at this point we should take any good news we can get."

"The more I think about it, the more I'm certain that the law suit has something to do with Chapeau. I just can't figure out how."

"But Chapeau admitted that she was trying to hit me," Sean said. "What would anyone gain by hitting you?"

"I have no idea."

"Like I said before, maybe the person that wrote the note saw you get hit by the car and nothing else. It might be completely unrelated. Listen, I need to make another call, so I'm heading home. I'll talk to you later," Sean said hanging up the phone.

As he walked back to his apartment, he saw Ankur Gustav approaching from down the street. Sean's stomach tensed. His hand instinctively curled into a tight fist. As the two neared, Gustav just passed Sean with a small grin on his face. Not a word was said. Sean exhaled slowly. Gustav had become the least of his concerns.

Once back at his apartment, Sean called information for the telephone number for Double Helix Laboratories. The operator told Sean that the lab was located in Van Nuys, just outside of Los Angeles. Sean dialed the number and asked to speak to the records clerk.

"This is Gabe, how may I help you?" the man on the other end asked.

"Hi, my name is James Mason, and I work in the New York Office of the World Health Organization. I'm hoping that you can help me locate an order that one of my colleagues placed with your firm several years back."

"I'll see what I can do. What information can you give me?" the clerk asked.

"I have an approximate date range and the name of the individual who probably placed the order."

"Alright. Those will help."

Sean gave the clerk what he thought would be the right dates. "As for the name, I believe it would be Lawrence Needham or Valerie Chapeau."

The clerk took notes as Sean spoke. "Okay Mr. Mason, if you give me a number where I can return your call, I'll get on this right away. I should be able to get back to you within the hour."

Sean thanked the clerk and gave him his home number. After hanging up, he reclined on his couch, pondering everything Chapeau said that morning. Fifteen minutes later the phone rang.

"Mr. Mason? This is Gabe at Double Helix. I found the order you were looking for."

"That was fast."

Proud of his work, the clerk smiled to himself. "The only thing is that my supervisor just reminded me that the information is confidential, and without the proper authorization, I can't give it out."

"I understand," Sean said. "But I think you'll agree that this is an unusual case. You don't recognize the name Lawrence Needham, do you?"

The clerk hesitated before answering, "No, I don't."

"He's my boss and he's the Director-General of the World Health Organization. He's currently in Geneva at a conference and he's asked me to get this information. Now if you or your supervisor wants to check on that information, be my guest. But we're just wasting time."

Sean heard the clerk place his hand over the phone before speaking to someone else in the room. Then he spoke to Sean, "I guess this is okay."

"That's good to hear."

"I found no orders placed by Valerie Chapeau, and several by Lawrence Needham. Fortunately there was only one in the time frame you gave me. And it was the last one that Needham made."

"Great. Could you tell me what the order requested?" Sean asked.

"It was a relatively large order. He requested large quantities of two products. The first was simple penicillin—"

"The syphilis project," Sean mumbled.

"—and the second was provided by Needham. It was an experimental drug, a vaccine or antibiotic I suppose, that we simply packaged for distribution."

"What do you mean 'packaged for distribution'?"

"We divided it into several ten-milliliter injection vials."

"And you don't know what it was?"

"No. We don't run tests on experimentals. We only test the products we produce on site."

"By any remote chance would you happen to have any of the experimental solution?"

"Of course. We keep at least one sample of everything that comes through the lab."

"How long would it take to run some tests on the solution?" Sean asked.

"It depends on the tests. What did you have in mind?"

"I need you to test it for hepatitis C," Sean answered.

"Excuse me? Did you say hepatitis C?"

"Yes. How long will that take?"

"Evidence of HCV doesn't normally exist in solutions like this."

"I realize that, but all the same, I need you to test it."

"Alright. That shouldn't take too long. What else?"

"Is there any way to determine if the solution came from an animal?" Sean asked.

"Hold on a second," the clerk said, again covering the phone and speaking to the other person in the room. "Yeah, we can do that. What kind of animal were you looking for?"

"A lion."

"Okay. My supervisor said that that could take some time."

"I don't have much time."

"We'll do it as quickly as possible."

"I'll need a copy of the results," Sean said.

"As soon as we get them, we'll overnight them to you."

"Great," Sean said. He gave the clerk his address.

"I thought you said you were in New York," the clerk said looking at Sean's address.

"That ... that's where the office is, but I'm currently on assignment in Boston."

"Oh. Is this something big?"

"You could say that," Sean answered.

JUST before he sat down to eat dinner, Sean took a call from Valerie Chapeau's lawyer. Chapeau would be arraigned the following afternoon. She was in the lockup at the Stamford Police Station. She had requested to see Sean. For the second time that day, Sean headed to southern Connecticut.

Chapeau's lawyer met Sean in the foyer of the station.

"Mr. Graham, I'm Cliff Bradley, Ms. Chapeau's attorney," the tired looking man said. He handed Sean his business card. "Thanks for coming down."

"No problem."

"She's pretty out of it. She said she wouldn't talk to anyone except you."

An officer let the two men into an interview room. The room was cold. A steel table and four chairs sat in the center of the room.

"I'll go get your client," the officer said. He returned shortly with Chapeau. She was dressed in a gray jumpsuit that was too large for her. The cuffs of the sleeves and legs were rolled several times. She looked awful. Dark, heavy circles engulfed her eyes. Sean saw that she had been crying.

She took a seat opposite Sean at the table. She looked at her lawyer. "Could you leave us for a bit?" she asked. Her voice was quiet.

Bradley didn't like the idea. "Are you sure that—"

"I'm sure," Chapeau said.

"Okay. Just remember that what you two discuss is not privileged. The DA can ask Mr. Graham about anything you say in here. I'll be right outside," he said leaving the room.

"I apologize for asking you down here so late in the day," Chapeau said, her voice little more than a whisper.

Sean shrugged, not knowing what to say.

"When I first got into medicine, I thought I could change the world. I thought I could make a difference in people's lives. I think that's why most people go to medical school in the first place. But then I started working with real patients. There's a hell of a difference between learning medicine in books and learning medicine working on real people. Sooner or later you realize that in spite of your best efforts, people die. Or even worse, they live. But they live with a machine hooked up to them to help them breath for the rest of their lives. There's always something that can go wrong. One day I realized that I was tired of working with people, so I turned to research. I figured I could get away from the human element of medicine," she said. She slouched into the back of the chair.

Sean stared at her, trying to predict what she was getting at. Her expressionless face told him nothing. He continued to sit and listen.

"So I took the job at SISS. The pay wasn't spectacular in any way, but at least it got me away from all of the sick people. SISS was a good place to work. Nice people, nice hours. I remember your friend Marcus Tran."

Sean leaned forward in his seat.

"He tried hard to fit in. You could tell that he tried to cover up the fact that he was an immigrant. It was funny how he was always throwing around the newest slang terms. He was in love with LA. I always thought that he was just a harmless kid. I guess he was until the whole serum thing reared its ugly head. Nobody thought anything of it until the CDC showed up. And of course Larry Needham made his way back into my life. I hadn't seen him since med school. He had broken my heart. When I heard he was in LA again, I was all too willing to let him break it again. I did plenty of stupid things for him, not the least of which was burning the place down."

Sean's eyes came to life. "So you did start the fire."

Chapeau ignored him. She began to speak with more

animation, her voice growing angry. "I figured that it would have been enough to let the place close. I mean it looked legitimate that we would close after we failed to receive any federal grants for our research. That was no fluke either. We had received grants every year like clockwork. A research facility might get weaned from its federal funding, but to go cold turkey was ridiculous. 'Burn it down. There's too much evidence,' he said. And who was I to argue. I thought we were going to run off together. I didn't even know what he was up to. All I cared about was being with him."

"So it was all a cover up," Sean said.

Chapeau grew increasingly agitated. "Of course it was a cover up. But I had no idea what I was hiding. I was ready to skip town with Larry. I figured we were going to make a life for ourselves somewhere else. But he saw it differently. He was gone before the match even hit the floor." After a few deep breaths, she gained her composure. "But I'm not a murderer," she said, looking at Sean.

"But you tried to run me over. You almost killed my friend," he said.

"I was desperate. I'm not asking you to forgive me. I know you won't. I'm not asking you to understand either. I know I'm guilty. But my sin is greed. When Larry left me, my life turned upside down. For some reason I thought that if I became filthy rich, I could forget about him. So I set out to make as much money as possible from him."

"What are you talking about?"

"We had a deal, me and Larry. He got the serum and my silence, I got the money."

"What money?"

"You know that he got me the job at NEIL. When NEIL first broke onto the scene, it was primarily a cancer research firm. That was a front. When I took over, we still did cancer work, but our biggest sellers have been hepatitis related drugs. We patented the drugs Interferon and Ribavirin, both used to treat the disease."

"So?"

"So Needham bought my silence. He got the serum, I got the curing business. He keeps NEIL one step ahead of the competition."

"I'm not sure that I understand."

"He knows all there is to know. He filters information to

my company so that whenever anyone catches up with our technology, we break further ahead. We're always one step ahead of the competition."

"And ultimately some of the money makes its way back to Needham through NEIL's parent company Hydan International Enterprises," Sean said.

Chapeau smiled. "I'm glad you came along, Sean Graham. I've carried this guilt on my shoulders for too long. For a while I thought that the house, the cars and the lavish Caribbean cruises could mask it, but I was just fooling myself. When you first walked into my office, I knew that it was just a matter of time."

Sean pushed her for more information, "You said that Needham kept you ahead of the others. How?"

She smirked again. "You already know. You just want to hear me say it."

"Then say it."

She paused, enjoying Sean's tension. "Needham knows the cure for hepatitis C."

Sean stared at Chapeau. "You know this for a fact?"

"No, but I have a very strong suspicion that he does. If he doesn't know the cure, he at least knows a vaccine. I didn't know what evil he had done, and he paid me very well not to ask," she said. "I started putting the complete gestalt together after you began asking questions. I didn't see the link until you asked me about radiation causing a mutation in feline hepatitis to become HCV."

Sean stood from the table. "You're all I need to nail him. Somehow I'm getting you out of here and we're going to confront him. I'll even post bail," Sean said excitedly. He started for the door.

"I'm not going anywhere," she replied. "I won't put my family through this. It's over."

"What are you talking about? You have to help me."

Her chin dropped to her chest. She shook her head slowly. "It's over. If you mention anything I've said to anyone, I'll just deny it. Without me, there's no proof."

The excitement faded from Sean's voice, "You have to help me."

She continued to shake her head. "No. It's over."

EARLY the next morning, Bob Sauganash turned the VCR

on again. He was the Director of Security at Northeastern America Bank. Over the past two days he had reviewed several hours of video tapes from the bank's ATMs. One of the bank's account managers noticed that a large sum of money had been withdrawn from an account during a single afternoon. Sauganash attempted to determine by whom. From the ATM transaction log, he knew the times of the withdrawals. Now he sought the corresponding footage from the ATM videotapes.

Sauganash heard someone enter his office. He didn't turn to see who it was. "How much did you say this person made off with?" Sauganash asked.

"About twenty-five thousand over eight withdrawals," the account manager replied.

"How could they withdraw that much money from the ATMs?"

"The account holder requested that all limits be lifted from his account. And it is a rather substantial account," the manager said, handing Sauganash the balance sheet.

"Wow. And except for some change, the bulk of it was all recently deposited," Sauganash said, turning his attention back to the monitor. "Tell you what, that certainly doesn't look like a Sean Graham to me."

"No, but she's quite attractive."

Sauganash picked up the phone and dialed a number.

"Hello?"

"Hello. Is Mr. Graham in?" Sauganash asked.

"Speaking," Sean said, as he finished smearing cream cheese on his breakfast bagel.

"My name is Bob Sauganash. I'm the Director of Security over at Northeastern America Bank in Harvard Square. I was hoping that you could come over so that we could talk about some recent activity in your account."

"I'm really busy. I don't think that I can make it by today."

"Mr. Graham, this is important. Did you withdraw any money from your account recently?"

"No. Why?"

"Because someone withdrew twenty-five thousand dollars from your account the other day."

"What? There has to be some mistake."

"I'm afraid not. Did you ask someone to withdraw any money for you?"

"No."

"Well we'd like you to come over and look at some video-tape. Maybe you'll recognize the person. You didn't happen to give someone your PIN number, did you?" Sauganash suggested.

Sean looked at Sam as she entered the living room. "I have to go," he said, hanging up the phone.

"Who was that?" Sam asked.

"It was the bank. Someone stole twenty-five thousand dollars from my account."

"Oh my god. Do they know who?"

"No. I have to run," Sean said, grabbing his jacket and racing out of the apartment.

A pleasant looking middle-aged woman showed Sean into Bob Sauganash's poorly lit office at Northeastern America Bank. Sauganash sat behind a desk smoking a cigarette. Sean counted a dozen or so extinguished butts in his ash-tray.

"Mr. Graham, thank you for coming by. Have a seat," Sauganash said.

"Thanks."

"Mr. Graham, yours is an unusual account. At your request, we lifted the ATM withdrawal limit on your card. As you know, there are several other fees and restrictions that we've waived as well. It was only the attentive eye of your account manager that caught the recent unorthodox activities on your account. Had she taken another day to identify the withdrawals, you'd be out of luck. You see, we recycle our videotapes every three days. The evidence we have would have been lost. As fortune would have it, however, we caught the fraud in time. Before we take a look at the tapes, I need to ask you a few more questions."

"Go ahead," Sean said.

"I asked you on the phone whether or not you'd ever given your PIN number to anyone. You didn't respond."

Sean nodded. "I think I might have."

"Fine. I thought that might be the case," Sauganash said. "Perhaps you gave it to a now spiteful ex-girlfriend?"

Sean didn't answer.

"I only ask because if that's the case, even with the video tape, it will be awfully difficult to recover your money, and prosecution is pretty much out of the question. I've been in this business a long time. I've seen things like this happen. I wouldn't get your heart set on seeing that money again," Sauganash said picking up the VCR remote control. "Well, without further ado, let's roll tape."

He turned to face the bank of monitors on the wall. On the center screen a fuzzy black and white image took motion. It was a tight shot of a man standing at the ATM. As he punched the numbers on the keypad, he looked nervously over his shoulder.

"I have no idea who that is," Sean said.

"Just wait. He's not the one."

After placing the cash in his wallet, the man walked away. Moments later a woman wearing sun glasses approached the ATM. She read from a piece of paper before punching in the PIN number. Sean shook his head. He recognized Sam immediately. Sauganash saw the look on Sean's face.

"That's what I thought," the security director said. He lit another cigarette. "Do you want to consider pressing charges?"

"No. I'll handle this on my own," Sean answered.

"You're certain? I don't recommend going out and doing anything foolish."

"Don't worry, I'm not crazy."

"Well, I'd at least consider reinstating the limits on your ATM withdrawals."

Sean walked to the door. "That won't be necessary."

WHEN Sean returned to his apartment, he found Sam in the living room. Her suitcases were sprawled across the floor. Sean sat on the couch in front of her.

"I figured I'd get a head start on packing. I usually do it last minute and always end up forgetting something," she said smiling at Sean.

He didn't know how to begin. He thought that there had to be an explanation.

Sam saw the look on his face. "What's wrong?"

"Sam, I know that there must be a reason, but for the life of me, I can't imagine what it could be."

"What are you talking about?"

"You know what I'm talking about."

"No. I really don't."

"I just had a rather painful meeting with the security director over at my bank," Sean said. Sam's face went pale. "I'm sure you have at least some idea what we talked about."

"Sean, it's not—"

"Wait," Sean cut in, "before you lie to me, I should tell you that the bank had a pretty sophisticated video surveillance network. I never would have believed it if I hadn't seen you on the tape."

Sam quickly moved to Sean's side. "Sean, you have to believe me. It's not what you think."

"And what is it that I think? That you stole money from me?"

"I had too. They made me do it."

"They? Who are they?" Sean yelled.

"I ... I can't tell you. You have to believe me. I would never do something like this. You know I wouldn't."

"That's what I thought until I saw the tape."

"Sean I can explain," Sam said.

The buzzer to the apartment rang. Sean went to the intercom. "Who is it?" he barked.

"I have an overnight parcel for a James Mason."

"Come on up," Sean said. He stood at the open door waiting for the deliveryman. Sam sat quietly on the couch.

The courier walked down the hall and handed Sean the letter-sized envelope. "I just need you to sign here," he said. Sean signed the receipt and closed the door.

He opened the envelope and withdrew two pages. He read both in their entirety. His hands trembled a bit as he stuffed the pages back into the envelope. He turned his attention to Sam. "Come up with a good excuse. I'm out of here."

"Sean, we need to talk."

"It'll have to wait."

"Where are you going?"

Sean grabbed his keys from the kitchen counter. "To show Needham that I have him by the balls."

"Sean wait. We really need to talk," Sam called after him, but he had already left the apartment.

SEAN exited the elevator at Massachusetts General Hospital and walked to the nurses' station.

"Can you tell me what room Lawrence Needham is in?" he asked.

"Just a moment," the man behind the desk said. He typed a few words into his computer. "He's in 2217. Down the hall, second to last door on the left."

Sean walked stiffly down the hall, envelope in hand. When he got to room 2217 he peered through the open door. Needham's wife sat by his bedside. Sean knocked as he entered the room.

Gayle Needham turned to see who it was. "Oh, Sean. Come on in. He just woke up from a nap." She returned her attention to her husband. "Look who's here honey. It's Sean Graham."

Needham turned slowly to see Sean. There were several machines hooked up to him. He looked sickly. His face was thin with a yellowish hue to it. His blue eyes had sunk into dark caverns. Sean estimated that he weighed no more than one hundred pounds.

"Mrs. Needham, I need to speak with your husband in private," Sean said. His tone was more of a demand than a request.

She looked at her husband. He nodded to her. "Well okay. I'll be just outside," she said before exiting the room.

With a hand held control, Needham adjusted the head of the bed until he sat in an upright position. He fixed the blankets at his waist. "What can I help you with Sean?"

Sean stood at the foot of the bed. His arms were limp at his sides.

"Why don't you have a seat," Needham suggested.

"I'd prefer to stand."

Needham detected the sense of urgency in Sean's voice. "Is something wrong?"

"You could say that," Sean replied.

Needham waited for Sean to continue, but he didn't. "Well would you like to tell me what it is?"

"I can remember when I was growing up people asking me what I wanted to be when I was older. Like everyone else I wanted to be a professional baseball player or an astronaut. But as I got a bit older I remember admiring real life heroes—firefighters, police officers and doctors. They had great jobs. Their lives were devoted to helping people. As I got even older, I began to realize that those jobs weren't for everyone, but the respect I had for those people was just as strong. What I'm getting at here is that people in certain professions are trusted by the public simply because of the uniforms they wear—whether its a badge or a white lab coat. You took that trust and preyed on it. You used your lab coat as a shield, concealing from the world what you were really up to."

Needham looked at Sean with a shocked expression—somewhere between confusion and disbelief. "What in god's name are you talking about?"

"You know what I'm talking about."

"I'm sure that I don't have any idea."

"You intentionally spread hepatitis C across the globe."

Needham let out a single laugh before launching into a fit of coughs. When he caught his breath he chuckled quietly. "Is this some kind of joke? I'm sitting here literally on my deathbed and you accuse me of spreading HCV to the world. I must say, your imagination gets better every time I see you. First you tell me that I unknowingly spread HCV. Now you say it was my intent. It's no wonder they're considering kicking you out of school. Your imagination is better suited to Hollywood than academia."

"You can deny it all you want. I have proof."

"Proof? Proof of what? You're crazy. Now leave my room and ask my wife to come back in."

"I'm not going anywhere. You're not fooling me. Chapeau told me everything," Sean said.

"Chapeau," Needham repeated, his voice more subdued.

"Yes, Valerie Chapeau. She told me how you paid her off in exchange for her silence. It all comes back to the serum, doesn't it? She's behind bars right now, so I'm sure that she'll be more than willing to cooperate."

Needham smiled. "She won't cooperate with you"

"I'm sure she will. She's in jail right now for attempted murder. It might take a while, but I'm sure she'll see the light."

"Oh she's seen the light," Needham said.

"Smile all you want, her words are going to hang you."

"No pun intended."

"What are you talking about?"

"Valerie Chapeau is dead. She hanged herself with her trousers last night in her jail cell."

"What?"

"It's quite true. Call down there if you like, use my phone," Needham said, picking up the handset.

"I don't need Chapeau. I have all of the evidence I need."

"You're living in a dream."

"The timeline for the spread of hepatitis C in sub-Saharan Africa matches exactly the timeline of your African syphilis project."

"Coincidence," Needham said confidently.

"Maybe without this," Sean said holding up the envelope. He pulled the two pages out. "This first page is the order form you submitted to Double Helix Laboratories. The date of the order is exactly one week before you embarked on the syphilis project. The order requested the preparation of two hundred ten-milliliter injection vials of penicillin. It also requested the preparation of a smaller number of ten-milliliter injection vials containing an experimental drug submitted by you."

"What are you getting at?"

"Let's move on to page two."

"Yes, let's."

"Page two details lab results on tests performed yesterday at my request. Allow me to read a portion: 'Preliminary DNA analysis of the solution confirms that it originated from a feline source. Degree of certainty is one hundred percent. More extensive analysis is required to determine if feline source was *Panthera leo*—or African lion.'" Sean looked up at Needham before he continued. "Let me skip down to the bottom. 'After standard infectious disease analysis, it is confirmed that the solution demonstrates characteristics consistent with HCV infection.' That's no coincidence," Sean said. He handed both documents to Needham who read them silently.

As Needham examined the documents, there was a knock at the door. Both Sean and Needham turned to look. Sam entered the room.

Needham smiled. "Perfect timing Samantha. Please come in."

Sam walked over to Sean and took him by the elbow. "We need to talk."

"It'll have to wait," Sean said gruffly.

"It can't wait."

Sean pulled away from her.

"Why don't you come over here," Needham said, his eyes fixed on Sean. Sean walked to the side of the bed.

"Closer. I have a question for you."

Sean leaned closer to the sickly doctor.

"Closer."

Sean leaned further, their faces inches apart. Needham put his mouth up to Sean's ear and whispered, "Tell me, how difficult is it to keep a secret?"

"What?"

"You heard me. How difficult is it to keep a secret? You know, everyone is always gossiping about this or that. They tell you not to tell a soul, and we promise not to. But how often do we actually keep that promise. Not often, right?"

"What are you talking about?" Sean asked, beginning to pull away. Needham grabbed his shoulder firmly and pulled him back.

"I have a secret for you. But first a question. How hard is it to commit murder?"

Sean didn't respond.

"Okay. You would imagine that it's rather difficult, wouldn't you? That being said, how difficult is it to commit genocide?"

Sean continued to stare blankly.

"Sean, the things I have done make Hitler and Pol Pot look like choir boys. They were tyrants. They had strong, unconscionable views that they imparted on the world. They will forever be remembered as evil incarnate on earth. Their methods were medieval. My legacy is entirely different. When it is my time to leave this world, I will be remembered as a saint. The global community recognizes me as nothing more than a healer. In some aspects, this is exactly what I am. But there is a side to my work that most people can't understand; they lack the intellect. They can't comprehend the scope of my work. You're right Sean, years ago, I released a plague on the world. A silent plague whose wrath fits into the natural rhythms of life on earth. Disease is the way that nature keeps humanity in check. I just gave nature a helping hand.

"Don't act surprised. I know you understand my motivations. The Africans are little more than animals. Fifteen well placed prostitutes acted as the catalysts for a naturally occurring cleanser. Along a road the virus traveled, striking everyone who came in contact with it. I did little more than to start the ball rolling. Their savage lifestyles provided the perfect boiling pot. Their tribal wars saw soldiers running wild across the landscape, raping every woman in sight. Soon entire armies of virus-laden men roamed the lower continent. Then add all of their tribal circumcisions, tattooing and body piercing. Not even I could have imagined that the virus would spread so efficiently. And it is the horrid lifestyle of these very same slovenly people that hides the true source of the virus. No one would ever believe that a confused little lab technician with a strange fetish started the whole thing when he got a little creative and injected the plasma from a lion into his scrotum. I'd seen the potential for this virus before the world ever heard of Marcus Tran, but I would never have had the courage to act on it. Then the Tran case opened the door. All I did was walk through and provide a little guidance. When this virus has run its course, a continent in turmoil will get a fresh start. Ultimately the world will be better off."

Sean was shocked by Needham's composure. "Rationalize your actions all you want. You killed innocent people. People that had nothing to do with the unrest in Africa," he said.

"Innocent? Who, the sex fiends and drug addicts? Mine is the hand of the lord, striking down those who pollute his garden. Everyone bitches about these degenerates. I alone had the courage to act. And when all is said and done, I'll be received as a hero. One day you'll learn that no one is innocent."

Sean struggled to find words, "It's not your place to judge."

Needham calmly adjusted the pillow behind his back. "And it's yours to judge me? You obviously don't read your bible. 'Let he who is without sin cast the first stone'. My conscience is clear. I'm ready to see the face of God."

"They've never seen God where you're going. I've caught you. You'll be exposed for the person you really are."

Needham let out a chuckle. "You'll make me a bigger hero than you can imagine."

"You're crazy."

"I'm not crazy. I'm simply certain that you won't say a word of this to anyone," Needham replied.

"Don't bet on it."

"Why don't you ask Sam why you'll keep quiet? Tell him Sam. Tell him how I wasn't even in Africa at the time of the syphilis project."

Sean turned to Sam. “What is he talking about?”

Sam didn’t answer.

“Go ahead Sam, tell him,” Needham repeated.

“Needham, your name is all over the project,” Sean said.

“How naive are you? Do you think that in archaeology all of these old professors are out in the field digging for tiny bones? Don’t be ridiculous. That’s what graduate students are for. They do the work, their professors get the credit. Your work for Richard Fulsonmayer is a case in point. You did all of the leg work, yet when all is said and done your name is lost somewhere at the bottom of page sixteen between the footnotes. I wasn’t there.”

Sean’s head was full of confusion. “What are you saying?”

Needham smiled again. “Your friend Sam did it all.”

Sean turned to Sam. She stared at the floor.

“Sam,” Sean said. She didn’t respond. “Sam. What’s he talking about?” He knew the answer by her look.

He turned to Needham. “But at least your name is on this work order for Double Helix Labs,” Sean said, holding up the document. “That shows your intent.”

“Wrong again, Sean. Take a close look at it. Sure, my name is there, but I never signed the order. Examine the initials at the ‘X’.”

“SF,” Sean said. He looked at Sam. She continued to stare at the floor.

“I swear to you, I didn’t know,” she said.

“Just like with my money.”

“No, not like the money. You have to believe me, I didn’t know.”

Sean turned back to Needham. “In the very least you were negligent. I’m sure an investigation would turn up even more than I found.”

“I don’t think so. I’ll take my chances. You see, I have a card I have yet to play. I’m sure Valerie Chapeau told you.”

“The cure,” Sean said quietly.

“Yes, the miracle elixir.”

“So you do know the cure.”

“Oh yes, and I’ll give it to the world. Just imagine, the final heroic act of a dying genius. That’s how this will play out. I’ll need a day to prepare, but in two days I will hold my final press conference, at which time I will reveal two things to the world. First I will demonstrate how the virus spread.

Of course Samantha will be another unfortunate casualty. But what's a great plan without a scapegoat? After I've retraced the virus's spread, in, might I add, much greater detail than you just have, I'll drop one of the biggest public health bombs since penicillin. Hepatitis C will be a thing of the past. Sure, I may have been negligent in giving my student such freedom, but the cure will undoubtedly exonerate me of all my sins. Like I said, Sean, my conscience is clear."

15

TWO hours after he witnessed Sean and Sam leave Massachusetts General Hospital, Santiago sat in his rental car listening to the radio. Needham's plan to hold a press conference had just been announced over local news outlets. It would go national on the nightly news.

"Shit," he said. He pulled a piece of paper from his wallet and dialed the number.

"Hello?"

"It's Santiago."

"How did you get this number?" Claris asked.

"I'm a PI remember? You're not invisible."

Claris shifted uncomfortably on his favorite park bench. "Why are you contacting me? You know the protocol."

"Yeah, but I figured you'd want to hear this."

"What?"

"Needham just announced a press conference."

"For what?"

"They didn't say."

"When?"

"Two days from today. It'll be over at the Harvard School of Public Health."

"Shit. Do you have any idea why he's holding it?"

"No, but Chapeau is dead. That might have something to do with it."

"What happened to her?"

"Suicide. I told you how Graham visited her at the jail. Well she hung herself later that night. Graham and Ferson went to visit Needham in the hospital today, and now Needham wants to talk to the media. The radio quoted Needham as saying that it was going to be something big, but he wouldn't be specific."

"I've got to get on a plane. I'll be there as soon as I can," Claris said. He hopped on his bike and rode home through the tropical heat.

SEAN sat silent on the couch in his apartment, his attention focused on the TV. CNN had just run its report on the Needham press conference. Sam sat on the couch next to Sean. "Are you ever going to talk to me?" she asked.

Sean didn't look at her when he responded, "Don't you have a plane to catch?"

"I'm not going anywhere until we talk."

"What's there to talk about?"

Sam didn't answer.

"Oh, I know," Sean began in a mocking tone. "How about you tell me why you stole my money? Or maybe you could start from the beginning. That sounds like a plan. You've known about the serum from the start. You just let me search blindly like an ostrich with its head in the sand. 'Trust me,' you said. What a load of crap."

"Sean I can explain."

"Go for it."

"Just to set the record straight, I never knew about the serum until you asked me about it after you got back from Tanzania. And you have to know that there's no way that I could have known I was infecting people with HCV. Please tell me you know that," she said.

"A week ago I would have believed that. You signed the work order and administered the injections. How couldn't you have known or at least suspected?"

"For the same reason that this has gone unnoticed for over two decades. This is the Director-General of the World Health Organization we're talking about. I'd worked closely with him and he'd never given me any reason to question him."

"But you've known for a while."

"I became suspicious when you showed me the CDC's locational timeline. Before that I figured you were just chasing your tail."

"How do you explain the money?" Sean asked.

"A few days ago a man approached me at the bookstore."

"I was there. You were there to spy on me," Sean interrupted.

Sam hadn't realized that he'd been at the bookstore. "So you had been spying on me."

"I was a bit suspicious too," Sean admitted. "So who was he?"

"The scary thing is that I still don't know. But he

threatened to tell you about my involvement in this whole affair if I didn't cooperate with him. I told him to get lost, but then he started giving me details about my involvement that I hadn't realized before. When he showed me his gun, I knew he was serious. He threatened to kill me, Sean."

"So what, you stole the money to prove your commitment to him?"

"Exactly. You have to know that I would never do anything to hurt you."

"Why didn't you just tell me the truth?"

"Because I thought that I could take care of everything by myself. But then things just got out of control. I knew that Needham was dying. I know it sounds awful, but I hoped that he would die before any of this came out. I'm sorry Sean."

"What about that guy from the bookstore? Have you seen him again?"

She shook her head, "Just to give him the money."

Sean sat quietly thinking to himself.

"You trust me, don't you?" she asked.

He looked at her before pulling her close. He kissed her forehead. "I trust you. I'm sorry I got us mixed up in this."

"Don't worry, we'll figure something out."

Sean leaned back into the cushions of the couch. "Do you think that he'll go through with the press conference?"

"Why wouldn't he?"

"I don't know," Sean said. "Maybe he doesn't really have the cure."

"I would bet that he does."

"Well if he's going public with this whole thing, I'm not letting him get away with the murders he committed. Your involvement is one thing, but the real issue is that he's made a name for himself while abusing the people who trusted him."

"I didn't know I was involved," Sam said.

"Pleading ignorance doesn't generally win support in the court of public opinion. I don't want to think what'll happen if Needham tells the world that you accidentally brought HCV to the human population in Africa. We need to find a way to stop his press conference. But we also need him to give up the cure."

"I can't even imagine where to begin."

"He couldn't have covered all of his bases," Sean said.

Sam took the TV remote from the coffee table and changed the channel. The networks were running their national nightly news. Every channel she chose ran the Needham story. Medical correspondents speculated on the nature of the press conference. Most thought that the conference would in some way relate to AIDS, but none even suspected what Needham was planning.

"This is huge," Sam said.

"I'm starting to realize that too."

THE plane had sat dormant on the runway for fifteen minutes before the captain came on the cabin intercom, "Ladies and gentlemen, this is Captain Reyes. We're sorry for the delay. We have a bit of a problem with the navigation system. We thought that we could correct it from here, but it now appears that we have to return to the terminal and have our engineers take a look at it. At this point we're expecting a delay of two hours. Unfortunately due to the fact that this is an international flight, we can't allow you to leave the plane. Again, we're truly sorry for the delay. Please let any member of our cabin crew know if there's anything we can do to make you more comfortable. We'll keep you updated. Thank you."

The plane began a slow arcing turn back to the terminal. Claris groaned. His timing would have been tight even without the delay. Now it appeared that he might not even make it to his connecting flight in Tokyo.

As the deadline for the two hour delay approached, the captain addressed his passengers. "Ladies and gentlemen, this is Captain Reyes again. It looks like it's going to take a bit longer than we had initially thought. We're looking at another two hours here on the ground. We'll keep you posted. Again, thank you for your patience."

Claris's stomach churned. His plan was quickly crumbling before his eyes.

LONG after midnight, Sean and Sam sat brainstorming at the dining room table. All of Sean's research material was strewn across the room. They had tossed ideas at each other for over four hours, but each idea eventually led to a dead end.

"Do you mind if I clean some of this up?" Sam said looking at the mess on the table. "I can't think straight with this stuff thrown all over the place."

"Be my guest. I'll put on another pot of coffee," Sean said heading to the kitchen.

Sam pulled all of the material together into neat piles. "Do you need this envelope for anything?" she called to Sean in the kitchen.

He looked her way. "What is it?"

"It's the overnight envelope addressed to James Mason."

"No, you can toss it."

Sam walked into the kitchen and dropped the envelope into the garbage. "Didn't you feel a bit strange using the name of a man who was just murdered?"

"No. And they don't know—" Sean stopped.

"They don't know what?"

"They don't know if he was murdered," he replied. "What day was that?"

"I don't remember exactly," Sam said. "But I think we'd gone out for dinner with Ian that night."

"I think you're right. And if I'm not mistaken, that was the same day that Needham left town for a day. Something about seeing a specialist."

Sam thought for a moment then shook her head, "What you're thinking is impossible."

"In light of recent revelations, I don't think so."

"Mason was crazy."

"Maybe so, but if he really had someone following him that day, his paranoia was obviously well founded."

"So how do we find out if Needham was in Chicago?" Sam asked.

"We call the airlines."

"They won't give us that kind of information."

"Maybe not us, but Ian can find a way," Sean said.

Sam smiled for the first time in an eternity. She walked to Sean and hugged him. "I have a good feeling about this. We're going to nail Needham."

"If he was involved in Mason's death, we'll be able to get him to give up the cure and nothing more at the conference."

"I hope you're right."

"Let's call Ian."

They returned to the living room. Sean picked up his cellphone.

"Why are you using that?" Sam asked.

"It's a long story."

Sean dialed the number to Ian's parent's house. He pressed SEND on the phone. Nothing happened. "Damn it," he mumbled.

"What's wrong?" Sam asked.

"It's this cellphone. It's been acting up again. I can never get it to work."

He dialed the number again. This time it connected.

After several rings Ian answered the phone. "Hello?"

"It's me," Sean said.

"What time is it?"

"Late."

"So what's Needham going to say at this press conference?" Ian asked.

"So you heard."

"Must be a slow headline day because it's the only thing on the news."

"I know."

"So what's up?" Ian asked.

"We can't let Needham give that press conference."

"Why not?"

Sean explained how Needham planned to use Sam as a scapegoat.

"What about Chapeau?" Ian asked. "If Sam's just a scapegoat, Chapeau will say so, won't she? You said she was coming clean on everything else."

"Chapeau is dead."

"No way. How?"

"Suicide."

"Tell me something," Ian said. "Did Sam steal your money?"

"Yes."

"I knew it. Then she's got to be involved."

"Only marginally."

Sean went on to tell Ian about the mystery encounter at the bookstore.

"So you still trust her?" Ian asked.

"Yes. Needham's selling her down the river. She didn't know any of this."

"So who was the guy at the bookstore?"

"We don't know, and we don't have time to find out. We have to stop Needham."

"But you said that he's going to announce the cure. You can't stop Needham even if he's going to implicate Sam. This is a major disease we're talking about here. Sam should take one for the team."

"Ian, Chapeau even said that she wasn't sure if he had the cure. I'm not sure how yet, but if Needham does have the cure, I'll get it from him. He's guilty of murder, and somehow I'm going to expose him. And as for Sam taking the hit, that's not an option," Sean said.

Ian sighed, "I figured it wouldn't be. What do you have planned?"

"Blackmail seems to be the weapon of choice lately."

"No kidding. But what can you blackmail Needham with?"

"If my intuition is right, he killed James Mason in Chicago."

"I thought Mason was drunk driving."

"The police said that he was drunk at the time, but that he'd suffered blunt force trauma to the head which may or may not have been a result of the car crash."

"But was Needham ever in Chicago?"

"I have no idea. That's why I called you. Is there any way you can come back here and give us a hand? I don't think that Sam and I alone can cover all of the bases. We could really use your help. I know that you could figure out a way to find out if Needham was in Chicago."

"I'll do my best to help, but I can't come back to Cambridge. I'm on a flight to Georgia at seven this morning. I called the court down there yesterday. The judge is due in today. One of his kids got sick so he cut the vacation short. I'm not sure how to approach this, but I have a feeling that being down there will help me think. Tell you what, I'll make a few calls and get the ball rolling, but don't get excited because this could take some time."

"Time is a luxury we don't have," Sean said. "We need this now."

"I'll see what I can find. This is a tough one, Sean. I can't do it myself. I'll have to have someone at the firm look into it for me. Don't bother waiting by the phone, it'll take a while."

"I know. Just work as fast as you can. Thanks Ian. Good luck in Georgia."

"You owe me," Ian said hanging up.

Sean put the phone down.

"So now what?" Sam asked.

"Let's get some sleep. My brain is turning to mush."

WHEN Sean first woke up he rolled over to look at the clock. It was nine AM. He got out of bed to look for Sam. She was nowhere to be found. After putting on yet another pot of coffee, he sat down at the table and stared at all of the research material. Was there anything else that he had missed?

He picked up Tran's file and slowly paged through it for what seemed like the hundredth time. He gained no further insights. After closing Tran's file, he found the computer printout of the names from the CDC's LA team. Would calling Carl Tessum out in San Francisco yield more answers? Sean doubted it. The Mason link looked like the only chance they had to stop Needham.

At noon, Sam returned to Sean's apartment. Sean was still toiling over the numerous documents. He looked up when Sam walked in. "Where have you been?" he asked.

"I was down at the school of public health. I thought that maybe we were just looking in the wrong place for the answers."

"And?"

"And I couldn't find anything down there either. I think Mason is our best bet. Any news from Ian?"

"Not yet."

"I'm getting a bit nervous. There are already at least fifteen of those huge news trucks with the giant satellite dishes camped out in front of the auditorium down there. The conference was all anyone was talking about."

Sean shook his head in dejection, "I hope Ian finds what we need, because I'm stumped for any more answers."

Sam rubbed Sean's shoulders. "He'll come through. He always has."

"I know, but the law of averages has to catch up to him sooner or later."

"So what do we do now?" Sam asked.

"We keep looking for other angles to go at him with. There has to be something we missed, something that directly links Needham to the serum."

"You mean other than me," Sam said as she sat next to him at the table.

"Yes, other than you."

"What would happen if I went to the press first, with the real story?"

Sean thought about the idea. "Same outcome. Other than admitting that he was negligent in giving you so much leeway, Needham would deny everything and focus all of the blame back on you. I hate to admit it, but I think that most people would end up believing his side of the story."

"What else can we look into?" Sam asked. "We have twenty-four hours."

"What about Barnard Claris?"

"What about him?"

"Is there anything that we overlooked?" Sean asked.

"Like what? We really don't know too much about him."

"We know that he's involved. Hydan International Enterprises pays out to an account in American Samoa. That's where Claris is. So what's the link?" Sean said.

"He has to be in on it," she replied. "Hydan's only other link was to Chapeau at NEIL. So what's Claris's role?"

Sean tapped a pen on the table as he thought. "I have no idea. What could he possibly have done from Samoa? The only thing that makes me think that he was involved was his reference to Double Helix Labs. You don't really think that was a coincidence, do you?"

"If it's not a coincidence, you're saying that he was tipping you off."

"Maybe it just slipped out. If he's involved and the link between Hydan and American Samoa is actually a link to him, then he'd be giving himself away. I don't think he'd do that. I'm convinced that he just said Double Helix when he meant SISS; a Freudian slip type of thing."

"So what do you propose to do?"

"I have no idea. It took Ian a while just to find Claris's address. We're not going to find his phone number," Sean said, putting on his jacket.

"We'll never know until we try."

"Then let's get to the law school library. They have the best databases on campus. If we can't find him in twenty-four hours, he can't be found."

DRESSED in his best suit, Ian entered the relatively quaint courthouse in Wilkes County, Georgia. The security guard told him that the intake room for civil cases was at the end of the hall on the second floor.

After climbing the flight of stairs, Ian entered the small office. The two clerks looked up from their desks when the door opened. One was a sixty year old woman whose glasses hung on a thin silver chain around her neck. The other was an attractive young woman in her late twenties.

Both stood and walked to the counter to help Ian. The older woman spoke first, "How can I help you?"

"I'm here to check on the status of a case to be heard by Judge Reynolds."

"Who are the parties?" she asked, as the younger woman returned to her desk.

"Westons versus Homestead Savings Bank."

"Just a moment," the clerk said, walking to a file cabinet.

The younger woman immediately returned to the counter with a document in her hand. She smiled as the older woman mumbled at the file cabinet. "Here it is," she said, handing the document to Ian. "Judge Reynolds returned today, but didn't take any of his new cases. This one goes up to him first thing in the morning."

"Thank you," he said. He held the law suit in his hands. A nervous sensation took over his body as he paged through it. He wanted to run from the building with the document and end the charade, but he knew that he'd never make it past the security guard at the front door. He handed it back to the young clerk. "When did you say that Judge Reynolds will get this?"

"First thing in the morning. He usually goes through the new cases during breakfast. It's common to find coffee stains on briefs he's read through. He's not the neatest man, but he's a stickler for procedure. So if you ever go before him, look sharp. He'll excuse you from his court room if you're not." The clerk smiled at Ian again. "Well I'd best tell Phyllis to stop looking for this before she gets crazier than a raccoon.You have yourself a nice day."

"You too," Ian said before leaving the room.

BY late afternoon a cold wind blew across the campus, a sign that chilly fall weather would arrive soon in Cambridge. After several hours of tracking down leads at the law school library, Sean and Sam took a break. They walked into the Square to buy coffee. News of the press conference was everywhere. Fluorescent pink and yellow flyers were taped to kiosks and light posts announcing the event. As with all high profile events at the university that expected a large audience, student admission was determined by a lottery system. The brightly colored flyers gave details on where to register.

Sean pulled one of the notices off a light post. "The school of public health is playing up this press conference like it's some mystery revelation," he said.

Sam nodded. "It is."

"There's going to be a huge turnout. Even people at the law school are talking about it. You'd think that the chairman of the Fed was announcing a change in interest rates."

"Needham's an important man. I overheard somebody saying that the school has already issued three hundred fifty press credentials. They're moving the conference to the largest assembly hall at the school of public health."

"I wish that we had something concrete to stop it with. I can't believe that Ian hasn't called me yet," Sean said.

They sat down on a bench. After hours of research, they still had no leads of their own. Ian's information on Needham's whereabouts on the day Mason died was still their only hope.

"My idea-well has run dry, and my stomach can't handle anymore coffee," Sam announced, throwing her cup in the trash. "I'm starting to go crazy."

Sean put his arm around her shoulder. "I know. We still have time. We'll come up with something."

"I hope so."

Sean stood and took Sam by the hand. They began to walk back to the library. "I've been thinking about Hydan International Enterprises," he said.

"What about it?"

"It's one of the key links in the puzzle."

Sam wasn't sure what Sean was getting at. "And?"

"And it's not like I found the link. It just showed up out of the blue. That guy jogging passed it to me. I'm positive. I didn't have time to give much thought to it then, but now I'm beginning to think that I know who he was."

"Who?"

"If I'm right it was Trevor Matthews."

"Who's that?" Sam asked.

"He was one of the guys on Needham's team in LA."

"What makes you think that it was him?"

"A hunch more than anything else. Everything about that jogger was wrong," Sean said. A small grin came to his face when he pictured the disheveled man running toward him.

"Like what?"

"I don't know. When you've run for as long as I have you notice things. First, he was way too wobbly to have actually been a runner."

"Maybe he was a novice."

"Maybe, but he was also fresh from the bush."

"How could you possibly notice that?" Sam asked.

"He was too tan to be a local."

"So maybe he was recently in Florida."

"And then there was the look," Sean said.

"The look?"

"Yeah, culture shock. The same look that the American tourists had in Africa. The look I'm sure I had when you first saw me. And the look that I'm certain I had when I first got back here. That puzzled expression that gives away the fact that you're not quite used to your surroundings. It was all over his face."

Sam smiled. "I know that look. You're right, when you see it, there's no mistaking it for anything else."

"When Ian and I were first looking for leads, Matthews' name came up, but Ian couldn't find anything on him because he was overseas. I bet that jogger was him. We'll find him tonight," Sean said, opening the library door for Sam.

JUST before midnight, the librarians made their rounds of the law school library, shooing any remaining students. One of the librarians found both Sean and Sam asleep among piles of Sean's research material.

"Young man," she said, tapping Sean on the shoulder. "You and your lady friend have to find another place to sleep for the night. The library is closing."

Sean nodded and woke Sam. "What time is it?" she asked him.

"Midnight."

"How long have I been asleep?" she asked.

"I have no idea. I just woke up."

They packed their bags and walked out of the library. It was cold outside and a strong wind blew at the leaves in the trees. They walked in the direction of Sean's apartment.

"So did you find anything on Trevor Matthews?" Sam asked.

"Nothing. As far as I could find, he's not on the faculty at any university overseas."

"Forget about it," Sam said. "That jogger probably wasn't him anyway."

"It's already forgotten. The jogger's identity isn't nearly as important as finding another way to stop the press conference."

Sam nodded in agreement.

"This has been one of the worst days of my life," Sean said.

Sam laughed.

"What? It hasn't been bad for you?" he said.

"It's been bad, alright, but I wouldn't say it was my worst," she said, still laughing.

"What's so funny?"

"I was just thinking about the dog I had growing up. She was the source of the worst day of my life."

Sean cracked a small smile. "How so?"

"When I was thirteen, I had this enormous Siberian Husky named Oreo. She shed all over the place so she was never allowed on the furniture, much less the beds. One night I convinced my parents to let her sleep in my bed with me. To this day I can't figure out why they agreed. Anyhow, early the next morning my parents went on a day trip to Napa and left me and the dog home. In and of itself, this wouldn't have been a problem. What was a problem was that the head gear I had to wear for my braces got tangled in her hair as I used her for a pillow. When I woke up in the morning, I was firmly stuck to Oreo's side. Whenever either of us moved it caused both of us to shriek in pain. Every time she moved, I swore she would rip the teeth right out of my mouth. The more I struggled to remove the head gear, the more frantic the dog became. I laid in my bed the entire day crying. The worst part was that neither me or the dog could get out of the bed to go to the bathroom. Of course when my parents came home all they cared about was that the bed had been wet—by me and the dog. They ignored the fact that their tortured daughter was permanently attached to the family pet."

Sean laughed. "Put in that light, my day hasn't been so bad. Let's just hope that Ian has some good news," he said as they entered the apartment.

Sean plopped down on the couch and turned on the TV. CNN reran the day's headlines. The first story was about Needham's press conference. The reporter stood in front of the school of public health. Sean could see several other reporters in the background giving their own reports. The conference was set for nine in the morning.

After changing into her pajamas, Sam joined Sean on the couch. "Aren't you going to call Ian?" she asked.

"He's in Georgia and I forgot his cellphone number. I'm sure he'll call any minute."

Sam looked at the TV. "It's still big news, isn't it?"

Sean nodded.

"What if Ian doesn't have good news?"

Sean shrugged. "Then we bluff. I just hope that it doesn't come down to that."

It had started raining outside. The drops tapped lightly at the window. A distant thunderclap softly rumbled.

"I love thunderstorms," Sam said, snuggling closer to Sean. He put his arm around her. "Do you remember that night in the Serengeti when the Land Rover broke down and we had to camp at Barafu *kopjes*?"

Sean smiled. "It rained for twenty straight hours. We barely left the tiny tent that entire day."

Sam kissed him. "I think that's when I started falling for you."

"Why?"

"It was the way—" Sam began, but was interrupted by the ringing of Sean's cellphone.

"Hold that thought," Sean said before answering the phone. It was Ian. "So what's the news?" Sean asked.

"My friend at the firm confirmed that Needham was out of town on the same day that Mason died."

"And?"

"And you were right. He had a United flight that arrived

at Chicago's O'Hare airport at noon. His return flight was at nine that night."

Sean looked at Sam, "We got him."

"So what now?" Ian asked.

"We stop him before he even leaves the hospital for the press conference. Then we call the Chicago Police. Thank god you found this. We were out of answers up here."

Ian was silent on the other end.

"What's wrong?" Sean asked.

"The judge is back in town."

"What happened today?"

"Nothing. My case is still in limbo, but he'll get to it tomorrow."

"What are you going to do?"

"The way I see it I have two choices. I can try to explain to the judge what's going on—even though I don't really know—or I can just wait and see what happens when the judge realizes that I'm not a member of any state bar association."

"What about the police?" Sean asked.

"I don't think that I can take that chance. By the time we talk tomorrow, one way or another, my fate will be decided."

"We'll come up with something," Sean assured his friend.

"I have to go think," Ian said. "I'll talk to you tomorrow. Good luck."

"You too," Sean said before hanging up the phone.

"Good news?" Sam asked.

Sean smiled. "Needham was in Chicago for nine hours the day Mason died. I think we've got him."

Sean took Sam's hand and led her to the bedroom. "The press conference is scheduled for nine o'clock. Let's get up at six," he said. He set the alarm on every clock and watch he could find, before joining Sam in bed. "There's no way I'm sleeping through this."

At half past four that morning, Sam rolled over and saw that Sean was sitting up in bed. "What's wrong?" she asked.

"Nothing. I guess I'm just nervous."

Sam hugged Sean. "I know that a lot of what you're doing is because of me. But you have to realize that there's much more than me and my reputation at stake here."

Sean looked at her without speaking.

She continued, "Quite a while back, I worked in Tanzania trying to get teens to use condoms. They absolutely refused, because they thought that the condoms were a ploy by Westerners to give Africans diseases."

"That's ridiculous."

"Of course it is, but that's what they thought. It's taken decades for the international public health community to foster trusting relationships with people around the globe. If Needham goes through with his plan, those relationships will be destroyed. If it comes out that the spread of hepatitis C on the African continent was due, in large part, to the practices of the Western public health community, it's all over."

"I hadn't thought of that," Sean said. He closed his eyes trying to sleep. After another hour of staring at the ceiling, he left the bedroom and sat alone at the dining room table. He ran through the accusations he would aim at Needham. He pictured Needham's face. An awful smile crossed it. Sean knew he was still missing something.

16

THE alarms of two clocks and a wristwatch woke Sam at six in the morning. She sleepily wandered out of the bedroom to find Sean. He had just finished his shower.

"What time did you get up?" she asked him.

"I never slept."

"How do you feel?"

"Surprisingly awake."

"So what's the plan?"

"I think we should head over to the hospital before Needham leaves for the conference. It'll be a zoo over there, and I imagine that we won't be able to get close to him."

"I need ten minutes," Sam said.

"The clock's ticking."

SEAN turned the radio on in his small Ford as he drove with Sam to Mass General. He had a nervous pit in his stomach.

"What if he won't talk to us?" Sam asked.

"He will," Sean said, knowing that it was possible that he wouldn't.

They rode the elevator to the second floor of the hospital. Sean turned to Sam. "What are Needham's chances of surviving?" he asked.

She shook her head. "This far gone his only chance is the transplant, and his name is still way down the list."

When the doors parted, they exited into a swarm of news cameras and reporters each hoping to get a preview of the conference's topic. Sean quickly realized that their chances of making it through the crowd and into room 2217 were slim at best.

He walked to the nurses' station opposite the elevator.

The nurse behind the desk glared at him in annoyance. Her appearence revealed that she had worked the night shift.

"You're here for Dr. Needham, right?"

Sean put on his best smile and nodded. "It's been a long night, hasn't it?"

"You're telling me," she answered, starting to let her guard down.

"How long have these guys been camped out here?"

"The first crew arrived just after midnight. The crowd started to form at about five this morning."

"There's no way I'm going to make it past that mob to see Larry, is there?" Sean said.

The nurse shook her head. "I don't think so."

"Is there any way you could call him and let him know I'm here? I'm one of his students."

"You seem like a nice guy, and I would. But I can't," she answered. She motioned for Sean to lean forward. She whispered into his ear, "He's not even in there. We moved him last night because we knew this would happen."

"So where is he?"

With ten minutes remaining in her shift, the nurse was no longer concerned about the confidentiality of Needham's whereabouts. "He's up on eight," she answered.

"Thanks," Sean said. "I hope you have a quiet day when you get off."

The nurse smiled at him as he disappeared with Sam into the elevator.

At the nurses' station on the eighth floor, Sean made the same request.

"He left about an hour ago," the nurse behind the desk said.

"You're not just saying that to get rid of me, are you?"

"No. His wife pushed him out in his wheelchair an hour ago."

Sean turned and walked over to Sam. "He's already gone. We have to get over to the school of public health."

THE area within five blocks of the school of public health was heavily congested. Large media trucks with satellite dishes lined the streets. Thick cables linking the crews to their trucks crossed the roadway leading to the building where the press conference would be held. After searching for five minutes for a parking space, Sean finally pulled into an alley and left the car parked illegally. Sam didn't comment on the obvious.

Together they ran across the street past media camera crews. A crowd had formed at the doors to the building. Sean looked up at a news helicopter taping footage of the scene for the midday report.

"I never would have imagined that this many people would show up to hear Needham speak," Sean said, shoving his way into the middle of the mob.

When they finally reached the front of the line, one of the two guards stopped them at the door. "Tickets," was all the guard said.

Sean looked at Sam. "We're students," he said to the guard.

"Yeah, so are the other million people out here. No student lottery ticket, no show." The guard turned to the next people in the makeshift line.

Sean pulled Sam aside. "We have to sneak in. There has to be another door," he said.

"Be realistic. I'm sure all the doors are covered."

"Damn it," Sean said. He looked at the mob slowly funneling through the door. About half of them had bright red tags hanging from strings around their necks. They were press passes. Sean scanned the area in front of the building.

"Stay right here," he said to Sam before running across the street.

Sam stared at the line of people moving into the building. It was growing. She looked at her watch: 8:45. They were running out of time.

Sean returned with a cup of coffee. He handed it to Sam.

"What's this?" she asked.

"Do you see that folding table over there?" Sean said pointing to a table beyond the line of people waiting to enter the building.

"Yes."

Sean loosened the lid to the coffee. "I want you to walk over there and ask the woman behind the table what time it is. When she looks at her watch, spill the coffee. Try to get some on her. Apologize and leave."

"What?"

"Just do it. I'll meet you back here."

Sam walked quickly over to the folding table. The woman behind it smiled as she approached.

"Can I help you?" the woman asked.

"I was just wondering if you happened to know the time," Sam said, coffee poised.

The woman behind the table pulled the cuff of her jacket up and looked at her watch. Sam tossed the cup. The coffee splashed across the table and onto the woman. She jumped up from her seat.

"Oh my god, I'm so sorry," Sam said.

The woman stood in disbelief, shaking the hot liquid from her pants. When she looked up to yell at Sam, she was already gone.

Sam found Sean deep in the crowd. "Can I ask what that was all about?" she said.

Sean showed Sam the red tag around his neck. He put one over her head. "She was checking ID for the press badges. Now if we can fight through this crowd, we're in."

"He's on in ten minutes," Sam said.

"I know."

IAN sat on a hard wooden bench outside of Judge Reynolds' chambers. The judge had yet to enter the courthouse. Ian fidgeted nervously in anticipation. He had no plan.

He sat flipping through the local newspaper when his cellphone rang. It was Sarah calling from the law firm.

"How are you, Ian?" she asked.

"I've had better days."

"Do you want to talk about it?"

"Not really. What's up?"

"I had a bit of an oversight yesterday. I found out a little more about that doctor's Chicago itinerary for you. What was his name again?"

"Needham," Ian replied.

"Right, Needham."

"What is it?" he asked.

She proceeded to give him the latest information. Ian shook his head. He repeated the name, "Great Lakes Regional Airlines. Are you sure?"

"I'm positive, I have the information right here," she answered.

"Shit."

"Is something wrong?" she asked, hearing the tension in his voice.

"I have to go," he said hanging up the phone.

He dialed Sean's cellphone number. It rang, but then disconnected. He tried again. Same result.

"Pick up, Sean."

ONCE inside the doors of the school of public health, Sean and Sam hit gridlock in the hallway leading to the auditorium. The corridor was packed from wall to wall with people. Sean could hear a man speaking over the microphone in the auditorium. He was telling people to take any available seat: "And we need to clear that corridor up there. It's a fire code violation to block that door. If you'd all just move down to the front, there's plenty of room to sit here on the floor. You're all going to have to scrunch if we're going to get everybody in."

Sean and Sam got separated in the confusion of the crowd. Sean made his way up to the auditorium door, but the line stalled again. He realized he was sweating. He looked at his watch. Needham was due in less than two minutes.

Sean began to push the two men in front of him.

One turned around and shoved back, "Settle down pal. This line's not going anywhere."

From inside his coat pocket, his cellphone rang. Before he could answer the call, the phone died. He looked at its display: RECHARGE BATTERY. "Damn it," he said aloud.

His heart raced wildly. He wasn't getting into the auditorium. He wouldn't be able to stop Needham.

Further down the corridor, away from the entrance where the crowd poured in, Sean saw a group of uniformed campus police officers approaching.

"Clear the way," one officer shouted. "Make a path. Coming through." As the six officers approached, Sean saw that they surrounded a wheelchair. He couldn't see Needham behind the human shield. The only wheelchair accessible entrance to the auditorium was through the same door the crowd had formed at.

Sean ran to the approaching men. Thinking that Sean was a threat, the lead officer intercepted him ten feet in front of Needham's entourage. "What the hell are you doing?" he said.

"I need to speak to Needham."

"Get lost, we're already running late," the officer replied, pushing Sean back toward the crowd.

Sean yelled past him, “Dr. Needham, it’s me, Sean Graham. I have new evidence. You have to listen to me.”

The guard kept pushing Sean backward in spite of his struggling.

“Let him through,” Needham said in a weak voice.

The officer didn’t hear him. He kept pushing Sean back.

“Hey Cahill,” the officer at Needham’s side called. “Dr. Needham said to let him through.”

Officer Cahill stopped pushing Sean. Sean knocked the officer’s hands from his chest. He ran to the group of men. For the first time, he saw Needham. He looked even worse than before.

Needham cracked a small smile as Sean approached. “You came to see this in person. I’m glad.”

“Listen to me,” Sean said. He stopped and looked at the policemen. They all backed away.

“What is it?” Needham said. “You’re delaying my moment of glory.”

“I know about Chicago.”

“What about Chicago?”

“You killed Mason.”

“You’re crazy. He died drunk driving.”

“Murder hasn’t been ruled out. I’m calling the Chicago Police to let them know that you were in Chicago on that day.”

“Sure I was in Chicago, but I was only there on a half-hour lay over. I got right back on a plane and flew to Milwaukee.”

Sean shook his head. “No you didn’t. You flew in and out on United. You had nine hours.”

Needham laughed at Sean. “You’re right, I flew in and out of Boston on United, but your research is incomplete. I flew Great Lakes Regional Air out of O’Hare to Milwaukee. United couldn’t connect me to Milwaukee on such short notice. Call Great Lakes and Dr. Chauncey in Milwaukee. They’ll both tell you. Sorry Sean. That’s strike three. Now if you’ll excuse me, I have a press conference to deliver,” Needham said. He turned his attention to his escorts. “Gentlemen, whenever you’re ready.”

Sean stood aside as the group continued down the hall. He followed at a short distance, suddenly finding himself completely exhausted.

The police officers cleared a path for Needham's wheelchair. As he rolled past, reporters shouted questions at him. The noise from the crowd crescendoed. Sean felt like he was in a football stadium. He watched as the people in the long descending aisle parted for Needham and then collapsed again in his wake.

Sean searched the faces of the crowd for Sam. He couldn't locate her. He stood at the crowded door to the auditorium in a shocked daze of defeat. He looked around blankly, searching for any guidance.

A strong hand gripped Sean's upper arm, pulling him from his stupor. Sean turned to find a very tanned man in his mid-fifties holding his arm.

"Don't let him take the podium," the man said.

Sean continued to stare blankly forward. The man shook Sean hard. "Did you hear me? You can't let him speak," the tan man repeated.

Sean noticed the man was sweating profusely. The man jabbed a hand-held tape player into Sean's stomach. "Play this for him. Then we can go home."

Sean shook his head. "I don't understand."

"There's no time to explain. Tell him Salieri is in the building," the man said before turning to the man at his side.

"Salieri?"

The man spoke to his companion, "Get him to the stage before Needham."

The other man nodded and took a firm grasp of Sean's arm. He dragged Sean quickly through the wall of people standing in the aisle leading to the stage. His grip on Sean's arm was incredibly strong. At one point, the man turned to look at Sean. Sean recognized him as the tourist he had knocked over in Harvard Square. He felt sick to his stomach as another wave of confusion crashed over him. His knees weakened, but the man continued to pull him forward, pushing people aside without a word.

The man shoved Sean forcefully into the last officer in Needham's convoy just as they arrived at the base of the stage. The officer wheeled about and took hold of Sean.

"You again?" he said.

"Dr. Needham," Sean called.

Needham stopped and addressed Sean without turning

his head to look. "You're too late, Sean. But I do admire your efforts." Sean struggled to hear Needham's voice over the din of the packed auditorium. Needham continued, "I hope you don't mind, but I'm going to ask Officer Cahill here to escort you from the building."

Cahill smiled at the prospect.

Needham began to wheel forward again.

Sean shouted after him. "Salieri wants me to play this tape for you. He's in the building."

Needham stopped abruptly. He turned his chair slowly and wheeled to Sean. "What did you say?"

Sean held out the small tape player. "Salieri wants me to play this for you. He's standing in the corridor outside."

"Salieri," Needham whispered. He looked at the guards surrounding him. "Bring Mr. Graham with me," he said.

Sean followed as the group wound its way up a wheelchair ramp that led to a backstage area, concealed from the auditorium by a crimson colored velvet curtain.

Needham motioned for the men to leave the two alone. "Salieri," he whispered again. "How did you find him?"

Sean shrugged, not knowing how to answer.

Needham pressed the PLAY button on the tape player. The first voice Sean heard was distinctly Needham's:

All you have to do is take the money and look the other way. When I first proposed the idea you were all for it. Now, all you have to do is let it go. No one knows about the serum but you, me, Matthews and Valerie. Hell, the other two don't really even know what the serum is. I offered both of them the same thing I'm offering you. Chapeau already agreed. Matthews has gone AWOL, but I'm not concerned about him. He's a coward. He'll never make any noise. Barnard, this is easy ...

Sean realized Needham was talking to Claris.

... just take the money and go away. Do you realize how comfortable you can live? We're onto something huge here. And nobody is going to realize what it is until it's too late. You said yourself that this virus could be the panacea for all that is rotten in the world.

Finally Claris responded:

In theory Needham. In theory. You've intentionally unleashed a virus on a continent. I can't let you get away with that.

Needham interrupted him:

Take that fucking money and look the other way. If you don't and consider selling me out, I'll take you down with me. You know I will. Be smart. Take the money.

Needham stopped the tape player. Sean took it from him, removing the tape. "This tape is yours if you call this whole thing off. If not, I go public right now. There are a hundred news crews outside and I could get this on every network worldwide in five minutes."

After a brief moment of consideration Needham nodded, extending his hand. Sean gave him the tape.

Needham placed it in his sport coat pocket. "Mr. Graham, please wheel me to the microphone. You have my word, this ordeal of ours will not be mentioned."

Sean pushed Needham from behind the curtain onto the large stage. Applause erupted in the auditorium.

Sean helped Needham adjust the microphone before leaving the stage.

He held his breath as he waited for the doctor to speak.

Needham cleared his throat. "Ladies and gentlemen, I thank you for taking the time to come listen to me speak today. Unfortunately the speculation over the nature of my announcement today has caused a media feeding frenzy. It is unwarranted. I stand—or rather sit—before you today in failing health to announce nothing more than my resignation as Director-General of the World Health Organization. My resignation is effective immediately. I thank you for all of your support throughout my career. Please continue to fight diligently for the health and human rights of all people across the globe. Thank you."

Needham wheeled himself away from the microphone as quickly as possible. The murmur in the crowd grew to a steady clamor again.

Sean watched Needham as he neared. The brief speech had taken all of what remained of the doctor's strength.

Needham stopped in front of Sean.

"My question is obvious," Sean said to Needham. "Why?"

He stared into Sean's eyes before he spoke.

"Did I tell you about the first time I went to Africa?" Needham asked, his voice failing him.

"No."

Needham pulled a billfold from his sport coat. He opened

it and removed a piece of paper that was brown with age. It was an old newspaper clipping. He stared at it as he spoke to Sean.

"I was a little younger than you. When you flew over to Africa, I can imagine that as you sat on that plane while it taxied down the runway in Boston or New York, or wherever you were leaving from, that the blood pumped quickly through your veins driven by the excitement of the unknown. And when the plane left the ground and headed out over the whitecaps of the Atlantic you were gripped by fantasies of a mysterious ancient land. For most people, this is what Africa represents."

Needham rubbed the clipping gently before continuing. "I too remember my first flight over there. But I wasn't going on safari or doing research or volunteering for the Peace Corps. There was no pretty girl at the airport welcoming me to the Dark Continent. An hour after I landed in Dar es Salaam I was escorted into a small basement room. I'll never forget that room. So damn hot. Under a lone hanging light were two covered gurneys. As I walked around the gurneys, I clung to the hope that my trip was all a big mistake. But when I pulled back the sheets, the reality hit me," Needham said with a slow sigh. "The coroners had done their best to preserve the bodies, but after a month, human flesh loses its staying power. You can't begin to imagine the horror of seeing your father's decapitated head staring at you. Or the smell of your mother's rotten flesh. I left Africa that very same day accompanied by my parents. They, of course, rode with the luggage. So you ask me why, and now you know. The atrocities committed by those animals hit home. No one is innocent."

Sean shook his head.

"Hepatitis C came along under ideal circumstances," Needham continued. "Marcus Tran was the source. We know that. Whether or not he was a sex addict or a druggie is irrelevant. He associated with people that were. The fact that some of his friends in the degenerate community caught the infection played right into my plan. The virus spread like wildfire through the urban centers of the United States. But because of its long latency period, not too many people died right away. And look who it killed: hookers, queers and druggies. Who cared?"

"So the name Non-A, Non-B virus was intentional," Sean said.

Needham nodded. "And it worked like a gem. Nobody else discovered the true agent until almost a decade later. Now, over a hundred million people in Africa have it. It's too late for them. Just as with AIDS, nobody will care until the respected people in their own communities start dying. This disease is just like AIDS, but with a larger scope. And nobody cares. But they will. Trust me, they will."

"What about the cure?"

Needham shook his head, "I'm going to die very soon of liver failure. Ironic, isn't it? Your selfishness has prevented me from my greatest moment. All you had to do was offer Samantha up in exchange for the cure. Now you want it all. It's not that simple. I will die and the cure will die with me. But you're a smart young man. You'll look in the right place. All of these scientists working with Interferon and Ribavirin—they're all minor successes. These people are looking too hard. The answer won't be found under a microscope. Go to the origin. You'll find it there. You saw it there in writing."

Sean thought of the leather-bound research log in the Serengeti.

"Now if you'll excuse me," the frail doctor said, "I have to go remove my name from the transplant waiting list."

Needham rolled past him without another word. He looked to his police officer escorts. "Please have the ambulance pick me up at the back door to take me back to the hospital. I'm in terrible need of rest."

Sean waited backstage as the lingering crowd slowly exited the auditorium. When only a few stragglers remained, Sean walked up the aisle. Sam sat in a seat by the exit.

She stood up and hugged him. "What just happened?"

"I'll explain on the way home."

AFTER finding a parking space, Sean and Sam walked toward his apartment. Three police cruisers were parked in front. Two officers appeared from the building, leading Sean's superintendent away in handcuffs. As Sean and Sam neared the walkway leading into the building, a man in a dark suit approached them. Sean recognized him as Chapeau's attorney.

"Mr. Graham, I was hoping to speak with you."

"What's going on Mr. Bradley?" Sean asked.

"Before she died, Valerie Chapeau wrote an affidavit. In it she gave the details of how she had paid your superintendent to break into your apartment on several occasions. On one such occasion he was to leave a syringe on your pillow. I guess it was supposed to scare you off."

"What?" Sean said in disbelief.

"I forwarded the affidavit to the proper authorities who passed the case on to the Cambridge Police Department. They obtained a warrant this morning to enter his apartment. They found several of your belongings there, including the computer you reported as stolen. Detective Matteson will want to speak with you," Bradley said, pointing to a man by an unmarked police car.

"Thanks," Sean said leading Sam toward the building. Before they went through the door, Sean spotted a man seated alone on a bench at the bus stop across the street. "Here are the keys. I'll meet you upstairs in a second," he said to Sam.

He crossed the street and joined the man on the bench.

Sean spoke first. "So you're Barnard Claris."

The tan man nodded as he lit a cigarette. He held the pack out to Sean.

"No thanks," Sean said.

Claris took a long drag and exhaled slowly. "You've sure stirred things up, Sean Graham. I didn't think I'd ever see the day that this wall would come tumbling down."

"Why did you come?"

Claris chuckled at the question. "Because I didn't know what you knew. I got that letter from you and it scared the shit out of me. Then my man tells me that you're on to something."

"Your man?"

Claris pointed to a table at the cafe just down the block. "He's been following you for quite some time."

Santiago nodded in their direction. The sick feeling returned to Sean's stomach.

"Don't worry, he's leaving today," Claris assured Sean. "As for me, I had to come. When Needham announced the press conference, I knew what he was going to do. He would implicate me in one way or another. Sooner or later, some of the money trail would lead to me. I couldn't let that happen. You heard the tape. All I did was take the money. I looked the other way when we turned in the original CDC report. I knew it had flaws. So did everyone else. I suppose that I could have been like Matthews and fallen off the face of the earth, never to be heard from again, but if I was going to be exiled, you can be sure that it wasn't going to come cheap. Spending the last two decades of my life on that damned island has been my penance."

Sean nodded in understanding.

"You can tell Ian to come back from Georgia. The case will mysteriously disappear tonight," Claris said.

"You were the one who blackmailed Ian? Why?"

"Because I didn't know if Ian would keep what he learned just between the two of you. By getting him preoccupied with something else, he was removed from the picture."

"Why didn't you stop me from moving forward?"

"Because I thought that it was about time that Needham got what he had coming. But I had to keep an eye on you so that you didn't take me down with him," Claris said, dropping the cigarette and extinguishing it with his shoe. "As for your friend Samantha, she was an unwilling party all along. She didn't know about any of it. Needham just used her as a pawn. I had my man approach her and threaten to tell you everything about her involvement if she didn't help us. That's why she stole the money. Don't worry, it's being wired back as we speak."

Sean was amazed that Claris had turned out to be the key. "What will you do now?" he asked.

Claris grinned. "I'll disappear again. Don't try to find me. You won't. I won't register to vote again."

Sean returned the smile.

Claris stood and extended his hand. "It was nice to meet you Sean Graham. Stay out of trouble."

"I'll try."

He watched as Claris walked away down the brick sidewalk.

EXACTLY one week after the press conference, Sean and Ian ate lunch together at a sidewalk cafe just off of Boston Common.

"You sure took your sweet time getting back to Boston," Sean said looking over the menu.

"What, did you miss me or something?" Ian joked.

"No, I was just saying that you stayed out at your parents' place for a nice little extended vacation."

"Oh, I get it. Now that Sam's gone, you need to hang out with your best friend again. When did she leave?"

"Two days ago."

Ian gestured to the waitress, but she didn't see him. "She's completely ignoring us," he said to Sean. "So how did the Ad Board meeting go?"

"Not as poorly as it could have. One of my students, Michael Rubicon, went before the Ad Board to testify—if that's the right word—that he overheard Gustav and Courtney on several occasions planning to set me up. It helped, but Dean Blackwell still felt that I behaved inappropriately."

"So what's the bottom line?" Ian asked.

"They took what Rubicon had to say into consideration, but I still have to take a leave of absence."

"That's pretty harsh. How long?"

"I can return next fall."

"Could be worse." Ian again attempted to signal the waitress. "What's her deal? We've been here for ten minutes."

"She's playing hard to get."

"You know, that's the worst part of this whole thing. Why did Claris have to use a pretty girl to play the role of Jessica Weston? I was so psyched to have her live across the hall."

"I think that's the funniest part."

Ian shrugged. "So what about Needham? Are you planning to expose him?"

"No. He's on his death bed. What's the point? It wouldn't do any good."

"So you're just taking off and forgetting about him."

"Pretty much. I spoke to my brother yesterday and he said that he's feeling healthy and for me not to worry. His health was the only reason I'd consider staying here. But he's okay so I'm leaving."

"What does your dad have to say?"

"He was in town yesterday and I asked him to dinner. Remarkably we had a civilized conversation. He didn't freak out when I told him about the Ad Board or about my going away. He even kept his cool when I told him that I donated half of my trust money to a hepatitis research foundation. I guess things are finally beginning to change between us. It may take a while, but we're moving in the right direction."

"And what about Fulsonmayer?" Ian asked. "Have you spoken to him since the Ad Board?"

"No. He keeps blowing me off. He's too caught up in getting his research published to care about what happens to me."

"Then you're better off without him."

"I guess so."

Ian took a sip of water. "I can't believe you're taking off again."

"I know. It hasn't really hit me yet."

"Outlandish. Here today, gone tomorrow," Ian said with a smile. "Tell me something. Why can't you let this drop now?"

"I don't know. Something inside me keeps me going. It's like this dream I keep having of this car accident I saw. In the dream, I see all of these injured people all over the road, and I drive past them in slow motion. I know that there's absolutely nothing I can do for them. If I stopped, I'd just be in the way. I think that's why I've kept pushing this HCV thing. Because there's something that I can do. For once I can make a difference."

"Don't get overzealous on me. You're one man."

"I know, but Needham proved that one man can change the world."

Ian nodded as he raised his glass of water. "Well, since our waitress has forgotten us, water will have to do. To your continued success. Let's hope you don't dig up any more controversy."

Sean touched his glass to Ian's. "I'll drink to that."

EPILOGUE

Serengeti National Park, Tanzania

AS the Land Rover began its descent of the hill leading to the southeast entrance of the Serengeti, the water hole came into view. Sean had looked forward to seeing it for hours. He turned the truck off the main road and drove in the direction of the solitary oasis. It was the largest permanent source of water for miles in any direction. A single tree provided shade for the numerous animals that drank in the hot afternoon sun.

As he parked at the water hole, he listened to the latest BBC news. In his British accent, the newscaster announced a breaking story, "Here's Gloria Lancaster with the latest from the New York Desk."

A woman with a surprisingly deep voice took over the report:

Doctors from Boston's Massachusetts General Hospital are reporting that recently resigned Director-General of the World Health Organization, Dr. Lawrence Needham, died early this morning from complications arising from liver failure. Needham died after being in a coma for a week. He was the world's preeminent authority on HIV and AIDS. His accomplishments in the field were numerous. Prior to being named Director-General of the WHO, Needham was the founding Director of the WHO's Global Program on AIDS. In recent years, he has been credited with ...

Sean switched the radio off and slowly stepped out of the Land Rover. On the other side of the water hole, fifteen zebras kept a suspicious eye on him as he walked to the water.

He reached into his pocket and withdrew the wishing stone his brother brought home from Alaska. He thought for a moment, rubbing the smooth stone between his fingers. Standing at the water's edge, he tossed the black rock with its thin white band. It skipped twice across the surface of the water before disappearing.

Sean smiled at the thought that the stone had traveled half way around the world before coming to its final resting spot at the bottom of the water hole.

He watched the water until the ripples from the stone had vanished, once again leaving the water in a smooth glass-like state.

He returned to the Land Rover and proceeded to the park gate where he parked the truck at the ranger outpost. As he had several months earlier, he would register in the leather-bound research log.

Before exiting the truck, he turned and looked into the back seat. He touched Sam gently on the knee, waking her.

"We're here."

The End.